TROJAN GOLD

Also by Elizabeth Peters
In Thorndike Large Print

Lion in the Valley

TROJAN GOLD

A Vicky Bliss Mystery

ELIZABETH PETERS

THORNDIKE PRESS • THORNDIKE, MAINE

Library of Congress Cataloging in Publication Data:

Peters, Elizabeth.
  Trojan gold.

  1. Large type books. I. Title.
[PS3563.E747T7 1987b]   813'.54   87-11258
ISBN 0-89621-818-X (lg. print : alk. paper)

This novel is a work of fiction. Any references to historical
events; to real people, living or dead; or to real locales are
intended only to give the fiction a setting in historical reality.
Other names, characters, and incidents either are the product
of the author's imagination or are used fictitiously, and their
resemblance, if any, to real-life counterparts is entirely coin-
cidental.

Large Print edition available in North America by arrangement
with Atheneum Publishers, New York.

Large Print edition available in the British Commonwealth by
arrangement with Piatkus Books, London.

Cover design by Armen Kojoyian.

TO **DOMINICK**
*with respectful admiration, admiring respect,
and much affection*

ONE

Fire stained the night. The sky above the dying city was an obscene, unnatural crimson, as if the lifeblood of its people were pouring upward from a million wounds. As he fought through the inferno he missed death by inches not once but a dozen times. The conquerors were already in the city. Another enemy army was closing in from the west; but the horde of refugees, of whom he was one, fought their way westward with a desperate, single-minded intent. Throughout history, always the barbarian hordes had come from the east.

Unlike the others, he was not concerned with his own survival, except insofar as it was necessary in order to ensure the survival of something that meant more to him than his own life. This city would fall to the barbarians as other imperial cities had fallen — Rome, Constantinople — and the battle and its aftermath would add more wreckage to the monstrous mound of shattered beauty — dead children and mutilated women and torn flesh, burning books, headless statues,

7

slashed paintings, shattered crystal. . . . One thing at least he would save. How he would do it he did not know, but he never doubted he would succeed. He knew the city, knew every street and building, though many of the landmarks had vanished in pillars of whirling flame and heaps of smoldering rubble. He would get there first. And in the lull between the flight of the vanquished and the triumph of the conquerors, he would find his chance.

He was more than a little mad. Perhaps only a madman could have done it.

That's how I would begin if I were writing a thriller instead of a simple narrative of fact. Exactly how he accomplished it will never be known; but it may have been something like that. I only wish my part of the story had started with such panache – the death throes of a mighty metropolis, the fire and the blood and the terror. . . .

What am I saying? Of course I don't really wish that. But I could wish for a slightly more dramatic start to this tale than a stupid petty argument with my boss's secretary over a stupid petty bit of office routine.

I love my work, and I don't really hate Mondays. I hated this Monday morning, though, because I had a hang-over. I am not a heavy drinker – I know, that's what everybody says, but in my case it's true. I make it a rule not to overindulge, in any fashion, on a work night. There were reasons – not good reasons, but reasons – why I had broken the rule that Sunday. They have no bearing on this story and they are nobody's business but my own. Suffice it to say that I was late to work and not happy to be there. If I had been in my normal sunny morning mood, I probably would not have overreacted when I saw what Gerda had done.

Gerda is, as I have mentioned, my boss's secretary; and my boss is Herr Doctor Anton Z. Schmidt, director of the National Museum in Munich. The National is small but what's there is "cherce," to quote one of my favorite film characters. The building and the basic collections had been contributed to the city back in the eighteen hundreds by a Bavarian nobleman who was as eccentric as he was filthy-rich, which is one of the reaons why our present collections are a bit unusual. For example, we have the most extensive collection of antique toys in Europe. We have a gem room, a medieval-art section, and a costume room. The noble Graf von und zu Gefenstein also collected ladies' underwear, but we don't display that collection, fascinating as it is to students of costume. At least the people who request access to it *say* they are students of costume.

The point of all this, in case you are wondering, is that our staff isn't large. Although Gerda has the title of Secretary to the Director, she types all our letters and takes care of most of the office work for the staff. No problem for Gerda; she is inhumanly efficient. She is also very nosy.

Since I was late, I wasn't surprised to see that Gerda had taken advantage of my tardiness to mess around with my things. I wasn't surprised, but I was irate. If I had told her once I had told her a hundred times to leave my desk alone. Those heaps of debris are sacred to me. I know where everything is. If people start tidying up I can't find anything. Gerda had stacked everything. She is a great stacker — nice neat piles, sorted by size instead of content, every corner squared.

She had also replaced my desk blotter. The new one lay there pristine and dead; gone was the old one, with its vital store of information — telephone numbers, shopping lists, addresses of shops, and notes on books I wanted to read. . . . And smack in the center of the nice new blotter was my mail. She had opened every letter and every parcel. The envelopes were stapled to the letters, which meant that in order to avoid tearing the latter, I would have to pry off the staples, breaking half my nails in the process.

I kicked the nearest filing cabinet. Hopping and swearing, I went behind the screen that concealed the really important objects in my office – the sink and hot plate and coffee maker – and plugged in the last-named article. I fully intended to kill Gerda, but I figured I had better have a cup of coffee first. Otherwise I might stumble on the stairs and break a leg before I got my hands around her throat.

While I drank my coffee, I glanced through the mail but found nothing that improved my disposition, especially after I broke a nail prying off a staple. It was the usual assortment; notices of meetings, circulars from academic presses offering books nobody could afford on subjects nobody knew anything about, and letters from students asking permission to use the collections or to reproduce photographs.

The stack of mail was pyramid-style, with the largest items on the bottom. I worked my way grimly down to the base – a coarse brown envelope approximately 8 by 10 inches in size. One of those well-known plain brown wrappers? It was plain enough; no sign of writing, not even my name. The heavy tape sealing the flap had been slashed, leaving edges so sharp I cut my finger when I reached into the envelope. Gerda's famous paper knife, honed to the keenness of a headsman's sword. One of these days someone was going to stab her with that knife. It might be me.

She hadn't stapled the enclosure to the envelope, probably because her diabolical tool could not penetrate the heavy cardboard on which the photograph was mounted. It was a black-and-white photo, probably enlarged from a snapshot; the faintly fuzzy focus suggested amateur photography. As I stared at it, a flash of memory rose and fell in the murky depths of my alcohol-fuzzed mind, but I couldn't get a grip on it. Yet I knew I had seen a photograph like that before.

The subject was a woman. The skin of her face had sagged and her thin mouth was set in a straight, expressionless line. She could have been any aging *Hausfrau,* except for her costume. A fringed diadem several inches wide encircled her brow. From it dangled ropes and chains of some metallic substance. Her earlobes were pulled down by more chains and dangles; the bodice of her plain dark dress was almost hidden by necklaces, row on row of them.

I turned the photograph over. The back was plain gray cardboard, with no inscription or photographer's imprint. Why the hell had someone sent me a picture of his mother dressed up for an amateur theatrical performance? His mother the soprano? She didn't resemble the conventional contralto stereotype; her chin sagged with the weariness of age, and her features were pointed and meager, like those of a rain-soaked bird. But the gaudy fake jewelry suggested one of the more exotic operas, such as *Lakmé* or *Aïda*.

I inspected the envelope again. It was still blank.

Eventually the caffeine penetrated my brain, and I gathered enough strength to pry myself off my chair. There was a pile of work waiting for me, but I decided that first I would go and kill Gerda.

My office is at the top of one of the towers. There are four towers, one on each corner, plus battlements and machicolations and all the other accouterments of nineteenth-century pseudo-medievalism. The Graf was as loony as his king, mad Ludwig of Bavaria, and both of them loved to build castles. It's fashionable to sneer at Ludwig's taste, and I admit he went overboard on the interior décor – all that writhing gilt and those enormous Wagnerian paintings – but anyone who can contemplate unmoved the fairy-tale towers of Schloss Neuschwanstein framed by the misty mountaintops hasn't got an ounce of romance in his/her soul.

I chose my office in part because of the view.

There are windows all around, looking out over the rooftops and towers of the city that I love like a native daughter – the twin green onion domes of the Frauenkirche and the lacy stonework of the Rathaus tower, the Isar winding gracefully between banks that are green in summer and snowy-white in winter, and the bustling traffic of Karlsplatz with the clock tower and the gates and the shops. You can keep your Parises and your Viennas; give me Munich any day. It's one of the happiest, handsomest cities in the world.

Another reason I chose to perch up in my airy aerie was for purposes of privacy. There is no lift, and people who want to see me have to want to see me very badly before they will tackle five flights of stairs. Even Gerda doesn't do it often; I suppose the chance to pry during my absence had been too strong to resist. I keep telling myself that climbing stairs is good for the figure, but I must admit that I don't tackle them myself unless I want something rather badly. This morning I wanted Gerda.

The director's office is on the second floor, but I had to go all the way down and then climb the central stairs, since the towers connect to the main building only on the first level. By the time I reached Gerda's room, I was full of adrenaline and pent-up rage.

She had been expecting me. I heard her type-writer start to rattle as I opened the door. She kept on typing, pretending she hadn't noticed me, even after I stamped across the room and stood beside her desk. When I saw what she was wearing, I became even more annoyed. The turtle-neck knit shirt, in bright stripes of shocking pink and pea green, was an exact copy of the one I had worn to work the week before.

This was a form of flattery, and it should have touched me. My hair is blond; Gerda's is brown. Gerda is five feet and a fraction; I am a fraction less than six feet. I am a bean pole, Gerda is a dumpling. For some crazy reason, she wants to look like me.

What woman in her right mind would want to be six feet tall? How can you look coyly up at a man from under your lashes when your eyes are on the same level, or higher? How can you find skirts long enough to cover your knees? Put a pitchfork in my hand, and I look like a farmer; put a spear in my hand, and I look like an undernourished Valkyrie. I'd much rather be cute and cuddly like Gerda — well, maybe not quite that cuddly — and it infuriates me when she tries to imitate me, especially since the clothes that look okay on me don't suit her at all.

I slapped the edge of the desk with the photograph. It cracked, like a pistol shot. Gerda jumped. "What's the idea of opening my mail?" I shouted. "How many times have I told you not to open my mail?"

I yelled in German. It's a good language to yell in, and I added a few expletives to my rhetorical question. Gerda answered in her meticulous, stilted English.

"That is impossible to calculate. It is also a meaningless question. To open the mail, it is my duty. In order to direct each piece of mail to the proper destination within the museum, it is necessary that I should investigate—"

We went on that way for a while, in a mixture of languages. My voice kept rising: Gerda's remained studiously calm, but her cheeks got pinker and pinker till she looked like a kewpie doll. The whole thing was ridiculous. Yelling was making my head ache, and I regretted having started the fight. We all knew Gerda's habits, and we all made damned good and sure none of our personal mail was directed to the museum. I wondered why I was doing this and how I could stop.

I was saved from retreat by Schmidt, who came barreling out of his office and added his bellow to the general uproar.

"Was ist's, ein Tiergarten oder ein Museum? Cannot a man absorb himself in study without

two screaming females interrupting his thoughts?
Die Weiber, die Weiber, ein Mann kann nicht —"

"You sound like *The Merry Widow,*" I said.
"Calm yourself, Herr Direktor."

"I calm myself? Whose screams were they
that interrupted my contemplation?"

"Not mine," said Gerda smugly.

"I knew that," Schmidt said. "What is it this
time?"

"You know," I said. "You've been listening
at the keyhole. You couldn't have heard us unless you *were* listening. That door is six inches
thick."

Schmidt's pudgy little hand stole to his mustache. He started growing it to compensate for
the complete absence of hair on his head, and it
has got out of hand. I think his initial model
was Fu-Manchu, for Schmidt has a deplorable
taste for sensational literature. Unfortunately,
Schmidt's mustache came out pure-white and
bushy. He's about Gerda's height, a foot shorter
than I, and that damned mustache was the only
touch needed to turn him into a walking caricature of a quaint German kobold or brownie —
round tummy, twinkling blue eyes, and an
adorable little pink mouth, like that of a pouting baby.

He didn't deny the charge. "The post," he
said. "Again the post. What is it today — a

letter from, er, grr, hm, a close friend, *vielleicht?*"

He leered and sidled around the desk trying to sneak a peek at what I was holding. I handed it to him.

"Sorry to disappoint you, Schmidt. My er, grr, close friends don't send passionate love letters to me at this address. If they did, they would cease to become close friends. I don't know who sent this, because Gerda had removed the outer envelope and, probably, an enclosed explanatory letter. Now I haven't the faintest idea what it means or what I'm supposed to do about it."

Schmidt's pink forehead crumpled into rows of wrinkles. *"Sehr interessant,"* he muttered, worrying his mustache. "Now where have I seen this face before?"

"Something strikes a chord," I agreed. "It looks like a theatrical costume. Hardly the sort of thing we'd want for the collection."

"Nein, nein. And yet . . . What is it that strikes me?"

Gerda cleared her throat. "I recognized it at once, Herr Direktor. When I took the course at the university last spring – or perhaps it was summer – yes, it was the Herr Professor Doktor Eberhardt's course in the minor arts of Asia Minor –"

I was tempted to lunge at her. She'd had

hours to check on that photograph and make fools of her two educated bosses. Schmidt was just as infuriated. "Get to the point," he shouted, glaring.

Gerda looked smug. "Surely the very-highly-expert doctors recognize the photograph. It is that of Frau Schliemann wearing the treasure of Troy. If you recall, it was in 1873 that the distinguished archaeologist found the mound of Hissarlik, in what is now Turkey, and identified it as—"

"You need not summarize the career of Heinrich Schliemann," said Schmidt, with heavy sarcasm. "Hmm. Yes. Possible you are correct. It is not, of course, my field."

It wasn't my field, either. All the same, I should have identified the photograph. Every art historian takes introductory courses, and every woman worthy of the name is fascinated by jewels. Gerda had one-upped me with consummate skill, and it was for that reason, I think, that I pursued the matter. On such low-down, petty motives does our fate depend. If Gerda had not tried to show off, and made me look stupid — if I hadn't been suffering from a well-deserved hang-over — I would probably have returned to my office, tossed the photo into a "pending" file, and awaited the expected, irate inquiry from the sender.

Which would not have come.

Instead, I said sharply, "What did you do with the outer envelope?"

Schmidt was still studying the photograph with a puzzled frown. Without looking up he asked, "How do you know there was another envelope?"

"Because this one is blank — no address, no stamps, no postmark. Come on, Gerda; there had to be an outer envelope. What happened to it?"

Gerda's eyes shifted. Mine followed the direction of her gaze. Her wastebasket was not only empty, it was as clean as my kitchen floor. Cleaner — I have a dog. "You threw it away?" I yelled.

"It was covered with filth," Gerda said, with a fastidious curl of her lip. "Stained and dirty — one could scarcely read the name."

"Was there a return address?"

"None that I could read. The dirty stains—"

"Postmark?"

Gerda shrugged.

Schmidt followed me out of the office. I asked him where he was going, and he said simply, "With you."

"Why?"

"You are going to look through the trash for the missing envelope." Schmidt savored the phrase. "The missing envelope...A good title for a thriller, *nicht?*"

"It's been used. Probably by Nancy Drew."

Schmidt didn't ask who Nancy Drew was. Maybe he knew. As I said, he has deplorable tastes in literature. "And," he went on cheerfully, "a good beginning for an adventure."

"What makes you think this is the beginning of an adventure? If," I added, "one can apply that melodramatic word to the unfortunate incidents that have marked my academic career."

"I hope it is. It has been eight months since our last case. I am bored."

Since Schmidt's only contribution to my last "case," if it could be called that, was to be pushed into the local slammer by a group of suspicious Swedes, his use of the plural pronoun might have been questioned – but not by me. He was still sulking about missing most of the fun. I didn't want to hurt his feelings, but I didn't want to encourage him either. I had had enough "cases," or "adventures," or, more accurately, "narrow escapes."

Not that I expected the mysterious photograph (damn! another thriller title) would lead to any such undesired development. It wasn't really mysterious, only odd, and if I could find the covering letter – there must be one, Gerda had simply overlooked it – the oddity would turn out to be odd only in the academic sense. Like most academicians, I had received my share of crank letters. Some were communiqués from the lunatic fringes of historical scholarship – like the woman who claimed to be possessed by the ghost of Hieronymus Bosch. Before her family got her committed, she sent me fifteen huge canvases she had painted under his spiritual direction. Some were from amiable ignoramuses who hoped to sell us some piece of junk they had dug out of the attic. This would probably turn out to be something of that sort, and my present quest was a real waste of time and effort. Possibly an explanatory letter had been sent under separate cover and had been delayed in transit. In any case, if the idea was important enough to the sender, he or she would write again when I failed to reply.

Having arrived at this reasonable conclusion, did I return to my office and my duties? No, I did not. I was still annoyed with Gerda, and an odd, provocative sense of something not quite right about that photograph was beginning to trouble my mind. With Schmidt trotting happily at my heels, I threaded a path through the maze of corridors and rooms that constituted the basement of the museum. The plan represented the Graf's vague idea of a medieval undercroft, complete with model dungeons and torture chambers. Schmidt had tried to set up the usual labs and studios, but the workers had gone on strike, even after fluorescent lighting had been installed and the rusty shackles and implements of torture had been removed. Von Blauert, our chemist, complained that he kept having nightmares about being shut up in the Iron Maiden. So Schmidt resignedly moved the whole lot up to the top floor, and the cellars were used only for storage of nonperishable items. There was also a door opening into the sunken enclosed courtyard behind the museum, where the trash from the museum ended up in big bins that were picked up bi-weekly by a local firm. The courtyard did double duty as a staff parking lot, which was how I knew about the trash.

Hearing our footsteps ring in dismal echoes along the authentic-stone-paved passageway, Carl, the janitor, opened the door of his room. His face lit up when he saw me, and he greeted me with flattering enthusiasm. At least it would have been flattering if I had not known that I was not the object of his adoration. It was my dog he doted on.

There's an antique witticism that runs, "I don't have a dog, he has me." Caesar is a Doberman, big as a pony and slobberingly affectionate. I had to bring him to work with me one day when the exterminators were dealing with an infestation of some strange little purple bugs in my house. Carl was in the courtyard when we arrived, and it was love at first sight, on both parts. Carl was in the habit of paying a formal call on Caesar every few weeks; he always brought presents of bones and took Caesar for a long walk.

I had to give him a detailed rundown on Caesar's health before he allowed me to question him. Yes, he had emptied Gerda's wastebasket that morning. He emptied her wastebasket every morning and every afternon. No, the trash men had not collected that day: Tuesday and Friday were their regular days. Certainly, we could prowl around in the trash all we liked. He hoped we enjoyed ourselves.

He didn't offer to help, and I didn't ask, since I couldn't tell him what I was looking for. I only hoped I would recognize it if I saw it.

Snowflakes trickled down out of a pewter-gray sky as I climbed on a packing case and peered down into the bin which, according to Carl, held that day's garbage. Schmidt, who would have needed a ladder to reach the same height, jumped up and down to keep warm and demanded that I toss down an armful or two so he could help me search. I was tempted to give him a bundle of the riper refuse — the remains of people's lunches, from the smell — but controlled myself. A handful of papers stopped his outcries; he hunkered down in the lee of the bin and began sorting them, happy as a puppy with a moldy bone.

Cold had turned Schmidt's pink face a delicate shade of lavender by the time I found the envelope. It should have been on the top of the heap; but in the manner of all desired objects, it had slid down into a corner, behind a soggy paper bag containing two apple cores and the crusts of a Gorgonzola-and-wurst sandwich. For once Gerda had not exaggerated. The paper was filthy. A disfiguring brown stain covered much of the envelope. It was an old stain, hardened and dark; and although I am not particularly fastidious, my fingers were slow to close over it.

A shiver ran through me. The shiver was not one of apprehension; it was freezing out there. I only wish I did have premonitory chills when something awful is about to happen to me. Then I might be able to avoid it.

I dragged my purpling superior from the papers he was examining. Once inside, we examined my find.

"Ha," Schmidt cried eagerly. "Blood!"

"Mud," I said shortly. "Schmidt, your imagination is really deplorable."

"There is no return address."

"Oh well, I tried. Now I can forget the whole thing."

"But, Vicky—"

"But me no buts, Schmidt. Don't think it hasn't been fun; we must meet and pick through garbage again someday."

"Where are you going now?"

"To the library. I have work to do."

I had work to do, all right, but not in the library. I stayed there only long enough to get the book I wanted. Then I took it upstairs to my office.

The snow was falling more heavily now; it formed a lacy, blowing white curtain around the walls of my room. I felt much better. Nothing like a little exercise and a yelling match to restore a lady to perfect health after a night on the town. I spread my clues out on the desk and settled down to study them.

The envelope first. There was no return address, at least not on the part of the envelope that had escaped the obliterating stain. After prolonged rummaging in my desk drawers I found the magnifying glass Schmidt had given me for Christmas one year. Schmidt expected me to use it while I crawled around on the floor looking for clues in the dust — something I hardly, if ever, do. I actually had used the glass a time or two in the preliminary stages of authenticating a work of art; sometimes all it takes to spot a fake is a close-up look at the brush strokes or the machine-drilled "wormholes."

On this occasion the Holmesian accessory was of no help. Under magnification, the blurred letters of the postmark were larger but no more legible. The first two letters might have been a *B* and an *A*. Bad something? There are hundreds of towns in Germany named Bad Something. The opaque dark stain covered most of the back of the envelope and a good third of the front, including the areas where one might have expected to find a return address. Even under the lens I couldn't see any traces of writing.

I filled my sink with water and dunked the envelope. It was of heavy paper coated on the inside with a thin layer of plastic, which had prevented the stain from spreading to the inner wrapping. I was wasting a lot of time on something that was probably a peculiar practical joke; but when I returned to my desk and opened the reference book from the library, I knew why my curiosity had been aroused. Gerda had been only half right. Superficially the photo I had received did resemble the famous photograph of Sophia Schliemann decked out in the gold of Troy. But mine was not a picture of Sophia. It was of a different woman – wearing the same jewelry.

Not the same jewelry – a copy. It had to be a copy, because my photograph had been taken quite recently. The woman's hairstyle, the photographic technique, and a dozen other subtle clues obvious to a great detective like Victoria Bliss proved as much.

Besides, there was a calendar on the wall, visible behind the woman's shoulder. It read "May 1982."

The gold of Troy had vanished, never to be seen again, in the spring of 1945.

I felt it begin – a warm, delirious flush of excitement rippling giddily through my veins. A harbinger of adventure and discovery, of mysteries solved and treasure restored to an admiring world? More likely a harbinger of certifiable lunacy. I slammed the book shut and planted both elbows on it, as if physical restraint could contain the insanity seeping from those pages like a dark fog, inserting sly tendrils into the weak spots of my enfeebled brain. I swear the damned book squirmed, as if struggling to open itself.

I pressed down harder with my elbows and dropped my head onto my hands. I knew what was wrong with me. I was bored and depressed and disgustingly sorry for myself, otherwise I would never have given the insane hypothesis a second thought.

Christmas was only a few weeks away, and this year I couldn't afford to go home to Minnesota. They would all be there for the holidays — Grandmother and Granddad Anderson, my brothers and their families, including Bob's new baby son whom I had never seen. Mother and Grandmother, the world's greatest Swedish cooks, would be baking, filling the house with the warm rich smells of cinnamon and cloves and chocolate and yeast; Dad would be decorating the tree and Granddad would be sitting in his favorite chair telling Dad he was doing it all wrong and trying to pick fights about politics with his "damned liberal grandchildren"; and the kids would be screaming with excitement and punching each other and trying to figure out how to break into the closet where their presents were hidden. . . .

I was all alone and nobody loved me.

But even as I watched a fat tear spatter on the cover of the book, my unregenerate memory was trying to recall what I knew about the gold of Troy.

My field is medieval European painting and sculpture. However, in my line of work, it is necessary to become something of a Jack-of-all-trades, since museums can't afford to hire experts in every specialty of art history. I had had to learn about jewelry, since we have one of the best small collections on the Continent. And the career of Heinrich Schliemann is a fable, a legend, a children's book come to life.

Schliemann was the original Horatio Alger hero. He began his career as a stock boy, sleeping under the counter of the store at night, and ended up a millionaire merchant. Once he'd acquired his wealth, he dumped his business interests and turned to the subject that had obsessed him since his daddy had read to him from Homer. Unlike most historians of his time, naïve Heinrich believed the Homeric poems were literally true. The credulous merchant was right, and the historians were wrong. Schliemann found Troy. At the bottom of the trench he had cut across the city mound, he came upon a disintegrated wooden chest that held the treasure of a vanished nobleman.

Schliemann had found more treasures than any amateur deserves to find. He'd dug up another hoard at Mycenae a few years later. But it was the first one, the Trojan gold, that fired his imagination. He decked his beautiful wife Sophia in the jewels for the picture that had been so often reproduced. Perhaps the divine Helen had worn these very diadems, earrings, chains, and studs. . . . Actually she hadn't. The gold didn't come from Priam's Troy, but from a period a thousand years earlier.

That was about the extent of my knowledge of Schliemann's find. I knew even less about the disappearance of the treasure, though that event was as dramatic as the circumstances of its discovery.

Schliemann had presented the gold of Troy to a German museum, over the objections of his Greek wife, who felt it ought to remain in Greece. The Turks also claimed it, since Hissarlik, the site of Troy, was on Turkish soil. If the gold had turned up — which of course it hadn't. . . But if it had, the question of legal ownership would present an interesting tangle.

Nowadays, excavators can't remove a potsherd without the permission of the host government, but in the nineteenth century, archaeology was a free-for-all, and possession was nine-tenths of the law. The major museums of the world owe their collections of ancient art to methods that are at best highly dubious and at worst downright dishonest. The Greeks have never stopped complaining about the Elgin marbles and the Aegina sculptures; the Egyptians still want Nefertiti to come home. But the marbles remain in the British Museum, and the Aegina pieces are in the Glyptothek in Munich, and Nefertiti has gone back to a case in a Berlin museum after a brief vacation in a bomb shelter.

Like Nefertiti, the gold of Troy had been removed from its museum during World War II and placed in safekeeping. Somewhere in Berlin, that was all I knew. The Russians had been the first to reach Berlin. And that was the last anyone had seen or heard of the Trojan gold.

If I had given much thought to the matter, which I had not, I would have assumed the Russians had taken the gold to Moscow, along with other little odds and ends like factories, the Pergamum altar sculptures, German nuclear scientists, wrist-watches, and the like. But surely, I mused, most of that stolen property had eventually resurfaced – hadn't it? The factories had turned out steel and concrete for Mother Russia, the scientists had helped build lots of lovely missiles; even the Pergamum sculptures had been returned to a museum in Berlin. East Berlin, that is.

If the Soviets had returned masterpieces like the Pergamum sculptures, why hadn't they returned the gold of Troy?

The book popped open again; I'm sure I never touched it. I placed the two photos side by side and picked up my trusty magnifying glass.

The reproduction in the book was of poor quality, and my photo was grainy and blurred. I couldn't make out the finer details. I could see, however, that there were minor discrepancies I had not observed earlier. The pieces were the same — necklaces, earrings, diadem — but they weren't arranged in quite the same fashion.

Since I knew that Sophia's jewelry was the genuine article, the differences should have convinced me that the second set was a careless copy, right? Wrong. You see, the museum displays of ancient jewelry, all shiny and polished and pretty, are the result of long months of repair and restoration. The originals didn't look like that when they were found buried deep in the earth; they were often tumbled, twisted heaps of bits and pieces, and sometimes it is anybody's guess as to how the pieces went together. Was this flat jeweled ornament attached to that golden chain, or did it form part of the beaded girdle whose beads have tumbled from the rotted cord? Was this dangle an earring or a pendant or part of a crown? I could not remember what condition the Trojan gold had been in when it was discovered, but it was a safe bet that a certain amount of restoration had been necessary. The differences between the two sets were the sort one would expect to find if two restorers — two authorities — had disagreed.

My copy certainly was a first-class forgery.

Another tear plopped onto the book, spotting Sophia's face. I scowled and wiped it off with my finger. I ought to be ashamed of myself, succumbing to self-pity and *Heimweh*. That's all it was, a touch of homesickness. Nothing to do with...anything else.

TWO

"They" say hard work is the best cure for depression. I can think of several things that are more effective, but since none of them were immediately available, I applied myself diligently to a long-overdue article for a professional journal and didn't stop until I was interrupted by the telephone. It was Schmidt, inviting me to lunch. He takes me to lunch once or twice a week so I can regale him with Rosanna's latest escapades.

Rosanna is the heroine of the novel I've been writing on and off for nigh onto five years. I suppose you could call it a historical romance, though the history is wildly inaccurate and romance is a very feeble word for Rosanna's love life. So far she has been abducted by sultans, outlaws, highwaymen, degenerate noblemen, Genghis Khan, and Louis the Fourteenth, to mention only a few. (I *said* the historical part was inaccurate.) Rosanna has never been raped because it is against my principles to contribute, even by implication, to the "relax and enjoy it" school of perversion. However, she has had quite a few narrow escapes, and I wouldn't exactly claim she was celibate. I have given up any idea of submitting the book to a publisher, since it has become too absurd even for a historical romance, which, believe me, is very absurd indeed. I go on with it because it amuses Schmidt – and me.

Some instinct told me that Schmidt had an ulterior motive that day, but I accepted anyhow. After I had put on my boots and coat, I looked at the sink.

The water was a sickly, sickening brownish red. I pulled the plug and let it run out.

Schmidt never climbs the tower stairs except in cases of dire emergency, which is one of the reasons why I chose that particular office. He was waiting for me in the Hall of Armor, adjoining the tower; as I descended, I heard him talking to the guard on duty. I caught the punch line – "But, *mein Herr*, it is your mustache!" – followed by a chorus of guffaws from Schmidt and his stooge. Everybody laughs at Schmidt's jokes, even though they are all culled from the Bavarian equivalent of Joe Miller's book. A director has certain prerogatives.

I stepped over the velvet rope with its *"Eintritt verboten"* sign, greeted the guard, tucked

Schmidt's scarf into his collar, and led him out. It was still snowing. There was almost no wind, and the soft white flakes fell gently from the tarnished silver bowl of the sky. Traffic had stirred the streets into a sloppy slush, but the towers of Munich's myriad churches looked as if they had been frosted with vanilla icing.

We went to our favorite *Bierstube,* which specializes in a particular variety of heavy dark beer to which Schmidt is addicted. (There are few varieties of beer to which Schmidt is not addicted.) Schmidt ordered *Weisswurst* and got it, even though the church bells had already chimed twelve. He ordered a lot of other things, too, including an entire loaf of heavy black bread and a pound or so of sweet butter. I sipped daintily at my own beer and waited for him to get to the point, knowing it wouldn't take long. Schmidt thinks he is sly and subtle, but he is mistaken.

After the waiter had brought the first course, Schmidt tucked his napkin into his collar and stared fixedly at me.

"That was not Frau Schliemann in the photograph."

"I know."

"You know? Oh yes, you, you always know." Schmidt stuffed his mouth with wurst and masticated fiercely. Then he mumbled, "Mrshwenill."

"I beg your pardon?"

"Miss Know-It-All."

"Ms. Know-It-All, *bitte.*"

Schmidt grinned. I reached across the table and removed a speck of wurst from his mustache.

"So what shall we do?" he asked.

"What can we do?"

"Have the wrapping examined to see if the stain is blood," Schmidt said promptly.

"We could." And of course I would. I had known that ever since I saw the brown-red water. Since we did a lot of work with fabrics, we had a fairly well-equipped lab at the museum. If that particular test was beyond our chemist, I had several pals in the police department.

"But what if it is blood?" I went on.

"Human blood!"

"So what if it is human blood? We can't trace the damned thing; there is no return address. Perhaps the sender will follow up with a letter."

"And perhaps he is no longer in a position to do that," said Schmidt. "It took a lot of blood to make a stain that size, Vicky."

His illogical, melodramatic conclusion irritated me all the more because it was exactly what I had been thinking.

"You ought to write thrillers for a living, Schmidt," I snarled. "Which reminds me. Madly jealous at being supplanted in the affections of the King, Madame de Maintenon has accused Rosanna of practicing witchcraft. Would you like to hear—"

"No, I would not. At least not at the present time. Why do you refuse to discuss this matter? Most probably the photograph is a childish joke, but if there is the slightest chance it is anything else... You have a flair for such things, Vicky. All of us develop a certain instinct, which is nothing more than long years of experience working with antiquities; but yours is stronger than most. If the jewelry in the photograph is not the original, it is an excellent copy, *nein?*"

"Yes," I said.

Schmidt's fork, with its impaled chunk of sausage, stopped midway to his mouth. *Weisswurst* is really quite revolting in appearance; I will spare you the comparisons. I averted my eyes.

"What is it?" Schmidt asked solicitously. "There is in your voice a note of grief, of tears repressed—"

"There is nothing of the sort. Your imagination is getting out of hand."

"*Ach, so?* Then with the tactfulness for which

I am well known, I will pass on to matters of documented fact. Since you are this Ms. Know-It-All, I presume you are well acquainted with the details of the fall of Berlin in 1945."

"No, I am not, and what's more, I don't want to be. Art history may be a cop-out, but at least it enables me to focus on the positive achievements of the human race."

I had meant the statement as a criticism — an indictment, if you will — of myself; but Schmidt's sudden sobriety showed I had hit a nerve. Then, too late, I remembered something I had been told by Gerda, who really was Ms. Know-It-All. Schmidt had been a member of the White Rose, the Munich student conspiracy against Hitler — and he had lost many of his friends, including the girl he had hoped to marry, when the plot was discovered and the ringleaders were savagely executed. If the story was true, and I had no reason to suppose it was not, Schmidt had even stronger reasons that I to retreat from the contemplation of man's inhumanity to man.

I didn't apologize, since that would only have made things worse. After an interval, Schmidt's cherubic countenance returned to its normal, cheerful expression. He went on without referring to what I had said.

"The most valued exhibits from the Berlin

museums had been removed to a bunker in the Teirgarten — the zoo."

"I know what *Teirgarten* means."

"Ha! But you don't know, I will bet you, that many of the objects taken away by the Russians when they entered the bunker have now been returned. The Gobelin tapestries, the Pergamum sculptures, the coin collection of Friedrich the Great..."

One up for Schmidt. I had known of the Pergamum sculptures, but not the other things. Naturally, I wasn't going to admit my ignorance.

"All right," I said, with an exaggerated sigh. "Let's admit for the sake of argument that both preposterous premises are right. The gold in the photograph is the genuine article and the stain on the envelope is human blood. We're still up the creek without a paddle. We have no idea where that photograph came from."

Schmidt's cheeks gyrated as he tried to chew and nod at the same time. Swallowing, he patted his mouth daintily with the tail of his napkin and then remarked, "Too true. What a pity that the one man who might lead us out of our dilemma is no longer among the living."

I reached for a piece of bread and busied myself breaking and buttering it.

Schmidt is so classically, overpoweringly cute

that people tend to forget how intelligent he is. And I swear there are times when I think he can read my mind. Not that a high degree of ESP was required in this case. The word "copy" inevitably brought John to mind. Also the words "fraud," "fake," and "crook."

Sir John Smythe he called himself, among other names – none of them his real one. The title was equally apocryphal. He had once admitted that John was his first name – not very informative, even if it was true, which it might not be. He was the most accomplished liar since Baron Münchausen.

His physical appearance varied as extravagantly as his name. The underlying structure, the basic John Smythe, was inconspicuously average – about my height, rather slightly built, with no identifying characteristics. In repose his features could only be described as pleasantly unmemorable, but they were capable of a rubbery flexibility any actor would have sold his soul to possess. The color of his hair and eyes varied, according to the circumstances (usually illegal); but, as I had good cause to know, he was fair-haired and blue-eyed. The only features he had trouble disguising – from me, at least – were his lashes, long and thick as a girl's, and his hands. Deft, skillful hands, long-fingered, deceptively slender...

"Shall I ask the waiter for more butter?" Schmidt asked sweetly.

I looked at my plate. On it were five pieces of bread, each buried under a greasy yellow mound.

"No, thanks, this will do," I said, and bit into one of the slices. The slippery, sliding texture of the butter against the roof of my mouth made me want to gag.

Schmidt is a canny little kobold. He didn't refer to the subject again. He didn't have to. The damage had been done, though not by him. By the photograph, the fake, the fraud.

I left work early, and when I got home that evening I did something I had sworn I would never do again. The portrait was buried deep under a pile of cast-off, out-of-date business papers. Usually it takes me days to find a needed receipt or letter, but I had no trouble finding this particular item.

The portrait was not a photograph, or a sketch, or a painting. I had no snapshots of John; I doubt if many people did. He had good cause to be leery of cameras. But the silhouette had been cut by a master of that dying art; the black paper outline captured not only the distinctive bone structure and the sculptured line of that arrogant nose, but also a personality, in the confident tilt of the chin and the suggestion of a faint smile on the thin, chiseled lips.

People claim wine is a depressant. It never depressed me until that evening. I sat on my nice newly upholstered couch with my nice friendly dog sleeping at my feet, sipping my nice chilled Riesling *Spätlese*, and my mood got blacker with every sip — black as the scissored outline at which I stared. It might have been the chilly hiss of sleet against the windows. It might have been Caesar, moaning and twitching in a doggish nightmare. Sometimes dogs seem to have happy dreams. I had always assumed they grinned and whined at visions of bones, and overflowing food dishes, and friendly hands stroking them. What then were the subjects of canine nightmares? Giant cats the size of grizzly bears? Perhaps Caesar was reliving the tribulations of his youth, before I adopted him. I would never forget my first sight of him, bursting with fangs bared and eyes blazing out of the darkness of the antique shop I happened to be burgling. His keeper had kept him half-starved and beaten him to make him savage. . . .

John was one of the gang — art swindlers, forgers of historic gems. He boasted that half the great art collections contained copies he had substituted for the priceless originals, and he was particularly proud of the fact that the substitutions had never been detected. Not for him the armed attack, the murdered guards, the crude, grab-it-and-run techniques of lesser craftsmen. John abhorred violence, particularly when it was directed against him.

However, he had killed at least one man. I couldn't complain about that since the man he killed had been doing his damnedest to murder me.

John had vanished under the icy storm-lashed waters of Lake Vippen eight months earlier, taking with him the aquatic assassin who had picked me as victim number one. The body of the man he killed had been found a few days later. John had never been seen again.

The scenario was as romantically tragic as any I could have invented for my unending novel; and all the surviving participants had been suitably moved, including Schmidt, who had insisted on helping erect a suitable monument to the fallen hero. Schmidt was determined to regard John as a kind of Robin Hood, which couldn't have been farther from the truth. John did confine his depredations to the rich, but that was only because poor people didn't have anything worth stealing, and the only charity to which he contributed was himself. Of course John had never happened to rob Schmidt's museum. And Schmidt is a hopeless sentimentalist.

Schmidt is not, however, a fool. He had enjoyed wallowing in sloppy tears over the heroic dead; but once the glow wore off, he had probably reached the same conclusion I had reached — namely and to wit, that the memorial might be a trifle premature. The event had given John a heaven-sent opportunity to avoid a number of people whose greatest ambition in life was to nail him to a wall by his elegant ears. The man he had killed was the head of a gang of thieves who would probably resent the death of their leader and the loss of their jobs, particularly since John had been trying to steal the loot from them all along. John was also an object of passionate interest to the police of several countries. His presumed death would wipe the slate clean and give him a chance to start over.

At first I didn't doubt he was still alive. For weeks I expected to hear from him — one of those absurd communications in which his quirky, devious mind delighted. Once he had sent me a forgery of a famous historic jewel. Another time, it had been a single rose — another fake, a silk copy of a real flower. But eight months had gone by without a word from him. . . .

Is it any wonder I thought of John when I received an anonymous photograph of what appeared to be an excellent imitation of a museum treasure? Cryptic messages, copies, and forgeries were the trademarks of Sir John B. Smythe. Was this the message for which I had been waiting? Waiting was all I could do. I did not know how to get in touch with John; I never had known. Of course, if I was mistaken about his survival, a spiritualist medium was probably my best bet.

Yet this particular communication had sinister overtones that were not characteristic of John. His frivolous attitude toward life in general and his dubious profession in particular had gotten him into a heap of trouble. As he had once sadly remarked, some of his colleagues had no sense of humor. They kept misinterpreting his little jokes (at their expense) and wanting to beat him up.

The grisly bloodstain on the envelope wasn't John's style. Unless the joke had backfired. Unless the blood was his.

The shiny white cardboard reflected the lamplight, enclosing the black profile in a soft golden halo. The inappropriateness of that image brought a sour smile to my lips. The smile turned to a grimace as I remembered what I had done that afternoon.

It had seemed like a good idea at the time. In retrospect it struck me as the most idiotic move I had ever made — and I speak as one whose career has not been unblemished by foolish actions.

I had put personal ads in the major newspapers of the world. All of them. *Figaro, Die Welt, La Prensa, Neue Zurcher Zeitung, Il Corriere della Sera, ABC,* the New York and London *Times....*

Even now I hate to admit I did it. However, a lot of underworld characters use the personals as a means of communication, and I knew John sometimes read them for the sake of amusement. I felt certain the message would capture his attention. It read: "Rudolph. Not roses, Helen's jewels. Michael and Rupert no problem. Contact soonest. Flavia."

It had seemed like a good idea at the time. Few people would understand that string of absurdities, but I knew John would; the single red rose he had sent me came from the same corny old novel. The reference to Michael and Rupert cost me an extra twenty bucks, but I thought I had a better chance of arousing John's interest if I assured him the villains were out of the picture.

Caesar moaned. The wind wailed. The sleet kept on falling. The wine was gone. I was all alone and nobody loved me. Worse than that — I was drunk and all alone and nobody loved me.

Which only goes to show that those boring clichés about optimism are true. "Tomorrow is another day; it's always darkest before the dawn." Unbeknownst to me, a lot of people were concerned about me — thinking, worrying, caring, talking. The most provocative of the conversations might have gone something like this:

It began with commiserations, half-ironic, half-furious, on her husband's death.

"But there was nothing else to do! He had made up his mind. He was actually on his way to the *Postamt,* to send the photograph. I had to act quickly!"

"Stupidly, you mean. You have silenced the only man who knew where it was hidden."

"Perhaps he told her. A note, a letter, sent with the photograph—"

"And now you've lost that too. What the devil could have become of it?"

"I tell you, I don't know! Someone may have found it lying in the snow—"

"Are you sure that was the only copy? Did he communicate with anyone else?"

"No — I don't think so. . . . How can I be sure? Any of them might—"

"Shut up and let me think."

A long silence followed. She ran shaking fingers through her hair, nibbled on her bitten nails. Then the voice at the other end of the wire said, "I have received nothing. That would suggest that she was the only one he confided in."

"Yes. Yes. We can deal with her—"

"As you dealt with the old man? I forbid it. Do you hear? Keep that degenerate follower of yours under control. Leave it to me."

"Yes, my darling. I am sorry—"

"Rather late for regrets, isn't it?"

Tears filled her eyes, smearing her heavy make-up. "Don't be angry with me. You will break my heart. I promise, I will do whatever you say."

"Do nothing. Keep searching. Notify me at once — at once, do you hear? — if she communicates with you. In the meantime, I will take steps to correct your mistake."

"You think you can—"

"I have several ideas," the far-off voice murmured.

For the next few days I was followed around Munich by little fat men — or, sometimes, little fat women. They were all Schmidt. He loves dressing up in funny costumes. I wouldn't dream of destroying his illusion that he is a

50

great detective, so I pretended not to recognize him. I didn't try to lose him either, which wouldn't have been hard.

I would have lost him if I had been doing what he thought I was doing — heading for a rendezvous with the mysterious, the enigmatic Robin Hood of crime. Schmidt assumed that though John had vanished from the rest of the world, he had kept in touch with the love of his life. Maybe he had — but obviously I wasn't it.

The stain on the wrapping paper was human blood, all right. This fact, among others, convinced me John was not the sender. The sight of blood made him sick — especially, as he had candidly admitted, his own. Nor would he have left me hanging in limbo. He'd have sent a follow-up message.

I studied that damned photograph, with the naked eye and the magnifying glass, until every detail was imprinted on my brain. If there was a hidden clue, I failed to find it. Schmidt had no better luck than I. He kept stealing the photo, and I had to keep stealing it back; and I knew that if he had found something I overlooked, he wouldn't be able to resist bragging about it. I made a point of arriving early at work so I could intercept the mail before Gerda messed around with it. I infuriated the switchboard operator with my daily demand of "Are you sure no one else called?"

She was sure.

Except for Schmidt's comedy routine, it was a dull week. Even his appearance as a pint-sized Erich von Stroheim, complete with monocle, didn't cheer me up. Schmidt's eye muscles weren't up to the job of retaining the monocle, it kept falling out, and whenever I looked back at him, all I saw was his rotund rump as he pawed at the snowdrifts looking for his prop. That pursuit ended when some woman started beating him with her purse and accusing him of trying to look up her skirts. I guess he talked her out of calling a cop. I didn't intervene, since I wasn't supposed to know who he was.

I'm not one of those unfortunate people who sink into a deep depression during the holidays. Usually I love Christmas, and *Weihnachten* in Bavaria is lots of fun. Streets and shops were strung with greens; Christmas trees sparkled in every square and plaza. The Kristkindl-markt was in full swing, as it had been for over a hundred and fifty years; booths and stands crowded the square under the shadow of der Alte Peter, who is not an elderly gentleman but an elderly church. In the evening, lanterns and candles and strings of rainbow lights shone like fallen stars in the blue dusk, and trumpeters on the church tower played the old carols; the clear, bright notes drifted down like music from heaven, blending with the gently falling snow. Every variety of Christmas decoration was for sale, from gilded gingerbread to handmade ornaments; and I lingered at the booths featuring the lovely carved crèches. I couldn't afford any of the ones I wanted, so I bought *Pfeffernüsse* and sugared almonds for Schmidt, and a gilded bare branch strung with hard candies — a kindly compromise of the old legend in which the saint brings sweeties to the good little children and switches to the naughty ones.

In other words, I did my damnedest to cultivate some Christmas spirit. I had only limited success. The gold bracelet I bought mother recalled the glitter of Helen's diadem; a street sign reminded me that the small town of Dachau was only a few miles away and made me wonder why I was worrying about the fate of a few chunks of lifeless metal, compared to the wreckage of human life in that awful cataclysm.

Even the toy stores didn't cheer me up. German toy stores are superb, but I was pretty sure my nieces and nephews would prefer copies of American superheroes made in Taiwan to the beautifully crafted castles and storybook dolls and stuffed, cuddly animals. I loaded up on heroes for the kids and consoled myself with a stuffed kitten. I adore stuffed animals, but I have a hard time building a collection because Caesar keeps eating them. The kitten was life-sized and amazingly lifelike — a Siamese with seal-brown ears and tail, a pink nose, and blue glass eyes. At the moment, however, I was not too fond of blue eyes, what with Schmidt dogging my every move and John not dogging me. . . .

I also bought a robe and nightgown. They were Italian-made, sheer white batiste dripping with lace and embroidery. After I got back to work that day, I spread the robe out across the desk and stared at it. I cannot honestly say I do not know what possessed me to buy such a useless, extravagant item. I knew exactly what had possessed me. It wasn't even my style; as my mother keeps insisting, I look better in tailored clothes.

When the telephone rang I lunged for it, hoping the caller would be someone interesting enough to take my mind off my increasing insanity.

At first I didn't recognize his voice. Even after he had identified himself, I remained doubtful. "Are you sick or something? You sound funny."

"Humor is not my aim," said Tony. "This is a business call."

"The word was ill-chosen," I admitted. "Seriously — are you all right?"

"Yes."

"Where are you?"

"I'm in Illinois, of course. Are you going to the meetings this year?"

"Which meetings? Oh — Turin. No, I don't think so."

"You went last year."

I had not taken him seriously when he said the call was business; one never knows when the IRS may be bugging one's telephone. But the formal, almost accusatory tone was not like the Tony I knew.

"Last year the meetings were only sixty miles from Munich," I explained patiently. "And there were several sessions on art history. Are you going?"

"Yes. I — uh — I had hoped to see you."

"Well, you won't unless you stop over in Munich."

"May I? I wouldn't want to interfere with your plans—"

"Tony, you sound like Miss Manners' older brother. I'd love to see you. I can't think of anything I'd like better. I have no plans — I'll be all alone—"

"What about that weird little boss of yours?"

"Schmidt," I said in exasperation. "His name is Schmidt, as you know perfectly well. I usually do spend Christmas with him unless I go home, but this year he's going to his sister's. He can't stand the woman — she's one of those tight-lipped disapproving types — and he hates her husband, too; but she trapped him and he couldn't think of an excuse—"

"Oh," Tony said, in a sepulchral bass rumble, like Boris Karloff. "All right. How does the twenty-first suit you?"

I assured him nothing in this world or the next would give me greater pleasure than to pick him up at the airport on December 21.

"Okay," Tony mumbled. "See you then."

The click of the far-off receiver caught me with my mouth open and my rapturous enthusiasm half-expressed. He sounded as if he was even more depressed than I was. Instead of cheering one another, we might end up in a joint suicide pact. Then something else hit me. Tony had not asked me to marry him.

Tony always asked me to marry him. He had been asking me for years. One of the reasons why he disliked Schmidt was that he blamed the old boy for luring me from the primrose path that led to the cottage door and the little frilly aprons and the houseful of babies. This was completely unjust, since I wouldn't have married Tony even if Schmidt had not offered me a job.

Not that I wasn't fond of Tony, who is tall (really tall, I mean, six inches taller than I am), dark, and handsome, if you like the lean aesthetic type, which I definitely do. I met him at the midwestern college where we were both starving instructors, and we had spent one wild summer in Germany on the trail of a lost masterpiece of medieval sculpture. The successful climax of the hunt had won me a job offer from Schmidt, and it hadn't hurt Tony's career either; he was now an assistant professor at the University of Chicago with a consultative post at the Art Institute.

I loved Tony, but I wasn't in love with him — nor was I in love with the idea of marriage as such. I'm not knocking the institution; it seems to work fine for a lot of people. But not for me. Not for a while, at any rate.

Anyway, he had probably decided to propose in person. That must be the explanation. I had only imagined he sounded odd. Maybe he was recovering from flu. Maybe my own evil mood had affected my hearing. He was always good company — dear old Tony — a face from home, someone with whom to share the festive season. . . .

I started to feel more cheerful. Things were working out after all. It was a good thing John had not responded to my loony message. There were no two people I was less anxious to introduce than John and Tony. Unless it was John and Schmidt.

John's failure to respond didn't mean he was dead. He might not see the advertisement. He might see it and choose not to reply. A superstitious man might regard me as something of a jinx. Not only had I wrecked several of his business ventures, but I had been indirectly responsible for the infliction of grave bodily harm upon his person. The ad had only appeared a few days ago. He might yet...

If I married Tony, I would never have to spend Christmas alone ever again.

When I realized what I was thinking, I was so horrified I rushed out of the office and then had to go back for my coat. I really must be cracking up if that struck my subconscious as a legitimate excuse for matrimony. Christmas comes but once a year, for God's sake.

The rest of the week was uneventful except for snow and sleet and Schmidt's incompetent imitation of Super-Spy. Like the dim-witted heroine picking wildflowers along the railroad track, I was blissfully unaware of approaching danger. Actually, that isn't a very good analogy.

Trouble came at me, not along a single track, but from all directions at once, and by the time I realized what was happening, it was too late to jump out of the way.

Gerda and I had a date to go and see the Christmas crèches at the Bayrisches Museum. We were friends again; we fight at least once a month, when she says or does something that bugs me and I yell at her, and then she cries and I apologize. It's a tradition. Visiting the crèches was also a tradition, by Gerda's definition. I think we had done it twice before. I agreed to go because she cried, and because it seemed like a fitting part of my campaign to work up some Christmas spirit.

The crèches really are sensational. Some are small settings of the traditional manger scene, like the modern versions people put under the tree, but the best ones are vast panoramas that would fill an entire living room — miniature reproductions of village scenes, with shops and stalls and houses, and all the inhabitants pausing in their daily chores to watch the Magi riding toward the stable. The most elaborate of them come from Italy, and they feature painted terra-cotta figures dressed in real velvets and brocades in the case of the Magi and their entourage, and detailed reproductions of contemporary peasant costumes in the case of the villagers.

Some of the scenes are so complex that you can see them over and over again and still find charming details you missed before. If I were a snob and a hypocrite, I would claim that Gerda's naïve enjoyment enhanced my own more sophisticated expert's appreciation, but in fact I got as big a kick out of it as she did.

"*Ach,* Vicky, see the little boy stealing apples from the fruit stand!"

"He's the spitting image of my nephew Jim!"

"Do you think they had apples in December in the Holy Land?"

"Who cares? Look at the woman nursing the baby and gossiping with her neighbor on the next balcony."

The corridors along which we moved with snaillike deliberation were dimly lighted in order to display the *Krippen* in their lighted cases to best advantage. The place was crowded, but the churchlike atmosphere kept voices low and manners gentle. Except for the children. The little ones squealed with delight, the older ones with frustration as they tried to squirm through the barricade of adult bodies between them and the exhibits.

I hoisted one little imp up onto my shoulder, winning a thank-you from his *Mutti,* who had a baby in one arm and a bag of baby paraphernalia on the other. Gerda wrinkled her nose and moved away; like many self-professed sentimentalists, she really hates children. The imp and I discussed the scene; he was far less interested in the Christ Child and *"die süssen Englekinder"* than in how the Kings stayed on the camels.

I put him down and joined Gerda at the next exhibit. She was showing signs of restlessness, for which I couldn't entirely blame her. Even the miraculous birth palls after a dozen repetitions. "Look," she muttered, poking me. "That man — he has been following me."

So had a lot of other men, women, and children. I glanced in the direction she indicated and decided she was engaging in some wishful thinking; the light was poor and her follower moved on as I turned, but I caught a fleeting glimpse of a clean-cut profile, spare and handsome as a hawk's, before darkness obscured it.

"He looks familiar," I said thoughtfully.

"I suppose you think he is following you," Gerda said.

"I don't think he is following either of us. Gerda, you're getting testy. Hunger, I expect. Let's have a little snack; we've improved our minds long enough."

After she had been stuffed with whipped-cream cakes and coffee, Gerda's temper improved. We returned to work arm in arm, figuratively speaking.

I never lock my office door. I don't keep anything valuable there, and the guard on duty in the Armor Room is supposed to prevent unauthorized persons from going up the stairs. I was only mildly surprised to discover that the lights were burning. Usually I turn them off when I leave, but I had been distraught, distracted, and bewildered when I left. I thought nothing of it until I approached the desk and looked at the untidy pages of my manuscript.

I'm always impressed by characters in books who can tell at a glance that their belongings have been searched. They must be compulsively neat people. Normally, I wouldn't notice anything unusual unless my papers had been swept onto the floor and trampled underfoot. But I distinctly remembered struggling over a description of a Holbein miniature just before Tony's call put an end to my labors. The page now on top of the pile began, "quivered as her slender aristocratic hands strove in vain to veil their rounded charms from the Duke's lascivious eyes."

Schmidt was the obvious suspect. He was always trying to find out what Rosanna would do next. But he wasn't desperate enough to climb all those stairs, and as I glanced around, I saw other signs of disturbance: the drawer of a filing cabinet gaping open, a pile of books spilled sideways.

My first reaction was not alarm or annoyance, but hopeful anticipation. I had been waiting for something to happen. Maybe this was it. It, not John; if he had searched the office, I wouldn't notice anything out of place.

Schmidt had finally gotten around to making a copy of the mysterious photograph. (I deduced that from the fact that he had stopped swiping it.) I kept it in the top right-hand drawer of my desk.

As I reached impetuously for the drawer, it did occur to me to wonder how the intruder could have passed the guard down below. He had been on duty when I came in; he had nodded and mumbled a sleepy *"Grüss Gott,"* but he had not mentioned a visitor.

There was a blur of motion and a grating rattle, and something sprang out of the opening, striking my hand with a sharp prick of pain. Something serpentine, brightly colored. I jumped back with a scream, nursing my stung finger, where a bright drop of blood gleamed like a ruby. The snake fell to the floor.

It was a toy snake. My scream turned to a roar of rage. There was only one person who would play a childish joke like that.

Not Schmidt. He doesn't have a dram of meanness in his whole chubby body, and it takes malice to make a practical joker. No, it had to be Dieter. Dieter Spreng, assistant curator of pre-classical art at the Antikenmuseum in Berlin, frustrated comic and would-be lecher. His credentials would have gotten him past the guard....And he was probably still in the office. Practical jokes are no fun unless you can observe the hysteria of your victim. I pushed aside the screen concealing my domestic appliances, the only place in the room where anyone could hide.

He was doubled up and shaking with suppressed mirth, his arms hugging his midsection. Finding himself discovered, he let the laughter burst out in a genial baritone shout that was so contagious I felt my wrath fading.

"All right, Dieter," I said. "Come on out and fight like a man."

He straightened up and brushed his thick brown hair back from his flushed, grinning face. "Caught you, didn't I? *Herr Gott*, what a scream! You could play Isolde—"

"Caught me is right." I displayed my finger. Dieter's wide mouth drooped; he caught my hand and pressed it to his lips.

"I will kiss it and make it well. *Ach*, Vicky, I

am so sorry; the spring must have broken—"

"Oh, yeah?" I retrieved my hand and retreated to my desk. In the act of sitting, I had second thoughts and sprang up as if I had been stung. Dieter's mouth still sagged in clownish chagrin, but his brown eyes sparkled with amusement as he watched me. "No, no," he said soothingly. "There is nothing on the chair; I have given up the whoopee cushion. It was too crude."

I lowered myself cautiously into the chair. Nothing burped, whooped, or grabbed my bottom, so I relaxed. Dieter picked up the little plastic snake and shoved it under my nose. "See, there is no needle or pin to sting. As I thought, the spring was too tight; the wire broke and scratched you. Let me kiss it again—"

"Never mind. I'll live." Studying his arrangement behind the screen — a chair, a half-drunk cup of coffee — I added, "You made yourself comfy, I see."

"But I could not smoke." Dieter lit one of his awful Gauloises and puffed out a cloud of blue smoke. "I thought you would smell it and be suspicious. Can I get you some coffee?"

"No, thanks, it might be loaded with saltpeter or laxatives. What are you doing here?"

He pulled up a chair and provided himself with an ashtray by dumping out the paperclips in a small ceramic bowl. He was dressed *pour le sport*, as he was fond of saying, in well-cut boots and ski pants and a cable-knit sweater in a heavenly heather blend that set off his rosy cheeks and bright brown hair. The antique silver ring on his right hand glowed in the lamplight as he knocked ashes off his cigarette.

"I am in Munich to consult with Frick at the Glyptothek," he explained seriously.

"No, you're not."

"Of course I am not." Dieter grinned. "I could not get the museum to pay my travel expenses unless I consulted with Frick. I am on holiday, in fact; I hoped I could persuade you to join me for a few days of skiing."

"No, thanks. When I go on holiday I want to relax, not be on guard for snakes in the bed and buckets of water on the top of the door."

"I don't play jokes on the ladies who share my bed," Dieter said, reaching for my hand.

"That's not what I hear. Elise—"

"Oh, Elise." Dieter's fingers wriggled under the cuff of my sweater and squirmed up my arm. "One cannot resist teasing Elise; she is so funny when she is angry. You are different."

"How?"

"You are much bigger than Elise," Dieter explained. "You might strike me."

"Good point." Dieter's arm was now entirely

inside the sleeve of my sweater, and his eyes were crossed in intense concentration as he tried to stretch his fingers a strategic inch farther. "What on earth do you think you're doing?" I inquired with genuine curiosity.

Dieter put his cigarette in the ashtray. "I am thinking perhaps it would be better to start from the other direction—"

I pushed him away and pulled my sleeve down. "You are weird, Dieter. If I ever did decide to play games with you, it wouldn't be in my office."

"In a mountain chalet, then, with the snow falling and a fire on the hearth and a large furry bearskin in front of the fire—"

"I'm afraid not. I can't get away right now."

"Next week, then?"

"Sorry, I'm busy."

"You are always busy." Dieter lit another cigarette. "Why is it you always say no to me?"

I wasn't sure myself. Dieter's round face and dimples made him look like a kid, but he was well past the age of consent and not unattractive. Stocky and compactly built, he was an inch or two shorter than I, a consideration that didn't seem to concern him any more than it did me. He was good company, when he wasn't pulling chairs out from under people, and very good at his job. In a few years, when Dr.

Fessl retired, he would probably be head curator — no mean accomplishment for a man in his mid-thirties. I loved him like a brother, when I didn't hate him like a brother. But I had no desire to go to bed with him.

"Maybe some day," I said soothingly.

For a moment I had feared he was really hurt by my excuses, but if so, he recovered quickly. "Who is my rival?" he demanded in tragic accents. "Who is it I must kill to win your love?"

"It's none of your business, actually," I said. "But if you mean whom am I seeing next week — it's Tony."

"Tony. Ah, dear Tony." Dieter chuckled and blew out a thick cloud of smoke. "He looked so funny, when the chair broke under him — those long, thin legs and arms entwined like pretzels. How is he?"

I coughed and brushed at the smoke. "He's fine, I guess. How is Elise?"

"I have not seen her for months. I hear her marriage is finally ended."

I wondered how much Dieter had had to do with the breakup of that marriage. To judge from Elise's complaints, it had not been a very stable arrangement anyway; but if her husband had got wind of her fun and games with Dieter during the meetings the year before...

We gossiped about old acquaintances for a while — academicians are no more immune from that vice than other people — and then Dieter got up to go. "I don't suppose you will have dinner with me," he said dispiritedly.

"Thanks, but I'd better not. I have to work late."

"I will see if Gerda is busy, then."

"You leave Gerda alone."

"Why? She is a little plump, but I like ladies with something to hold on to. And she deserves a thrill, poor girl—" He ducked my half-joking swing at him and ambled toward the door. "Perhaps I will telephone next week, if I am still in Munich. I would be so happy to see dear old Tony again."

I said that would be fine, though I had a feeling Tony wouldn't be so happy to see dear old Dieter. He had too often been the butt of Dieter's jokes.

Dieter didn't quite close the door when he left. I slammed it shut and heard a grunt of surprise and a chuckle, and then the sound of footsteps descending the stairs. A cursory search of the room confirmed my suspicions. He had been a busy little lad. There was prune juice in the coffee pot and another wind-up toy in the filing cabinet — a tin bird that flapped its wings and cackled maniacally over a tin egg.

These offerings having been disposed of, I went back to work and actually finished the Holbein section of the article. Crazy Dieter had cheered me, not so much with his antique pranks as with...Well, why not admit it? A girl wants to be wanted, even by a man who likes women he can hold on to. It never rains but it pours, I thought complacently.

Pride goeth before a fall, and complacency before a kick in the fanny.

I worked late, partly to make up the time I had taken off to gad with Gerda, and partly in the hope of avoiding the worst of the rush-hour traffic. I was still feeling quite pleased with myself when I wended my way through the dungeons and out into the parking lot.

My car wouldn't start.

I loved my little Audi, which I had owned for only a few months. It was the main reason I couldn't afford a plane ticket to Minnesota that year. It was cute and foxy-colored, in keeping with its name; it had fake velvet upholstery in an elegant pale gold shade, and a stereo and a tape deck and fancy wheel covers. It had given me faithful service, and it got fifty kilometers to the gallon.

So, naturally, I got out and kicked the tires and called it bad names.

The janitor had left, but the night watchman

was on duty. Hearing my curses, he emerged from his cubbyhole and joined me under the hood. The only thing he was able to contribute was a flashlight; he didn't know any more about engines than I did, and after we had tried all the obvious easy things, to no avail, he suggested a mechanic. I replied with only a forgivable degree of sarcasm that it was a brilliant suggestion that never would have occurred to me, and where did he think we would find one at this hour?

He said he'd get right on it. I decided I might as well go home — there was no telling how long repairs would take. I went grumpily back into the building looking for Schmidt. His car was in the parking lot, but Schmidt himself was nowhere to be found.

There was nothing for it but to take the tram and then a bus; I live in the suburbs, near Grünwald, on account of my dog needing a yard.

The trams were still crowded with late workers and Christmas shoppers. I had to stand, squashed in between ranks of wet, tired, annoyed people. Shortly after we left Residenz-platz, I spotted Schmidt. He was wearing a bright red-and-green babushka with strands of gray horsehair sticking out all around the edges, a pair of dark glasses, and a purple scarf over the lower part of his face, to hide his mustache. I had no trouble seeing him, despite his diminutive stature, because nobody was anywhere near him. It wasn't hard to understand why people were giving him a wide berth; he looked like an escaped lunatic.

There was a lot of inadvertent contact as people were shaken, jostled, and pushed against one another; but all at once a specific contact brought me bolt upright and fuming. I turned my head and found myself staring into the wide innocent hazel eyes of a man standing directly behind me. He was the only one who could have given me that impertinent pinch; but instead of voicing my displeasure, I stood gaping in paralyzed silence. The only thing that kept me upright was the press of bodies around me.

He was dressed like a proper young businessman, in a dark tweed coat and snappy Tyrolean hat with a *Gamsbart* in the band. A trim dark mustache framed his mouth. What had he done to make his mouth look like that — so soft, so pink, so primly innocent? His mouth wasn't soft; it was hard and knowledgeable and very far from innocent. . . .

My own lips felt as if they had been sprayed with quick-drying lacquer. They were still half-parted and incapable of speech when he turned away. His timing was perfect. Before I could get my shaken wits together, the tram jolted to a stop at one of the major transfer points and people crowded toward the doors. He mingled with the others; several other men were wearing hats like his.

I started clumsily after him, stumbling over shopping bags and feet, but I knew the futility of pursuit. He would have been among the first off the tram; and before I could follow, he'd be gone, swallowed up by the rainy darkness.

An acerbic comment from a stout *Hausfrau* called my attention to the fact that I was sitting on her lap. The tram had started, throwing me off balance. I apologized and removed my offending person. She touched my arm.

"Entschuldigen Sie, Fräulein — I did not realize. . . . You are ill? Sit down, here is a place. . . . "

By the time we neared the end of the line and my transfer point, I had recovered. The tram was almost empty. I checked to make sure Schmidt was sitting in splendid isolation at the far end of the car, his face concealed behind a book he was holding upside down, before I reached into my coat pocket.

My pockets are usually a disgrace, bulging with objects — tissues, half-eaten candy bars, coins, keys, receipts, shopping lists. I had no trouble identifying John's contribution to the clutter, though it was no wonder he had had a hard time squeezing it in. The stiff paper felt cold on my fingers as I pulled it out.

It was a postcard.

The Saint Columba altar piece is one of the gems of the Alte Pinakothek in Munich, and a picture of it is a reasonable method of indicating a rendezvous point – not only a specific building, but a specific room in a large, rambling structure. But surely it was a diabolical coincidence that he had chosen a card showing one of my favorite details – the head of a man, beaky and handsome as a hawk, oddly familiar.

When I got off the tram, my bus was waiting, headlights cutting through the fog, steam snorting from its exhaust like the extrusions of a dragon with stomach trouble. I started to board it. Then I turned toward the chubby shadow that hovered in the gloom behind the lights of the station.

"Come on, Schmidt," I said. "You don't want to miss this bus; they only run every half hour."

THREE

Schmidt had not observed the encounter. I
didn't think he had, but I wanted to make sure.
That was my primary reason for blowing his
cover, as he put it; but I was also concerned
about the little madman's health. When he removed his bright purple scarf and blew his
bright scarlet nose, I saw that he had the beginning of a nasty cold. I persuaded him to
retain the babushka, in order to protect his
bald head; although I must say the horsehair
and the mustache made an unusual combination.

He was a little sulky at being found out, but
the prospect of a convivial evening with his
favorite subordinate soon cheered him. (I know
I'm his favorite; it would be disingenuous of
me to deny it.) I told him about Dieter, and he
was chuckling over the plastic snake when we
reached the house.

Caesar was delighted to see him. Schmidt
was not so delighted to see Caesar. I helped

Schmidt up off the floor and settled him in a chair. By the time I had fed Caesar and let him out and let him in and wiped his paws and removed Schmidt's wet shoes and socks and rubbed his feet with a towel and hung his soggy babushka to dry and provided him with beer, food, and an ashtray for his smelly cigar, I was devoutly thankful I had not strayed down the path of domesticity, frilly aprons, and babies. On the other hand, a baby couldn't be more of a nuisance than Schmidt.

After he had had a few beers and eaten the gargantuan meal I prepared, he decided to spend the night. He often did that when he had had a little more to drink than was legal, or whenever he had left his car at the museum. I fished out the flannel nightshirt I keep for such occasions, stuffed him full of cold remedies, and tucked him in bed.

Then, at last, I had leisure to think about what had happened.

It wasn't John's reappearance that shook me so much as my reaction to his reappearance. Typical, that epiphany — including the pinch — but I wondered if he had chosen a personal appearance instead of a more discreet response, via letter or telephone, in the hope of getting an unguarded display of emotion from me. He had certainly gotten one. No vapid heroine in a romance novel could have put on a better show – sudden pallor, pounding pulse, weak knees. Worse still, I had recognized him instantly, disguise and all. "Love looks not with the eyes but with the heart...." Or was it "with the mind"? John would know. He was always quoting Shakespeare.

The back of the postcard was blank except for the printed legend identifying the picture and the artist: Rogier van der Weyden (1399/1400), *Anbetung der Könige*. My face must have looked just as blank as I studied it, for one essential piece of information seemed to be missing: the time of the assignation. Unless he expected me to stand obediently in front of the damned painting from opening hour to closing every day until further notice....

I worked myself up into a state of righteous indignation before I noticed the faint pencil line under one of the dates. Fourteen hundred...hours? Two P.M.

"Oh, cute," I muttered. Caesar raised his head and looked at me inquiringly. "It's all your fault," I told him.

The accusation was totally unjust, but Caesar lowered his head and looked guilty. That must be why some people like dogs; they can be made to feel guilty about anything, including the sins of their owners. Cats refuse to take the blame for anything – including their own sins.

Schmidt was fit as a fiddle the next day and generously credited my TLC for curing his cold. His gratitude did not prevent him from trailing me when I left the Museum for what was supposed to look like a late lunch. I ditched him without difficulty or compunction by running a changing light on Sendlingerstrasse, under the very nose of a traffic cop. Schmidt tried to go through on the red and of course got pulled over.

Since there had been no date or day of the week specified on the postcard, I assumed I was supposed to turn up at the earliest possible moment, i.e., the following day. I wondered what John would have done if Rogier van der Weyden had been born in, say, 1860 – and then cursed myself for stupidity. Naturally he would select a painter whose vital statistics coincided with the time he found convenient.

On a wintry weekday when most people were busy Christmas shopping, the museum was not crowded. There were only half a dozen art-lovers in the room dominated by van der Weyden's glorious rendition of the Nativity; a quick glance assured me that John was not one of them.

Strictly speaking, the painting is not a Nativity. Christian iconography is painstakingly specialized. Except for the Crucifixion, no subject was so popular with artists as the birth of Christ, and every separate incident has its own designation and its own artistic traditions. This painting, which had once adorned an altar in Cologne, shows the Adoration of the Magi — the *Anbetung der Könige*. Though the Virgin is not at the center of the canvas, the composition is so admirable that the beholder's eye is led inexorably to where she sits holding the Baby on her knee. A benevolent brown cow looks admiringly over her shoulder as the first of the Kings kneels to kiss the outstretched hand of the Child. The colors are wonderful, they smolder on the canvas — the Virgin's rich blue robe, the scarlet mantle of the second Magi, the crimson-and-gold brocade tunic of the third King.

I've had a crush on that King since I was sixteen. He is dressed in the height of fifteenth-century fashion, his full-flowing sleeves falling to the mid-calf, his legs (a little thin, but not bad) encased in skin-tight hose. He has just swept off his cap to honor the Holy Family and his brown hair falls in wavy disarray over his forehead. If I ever saw a man who looked like that...

Suddenly I realized that I *had* seen a man who looked like that. No wonder the half-glimpsed profile of the man who (Gerda hoped) was following us had looked familiar. The same oblique shadows under the cheekbones, the same sharp angle of the jaw, the same indentation at the corner of the firm lips. What was more, I knew that man – or his double. A man I hadn't seen for almost a year...

John had to jog my elbow before I noticed him. He begged my pardon in clipped idiomatic German and moved away, but not before I had seen his nostrils flare with annoyance. The conceited creature had expected to find me palpitating with girlish expectation, instead of intent on a work of art.

I followed him on a seemingly leisurely tour of the exhibits; actually it didn't take more than ten minutes for him to reach the exit. Once on the street, he set a pace sufficiently brisk that I would have had to run to catch up with him, which, for a number of reasons, I was not about to do. Turning the next corner, he stopped at a parked car and unlocked the door. I arrived as he opened it; he stood back, motioning me in with a graceful bow. Perfect timing, as usual.

The car was a BMW, the latest model, black, sleek, and glossy. I got in. John got in. Neither of us spoke while he drove, with painstaking attention to the laws of the road, along Gabes-bergstrasse, past Königsplatz, with its museums and its pretentious pseudo-Greek gateway, and finally onto a quiet side street where he pulled in to the curb and stopped. He sat watching the rearview mirror until a Fiat that had been behind us went on by. Then he turned to face me.

His eyes were still hazel, but the mustache was no longer in evidence. His eyebrows were darker and bushier; you would be surprised how drastically a small change like that can alter a person's appearance. There was a new scar on his face, perceptible only at close range — a thin white line running from the corner of one eye across his temple and under his hair.

I had thought of a number of things I wanted to say in that first private confrontation — some cutting, some subtly sarcastic, and all, of course, cool, calm, and detached. Now that the moment had come, I couldn't speak or move. All I could see was that small pale scar, surely the memento of his encounter with my would-be killer. It had barely missed his eye. I wondered how many other new scars marked his body. I wondered why he had taken such a terrible risk... and, most of all, I wondered why he just sat there, staring dumbly, as I sat staring back at him.

Finally his eyes shifted; they scanned my face, with painstaking slowness, feature by feature. Then he raised his hand. One fingertip touched my cheek and glided lightly from the cheekbone to the corner of my mouth, along the curve of my jaw up to my ear, where his other fingers joined it to twine through my hair, cupping the back of my head. I was not conscious of other movement, his or mine, until our lips met.

He withdrew as delicately as he had advanced, settling himself behind the wheel as behind a barricade and presenting another barricade in the form of a bland, impassive profile.

"Cigarette?" he inquired politely.

"I don't smoke. How trite of you, John."

"I have become trite — commonplace — conventional. High time, wouldn't you say?"

He was not as cool as he pretended. There was the slightest possible tremor of his hand as he reached for the lighter. I thought I was doing better until I realized I was still leaning toward him, lips parted and expectant, hands reaching. I sat up, smoothed my skirt, and folded my hands primly in my lap.

"So you've become respectable. What have you been doing since I saw you last?"

"As you say, I've become respectable. Nice

little cottage in the country, nice honest job..."

I laughed. I couldn't help it, any more than I could help asking the next question.

"Nice little wife?"

That shocked John out of his calm. "Good God, no. What a horrible thought."

I didn't say anything. After a moment, John inquired, "And you?"

"I don't have a wife either."

The curl of his lip showed what he thought of that cheap quip. I didn't think much of it myself.

"It's only been eight months," I said. "I'd have to be a fast worker to locate and capture a husband in that space of time."

"You're too modest. I assumed you always had a few candidates waiting in the wings."

"And that I would be so devastated by your presumed demise that I would seek solace in the arms of the first personable male who made me an offer?"

John blew out a smoke ring. "You knew I wasn't dead."

"I was...almost sure."

The catch in my voice was slight — and, I assure you, unpremeditated — but John caught it. I was afraid he'd laugh or make some mocking reply. Instead his bushy eyebrows drew together, and there was no amusement in his voice when he said, "I suppose you feel I ought to have sent you word."

"Not at all. Neither of us is under any obligation to the other."

"Neither? You ungrateful wench, I risked a horrible death for your sake."

Just like old times, I thought, and sailed happily into the fray. "My sake, hell. I may have been first on the death list, but you were a close second. It was kill or be killed, buster."

"That is a highly questionable assumption. I swim like an eel. I could easily have made my getaway while he was slaughtering you and the old gent."

"The old gent raised a memorial to you."

"I know. What a tasteless monstrosity," John said disgustedly. "Honestly, Vicky, couldn't you have exercised a little control? Those mourning cupids, with bums like cups of custard, weeping through their doughy fingers—"

"I designed those cupids, I'll have you know."

The muscles at the corner of his mouth quivered. I went on, "Unfortunately, I couldn't persuade him to use the motto I favored."

"Which was?"

" 'He hath no drowning mark upon him; his complexion is perfect gallows.' "

The muscles gave up the fight and stretched into a broad, appreciative grin. "Oh, lovely.

Couldn't have done better myself. Well, I appreciate the thought, darling. Shall we call it square? The absolute dreadfulness of that monument makes up for any neglect on my part."

"Square," I agreed. It was the only possible way of dealing with John, forgetting the past and letting bygones be bygones. If I started adding up all the aggravations he had caused me, I'd get mad, and I was about to ask his help.

"So what are you up to now?" John asked curiously. "I dare not hope it was for the sake of my *beaux yeux* that you framed that enticing advertisement."

"You are right about that. It was eye-catching, wasn't it?"

"Caught mine, certainly."

"In which newspaper?"

I hadn't really expected him to fall for it. He chuckled. "That would be telling. So what's the scam, love?"

I told him.

The story sounded even more tenuous and fantastic than I had realized. John didn't sneer or snicker, but he wasn't enthusiastic either. Lips pursed, he shook his head. "Is that all you've got? It's a picturesque scenario, my dear, but . . ."

"I can show you the photograph," I said. "If the jewels are copies, they are damned good ones."

"No need," John said abstractedly. "You're the expert; I accept your conclusions."

I was absurdly flattered by the compliment; he didn't hand them out freely. Then he added, looking at me from under those curly long lashes, "Did you by chance wonder whether I sent you the photo?"

I shrugged. "Your name does leap to mind whenever the question of art forgery arises."

"Thank you," John said sincerely. His brow clouded; he then said in a wistful voice. "I'm ashamed I didn't think of it. It could be the quintessential swindle of all time. Do you know what happened in Berlin on the night of May first, 1945?"

"Yes," I said shortly. I don't neglect essential research, even if it doesn't make for pleasant reading. "At least I know the outlines. Some of the most prized objects from the Berlin museums, including the Trojan gold, were in a bomb shelter in the Tiergarten bunker. It was a fortress — massive concrete walls, antiaircraft batteries bristling from walls and roof—"

"Containing troop quarters, a hospital, and an air-raid shelter for fifteen thousand people," John said. "Because of its strong fortifications and its location, in the grounds of the zoo in central Berlin, it was one of the last places to be taken. In fact, it wasn't taken; the com-

86

mandant surrendered after the general order had gone out at midnight on the first of May. The Russians entered the bunker several hours later — before dawn."

"So it was still dark," I said. "Raining, too—"

"Rain was the least of it." John lit another cigarette. "The city was a scene from the inferno — church spires burning like giant candles, Russian tanks rumbling along Unter den Linden and the Wilhelmstrasse, screaming mobs fighting their way through the flaming, rubble-strewn streets. There was a heavy artillery bombardment, and hand-to-hand fighting, throughout the zoo and park area. The commandant of the Tiergarten bunker told his men that those who wanted to try breaking out before the surrender could do so."

"So people were going in and out—"

"Mostly in," John said. "What you must realize is that the Russians were not a homogeneous group. The first ones to reach Berlin were highly disciplined shock troops; the terrified inhabitants, expecting the worst, were surprised and relieved when they were treated with relative decency. The second wave was something else again — a motley medley of illiterate tribesmen from the steppes — Karelians, Kazakhs, Tatars, Mongols, you name it — who could barely speak Russian and who had never seen a light bulb or a w.c."

"I know that. And I don't want to hear —"

John went on as if I had not spoken, his voice as cool and dispassionate as that of a lecturer. "There were thirty thousand people crammed into the shelter in the bunker — twice the number it had been designed to hold. There were patients in the hospital, nurses, doctors, guards. The commandant handed over the keys; the Russians went in. Then, to coin a phrase, all hell broke loose. Patients were shot in their beds, nurses—" He broke off at my involuntary gesture of protest and a bleak smile touched his lips. "War is hell, as they say. While all this was going on, the Russian troops reached the third level, where the museum treasures were stored.

"What happened then is anybody's guess. The Soviets never turned over the museum pieces to a joint commission on missing and stolen art. Some of them have resurfaced since, but it is conceivable that the gold of Troy is still thriftily stored away in a Kremlin vault. It may have been lost or destroyed during the journey east. A group of those untutored laddies from the steppes may have smashed it to fragments in the boyish exuberance of victory. They wouldn't have realized its value—"

"There is another possibility," I said. "Someone may have got to it before the Russians did. Someone who did know its value. In all that pandemonium, he could have smuggled it out of the building and out of the city. It didn't bulk that large. Schliemann bundled the whole lot into his wife's shawl when he removed it from the excavation."

"Anything is possible," John said. He thought for a second and then added, "Almost anything. See here, Vicky, there are a number of points about that scenario of yours that make my hackles rise. Why was the photograph sent to you? Why didn't the sender give you more information? Your advertisement was a wee bit misleading, you know. Black Michael and Rupert of Hentzau may not be hiding in the woodshed, but something nasty is; the bloodstain you described didn't come from a cut finger. If the sender is still alive, why hasn't he communicated with you?"

"He could have had an accident."

"Tripped on a cobblestone and cut himself on a beer tin," said John in his most disagreeable voice. "And some kindly passerby found the envelope and posted it?"

"You're contradicting yourself," I said. "First you tell me there's no evidence and then you imply—"

"That the only evidence is bloody," John said

poetically. "Either way, I don't like it."

"Then you're not interested?"

"No."

The flat finality of his refusal caught me unawares. I stared at him, disconcerted and surprised; he shifted uneasily and turned away. "Give it up, Vicky. You're wasting your time."

"Just tell me one thing. Are there any rumors in the art underworld about the Trojan gold?"

"I have severed my connections with that ambiance," John said primly. "I am leading a life of quiet, honest—"

"Sure you are. That's why you're in disguise — why you keep looking nervously in rearview mirrors, why you are so astonishingly well informed about the Battle of Berlin and the architecture of the Tiergarten bunker."

"Oooh, what an evil, suspicious mind you have," John murmured. "I know a lot about a lot of things, my dear."

"Military history is not your specialty. Would you care to swear on something sacred to you — your own precious hide, for example — that your interest in the gold of Troy has not been recently awakened by some of those rumors I mentioned?"

"You cut me to the quick." John pressed his hand against his presumably aching heart and gave me a soulful look. "In order to dispel your suspicions and restore that perfect amity that should mark our relationship, I will make a clean breast of it. I owe the information to my dear old dad."

The statement surprised me so that I forgot, momentarily, that he hadn't denied the allegation. One tended to think of John as self-engendered, like Minerva from Jove's headache.

He went on blandly, "You'd remember every grisly detail, too, if you had heard them as often as I did. The Battle of Berlin was the old boy's favorite topic of conversation when he got to reminiscing about the good old days in general and his own heroism in particular. He'd rave on for hours about how Churchill tried to convince the Allies to drive through to Berlin, and how bloody Eisenhower held back. He had studied the subject intensively, and I was the only one who'd listen to him. Or rather, who could be coerced into listening. I was young and frail and helpless—"

"And abused and whatever," I agreed. "Is that why you became a pacifist?"

"Because of Papa's ghoulish war stories?" John grinned. "I wouldn't call myself a pacifist. It's impossible to convince some people of the error of their ways without hitting them as often and as hard as one possibly can. I'm simply opposed to people hitting *me*."

"Emulating dear old Dad's heroism is not your aim?"

"Emphatically not. Which is why I am presently avoiding publicity. In case it has slipped your mind, I am still being sought by the police of several countries, including Germany."

"Public enemy number one."

"More like number one hundred and ten. I never aspired to greatness. Neither do I aspire to spending ten to fifteen years in prison."

"So you won't help me."

"No."

"All right." I reached for the handle of the door.

John's hand closed over mine. "Don't be a sorehead. Let me buy you a drink and we'll reminisce about old times."

"No, thanks. You can drop me at my car if you will. It's parked near the gallery."

Conversation during the drive back was minimal. His brow unclouded, his hands light on the wheel, John whistled tunefully as he drove. I recognized the song: "Oh Mistress Mine, Where Are You Roving?"

Good question. John acted like a man who was at peace with the world, having fulfilled a tedious duty to an old acquaintance. His behavior was unexceptional, his logic was unassailable — and he had been courteous enough to refrain from hinting, even obliquely, that I must have invented the whole preposterous story as an excuse for trying to locate him.

I could have killed him.

"That's my car," I said, pointing.

"I know," said John, driving past.

"Of course you do. I should send you the mechanic's bill."

"I trust it wasn't excessive," John said anxiously. "There were only a few minuscule wires dislocated." He turned the corner and stopped. "This is a bit more private," he explained. "I presume you'd rather not be seen in my company."

"You mean you'd rather not be seen in mine."

"Just a precaution. You do have an untidy habit of attracting predators." Before I could reply to this blow below the belt — the most recent set of predators had been put on my trail by John himself — he leaned across me and opened my door.

I took the hint. For fear of scraping his precious tires, he had stopped a safe distance from the curb, and I stepped out into six inches of icy slush.

I turned. "I won't bother putting an advertisement in the papers when I find the gold. You'll see the headlines."

93

"Would you mind letting go of the door?"

"Oh — sorry."

Instead of closing it, he remained stretched out across the seat, peering up at me from under lowered brows. "You aren't going to take my well-meant advice?"

"No."

John's frown deepened. "Do you know something you haven't told me?"

"A few ideas are swimming briskly about in my head," I said. "But they needn't concern you. You aren't interested."

Still prone, he took a card and a pen from his pocket. "I might be able to extend a few tentacles into the old-boy network. See if anything is stirring."

I watched him scribble on the card. "I'd appreciate that. But please don't bother giving me a phone number; it would just turn out to be the Soviet chancellery or the Society for the Prevention of Extramarital Sex."

John grinned reluctantly, but held on to the card. "I'll be in touch. We might have dinner. Or perhaps a spot of extramarital—"

"Sorry. I'm saving myself for Tony."

"Who's Tony?"

"An old friend of mine. He's coming all the way from Chicago to spend Christmas with me. He's an assistant professor — six-five, tall, dark, and handsome." I don't know why I went on talking; I couldn't seem to stop myself. "If Tony should fail me, I'm afraid I would have to consider Dieter's application before yours. He's shorter than you are, but he'll be a curator at the Antikenmuseum by the time he's forty. A nice, honest job."

John propped his chin on his hands and politely smothered a yawn. "Do go on," he urged. "How far down the list am I?"

The slush had soaked through my supposedly waterproof boots and my feet were getting numb. "Never mind," I snapped. "I'll be seeing you. Or not, as the case may be."

"Take this." He handed me the card.

"Well!" I said, examining it.

John's smile shone with seraphic innocence. "It's an answering service," he murmured.

The door slammed; the car pulled away.

"Bastard," I said, staring after it.

I had spoken English; but many *Münchener* understand the language. A woman passing along the sidewalk stopped and looked at me. "Aren't they all, dearie," she said.

It was a good thing I had to keep my foot on the gas as I drove back to work. Otherwise I'd have been tempted to kick myself.

Though I felt sure he hadn't meant to do so,

95

John had given me a clue with one casual question. He hadn't asked *why* the photograph had been sent to me; he had asked why the photograph had been sent to *me.* The stress made all difference. Why send it to me, of all people? And why in heaven's name hadn't it occurred to me to ask myself the question?

I knew why I hadn't asked myself, and the answer did me no credit. Vanity, all is vanity, saith the poet. Whom else would a repentant thief look up but the great Victoria Bliss, art historian extraordinaire and famous amateur sleuth?

Which was nonsense. I wasn't famous. In the field of pre-Hellenic art, I wasn't even well known. I had not written on the subject or lectured about it.

Somewhere, at some time, I must have met the sender of that photograph, talked to him — bragged, more likely — about my status and my expertise.

I had no opportunity to explore the hypothesis that afternoon. When I dashed into the museum, already ten minutes late for a meeting, Schmidt was lying in wait for me. He was furious — not because I was late, but because I had eluded him earlier — and I had to stand there in my wet, icy boots while he bawled me out.

The meeting lasted for over two hours, and

then I had a dozen odds and ends to deal with. When the long day was over, I drove straight home without bothering to see whether Schmidt was following me.

The first thing I did was to call the number on the card John had given me. It turned out to be an answering service, just as he had said. I had expected some kind of practical joke, and it wasn't until the bored voice asked for whom I was calling that I realized I didn't know.

"John Smythe?" I mumbled, making it a question.

"I am sorry, we have no client of that name."

Hot with fury and embarrassment, I was about to hang up when it hit me. "Schmidt," I said. "John – Johann Schmidt."

"Your message?"

"Never mind," I growled, and hung up.

Caesar growled too, and lunged for the phone. The strange black object had offended me; he was anxious to mete out the punishment it deserved. I pushed him away and was about to replace the phone when it rang. The caller was Schmidt, suggesting he drop by and take me out to dinner. I didn't ask where he was; I suspected he was calling from the kiosk on the corner. I told him no, I didn't want to go out, I was catching a cold, I had a headache and a lot of work to do. He didn't believe me.

Finally I hung up on him.

The phone kept ringing. Schmidt again; then Gerda, wanting me to go out with a cousin of hers who was in town for the holidays. I know what Gerda's cousins are like – she had set me up with a blind date once before – so I declined. Schmidt called again. Another friend called, asking me to a party I didn't want to go to. Schmidt called again. After that I unplugged the phone.

It took me some time to get the things I wanted together. The appointment books, receipts, and letters made a dusty, depressing heap on the coffee table – four years of my life reduced to a pile of papers. There was a pot of black coffee on the table, too, and Caesar's head was on my feet. I didn't have the heart to push it off, even after my toes went numb. Poor guy, he led a boring life – not even a pile of paper to remind him of past triumphs and past failures. He was alone all day; though he definitely preferred people to other forms of animal life, I suppose he'd have settled for a squirrel or even a mouse to keep him company. I had no mice, and although there were plenty of squirrels around, I couldn't leave Caesar outside when I was away from home. Not only did he bark maniacally at the slightest sound or movement – to the extreme annoyance of my neighbors — but he could get over or under or through any fence constructed by human hands.

I sipped my coffee and gloomily contemplated the pile of papers. I had been meaning to organize them for lo these many years.

Somehow I wasn't at all surprised when the first paper I plucked out of the pile turned out to be the bill from that funny little hotel in Trastevere. A bill for one night...and I had spent the first few hours of that night repairing the damages John had sustained during what someone — not me, I assure you — might refer to as the Roman caper. The bruises, cuts, and bullet holes had not impaired what he quaintly referred to as his vital functions.

I caught a glimpse of my reflection in the mirror across the room, and even though nobody could see me but Caesar, I hastily wiped the foolish smile off my face. Damn the man, why couldn't I stay mad at him? And why had I kept the hotel bill? I had been on an expense account, but I had not submitted that bill because I'd have had to explain to Schmidt why it was for a double room and a quite excessive amount of room service....Actually, I had planned to present the bill to John. He had left it for me to pay — the first time, but not the last, he had pulled that stunt.

"Bastard," I said halfheartedly.

"Grrrr," said Caesar.

I threw the hotel bill in the wastebasket. Next to go were a few crumpled travel brochures from Rothenburg, the delicious little medieval town in Bavaria where Tony and I had spent one summer tracking down the Riemenschneider reliquary. More fond memories evoked — the grim black tower and the grisly crypt at midnight, the mummified face of a long-dead count of Drachenburg glaring up at us from the coffin we had violated, Tony bleeding all over my best nightgown after being stabbed by a walking suit of armor.... The men in my life didn't have an easy time of it. One could not help wondering why they kept coming back for more.

Tony really had not sounded like himself. Had that worm finally turned? If the data for which I was presently searching substantiated my half-formed hypothesis, the question might have a new and poignant meaning.

The next lot of papers was quickly sorted — family letters, pictures of nieces and nephews, postcards, more travel folders. Among them was a letter from my friend Gustav in Sweden, enclosing a snapshot of the famous memorial to John. It was even worse than I had remembered. Weeping cupids, a lugubrious life-sized angel with ragged wings draped unbecomingly over her bowed head, scrolls and drooping flowers and banners hanging limp at half-mast, and, as a crowning touch, two huge lions, modeled after the one at Lucerne, with muzzles resting on their outsized paws.

I fished the hotel bill out of the wastebasket and put it in an envelope with the snapshot and a few other odds and ends — every scrap in my possession that had reference to John Smythe, Esquire, alias Johann Schmidt, alias Al Monkshood, etcetera, etcetera, ad infinitum. Mark it "Bygone follies of my youth" and file it...in the fire.

However, I do not have a fireplace, so I crammed the papers back into the carton from which they had come and got down to business. The brief journey into nostalgia had convinced me that my hunch was correct, and that I had not overlooked any other possibility. I knew what I was searching for. I had taken the pictures only the year before, but they were jumbled in with all the snapshots I had been meaning to sort and put in albums for ten years, so it took a while to find them. I spread them out across the coffee table.

I am not a good photographer and my camera is a cheap Instamatic, but it is hard to take bad pictures of Garmisch-Partenkirchen when the mountains are capped with snow and the wind blows strong from the south, producing brilliant blue skies and air clear as crystal. Garmisch is in the Bavarian Alps, about sixty miles south of Munich. The Winter Olympics were held there — long before my time — and the facilities provided for the Games have made Garmisch a popular winter resort. It is also an ideal spot for a conference — lots of hotels and meeting rooms, as well as certain sources of entertainment, such as bars and restaurants, which are just as important, even to serious souls like the members of the International Society for the Study of Ancient and Medieval Antiquities.

A group of us had decided to avoid the high-priced hotels of Garmisch in favor of a more picturesque ambiance. The gang of six, Dieter had named us; and it was Dieter — wasn't it? — who had found the hotel in a small village southeast of Garmisch. Transportation was no problem since three of the group had their own cars, and there was a little, lumbering local bus. Anyway, we didn't attend many of the meetings.

Gasthaus Hexenhut was as charming as Dieter — if it was Dieter — had claimed. I had taken several pictures of it, with the pointy-topped hill that had given it its name looming up behind it. The sign over the door claimed *"seit 1756,"* and although the hotel might not have been that old, the building certainly was. It had green shutters and wooden scrollwork under the eaves, and painted sprays of flowering branches encircling the doors and windows. Balconies outside many rooms offered guests spectacular views of mountain scenery, crowned by the perpetual snows of the Zugspitze. The big comfortable rooms were furnished with antiques and with magnificent tile stoves, warmer than central heating. There were down comforters on all the beds, and the restaurant featured food as unpretentious as it was excellent.

I had persuaded one of the waiters to take a picture of the entire group in front of the hotel. There was Tony, towering over the others; me next to him; Dieter next to me – his left hand was behind my head, making a graphically suggestive gesture. Then Elise Cellier of the Louvre, slim and petite in her fancy blue ski outfit. Rosa D'Addio from the University of Turin was as dark as Elise was fair and as sternly intellectual as Elise was frivolous. Sandwiched between them was a man I had known only by reputation until that meeting: Jan Perlmutter from East Berlin. He was built like one of the Greek statues in the museum of which he was an official, but his most conspicuous feature was his hair — tight fair curls that clung closely to his beautifully shaped skull and shone with the rare glint of true red-gold.

Poor Rosa had taken one look at Jan and had fallen flat on her face, literally as well as figuratively; there was an icy patch on the pavement, and she was so busy staring at him she forgot to look where she was walking. Though Elise was supposed to be with Dieter, she was not unmoved by the Greek god; Jan spent a good deal of his time trying to elude one or the other or both. Maybe he didn't always try. I paid little attention to the proceedings; Tony and I were renewing old acquaintances. If Tony hadn't been there, I might have taken a friendly interest in Jan myself. Or I might not; his humor was a bit too heavy-handed and his manners were too formal for my tastes. In fact, I had been a little surprised when he asked to join our frivolous group.

The conference had officially ended the morning I took the pictures. We were celebrating, looking forward to a few days of skiing, drinking beer, and so on. Especially so on. We must have had a few beers already, to judge from some of the antics I had photographed: Dieter burying a wildly gesticulating Elise in a pile of snow; Dieter upside down in a snowbank with only his feet protruding; Jan gravely constructing a snowman as anatomically accurate as the medium allowed, assisted by both Elise and Rosa; Tony leering insanely into the lens of the camera in blurred close-up.

That was the last of that group; dodging Tony, I had slipped and fallen and sprained my ankle. So, while the rest of them were on the slopes the next day, I languished in the hotel with my foot up.

The manager of the hotel couldn't have been sweeter. When he learned of my misadventure, he sent flowers, food, wine, and his own cane — a stout, solid article decorated from foot to curved handle with the little metal-and-enamel insignia that are the badges of local hiking societies. Reading the cane occupied me for a good fifteen minutes and amused me no end. With its aid, I was able to hobble around; and later that evening, when my so-called pals had abandoned me to whoop it up in the nightclubs of Garmisch, Herr Hoffman invited me to join him for a brandy.

He explained with grave courtesy that he thought I might be getting bored with the four walls of my room, and that was certainly true; but the contents of his private sitting room would have been worth a visit even if I had been able-bodied and otherwise occupied. There were several examples of the painted peasant furniture called *Bauernmalerei,* including a huge *Schrank,* or cupboard, as fine as any I had seen in the Bayrisches Museum. Each of the double doors had a pair of painted panels – formal bouquets of tulips, roses, and lilies. The creature comforts were nice, too – twenty-year-old brandy; a fire blazing on the open hearth; a fat, purring Siamese kitten to warm my knees and lick my fingers; and a Brahms quartet playing softly in the background.

I had asked Herr Hoffman to pose in front of the hotel the day we left. I had meant to send him a copy, but had never gotten around to it. One doesn't get around to things, that's the trouble with the world. But I had had the decency to make a small return for his kindness, stopping in Garmisch and ordering flowers to be sent to his wife, who was in the hospital.

He hadn't dwelt on the fact, had only mentioned it by way of apology for her absence, but I could tell he was deeply devoted to her and very worried about her condition. They had been married for almost forty years. It was hard to tell how old Hoffman was; his hair and eyebrows were pale pure silver-blond without a touch of gray, and he had one of those faces where the skin looks as if it had been glued to the bones, with no excess left to sag. Not handsome, probably not even in youth, but distinctive and distinguished-looking.

I didn't have to look for additional evidence. I knew. But I looked anyway. The receipt for the hotel bill wasn't among the miscellaneous papers I had examined. Since I had been an official representative of the museum and expected to be reimbursed for my expenses, I had filed the bill with my business papers, so I found it without difficulty. The Gasthaus Hexenhut wasn't one of your modern computerized chains. Hoffman had written the bills himself. I had studied the stained envelope till my eyes ached; the spiky angular handwriting was as familiar as my own.

There had been six of us at the hotel that week — myself and five others. In the past few days, I had heard from two of the five. Tony had gotten a sudden urge to visit me, and Dieter had shown up in my office with a plastic snake. Perhaps the answer to John's casual question was more complex — and more egodeflating — than I had realized. Perhaps I was not the only one to have received a photograph of the Trojan gold.

Hoffman had spent more time with me, but he knew the others and their credentials. We had all registered under the names of the institutions we represented. It wasn't too unusual

107

for Tony to pay me a visit. It wasn't unlikely that Dieter should drop in. But that made two out of five, and unless I was getting paranoid (which was quite possible) a third member of the group might also be in Munich. I had not know Jan well, and I hadn't noticed his resemblance to the man in the painting by Van der Weyden, probably because of Jan's hair, which was so conspicuously gorgeous, it drew the eye away from his other features. (The principle is well known to experts in disguise, I am told.) I had not seen the hair of the man Gerda had pointed out, only his spare, unadorned profile. If it wasn't Jan Perlmutter, it was Jan's twin brother.

I was sitting there pondering the meaning of it all and wondering what I was going to do about it when the doorbell rang. The sound split the stillness of the room like a scream; I jumped, and Caesar bounded to his feet howling like the hound of Baskervilles as he plunged toward the front door. A crash from the hall marked his progress; it also marked the demise of my favorite Chinese vase.

I kept the chain in place when I opened the door. It had stopped snowing and the wind was rising. Schmidt's mustache flapped wildly in the breeze.

"*Abend,*" he said brightly.

"What are you doing here at this hour?"

"It is only ten o'clock. You have not gone to bed."

"I was just about to."

Schmidt stamped his feet and hugged himself, pantomiming incipient freezing to death. "Let me in."

"By the hair of your chinny chin chin," I muttered. "Oh, hell. Come in."

Schmidt led the way to the living room, shedding his hat, coat, scarf, and gloves as he went. I picked up the coat, hat, scarf, and one of the gloves, and pried the other one out of Caesar's mouth.

Already comfortably settled on the couch, Schmidt awaited my attentions. "Coffee?" he said in contemptuous disbelief, indicating the pot.

"What did you expect, Napoleon brandy?"

"Yes, thank you," said Schmidt.

"No brandy, Schmidt."

"Beer, then."

"No beer. You are not spending the night and I am not going to drive you home and you are not leaving my house in a state of vulgar inebriation."

Schmidt sighed. "Coffee."

"Coffee," I agreed.

When I came back from the kitchen with a

fresh pot and an extra cup, Schmidt was looking at the snapshots. His mustache was twitching with pleasure. Schmidt loves looking at snapshots. He also loves having his picture taken. If he is anywhere in the vicinity when a photographer is at work, the finished product will have Schmidt or part of him somewhere in the background.

"You have not shown me these," he said indignantly.

"I had forgotten about them." I sat down on the couch beside him. "I took them at the ISSAMA meetings last winter."

"I had deduced as much," said Schmidt, contemplating a photo of Tony, who was pointing, in the idiotic way people do, at the Zugspitze. "It is not good of Tony. He looks drunk."

"It was cold. That's why his nose is so red."

"Ha," said Schmidt skeptically. "Oho, here is Elise. I have not seen her for two years. She should not make her hair that strange shade of pink."

So it went, with Schmidt making catty remarks about his friends. Schmidt knows everybody and he adores conferences; he had been sick in bed with flu that year, or he would have insisted on going along. I expected his encyclopedic memory would falter when it came to Jan, but I was in error.

"Perlmutter," he announced. "Bode Museum, East Berlin."

"Very good, Schmidt."

"I have an excellent memory for faces," Schmidt said, twirling his mustache complacently. "I have met this Perlmutter only once, but never do I forget a face. It was in Dresden; he studied then under Kammer. Young, he is, but brilliant, it is said. Hmmm. Now who..."

Frowning slightly, he studied the last of the snapshots. I said casually, "Oh, that's just the hotel where I stayed."

"But who is this fellow? Wait, no, don't tell me; I will remember in a moment. I never forget a face."

"You've never seen this face. It's the owner of the hotel."

"He looks familiar," said Schmidt.

"He does not. Come on, Schmidt, you've already scored, don't overdo it."

"I have seen him. I know I have seen that face somewhere. But I do not remember the hotel. In Garmisch, you say?"

"Uh — yes, that's right."

"What is his name, this man?"

"Hoffman."

"Hoffman...Yes, there is something familiar...."

I thought he was showing off. If I had known

he was telling the simple truth, I'd have changed the subject even faster than I did.

Schmidt wouldn't go home. After polite hints had failed, I told him point-blank I was tired and wanted to hit the sack. He waved my complaint aside. "It is a holiday tomorrow; you can sleep late."

"What holiday?"

"I have declared it," said Schmidt, giggling. "For me. I must do my Christmas shopping. I am the director; I can make a holiday when I want. I make it for you, too, if you are nice. We will go to shop at the Kristkindlmarkt."

"Depends on the weather," I said. "I feel a little snuffly tonight; the cold I mentioned —"

"Fresh air is good for a cold," said Schmidt. "Now let us open a bottle of wine and look at more photographs. Where are the ones you took of me at the Oktoberfest?"

I had not intended to take pictures of Schmidt at the Oktoberfest. I had intended to get an overall view of that giddiest and most vulgar of Munich holidays, not only for my own scrapbook, but to send home in the hope it would encourage my brother Bob to pay me a visit. Since my mother would see the pictures too, a certain amount of discretion was necessary; the snapshots had to be vulgar enough to entice

Bob and restrained enough not to scandalize my mother. I never sent the photos. Schmidt was in every damned one of them. I believe his aim was to demonstrate the variety of things that can be done with a stein of beer – in addition, of course, to drinking from it.

I did not open a bottle of wine. At midnight Schmidt switched from coffee to Coke and demanded more snapshots.

At twelve-fifteen the telephone rang. This prompted a ribald comment from Schmidt, which I ignored. Some of my friends have no idea of time, but I had a premonition about the identity of this caller; and I was right.

"I understand you telephoned earlier," said John brightly.

"I didn't leave a message."

"My heart told me it was you."

"Your heart, and the fact that you never bothered to tell me—" I bit my lip. The cold fury in my voice had aroused the interest of my inquisitive boss; he turned to stare and I moderated my tone. "So what's new?"

"Nothing."

"Nothing?"

"*Nihil, niente, nichts.* No rumors, no information, no news. If the subject we discussed earlier has aroused interest, it is not in the quarters with which I am – was – familiar."

"You're sure?"

"Absolutely."

"It didn't take you long."

"Efficiency is my most admirable characteristic."

"You have so few of them."

A chuckle from John and a more intense stare from Schmidt reminded me to control my temper and my tongue.

"My, my, what a sour mood we're in," said the jeering voice at the other end of the line. "I didn't expect gratitude, but you ought to be relieved at the absence of activity."

Since I could not think of a reply that would not further arouse Schmidt's suspicions, I remained silent. After a moment, John said, "Do forgive me, I neglected to inquire whether you had a guest."

"I do."

"Tony? Dieter? Tom, Dick—"

"Schmidt," I said between my teeth.

"Who is it?" Schmidt demanded. "Is it someone I know? Does he wish to speak to me?"

"Shut up, Schmidt," I said.

"Perhaps I had better ask leading questions," John said.

"Why bother?"

"Tit for tat. Have there been any new developments?"

"No."

"Hmmm," said John.

"You said you weren't interested."

"Not under any circumstances whatever. I cannot conceive of any contingency that would persuade me."

"Then you have no need to know."

"Er — quite. Look here, suppose I ring you tomorrow. A late report may yet come in."

"Fine," I said.

"Who was that?" Schmidt demanded as I hung up.

"A friend of mine."

"You did not sound very friendly," said Schmidt.

Schmidt finally left at about one-thirty. As I pushed him out into the night he called, "I will telephone you at nine o'clock. We must get an early start."

I nodded agreeably. At nine the next morning I expected to be halfway to Garmisch.

FOUR

At nine o'clock I was just leaving Munich. I had overslept. I figured Schmidt had probably done the same, so I wasn't worried about his following me. I was worried about two other people.

I lost more time taking a roundabout route through the suburbs instead of heading directly for the autobahn. The sun was trying to break through clustering clouds, but the side streets were slick with packed snow. I had to concentrate on my driving and try, at the same time, to keep an eye on the rearview mirror.

I didn't expect to have any difficulty spotting Dieter. He was such a ham he wouldn't be able to resist some silly trick. Having observed no bright purple Beetles painted with vulgar mottoes (Dieter's last-owned car) or vehicles driven by gorillas or mummies, I turned onto the autobahn and put my foot down. The suggested speed limit is 130 kilometers per hour, but nobody pays much attention to it; I got in the (comparatively) slow lane and gave myself up to introspection.

Painful introspection. I wasn't too pleased with myself. There is nothing wrong with having a positive self-image, but when self-esteem blossoms into conceit, it is apt to cloud one's judgment.

Whether the photograph was a hoax or a swindle or a sales pitch, it was reasonable to assume the sender would not limit himself to a single sucker. Until the previous day, I hadn't been able to pinpoint a particular group of prospects; but I should have made some phone calls to colleagues and asked whether they had received anything unusual in the mail.

On the other hand, nobody had telephoned me either. That made me feel a little less culpable. Either I was the only one Hoffman had contacted or the others were being devious — like me.

Schmidt it was who said it: "If there is the slightest chance..." The acquisition of the gold of Troy would be the museum coup of the century. Well, maybe not the century — there have been others — but a coup of mythical proportions. We're no nobler than anybody else. We talk about cooperation and mutual assistance in the lofty name of scholarship, but let some prize come on the market and we're in the arena with knives swinging. Competition stops short of assassination, but not by much. I could tell you some stories. . . .

It was hard to avoid the conclusion that Hoffman had communicated with the others. They might even have information I lacked — a return address that had not been obliterated, a note or covering letter of which I had been deprived by Gerda's interfering nosiness. They were behaving precisely as I would have expected if such a contingency had occurred.

Dieter would be intrigued and amused, and perfectly willing to spend a few days on a possible wild-goose chase, so long as the geese were nesting in one of his favorite vacation spots. Tony would call me on some pretense and wait to see if I would mention the peculiar photograph I had received from that dear old gentleman at the Gasthaus Hexenhut. My failure to do so would persuade him I was up to my old tricks, trying to track down a prize without cutting him in on the deal. Our first treasure hunt had begun with a challenge: "I'm smarter than you are and I'll prove it." I had no reason to suppose he had become any less competitive.

Jan was an East German. My vague notions of satellite politics had convinced me that half the people in Eastern Europe worked for the

KGB, if that's what they call it these days. He would have a stronger motive than any of us to locate the gold. If the Soviets didn't have it, their poor little feelings must have been badly wounded by the suspicions of the world; it would be a nice publicity ploy for them to rescue it and return it — to Jan's museum, where else?

So far, I hadn't seen hide nor hair of either of the women. That didn't mean they weren't around. It also didn't mean they were. Elise was not the world's brightest little lady, for all her academic qualifications, and her specialty was Renaissance sculpture; of all the group, she would be least likely to recognize or respond to the Trojan gold. Rosa was brilliant, but utterly devoid of imagination. I could see her glancing at the photograph and tossing it aside as just another crank communication.

There was only one jarring note in my composition. I simply could not see that gracious, kindly old gentleman as either a practical joker or a seller of stolen goods. That was why I was on my way to Bad Steinbach to confront him personally instead of calling or writing.

Still no purple Beetles in the mirror. Nor a sleek black BMW. If John intended to follow me, he wouldn't use a car I might recognize....

One might reasonably ask why, since I had

taken the trouble to locate John, I was now so determined to avoid him. I asked myself the same thing, and I knew the answer, even though I hated to admit it.

Putting that insane advertisement in the newspapers had been tantamount to yelling, "Anybody down there?" into the depths of the Grand Canyon. I had not really expected a response. In a way, I had not really wanted one.

Why do people have a hopeless need to glamorize things and people? It was impossible to turn John into a romantic hero when he was on the scene; he simply refused to behave like one. He was always making silly remarks or setting up a situation in which he looked like a fool. He could move fast enough and hit hard enough when he had to, and he could think even faster, but my most vivid memories of him were memories of deliberate foolishness. The only pure, unmarred memory was the last, when, stripped and sleek and deadly, he went over the side of that leaking boat into the icy water and risked his neck for someone else.

If he had never turned up again, I could have cherished that image and worked it into something beautiful. Or if he had come rushing to my side murmuring clichés – "I tried to forget you – I tried to stay away – It was for your sake, my dearest, I'm not worthy to black your boots — but I couldn't resist you, your image has been enshrined in my heart...." Hell, I could invent page after page of dialogue like that. So could John.

Instead he had popped out of nothingness like a demon in a horror movie, shocked me into a coma, pinched my bottom, handled me with the tolerant amusement of a man who had rediscovered some forgotten trinket — a toy he had enjoyed playing with once upon a time.... And he had turned me down flat when I asked for his help. Let's not forget that. He had turned me down. If he had had second thoughts, it was for reasons of his own, and that possibility made me very uneasy. I didn't believe his claims of virtue and respectability for a moment. He was still a crook, and a crook was the last thing I needed.

I was startled out of my sullen meditations when a car whizzed contemptuously past me and cut back into my lane so sharply that it grazed my left front fender. The driver was a little old lady with blue hair; she made a remarkably rude gesture at me as she went by. After that I concentrated on driving.

The streets of Garmisch were full of vacationers, winter-sports fans, and cows. The cows are part of the local color, and they have the right of way. They were not the only distractions; the shop windows bulged with goodies, including some gorgeous ski and après-ski costumes. I managed to get through the town without incident, bovine or otherwise, and took the road to Bad Steinbach.

The highway climbed steadily up into the foothills, passing through pine-shrouded shadows and out again into the sunlight of open meadows frosted with white. The sky ahead was a deep pure blue, framing the majestic outlines of the snow-capped Alpine peaks. I wished my mood matched the serenity of the scenery; the closer I got to Bad Steinbach, the more my vague sense of apprehension deepened.

The village huddles on a few acres of level ground, with the high hills enclosing it like a rampart. Some of the streets leading off the central square go up at a thirty-degree angle, and outlying houses cling precariously to the slopes. The roads that give access to them looked like tangled white ribbons against the deep green of the pine-covered hills. A broader panel of snow slashed across the side of the Hexenhut – the ski slope, one of the trickiest in the area because of the trees bordering it so narrowly. A lift operates from the station behind the hotel; I could see a bright car swinging in its ascent as I pulled into a parking place near the central fountain, with its oversized statue of Saint Emmeram. The fountain was dry now, and a fringe of icicles lengthened the saint's beard.

(In case you are interested – and I can't imagine why you should be – Emmeram was one of the first missionaries to the heathen Bavarians. He died in 715 or thereabouts.)

Most Bavarian villages look as if they had been designed for a production of *Babes in Toyland*. The Marktplatz of Bad Steinbach is no exception. On one side the serene, austere facade of the St. Michaelskirche gives no hint of the baroque fantasies within. The two adjoining sides are lined with houses and shops, fairytale quaint with their wooden balconies and painted fronts. Some of the balconies were draped with bright red geraniums, and I gaped at them for a moment until I realized they must be plastic. Facing the church, on the fourth side of the square, is the hotel. The only discordant note is the town parking lot, but it has to be there because they'd have had to blast out a piece of the mountain to get any more level ground.

In the summer, there are tables and bright umbrellas outside the hotel restaurant and the cafés. At least I assume there were, since that is the custom; I had never visited the village in the summer. There were no tables outside that day. However, the restaurant appeared to be doing good business, to judge by the people passing in and out.

Like the English, the Bavarians eat all the time. Unlike the English, they have not invented separate names for their various snack times; instead of elevenses and teatime and whatever, they refer to all of them as *Brotzeit*. It was just past 11 A.M. A reasonable time for *Brotzeit*.

The first thing I noticed was that the lobby had been modernized — not extensively, just enough to add a few jarring notes to what had been a charming period ambiance. There was a souvenir counter with racks of cheap beer steins and dolls dressed in Bavarian costume and pillows embroidered with mottoes like "I did it in Garmisch-Partenkirchen." The old wooden registration desk had been replaced by a shiny plastic structure. Hoffman wasn't on duty. The man behind the counter was someone I had not seen before — young and heavy-set, inappropriately attired in a short-sleeved gaudy print shirt. I didn't linger but went straight through into the restaurant.

It had undergone a similar transformation. The tables were more numerous and closer together, and each one boasted a vase of tacky plastic rosebuds. The bar was a modern monstrosity, frosted glass blocks with colored lights behind them.

Eventually one of the waitresses made it to my table. She was squashed into one of those Salzburger dirndls that you're supposed to buy several sizes smaller than your actual measurements. They are fastened across the midriff with hooks as stout as industrial steel, and the excess flesh thus ruthlessly compressed billows up over the low-cut bodice into the cute little white blouse, and sometimes beyond. When she bent over to ask for my order, I was reminded of a scene from one of my favorite movies — when Walter Matthau, confronted by a similar exhibition, screams, his eyes bulging, "Don't let them out! Don't let them out!"

They didn't get out. I ordered beer and examined the menu the girl had given me. The featured item was something called a Bavarian burger — ground veal and sauerkraut on a bun.

The omens were not auspicious. I had hoped I'd find Herr Hoffman in his usual place behind the desk. He might be elsewhere in the hotel or the village — or the world — but the implications of that bloodstained envelope were getting harder to deny. The refined old gentleman I had known would never have countenanced such vulgarities as plastic rosebuds and souvenir cushions.

I drank my beer and tried to figure out what to do next. There would be nothing unusual in my asking for Hoffman; anyone who had stayed at the hotel would remember him and he had been particularly kind to me. If my forebodings were mistaken, and I devoutly prayed they were, I would simply show him the photograph and ask him what it was all about.

If Hoffman was out of the picture, permanently or temporarily, it might be Frau Hoffman whom I would confront. I had never met her, but I assumed the woman wearing Helen's jewels must be she; she was the right age, at any rate. I couldn't think of any reason why I should not be equally candid with her. She was obviously in her husband's confidence.

If I asked for the manager and found myself facing a total stranger...Play it by ear? I keep thinking I'm good at that, even though events have often proved me mistaken. In this case there wasn't much else I could do. I paid my check and went back to the lobby.

The concierge behind the counter kept me waiting while he answered the phone and made busy work with piles of papers. He kept glancing at me out of the corner of his eye to see if I was impressed. At close range, I understood why he was shivering in short sleeves; every move he made was designed to show off his muscles.

126

Biceps bulged, pectorals popped, and everything else undulated. He had tousled his brown hair in deliberate imitation of a popular American movie star, and his full lips were set in a pout derived from the same source. After he had snapped at the girl at the switchboard, for no reason I could see, he turned to me with what he obviously believed was an ingratiating smile.

"Your pardon, Fräulein; we are very busy today."

Full pink lips and exaggerated pectorals happen to be the two male characteristics I most abhor. I didn't hold them against him; what I held against him was the smirk on his face as he looked me over.

"Are you?" I said.

"You wish a room? We are booked, but perhaps there will be a cancellation. . . ."

His hand — open, palm up — rested suggestively on the counter. I gave him a dazzling smile. His fingers curled like fat white worms exposed to the light.

"You weren't here last year," I murmured.

"No." He shrugged, setting off an obscene upheaval of chest and shoulder muscles. "This is not my profession, you understand. I am helping a friend in her time of need. My name is Friedrich Sommers — but I hope you will call me Freddy. As for the room—"

"No, thanks. I'd like to see Herr Hoffman."

Asking for the manager doesn't make you popular, even in big hotels. Freddy's smile wavered. "If there is a complaint, Fräulein—"

"Nothing like that. I just want to say hello to him."

"I am sorry to inform you that Herr Hoffman is deceased."

I had expected it, and, after all, I had scarcely known the man. But I didn't have to feign distress. "I'm so sorry. When did it happen?"

"Two weeks ago."

"Was he ill long?"

"He was not ill. It was an accident. He was struck by a car." Freddy's smile had passed into oblivion. "Are you by chance...Are you a friend?"

"No. I stayed here last year. He was very kind to me."

There was no obvious reason why I should have been so cagey, yet I found myself reluctant to give him my name. I didn't like Freddy. I had not liked his face or his muscles or his smirk, and I liked his suspicious scowl even less.

"Perhaps you would like to speak with Frau Hoffman," he suggested.

I had been about to ask if I might. The fact

that it was Freddy's suggestion made me wonder whether I really did want to. There was no retreating now, though, so I nodded and Freddy picked up the telephone. He raised one hand to his cheek when he spoke; it muffled his words to some extent, but my hearing is excellent.

After he hung up, he informed me that Frau Hoffman would see me, and indicated where I was to go. I remembered the corridor; it led to the room where Hoffman and I had spent such a pleasant evening a year ago. I must admit I felt a little like Alice falling down the rabbit hole.

Freddy must have been under the impression that I didn't understand German. That was stupid of him. I had not used the language when I spoke with him, but if he knew who I was, he must be aware of my proficiency in the language of the country where I presently resided. And he knew who I was. What he had said was: "She is here. Yes, the one you told me to watch out for. She is at the desk at this moment, asking for the old man."

Curiouser and curiouser, as Alice is reported to have remarked.

The friend Freddy was helping in her time of need had to be Frau Hoffman. I would not have expected the sedate elderly woman in the photograph to hobnob with a character like

Freddy, but people don't always behave the way you expect them to. The Hoffmans were childless. Maybe Freddy had appealed to the widow's frustrated maternal instincts. Or maybe he had a kind heart under an unprepossessing exterior. Be fair, Vicky, don't judge people by appearances.

A door at the end of the hall opened. Sunlight from the room behind the figure blurred its outlines; I was quite close to her before I realized she was not the woman in the photograph. She was much younger, probably in her twenties. Her face was vaguely familiar, though.

"Frau Hoffman?" I asked uncertainly.

"Yes." She stood back and motioned me to enter. "And you are the — you are a friend of my late husband?"

"I hope I may call myself that, though I only had the pleasure of meeting your husband once. You were in the hospital at the time, I believe."

I didn't really believe it, because I had remembered where I had seen her before. She had been a waitress in the restaurant. Friedl. The name came out of nowhere, as it does sometimes; I had heard it repeated often enough. The customers were always yelling for Friedl, especially the male customers. From waitress to wife to widow in less than a year...Quick work, and nice work if you can get it.

The promotion had not improved her looks. The waitress's uniform of tight-waisted dirndl and low-cut blouse had suited her slight but well-developed figure. She had had thick braids of brown hair that she wore coiled over her ears, and a fresh, pink-cheeked face. Now her hair was cut short and bleached almost white. She wore an ultrasuede suit that must have cost a bundle, but it was too tight across the chest and the apricot shade didn't flatter her complexion. She was heavily made up, and her nails were blood-red, long, and pointed.

"The hospital?" she repeated blankly. "That wasn't me. You must be speaking of my husband's first wife. She passed on last January."

"I'm so sorry," I said, and again I spoke sincerely.

She had certainly done her best to efface all traces of her predecessor. The room had been charming, filled with fine old furniture and beautiful shabby rugs. The painted *Schrank* was gone, as were the carved chest and the Persian rugs. Wall-to-wall carpeting in a shrieking shade of blue concealed the hardwood floor, and every stick of furniture was teak, glass, or chrome.

"Then you are the new owner of the hotel?" I asked.

"Yes." She snapped the word out, as if my

idle question had contained a challenge. "It has not been easy," she went on, with the same air of defiance. "But I can do it. Already I have made many improvements."

I couldn't bring myself to congratulate her on the improvements. Still feeling my way, I said, "I hope you have good help."

I was thinking of the hotel staff that had kept the place running so smoothly the year before, but Friedl interpreted the comment differently. With a betraying glance at a door that I assumed led to another room of her apartment, she murmured, "Freddy — Mr. Sommers — has been a great help to me. He is my — my cousin."

"I've met Mr. Sommers."

Belatedly remembering her manners, she offered me a chair, which I accepted, and coffee, which I declined. I had decided that my smartest move was to keep my mouth shut and let her make the first move. She didn't waste any time. "Did you get a message from my husband?"

I put on an expression of innocent bewilderment and countered with a question of my own. "Why, did he write to me?"

That was her chance. If she had said yes, and gone on to explain, I might have leveled with her.

Her eyes fled from mine. "I — uh — no, I

don't think...I wondered...Why did you come, then?"

"I just happened to be in the neighborhood. Herr Hoffman was very kind to me last year, so I thought I'd stop by and say hello."

"I see." She chewed on her lower lip and tried again. "He often spoke of you."

"Did he?"

"Oh yes. Often. He admired you. Such a learned lady, so clever, so intelligent. You had talked together – of many things...."

"Yes, we did."

She leaned forward, eyes narrowed. "What did you talk about?"

"Oh – lots of things. Art and antiques..." I paused invitingly, but the only response was a blank stare, so I went on, "Books, music – he was very fond of Brahms – cats...He had a beautiful little Siamese kitten. I hope it is flourishing?"

"Flourishing? Oh, the cat." Her mouth twisted unpleasantly. "I got rid of it. I hate the creatures. They are so sly. Besides, it was scratching my beautiful new furniture."

"I see."

"Did he speak of anything else?"

If I hadn't taken such an intense dislike to the wretched woman, I might have felt sorry for her. She was trying to find out how much I knew without giving anything away, but she was going about it so clumsily that she had betrayed more than she realized.

I said, "I see you've redecorated this room."

"Yes. Yes, I could not live with such dirty old things. This is much more cheerful, don't you think?"

"Cheerful" was not the word I would have chosen. In fact, the room was depressing, for all its bright colors and gleaming chrome. She had ruthlessly swept away not just inanimate objects, but the memories, the traditions, the long years of affectionate living they embodied. The fact that she had done it without deliberate malice only made the desecration worse; it was a symbol of the triumph of mediocrity over beauty and grace.

Ordinarily, I would not have been guilty of the bad taste of trying to buy a dead man's belongings from his widow of barely two weeks. In this case I didn't hesitate.

"If you haven't sold the furniture, I'd like to buy it."

"Buy it? All of it?"

"I was thinking of the *Schrank*. Perhaps some of the other pieces."

Again her eyes narrowed suspiciously. "Why would you want them?"

"Tastes differ," I explained patiently. "You

like modern, I like antiques."

"I have already sold them."

Couldn't wait to get them out of the house, I thought. Two weeks...

There was a sound from the next room — a muffled thud, as if someone had stumbled, or jarred a piece of furniture. Friedl started violently.

"Oh, do you have company?" I asked. "I'm sorry, you should have told me you were busy."

"Oh, no. No, there is no one.... It must have been the — the cat."

The cat that wasn't there. Quite suddenly I was overcome by a burning desire to escape from that sterile, horrible room and its occupant. I rose to my feet. "I mustn't take up any more of your time. Perhaps you could tell me to whom you sold the *Schrank*. He might consider an offer."

Now she seemed as anxious to be rid of me as I was to be gone. She gave me a name and directions, and let me show myself out. As I passed through the lobby, I noticed that Freddy wasn't at the desk.

The address she had given me wasn't far. No place in Bad Steinbach is far from any other place in Bad Steinbach. When I reached the fountain I stopped for a moment, to consider the new developments, and to get a grip on myself. The interview had left me shaken and off-balance.

Friedl and Freddy made a much more believable equation than Freddy and the late Frau Hoffman. I wondered whether Friedl had waited until after her husband's death to begin the affair.

I told myself I mustn't let my dislike of the woman prejudice my judgment, but it was no use; I felt about Friedl the way Friedl felt about cats. All prejudice aside, however, her behavior had been highly suspicious as well as highly inept. She knew Hoffman had intended to communicate with me. So why the devil didn't she come right out and say so? What was she trying to hide?

An answer came readily to mind.

If Friedl's intentions were honest and honorable, she should have welcomed the opportunity to confide in a responsible person — the very person her husband had planned to consult. If she knew about the treasure and intended to keep it for herself...I found that alternative much more plausible, and it explained some of the peculiarities in her speech and manner. She suspected Hoffman had written to me, but she wasn't sure. Then it had not been Friedl who mailed the envelope. Had Hoffman himself staggered, dying, to a postbox and pushed the envelope stained with his own blood through the slot with his last burst of strength? That scenario was a little too much even for my Rosanna-trained imagination. But then, who had mailed it? Was the blood Hoffman's? He had died suddenly, by violence. . . .

Much as I abhorred dear little Friedl, I wasn't ready to accuse her of mariticide. Not yet. It was no strain on my imagination to believe her capable of fraud, however. Yet even that assumption didn't explain her insistent questions. She had had two weeks in which to dispose of the gold, or move it to another location. That's what I would have done if I thought my husband had spilled the beans to an outsider. Then I'd sit tight and look innocent, and if some nosy female from a Munich museum came snooping around asking leading questions, I would tell her I hadn't the faintest idea what she was raving about. Gold? What gold? What would a simple Bavarian innkeeper be doing with a museum treasure? Sorry, Fräulein Doktor, but I'm afraid too much learning had addled your brain.

I had to allow for the obvious fact that Friedl wasn't the smartest woman in the world. I had not mentioned my name, to her or to Freddy, and she hadn't even had the basic intelligence to pretend ignorance of my identity. I hadn't d a single word that betrayed any knowledge of a secret or contradicted my statement that I was paying a simple social call; yet I had a feeling that Friedl was now as suspicious of my intentions as I was of hers, and for all the wrong reasons. My insistence on acquiring the *Schrank* had been a mistake, if an innocent one. I wanted it because it was beautiful; she thought of it only as a possible hiding place. Sometimes I think God must like stupid people, he gives them so many breaks.

Well, there was nothing I could do about it now. I brushed the snow from my pants and started walking across the Marktplatz. The shop she had mentioned was just off the central square, a couple of doors up one of the narrow streets. It wasn't an antique shop, as I had supposed. The sign read "Müller – Holzschnitzerei," and the small display window contained toys and ornaments carved out of wood, of the type sometimes referred to as "folk art."

Bells chimed softly as I opened the door. There was no one in the shop. From an open door at the back came the sound of tapping and a smell that made my nostrils quiver appreciatively. Fresh wood shavings, hot glue, and pipe tobacco blended into an aroma as seductive as the finest perfume. My grandfather's workshop smelled like that; I had spent many happy hours there as a child, hammering nails into wood scraps and making doll wigs out of curled shavings.

The tapping stopped. A man appeared in the open doorway, squinting at me through thick glasses.

He was short and square, with big gnarled hands. His shoulders filled the doorway from side to side. A light behind him made his hair shine like a silver nimbus.

After I had explained who I was and what I wanted, he put his pipe in his mouth and smoked in meditative silence for several seconds, without taking his eyes off me. Then he nodded and gestured. *"Herein, Fräulein."*

I followed him into the workshop. It was wonderful; tools were scattered over a long wooden table and sawdust had drifted like dun snow. He pointed, and then I saw it: a painted door, leaning disconsolately against the wall, splinters of wood hanging from the broken hinges.

"Oh, no," I exclaimed. "What happened to it?"

My unconcealed distress pleased the old man. His formal manner relaxed, and he said, "That is how it was when I found it, the pieces piled in the courtyard ready to be burned. She was good enough to sell it to me."

I damned Friedl with a few well-chosen

words — in English, since I knew a man of his age and background would think poorly of a lady who used vulgar language. He got the idea from my tone, if not from the actual words, and his eyes were twinkling when I looked at him.

"Just so," he said. "Don't distress yourself, Fräulein. I can repair it. That is my trade, at which I excel. I have no real talent for creating, you understand, but for restoration, there is no one better. Do you still want to buy it?"

"Yes. Please."

I didn't even ask the price. At that point, I'd have been willing to hock my car and mortgage my house; this was a rescue operation, not a commercial transaction. How could Friedl have done such a stupid thing? She must have hated him, to destroy an object that would have brought a fancy price from any antique dealer.

"What happened to the other furniture?" I asked.

The old man shrugged. "It went, I believe, to a dealer in Garmisch. I could not afford to pay so much as he. One moment, Fräulein, I must finish this piece before the glue hardens."

He settled himself on a stool, put his pipe carefully in an ashtray, and picked up the piece he had been working on — a carved head with a grotesque yet humorous grin — surely a caricature of a living model. The nose had been broken off; I stood watching as the old man carefully glued the nose, or a reproduction of it, into place.

"So," he said. Swiveling slowly on the stool, he faced me, his hands resting heavily on his knees. His face was as rigid as the wooden one he had just repaired, hardened by harsh weather and long years. His hair clung to his skull like a white fur wig. Then his leathery cheeks cracked into deep lines and his thin lips curled up at the corners.

"So," he repeated, "you are the so-learned *Mädchen* from the museum. Did you get the letter, then?"

"You sent it?" I gaped at him. "But how — why?"

His smile stiffened into sobriety, though a spark of amusement remained in the depths of his eyes. "I mailed it, I did not send it. There is a difference."

"You are right. There is a difference. I... Can I sit down?"

"Please."

He picked up an oily rag and passed it carelessly over a backless chair inches deep in sawdust.

"Thank you," I said meekly. "Would you mind telling me how it happened?"

"It does not take long to tell. I was working

late in the shop, as I often do. I heard the sounds from the Marktplatz. They were the sounds of death," the old man said simply. "The car did not stop; it accelerated and went on. I had expected him, you see. He had said he would come that evening. I went as quickly as I could, but there were others there before me; they made a circle around him. I saw only one shoe. I knew it, and pushed through them. His blood soaked the snow and spread as I bent over him. He knew me. He had no breath to speak, but he moved his hand — pushed the letter toward me. I knew what he wanted. We had been friends a long time."

He picked up his pipe and slowly tapped out the dead embers.

"I'm glad," I said. It was a stupid thing to say, but he understood.

"Glad there is someone to mourn him? Yes. The only one. She..." He turned his head aside and spat neatly into the pile of shavings beside him. Then he went on in the same calm voice, "It happens to old men, even those who should know better. After Amelie died, he was *verrückt* — crazy with grief. A man needs a woman, and *she* knew how to use her advantage."

"I'm sure she did. But...Do you know what was in the letter?"

"I do not open mail addressed to other people. It was so important to him that he thought of it with his last breath; that was enough for me. But I knew your name. He had spoken of you."

"What did he say?"

His eyes glinted. "That if he were forty years younger he would go to Munich to see you — and perhaps to do other things."

For some absurd reason I felt tears coming to my eyes. I gave him a watery smile. "If he had been forty years younger, I probably would have done them. He was a good man."

"Yes, a learned man. Not like me; I am only an ignorant worker, with no more than *Volksschule*. But he liked to talk to me."

"He never said anything to you about..." I didn't hesitate because I didn't trust him. I hesitated because I didn't want his blood reddening the snow in the Marktplatz. "About why he might want to get in touch with me?"

"No, nothing. When he spoke of you, it was in connection with art." The old man's face was stiff with pride. "Yes, we talked of such things, the scholar and the ignorant peasant. He loved beautiful things, and no craftsman worthy of the name can be indifferent to a fine work of art." His fingers caressed the surface of the sculptured head. "This would have hurt him. Often he spoke of the destruction of beauty – the statues broken, the paintings slashed by barbarians. So much lost. So much that can never be retrieved."

His voice was as deep as a dirge; it reminded me of the passage in the Brahms *Requiem* when the soft voices mourn in grieving resignation. "Behold, all flesh is as the grass, and all the goodliness of man is as the flowers of the field; for lo, the grass withereth. . . ."

I knew I was going to break down and blubber if I didn't get away. "I must go," I said, rising. "I'm afraid I am interrupting your lunch."

"No, I have this with me." He reached for a paper-wrapped sandwich. "Will you share? It is good ham and cheese."

I refused with thanks; but a rustling noise heralded the appearance of someone who was definitely interested in the offer. As the sleek fawn body slid out from under a bench I exclaimed, "Surely, that is Herr Hoffman's cat."

"Yes. Her name is Clara—"

"After Clara Schumann," I said with a smile. "The great love of Brahms's life. I'm so glad she's with you. Frau Hoffman said she had gotten rid of her, and I was afraid. . ."

"I would not let Anton's pet come to harm."

The cat leaped onto the table with the air of

spontaneous flight common to Siamese. It saun-tered casually toward the sandwich, looking as if food were the farthest thing from its mind. The old man pulled out a chunk of ham and offered it; after sniffing the morsel, the cat con-descended to accept it.

"I am not a lover of cats," Müller admitted. "And this one does not love me; she misses Anton. But we respect one another."

"That's about the most you can expect from a cat," I said, holding out my hand. I didn't expect the aristocratic animal to respond; in fact, her initial reaction was a long hard stare from eyes as blue and brilliant as — as other eyes I knew. After she had finished the ham, she sauntered toward me and butted my hand with her head.

"She does remember me," I said, flattered.

"No doubt. She is very intelligent, and very choosy about her friends. It is a compliment."

The cat began to purr as my fingers moved across its head and behind its ears. "Would you like to have her?" Müller asked.

I pulled my hand away. Deeply affronted, the cat turned its back and sat down with a thump. "Good God, no. I mean — I can't. I have a dog — a Doberman. They wouldn't get along."

"She is company for me," the old man admitted, lowering his voice as if he were afraid the cat would hear and take advantage. "But she will outlive me — she is not two years old. I would like to think she will find a home when I am gone."

"Oh, that won't be for a long time," I said firmly.

I gave him my card, and he promised to let me know when the *Schrank* was ready. Clara relented and allowed me to scratch her chin. I was almost at the door when Müller's quiet voice stopped me.

"There is some reason why you came, isn't there? Something beyond coincidence and kindness."

"I don't want. . ." I began.

"I don't want either." He grinned broadly. "At my age I have not the time or the strength for distractions. There is work I must finish before I die. But if there is a thing I can do for my friend, you must tell me."

"I will tell you," I said.

"That is good. Go with God, Fräulein. I hope you will not have need of His help."

I hoped so, too, but the picture was looking blacker and blacker. Müller's description of Hoffman's death had shocked me badly. Hit and run? There was no evidence of anything more sinister, but it was, to say the least, an ugly coincidence that Hoffman had actually been on his way to mail the letter to me when he was struck down.

I was so distracted I almost walked past my car. Pausing, I heard my empty stomach protest; Herr Müller's ham sandwich had reminded it that lunchtime was long past. I hesitated, trying to decide whether to eat in Bad Steinbach or drive on to Garmisch. Then I saw something that decided me. It was a familiar maroon Mercedes, parked, with unbelievable effrontery, only a short distance from my car.

I marched straight into the restaurant without going through the lobby; and there he was, at one of the best tables near the window. The table was piled with platters, some empty, some in the process of being emptied. He had been watching for me; he raised his hand and waved furiously.

"I saved you a place," he announced, indicating a chair.

"A chair you have saved, but not a square inch on the table." I sat down. "Don't tell me you followed me, Schmidt, because I know you didn't. How did you get here?"

Schmidt waved at the waitress. She responded a lot faster than she had done for me. "What will you have?" he asked. "The Bavarian burger is very *interessant*."

"I'll bet it is." There was enough food left on the table to feed a platoon. I ordered beer, then changed it to coffee, and began browsing among Schmidt's remaining entrees. He protested, but I told him it was for his own good. He ate too much anyway.

"So," I said, reaching for a sausage. "You haven't answered my question."

He was so pleased with himself he didn't bother bawling me out for trying to elude him. "Pure deduction," he said, grinning greasily. "Sheer, brilliant detective work. Ratiocination of the most superb intellectual—"

"Specifically?" I suggested.

"I recognized the man in the photograph you showed me." Schmidt snatched the sausage out of my hand. "I told you I had seen him before. You thought I boasted, but it was the truth. Never do I forget a face, or a name."

"Schmidt—" I began.

"I thought about it as I drove home last night," Schmidt went blithely on. "It worried at me, you understand. I thought he must be connected with art or antiquities, or I would not know him, and I had also on my mind this matter of the Trojan treasure; and suddenly, snap, click, the pieces went together. I had seen articles by this man in old journals. After I got home I found them. Guess, Vicky, what the articles were about?"

"Schmidt, please don't—"

There was no stopping him, he was so pleased with himself; his voice got louder and louder as he continued. "Troy! Yes, you will not believe it, but it is true, he was on the staff of Blegen during the excavations of the late thirties. To make it certain, I looked up the excavation reports and found in them a group photograph. He was there, standing next to Blegen himself — much changed, yes, but the same man, only a student at the time, but appointed in 1939 to the post of assistant in pre-Hellenic art at the Staatliches—"

His voice rose in a triumphant bellow. Half the people in the restaurant were staring. I picked up a piece of celery and shoved it into his mouth.

Schmidt's eyes popped indignantly. He hates celery, and any other food that is good for him.

"For God's sake, Schmidt, don't broadcast it to the whole town," I hissed. "You shouldn't have come here. They are already suspicious of me, and now you've made matters worse."

Schmidt swallowed the chunk of celery he had inadvertently bitten off, grimaced at the rest of the stalk and pushed it aside. He looked a little subdued.

"How can I help but make a mistake when

you lie to me?" he demanded. "You tell me the hotel is in Garmisch, which is not true; I must ask at the tourist bureau, to find the Hotel Hexenhut in Bad Steinbach. The earliest this morning I have telephoned you, to tell you what I have learned, and there is no answer. I rush to your house and no one is there — the poor dog, he is crying in the basement —"

"I called Carl and asked him to stop by after work, to feed Caesar and take him for a walk," I said. Schmidt had me on the defensive, and not just on Caesar's account.

"He needs a friend," Schmidt said seriously. "You should have another dog."

"Two dogs like Caesar and I wouldn't have a house," I said. "Don't change the subject, Schmidt. I didn't know about Hoffman's academic background."

"Ha, it is true?" Schmidt's pout changed to a broad, pleased grin. "Has Papa Schmidt put over one on the clever detective?"

"It's true," I admitted. "I underestimated you, Schmidt, and I apologize. That information answers one of the questions I've been asking myself: What was a Bavarian innkeeper doing with a museum treasure? It wasn't until late last night that I discovered he was the one who sent me the photograph. I — uh — I got so excited I went rushing out without calling you —"

"You see the difference between us," Schmidt said reproachfully. "I rush to see you, you rush away from me."

"All right, all right — I grovel, I apologize. Look here, Schmidt, the situation is more complicated than I thought. We are going to have to proceed with caution."

"Oh yes, I know." Schmidt nodded complacently. "I am very careful, Vicky, in what I say. And I have learned much. The woman in the photograph is the first Frau Hoffman—"

"I assumed it was."

"Yes, you assume, but I know. I have seen a picture of her, it is the same woman."

I put my hands to my head. "Schmidt. You didn't — you haven't seen Friedl?"

"If Friedl is the second Frau Hoffman, yes, I have seen her. By the way, that young man at the desk behaves very strangely, Vicky. When I ask for Herr Hoffman and explain I knew him once, many years ago, he turns a strange color and cannot talk sensibly. Do you suppose...What is the matter, Vicky? Have I done something wrong?"

"Yes, dammit! You shouldn't have...Oh well, maybe it doesn't matter. What did you say to her?"

Schmidt insisted he had given nothing away, and if his version of the conversation was correct, it was true — except that his mere presence was enough to alarm a conspirator. He had been deliberately vague about where and when he had known Hoffman, and he had (*aber natürlich!*) said nothing about the gold, or about a bloodstained envelope. How he had talked Friedl into bringing out the family album I could not imagine; I was surprised that she hadn't disposed of it as she had disposed of Hoffman's other personal possessions.

"Poor girl, she is in a state of great distress," Schmidt said sympathetically. "I advised her to go away for a holiday; her nerves are in terrible condition."

"Schmidt, you are such a push-over," I snapped. "She's a cheap little tramp who married Hoffman for his money and is now trying to steal his — his prize possession for herself."

"That is a terrible thing to say! How do you know?"

I gave him a brief rundown of what Friedl had said — and what she had not said. "What's more," I added, "I'm beginning to wonder whether she knows where — it — is. She tore that *Schrank* apart. Why would she destroy a valuable object unless she was looking for something?"

"It may be that she does not know for what she is looking," Schmidt said shrewdly. "It would not be necessary to destroy a piece of furniture to make certain there was not hidden in it something so large as — as what we are seeking."

"Good point. Maybe she hoped to find a clue — a map or a letter."

Masticating, Schmidt shook his head mournfully. "I cannot believe so lovely a young woman would behave with such duplicity."

"Believe it. I'll tell you something, though — I'm beginning to suspect she is not acting on her own. She is unbelievably stupid. When I was talking to her, I felt as if I were conversing with — with a ventriloquist's dummy, that was it. Someone had told her what to do, but not how to go about it."

"Aha," said Schmidt. *"Cherchez l'homme!"*

"I think you've got it, Schmidt. A woman like that always has to have a man around. Oh, hell. I don't want to discuss it here. Let's go."

Schmidt swept a measuring glance over the table, popped an overlooked morsel of cheese into his mouth, and nodded agreement. "The lunch, it is on me," he announced, summoning the waitress with a lordly gesture.

"It sure is," I agreed, surveying his bulging tummy.

Not until Schmidt had risen and was waddling toward the door did I get the full effect of his costume — bright red, fitting him like a second skin. It was so appalling I let out a yelp. "Schmidt!"

"*Was? Was ist los? Was ist's?*" Schmidt spun around like a top, bellowing in alarm.

A hush had fallen over the restaurant and every eye in the place was focused on us. I grabbed Schmidt by the seat of the pants (there was very little slack to grab) and the scruff of the neck and propelled him out the door.

We stood by his car arguing. Schmidt was hurt because I didn't like his outfit — "so fitting for the season of *Weihnachten*" — and he didn't want to go home. He was having fun.

We were still arguing when someone came running out of the hotel, calling my name. It was Freddy. "I am so glad I caught you up," he exclaimed. "Frau Hoffman hoped you would return; she said to tell you a message. There was a bridal chest, very old, belonging to Herr Hoffman, that was given to a friend of his. Perhaps he will be willing to sell to you."

Schmidt began bobbing up and down and gesturing at me. His face was almost as crimson as his suit, he was so excited. The word "chest" suggested an accompanying adjective — "treasure" — and he was reacting like a child reading Edgar Allan Poe.

"Where does the friend live?" I asked, hoping

it was someplace like Paris or Lhasa, and that I could talk Schmidt into catching the first plane.

"Not far from here. I can tell you. . . ."

He rattled off directions, adding helpfully, "It is only several miles from the town."

"I know it, I know it," Schmidt cried. "Thank you, my friend — *vielen Dank.*"

Freddy went running back to the hotel and Schmidt unlocked the Mercedes. "You are following me," he insisted, forgetting his grammar in his excitement. "I the way am knowing."

"Wait a minute, Schmidt —"

It was too late. He almost ran over my foot.

I got in my car and took off after the old lunatic, cursing aloud. If I had been on my own, I would have deliberated long and hard about pursuing that oh-so-convenient lead. I probably would have ended up pursuing it, if only for the sake of the chest, which I remembered well. It was a beauty. But I seriously doubted that it contained the gold of Troy.

The first few miles weren't bad going. Then Schmidt, who drove with an assurance that suggested he really did know where he was going, turned abruptly into a side road that plunged steeply up the mountainside. After a while I shifted into four-wheel drive. I'd have signaled him to stop if there had been anyplace to turn around, which there wasn't. Snowplows had carved out a single narrow lane; banks of glistening white rose high on both sides. I prayed he wouldn't meet a car coming down. Occasionally a sidetrack would wind off through clustered pines or up rocky banks toward an isolated dwelling. Otherwise there was no sign of human life.

I wasn't happy about the situation, but I didn't start to get really worried until after we had gone fifteen kilometers. The road had twisted and curved so often I had lost my sense of direction, but as it turned out, we weren't more than a mile from the town. I found out in the most direct possible fashion; rounding a sudden curve, I saw the damned place down below — straight down. The plows hadn't had any problem disposing of the snow in this spot; they had just pushed it off the edge of the cliff.

I leaned on the horn. Schmidt responded with a cheerful beepity-beep, and the Mercedes disappeared around another steep curve, its rear end wriggling like a belly dancer's navel. We went around a few more bends, with Bad Steinbach flashing in and out of sight down below; finally, to my relief, the road leveled out. It was then that the thing I had feared finally happened. Suddenly the Mercedes swerved, bounced off a snowbank, and headed straight for the opposite side. There was no snowbank on the side. The drop wasn't sheer — not after the first twenty or thirty feet.

I started pumping my brakes. Luckily the process had become automatic, because every ounce of my concentration was focused on the wildly weaving vehicle ahead. Schmidt was fighting the skid, but he was losing. There was something wrong with the Mercedes, it wasn't a simple skid....At the last possible second, he managed to sideswipe a tree. If he hadn't done so, he'd have gone over the edge.

I was out of my car before the echoes of the crash had died, running frantically toward the wreck. The Mercedes was skewed sideways; the front wheels were off the ground, still spinning.

Schmidt was slumped over the wheel, his poor pathetic bald head shining in the sunlight. Of course he wasn't wearing his seat belt; he never did, the damned fool....I wrenched the door open and reached for him.

The bullet spanged off the rear fender with a sound like a cymbal. The echoes rattled so furiously that I thought it was a semiautomatic. Before they died, another shot sent them flying again. Missed me by a mile...but there were a lot of potential targets. My tires, me,

Schmidt, the gas tank. . . As I tugged frantically at Schmidt's dead weight, I could have sworn I heard a gentle trickle of liquid. I didn't need my imagination to tell me the tank was already ruptured; I could smell the gas.

Terror lent strength to my not inconsiderable muscles; I gave a mighty heave, and Schmidt came out like a cork from a bottle. Somehow I kept my feet, towing him as I backed away. I might be doing him a deadly injury by moving him, but we'd both be fried like Wiener schnitzels if that gas tank went up.

God, he was heavy! I couldn't move fast enough. I felt as if I were towing a cast-iron statue, as if my feet were mired in glue. The air at the back of the Mercedes quivered, distorted by fumes, by heat. . . . How long before it blew?

Schmidt lay like a stuffed toy, his hands trailing limply. I could have sworn there was a smile on his face, damn him – bless him – oh, Schmidt, I thought, don't die. Don't just lie there and make me drag you.

I was still moving, but it didn't feel as if I were. My feet went up and down, as if on a treadmill, and the scenery didn't change, the wrecked car didn't get any farther away. It occurred to me that I ought to get myself and Schmidt behind that convenient snowbank. I could have managed the first part of the program, but not the second; dragging Schmidt was hard enough, lifting him was out of the question. Was that a flicker of flame I saw, in the shaken air?. . .

He only brushed me in passing, but my knees were like wet noodles, and when he hoisted Schmidt up over his shoulder, I sat down with a solid thud.

"For God's sake, this is no time to take a rest," he said breathlessly. A hand clamped over my arm and yanked me to my feet.

The hand was in the small of my back when we reached the snowbank, but I didn't need its pressure to send me up and over. I had a flashing glimpse of Schmidt sailing through the air like Santa Claus falling from his sleigh; then I landed face down in the snow and tried to burrow under it as the world went up in flame and thunder.

The echoes of the explosion went on for a thousand years. After they had died, I decided it was safe to raise my head. The first thing I saw was Schmidt's face, less than a foot away. Cold had reddened it to a shade only slightly less brilliant than the crimson of his suit, and rivulets of frozen blood traced fantastic patterns across his forehead. But his eyes were wide open and when he saw me, his chapped lips cracked in a smile.

I grabbed him by his ears and rained passionate kisses on his dimpled cheeks and bright red nose and grinning mouth. "Schmidt, you devil — you crazy old goat — are you all right, you damned fool? Oh, Schmidt, how could you be so incredibly stupid, you idiot?"

Schmidt giggled. A voice behind me remarked in saccharine tones, "This is the very ecstasy of love."

I rolled over. John was sitting with his back up against the packed snow of the bank, a cigarette in one hand. He was wearing a rather effeminate pale blue down jacket and darker pants. A ski mask, patterned in lozenges of navy and green, gave him the look of tattooed Maori warrior.

"Thank you," I said formally, "for saving our lives."

"A pleasure, I'm sure. And now, if you will forgive me—"

He started to rise. I threw myself at him and grabbed his ankle. "John, there's a man out there with a rifle—"

"Not any longer. However, if I don't waste any more time chatting with you, I may be able to discover which of your numerous enemies has been missing from his or her appointed place. Do excuse me."

"Wait, wait." Schmidt was snorting and flailing around in the snow like a red octopus. "I have questions – many questions –"

"I'm sure you do." Even white teeth flashed in the mouth hole of the mask.

I said resignedly, "Schmidt, meet Schmidt."

"Schmidt?" My boss's bellow of laughter made the echoes ring. "Ha, yes. Schmidt – Smythe – very good. I am so glad –"

"Yes, well, my rapture is also extreme," John said politely. He twitched his foot out of my numbing grasp and rose lithely to his feet. "Vicky, you'd better get Kris Kringle to a fire and a doctor. *Auf Wiedersehen.*"

He scrambled over the bank and disappeared from sight. I got to my feet, ignoring Schmidt's breathless appeals for assistance, information, and so on, and was in time to see the pale blue outfit disappear in the trees. A moment later an automobile engine started up, revved a few times, and faded. He had been following me the whole time. That diabolical road had required so much of my attention I hadn't watched for following vehicles.

Schmidt's Mercedes was blazing merrily away. I hoped it wouldn't start a forest fire. My own car was closer to the blaze than I liked.

"Wait here," I told Schmidt. "I'll turn around and come back and collect you."

By the time I had reported the accident and taken Schmidt to be overhauled by a doctor, night had fallen on the charming mountain village of Bad Steinbach. I was prepared to spend the night — though not, by choice, in the Gasthaus Hexenhut — if Schmidt's injuries demanded it, but he had come out relatively unscathed — only a bump and a cut on his forehead, which had hit the steering wheel. All those layers of fat had protected his body; he didn't even have a cracked rib. However, he was out of sorts because the doctor had slapped a large-sized Band-Aid on his wound instead of swathing him in bandages like a hero in the movies, so I agreed to stop in Garmisch to re-plenish his strength, i.e., eat.

He insisted on one of the best restaurants in town. He was paying, so I didn't object. When he had eaten his soup and a big hunk of saddle of venison, *mit Preiselbeeren* and all the rest, he announced that he was now feeling well enough to discuss our next move.

"What next move? We're going straight back to Munich and you are going straight to bed."

"There are many things we must discuss," said Schmidt seriously. "To think I have seen

162

him at last — the great, the famous Sir John Smythe!"

"The infamous Sir John Smythe. You didn't see him, you only saw that mask."

"I would have known him anywhere," said Schmidt romantically. "Who else would appear out of thin air to save us from a flaming death? But you, Vicky — you have deceived me. You were not surprised to see him. You knew he was still alive — you have been seeing him, making love with him all these months—"

"Schmidt, you ought to be ashamed of yourself. I think you're jealous."

Schmidt's petulant scowl relaxed. "It was very nice when you were kissing me," he said.

I couldn't help smiling. "I am rather fond of you, you old goat."

"Yes, but that is another thing. Always you say rude things to me, even when you thought I was dying. You blamed me for the accident, but it was not my fault, was it, if some madman shot out the tire of my car? I was driving magnificently until that moment—"

"You were driving like a maniac, as you always do. Hadn't it occurred to you that we had been sent on a wild-goose chase, possibly into a trap? If I had been alone, I'd have turned back long before it happened."

Since this was a valid complaint, Schmidt

chose to ignore it. "How did he get there ahead of us?"

Since this was a valid question, I chose to answer it. "I wondered about that myself. He might live up that way, in the hills; a telephone call from the hotel could have sent him out to ambush us. Or there may be a trail from the valley, a short cut."

"True." Schmidt ruminated. "I will have the gateau with rum and strawberries. For you—"

"Just coffee." After he had dealt with the pressing matter of dessert, he continued, "It was the concierge, you think? The fat boy who gave us the directions?"

"That's not fat, that's muscle," I said fairly. "Muscle enough to climb a mountain and get to the spot before us. But we haven't any proof. He may have passed on a message in all innocence."

Schmidt's curling lip showed what he thought of Freddy's innocence. He'd have preferred to make Freddy the villain rather than Friedl, lady's man that he was. I went on, "The police just laughed when I told them someone shot at us. They said it was probably a hunter."

"A bad hunter who could mistake a Mercedes for a deer," Schmidt grunted.

Schmidt slept most of the way back. He had eaten enough to render a gorilla comatose, but

I was worried about him. He was too old and too fat for such goings-on. His accusations had stung, though. I did have a tendency to denigrate him and underestimate him and treat him like a child. He enjoyed having me fuss at him — at least I thought he enjoyed it — but I was beginning to realize that the derogatory adjectives and the patronizing attitude might hurt an aging person who was already painfully aware of his increasing liabilities. I had to keep him out of danger without wounding his feelings and that wasn't going to be easy.

I took him home and tucked him into bed — not the first time I had performed that little job. I was reluctant to leave him alone, but he insisted he was okay, just tired; so, in keeping with my new policy, I said good night. Besides, I had a feeling. . . .

For once, my premonitions were right on the mark. It was long past midnight before I had tended to Caesar's needs and my own; when the summons came, I was ready. Caesar, sprawled on the bedroom floor, had keener ears than mine. He let out one short, sharp bark, and got up; then he loped to the window, his nails clicking on the bare boards, and began whining.

I turned off the light before I opened the window. The garden was white and dead and the high, distant moon cast long gray shadows across the snow. He looked no more solid than any other shadow as he slid over the balcony rail, but the arms that drew me to him were hard and real, and the lips that closed over mine were not cold for long.

FIVE

If my ears were burning that night I didn't notice. Some such omen ought to have occurred: people were talking about me again.

"Stop sniveling. Why the devil do you always snivel when I talk to you?"

"You are so cruel to me. It was not my fault. I didn't know he was going to do it."

"I told you to telephone me if she turned up."

"I did. It was only this morning that she—"

"And Schmidt too. That tears it. They know. If they weren't sure before, that moronic young thug has confirmed their suspicions. Where is he?"

Guiltily, as if the distant speaker could see her, she glanced at the closed bedroom door. "He is here."

"Keep him there. Keep him quiet."

"Yes, I will. *Liebchen*, no harm has been done. They were not injured—"

"And a damned good thing, too." After a long pause the voice said thoughtfully, "There

167

may be a way of turning this to our advantage after all. Now listen to me."

"Yes, I will. I will do exactly as you say."

"Then this is what you must do. . . ."

The smeared tears died on her cheeks as she listened, intent on every word. Freddy was a diversion, pleasant enough in his way; but the voice came from a world far beyond anything Freddy could offer — a world that would one day be hers, if she followed orders faithfully.

For some reason known only unto the great god Freud, I dreamed about babies. They were howling their little heads off because someone had stuck them upright in a snowbank, all in a row like ducks in a shooting gallery. One of them went on yelling after I woke up. It took me a minute to realize that it wasn't a baby, but Caesar, whining pathetically outside the bedroom door.

Sunlight slanting across the floor told me that Caesar's complaint was justified. It was long past his usual hour for R and R (relief and refreshment).

John was still asleep. Only the tip of his nose and a mop of ruffled fair hair showed over the blanket. I pulled it down with a careful fingertip, exposing his face. He murmured low in his throat, but didn't waken. No wonder he was tired. He had had a hard day — and night.

Propped on one elbow, I studied his sleeping face curiously. He was back to blond, sans mustache, beard, or other distractions — the original, the one and only. . . whatever his name might be. What's in a name, after all? A rose by any other name would smell as sweet — and its thorns would prick as painfully.

I slid cautiously out of bed and reached for the negligee lying crumpled on the floor. Goose bumps popped out all over me in a spontaneous explosion; I discarded the charming but chilly chiffon ruffles and made a beeline for the closet and my comfortable old furry bathrobe.

Caesar trailed me downstairs, whuffling appreciatively and licking my heels. By the time the coffee was ready, he had finished his breakfast — two gulps and a single comprehensive lick. I shoved him out the back door, fixed a tray, and carried it upstairs.

John was sitting up in bed, hands behind his head. He greeted me with a sweet smile. "Excellent service. I must come here more often."

"And no hotel bill," I said, putting the tray on the table. "Not that you ever pay them anyway."

"Didn't I ever reimburse you for that time in Paris?"

"No, you did not."

"A slight oversight." He stretched sideways, reaching for a cup.

The movement sent muscles sliding smoothly under his tanned skin; I wondered whether the tan had been acquired in a health spa or under a tropical sun. I didn't bother asking.

John would have considered Freddy's protuberant pectorals not only vulgar in the extreme, but also inefficient. His own body was above all else efficient-looking, as if he had deliberately designed it to do what he expected of it with the minimum of effort. It had a certain aesthetic appeal, however, at least to someone who prefers the lean grace of early classical Greek sculptures such as the Discobolus to the muscle-bound athletes of the later Hellenistic period. I had never mentioned my aesthetic tastes to John, since he was vain enough already.

Catching my eye, he pulled the blanket up to his chin. I laughed. "Surely modesty, at this stage in our relationship. . ."

"Cold, not modesty. Are you going to stand there like a statue of virtue all morning? ' 'Tis true, 'tis day; what though it be? O wilt thou therefore rise from me?' "

I sat down on the edge of the bed. That was a mistake. Or, to look at it another way, that was exactly the right move.

Caesar was howling plaintively in the garden

and the patches of sunlight had moved farther when I stirred. "I've got to let that damned dog in. The neighbors will complain."

"Never mind the neighbors. Or the dog."

"He remembered you."

"Of course. I'm unforgettable."

"In some ways," I agreed. "We have to talk about the gold, John. Are you in?"

"Not at the moment, but if you'll give me a little time—"

"I despise crude sexual double-entendres," I said crossly. "You used to quote Shakespeare. Last night all I got was Humphrey Bogart."

"There were occasional bits of Shakespeare. Even a smidgen of John Donne."

"Oh, really? 'License my roving hands, and let them go'?"

"I've always considered that one of Donne's less inspired passages. No, I believe, among other things, I remarked that 'Love's mysteries in souls do grow, But yet the body is his book.' "

"That's nice. I'm sorry I missed it."

"I expect your attention was on something else," John said, demonstrating.

"I thought you considered that one of Donne's less-inspired—"

"I was referring to the poetic spark — the divine afflatus. Insofar as practical advice is concerned..."

"John, if you don't stop that—"

"I thought you enjoyed it. Oh, very well. Lie still. I can't concentrate on crime when you squirm around like that."

"Is this better?" I curled up against him, my head on his shoulder.

"Not a great deal," John murmured. "But I will endeavor to rise above lesser distractions. What were we talking about?"

"Crime. If that's what it is."

"Taking pot shots at you is a crime in my book."

"Ah, so that's what convinced you I wasn't inventing wild stories in order to lure you back to my arms." John made a small sound, a mixture of protest and laughter, and I insisted, "You did think that."

"No, honestly."

"Yes, you did."

"I had enough confidence in your veracity to follow you to Garmisch. Damned lucky for you I did."

"Yes, I deeply appreciate it, but I can't help wondering why, if you had all that confidence in my veracity, you didn't say so in the first place."

"I thought you wanted to talk about crime."

"I am. I do. I just don't understand—"

John gave a long, exaggerated sigh. "My dear

172

girl, your initial scenario was pure fantasy. Attempted murder is a solid fact. People don't try to kill you unless you have done something to annoy them. What did you do yesterday?"

I gave him a brief rundown of the day's activities.

"Ve-ry interesting," John said thoughtfully. "Let's concoct a plot, shall we? I'll begin; feel free to interrupt if you have contributions or criticisms."

"I will."

"I'm sure you will. All right, here we go. Forty-odd years ago, Hoffman was an official of the museum where the Trojan gold was displayed. After the war—"

"Wait a minute, you're skipping. What was he doing during the war?"

"Irrelevant. We have to assume he was in Berlin at the end of the war and that somehow he managed to make off with the treasure. Otherwise we don't have a plot."

"Okay, I'll buy that."

"All the same, I wish I knew how he managed it," John mused. "It was one of the master scams of all time, played against a background of epic tragedy — Homeric tragedy, one might say. Crawling across a hellish no man's land pocked with bomb craters and fallen bodies, with shells bursting overhead and buildings flaming around him, clutching that precious bundle...We'll never know, I suppose." I nudged him and with a wistful sigh — the tribute of a master to a brilliant amateur — he resumed his narrative.

"After the war, he turned up in Bavaria, married the innkeeper's daughter, and settled into a life of quiet obscurity, giving up what might have been a distinguished academic career. The preservation of the Trojan gold had become an idée fixe, perhaps a symbol of all the masterpieces of art and learning smashed by the barbarians and never to be retrieved, as your friend the carpenter put it. Why should he hand it over to someone else? He had as much right to it as anyone — more, because he had saved it and they had threatened to destroy it. In his admittedly distracted mind, there was no difference between conqueror and conquered. One had bombed London and Coventry, but the other had reduced Dresden to rubble and gutted the Cathedral of Cologne. Well — what do you think?"

"Very literary, very intuitive, very profound. You may even be right."

"To resume, then. His first wife must have known about the treasure; he photographed her wearing it. Was it her death that made him decide to share his secret with someone else?

The inevitability of death is the one undeniable fact we all try to deny—"

"If I want more philosophy, I'll read Plato," I informed him. "Get on with it."

"His wife died," John said obediently. "He married again — a woman forty or fifty years younger. Did he tell her about the treasure?"

"Of course he did. Men do stupid things when they're in love."

"Dear me, what a sweeping, sexist generalization."

"I said, skip the philosophy."

"You were the one who...All right, what next? Did the second Frau Hoffman promise to carry on the trust? Or did she urge him to hand over the gold to the proper authorities?"

"Neither of the above. She's a greedy, ignorant little gold digger, John. If she found the True Cross, her first idea would be to hock it."

"I'll accept your evaluation — without," John added pointedly, "any sexist comments. The reaction you describe is unfortunately common to many members of the human race, male and female alike."

"So she said something like, 'Oh, Anton darling, think of all that money,' and he said, 'Bite your tongue,' and she...well, whatever she said, he realized he had picked the wrong lady. The minute he died, she'd have the treasure out of hiding and into the hock shop. That realization was what made him decide to pass on his trust to a more suitable custodian. Better it should end up in a museum than in the hands of — forgive me — someone like you."

I paused to give him time for rebuttal; he chose not to take advantage of it, so I went on. "He kept putting off the decision to act, however. How many people die without a will? Something finally forced him to make up his mind. I suspect — and there is some confirmatory evidence — that he learned Friedl had already betrayed him — gone behind his back. To — who?"

"Whom," said John. "Ouch," he added indignantly.

"Then don't be a pedant. You derailed my train of thought. Where was I? Oh — Friedl's extramarital activities. I'm sure she had plenty. Not only was Hoffman old enough to be her grandfather, but he was a gentleman — not her type. Freddy was definitely her type, and it wouldn't surprise me to learn that he is not unknown to the police. But he's even stupider than his lady. What Friedl needed was a person who had two specific qualifications: brains enough to comprehend the unique value of the treasure, and the right connections to dispose of it, quietly, lucratively, and illegally."

The taut muscles under my cheek quivered, and then relaxed. "It wasn't me," John squeaked. "Honest, lady."

"I believe you, darling. If she had approached you, you'd have taken care of the matter by now and left no loose ends dangling."

"Thank you."

"Bitte schön."

"Your hypothesis, though unsubstantiated, is worth considering," John said. "Where could she have met such a person? No, don't tell me, let me work it out for myself. At the hotel, obviously. All sorts of people go to hotels. They are known to enjoy skiing and other harmless sports; they eat, drink, and are merry. Perhaps it was a chance encounter (how romantic) that introduced Friedl to the man of her dreams, and while they were being merry she opened her little heart to him. She's the type that would babble in bed—"

"Unlike me," I said wryly.

"Quite unlike you. I've had a look at the lady, and she lacks your external charms as well as your ability to carry on a witty conversation even under circumstances of considerable distraction. . . . What was I saying?"

"It wasn't John Donne, but I liked it. Do go on."

"That's enough; I wouldn't want it to go to your head. We might try to have a look at the hotel register. This hypothetical expert of yours must have visited Bad Steinbach during the spring or summer of last year."

"She may have met him earlier," I said. "And remembered him when she learned about the gold. . . ."

John knew every nuance of my voice. He said alertly, "You've thought of someone."

"No. It's not only unsubstantiated, it's pure fiction."

The arm around my shoulders tightened painfully. "Don't hold out on me, Vicky. I'm willing to collaborate in this little venture of yours, but only if you tell me everything."

"Old habits die hard," I said apologetically. "In our past encounters, we've been on opposite sides. I'm not accustomed to trusting you."

The even movement of his breathing did not alter. After a brief, internal struggle, I said, "All right, then. I happen to know of five people – six, including myself – who had at least one of the necessary qualifications, and who were at the hotel last year."

"I think you may have something there," John said, when I had concluded the explanation. "While the old gentleman was learning to know – and of course, love – you, Friedl was learning to know someone else, in quite another sense of the word. Later, when the matter of the gold came up, she would think of him – or her?"

"Who's to know?"

"Who indeed? The encounter needn't have been heterosexual or even sexual. You say three of the lot have surfaced lately?"

"Yes, but that doesn't necessarily mean what you think. Suppose Hoffman contacted some of the others, as well as me? You and I know I'm uniquely wonderful, but Hoffman might have decided to check out a number of candidates before settling on one. We don't know how many copies of that photograph he mailed, or how much information he gave other people. I'm sure I would have received a letter or a phone call if he hadn't died."

"Or been murdered."

I moved uncomfortably. "I thought of that, of course. But much as I abhor the woman, I can't believe..."

"Always assume the worst; then you are never disappointed."

"John, I really have to get to work sometime today. Schmidt is sure to come looking for me—"

"Speaking of Schmidt – you don't mean to involve him in this, do you?"

"I wish I could keep him out of it. Your turning up didn't help. Schmidt is fascinated by you."

"I will endeavor to put a lid on my notorious charm when next we meet. Seriously, Vicky. I don't want to be constantly distracted by having to rescue Schmidt."

"And I don't want Schmidt to be in a position where he needs rescuing. We'll just have to elude the little rascal, that's all."

"Agreed. It behooves us, then, to investigate the people you mentioned. Their reputations, their recent activities, any suspicious circumstances. You might give me a list."

"I can do better than that. I have snapshots of all of them — they're in a box on the coffee table. You'll recognize the ambiance. There was Dieter Spreng from Berlin, Rosa D'Addio from the University of Turin, Tony..."

"Tony?"

"Tony," I repeated. Caesar was howling, the sunlight lay golden on the floor....I sat up with a gasp. "What time is it?"

For some reason, he was still wearing his wristwatch. "Two."

"Two P.M.? Oh, God! Wednesday. It's Wednesday, isn't it?"

"The last time I looked it was Tuesday. That was last night, so logic suggests—"

I jumped up and began groping for my clothes. "Tony. He's here. His plane lands at two. I told him I'd pick him up."

John sprang out of bed. Clad only in a wristwatch and a lordly sneer, he struck a pose like Jove about to hurl a thunderbolt and declaimed, " 'Yet she/Will be/False, ere I come, to two, or three.' Aren't you scheduling your appointments rather too tightly? Far be it from me to...Tony Lawrence from Chicago?"

Jeans, shirt, shoes..."Don't leave!" I ordered. "Oh, well – maybe you had better leave, come to think of it. Where can I reach you? Write it down. I want an address and a phone number – and a name! Any name so long as it's one to which you are currently answering...." I ran to the door.

John had dropped down onto the edge of the bed and changed his pose – Rodin's Thinker instead of Athenian Jove.

It's a wonder I made it to the airport in one piece. As I wove in and out of traffic, my brain felt like my spare-room closet, stuffed with odds and ends that had been shoved in, helter-skelter. It was all John's fault. Our discussion had clarified several of my amorphous ideas, but John Donne and the Discobolus kept elbowing into my attempts at deductive reasoning.

For God's sake, hold your tongue, John Donne, and let me think.

Tony. I had to concentrate on Tony; he was the most imminent of the concerns of the moment. I couldn't believe I had forgotten about him. Now that he had been recalled to my attention, I couldn't believe the things I was thinking about him.

I could handle the possibility that Tony might be one of several people whom Herr Hoffman had contacted, and that he was keeping mum about it because he hoped to outsmart me in a hunt for the Trojan gold. That possibility was looking less likely, though. According to what Müller had told me, there had only been one envelope. It was conceivable that Hoffman had dispatched other communications earlier (he certainly hadn't sent any later). But — call me egotistical — I couldn't believe that the old gentleman would have left me until last, or that he would have given me less information than he had given the others. It was one thing for me to take a day off work and drive sixty miles to check out a wild theory; for Tony to spend time and money on a trans-Atlantic flight, he'd need more to go on.

On the other hand, Tony said he had been planning to go to the meetings. If the trip had already been in the works, it wouldn't be much out of his way to stop over and find out what I was up to.

I wanted to believe it, because the alternative was an ugly one. If Tony was the faceless hypothetical conspirator John and I had invented, it would mean he was a cold-blooded, dishonest bastard who was ready to betray every ethical and professional principle – and that he had been making out with Friedl at the same time he was supposed to be enjoying my company. Guess which bothered me more.

I refused to believe it. There was a third possibility, and that was that Tony was completely unwitting. A man is innocent until proven guilty, after all. But if he was unwitting, I preferred to keep him that way. Tony and I had collaborated once before, with some success, but I didn't want to make a habit of it. Even if John had not turned up. . .

John. I should have locked him in the closet, tied him to the bed. . . . Not that he couldn't get out of any prison I could construct. He had gotten out of worse ones. What if he disappeared and never came back?

And then there was Schmidt. The thought of my boss, and of the possible permutations – all disastrous – of Schmidt and Tony, John and Schmidt, Tony and John, and all three – sent my brain into overload. The terminal was in sight. I decided to emulate Scarlett O'Hara and think about it tomorrow.

I had hoped the plane would be late, or that it would take Tony a while to get through customs. Both those contingencies would have occurred if I had been breathlessly anticipating the moment when I could fold him in a passionate embrace. Since I wasn't, they didn't. He was already there.

Though the terminal was crowded with holiday travelers, I had no trouble spotting him because he was a head taller than anyone else. He was bareheaded. His hair, thick and black and wavy, is the kind women love to run their fingers through, which is probably why Tony, thoughtful soul that he is, seldom wears a hat. He looks like a popular misconception of a poet (who usually looks like a popular misconception of a truck driver). He has delicate hollows under his cheekbones, and a thin, sensitive mouth, and a high forehead over which his hair tumbles in distracting curls.

I attributed his frown and his formal outstretched hand to annoyance at my tardiness, so I brushed the latter aside and flung myself into his less-than-enthusiastic arms. They were not unenthusiastic for long; as they tightened around me, and his lips warmed to the task at hand, I thought how nice it was to have to stand on tiptoe to kiss a man. After the first second or two I didn't make any other mental comparisons; it would be like comparing apples and oranges, each is delicious in its own way, it all depends on which you prefer. There is no doubt, however, that a certain degree of guilt increased the ardor of my embrace — though why the hell I should have felt guilty I don't know.

I freed myself, amid a spatter of applause from the watching tourists; after all, they had nothing else to look at. Tony was blushing furiously, as is his engaging habit. I linked my arm with his and led him toward the exit.

There wasn't much I could do but take him home with me. The Museum was out of the question until I could warn Schmidt not to give Tony the slightest hint of our latest scam — excuse me, investigation. John would surely have gone by the time we returned. I only hoped he had not left some intimate garment hanging on the bedpost or a message scrawled in shaving cream across the mirror. But so what if he had? Tony didn't own me. Fidelity had never been part of the deal. But I did owe him a place to stay, for old times' sake. He'd expect that much.

"I have a reservation at the Bayrischer Hof," he said, staring straight ahead. "If that's out of your way, you could drop me at a taxi stand."

My hands lost their grip on the wheel for an instant; I swerved back into my own lane amid the frenzied gesticulations of the wild-eyed driver of a Fiat on my right.

"What did you say?"

"I said, I have a reservation at the—"

"I heard you. What's bugging you, Tony? Just because I was a little late—"

"That has nothing to do with it."

"With what?"

"With the – er – the situation being what – er—" Tony let out a long, gusty sigh. "I'm engaged."

"To be married?" I gasped.

"That is the customary meaning of the word," Tony mumbled.

I cut across two lanes and finally found a place where I could pull off the road. I turned to face him. He wouldn't look at me; he continued to stare straight ahead, as if the bleak winter landscape held something of absorbing interest.

"That's very nice," I said. "Just one question, Tony. Why the hell did you come here?"

"It was her idea."

"Oh, was it?"

"It seemed like a good idea at the time."

"Oh, did it?"

He kept sliding down in the seat, his knees rising as his body sank. When his knees were on a level with his head, I couldn't control my laughter any longer. But I will admit that the laughter wasn't altogether merry.

"Look at me, Tony." I put one hand on his cheek; he shied like a skittery horse. "I'm not going to bite your head off," I continued gently. "Seems to me you're in enough trouble as it is. Who is this extraordinary female?"

The mildness of my voice reassured him. He pulled out his wallet. "Her name is Ann Belfort."

If he'd set out to find someone whose characteristics were the antithesis of mine, he had succeeded. A cloud of soft dark hair surrounded the girl's heart-shaped face; her eyes were as big and brown and melting as those of a Jersey cow. "Five feet two inches?" I inquired, studying the face I had always wanted to possess.

"Three and a half inches."

"Uh-huh. What do you do when you want to—"

"Now cut that out!" Tony sat upright, rigid with chivalrous indignation.

"Kiss her, I was about to say. I suppose you can always find a rock or a low table....Oh, hell, I'm sorry. Forget I said that. Belfort... Any relation to Dr. Belfort of the Math De-

187

partment at Granstock?"

"Uh — yes. His daughter."

"When are you being married? No, don't tell me. June, of course."

"That's right. I don't know why you—"

"Neither do I," I admitted. "I'm very happy for you, Tony. I honestly am. But I don't understand why you are here instead of in Illinois."

"She knows all about you," Tony said.

"*All* about me?"

"All she needs to know." Tony bowed his head. A lock of raven hair dropped adorably over one eyebrow. I repressed an urge to grab it and pull as hard as I could. "It was okay," he went on gloomily, "until about a month ago, when I woke her up calling your name."

"Did you really, you dear thing?"

"It wasn't so much what I said as the way I said it. 'Oh, Vicky — Vicky — oooooh...' "

He sounded like a dying calf, or a man in the last extremity of about-to-be-fulfilled passion. I grinned reluctantly. "I can see her point — though I still think this is stupid. She sent you back to your old love to make sure the incubus is exorcised?"

"Succubus," Tony said. "Incubi were masculine; the female demons whose diabolical sexual assaults on helpless innocent men—"

188

"Oh, right. Seems to me you're waffling, Tony. Either you're still lusting for me or you're not. What's the point of the Bayrischer Hof?"

"I don't really have a reservation."

"I thought not. It's a very expensive hotel."

"I had assumed I'd stay with you, of course. In a perfectly platonic way — no fooling around—"

My sympathy for cute little Ann began to dissipate. " 'I could not love thee, dear, so much, Lov'd I not honour more.' " But this was really too far out. Not love, quoth she, but vanity, sets love a task like...Like a weekend nose to nose and side by side with an old flame, with no moment of weakness, no — "fooling around," indeed.

"And you agreed?" I demanded incredulously.

"I didn't think there'd be any problem." Tony looked so hurt and baffled and young that I thought seriously of slugging him square in the chops. That boyish look gets all his women, but he was thirty-four years old, for God's sake. Old enough to have better sense.

"I mean, we were always good friends," Tony went on in an aggrieved voice. "I used to like to *talk* to you. If you hadn't kissed me—"

"I did it out of the kindness of my heart, you conceited male chauvinist! If you're going to let one friendly kiss get your male hormones in a whirl...Did this woman step out of some kind of time warp, or is she just emotionally retarded?"

"Of course a single experiment is not conclusive," said Tony, reaching for me.

Apples. Nice, crisp fresh apples, like Jonathans, with a little tang under the sweetness. Wholesome American fruit, no imports, nothing exotic. But the very best of their kind.

It was Tony who ended the kiss. I'd have gone on as long as he wanted; it was his experiment, not mine.

"Well?" I inquired. "Have you reached a scientific conclusion or is more research necessary?"

"I think," said Tony weakly, "I had better go to the Bayrischer Hof."

"You can't." I started the car and edged back into the traffic. "They'll be booked solid this time of year. Don't worry, you can always prop a chair against your bedroom door."

What I had said was true — most of the hotels would be full-up over the holidays. But the more I thought about letting Tony stay with me — chair or no chair — the madder I got. In addition to the other disadvantages, I resented being used as a bad-conduct prize.

After a moment of chilly silence I said,

"Scratch the chair. You can start calling hotels as soon as we get to my place."

The silence that followed was even chillier.

There was one positive feature to the situation, though. Now I could dismiss my suspicions of Tony once and for all. His odd behavior over the phone had bothered me more than I had been willing to admit; I hadn't even mentioned it to John, because I knew he'd pounce on it as further evidence of guilt. That was all explained by Tony's news; he had been apprehensive about breaking the news of his engagement and (the conceited thing) ditto my poor heart, and he must have known I would react profanely and angrily to Ann's loony experiment.

Tony stirred. "You've changed."

"How?"

"You didn't used to sulk."

"I'm not sulking. I'm thinking."

If I had been tempted to tell all to Tony and invite him to join the hunt, the news of his engagement had changed my mind. I had no right to push Ann's fiancé into possible danger. He would expect to see something of me, though, even if he stayed at a hotel. Could I keep him amused and unaware for a few days, and then send him off to Turin unscathed and unsmirched? The answer was yes, probably, if nothing untoward occurred and if Schmidt kept his mouth shut and if John stayed far away from me.

In my absorption, I almost drove past the house. I pulled into my driveway with an abruptness that wrung a rude comment on my driving from Tony.

I ignored the comment. "Here we are. We'll have a drink or two while you call hotels."

Tony looked hurt. I ignored the look, too. It had been his idea to stay at a hotel, hadn't it?

My house and its neighbors were part of the *Wirtschaftswunder* — the economic rebirth of Germany after the Second World War. Not a distinguished part, however. Like corresponding developments in the United States, there were only two basic plans, endlessly repeated, to which the architects had added minor details in the hope (unfulfilled) of making the houses look different. My neighbor on the north had a bay window in the living room, my neighbor on the south had a bay window in the dining room. I had a front porch. It wasn't much, just two walls with a roof on top and two teeny benches that nobody ever sat on.

Schmidt was sitting on one of the benches. If it hadn't been for that damned porch, I'd have spotted him in time and passed on by. To make matters worse, he had swathed himself in bandages that covered his forehead from eyebrows to hairline.

"Ah," he said, rising stiffly. "You have found him."

I looked at Tony. "You called the Museum?"

"You were late," Tony said sulkily. "I thought you'd forgotten. *Grüss Gott, Herr Direktor.* What the hell happened to you?"

"*Grüss Gott.* I came," Schmidt explained, "because I was concerned about you, Vicky. You were not in your office, you did not answer your telephone; and after what happened yesterday—"

"Never mind," I said.

"I am still sore," Schmidt said, rubbing his shoulder. "Being dragged by the arms and then thrown—"

"Never mind, Schmidt!"

"Dragged?" Tony repeated. "Thrown. What happened?"

I turned my back on Tony and made a face at Schmidt. It was a sufficient reminder; he was no more anxious than I to let Tony in on our "adventure."

"Never mind," said Schmidt.

I had just located my key when the door opened.

"What's wrong, love? Can't find your key?" John asked.

The artistic disarrangement of his ambrosial locks was supposed to suggest that he had just got out of bed. I've seen characters in soap operas look like that, but never a real person. His shirt was unbuttoned, and he was tucking it into his pants as he spoke. He was barefoot.

"I thought you'd gone," I stuttered.

"You begged me not to leave," John said.

When, oh when, I asked myself, was I going to stop playing straight man? I made an effort to get control of a situation which, I venture to assert, not even Emily Post could have handled neatly.

"Dr. Tony Lawrence, this is—"

"Sir John," Schmidt squeaked. "I am so glad to see you again. I have not yet thanked you for saving—"

"An honor, I assure you," said John.

"Sir John?" said Tony, eyebrows gyrating. "Saving—?"

I gave up on introductions. I gave up on everything.

I can't say that the next few minutes were comfortable. Tony refused to sit down; he stood in the middle of the living room like a Puritan divine about to thunder denunciations, and demanded the telephone. "I'll start calling hotels," he said stiffly.

"But my dear chap!" John's smile was a study

in guileless good will. "There's plenty of room."

"I wouldn't want to be in the way," said Tony.

"No, no. I must be off myself shortly; delighted to know Vicky will have someone to keep her company."

They went on like that for a while, with Schmidt listening in openmouthed fascination, until I got tired of the badinage.

"Sit down, Tony," I said sharply. "John, why don't you get us something to drink?"

I gave him a hearty shove to emphasize the suggestion, and followed him into the kitchen. "What do you think you're doing?"

"Trying to be a good host." John opened the refrigerator. "What are we serving?"

"He's not staying here." I pushed him aside and inspected the shelves. "Beer, I suppose. I always keep Löwenbräu for Schmidt.... As soon as I can find him a hotel room, he's leaving."

"Do as you like of course," John said smoothly. "But if I were you, I'd keep an eye on him."

"What do you mean?"

"He's one of the gang of six, isn't he?"

The opener slipped as I applied pressure and a fountain of beer shot heavenward. I tipped the bottle into the sink and turned on John. "Are you crazy? Tony wouldn't..."

John had already selected a tray from the rack under the counter; now he reached unerringly for the cupboard where I keep my beer glasses. He had certainly made good use of his time alone in the house. "Isn't he the chap you told me about – the one who was involved in the Riemenschneider affair?"

"Yes. He's a friend of mine, dammit!"

"Doesn't it strike you as a bit of a coincidence that he should drop in on you just now?"

"He explained that. He – it is a coincidence. They happen."

The swinging door opened and Schmidt slipped in. "Ah, you are still here," he said with satisfaction. He wasn't talking to me. "We must have a conference. Vicky, it was foolish of you to bring Tony here. We don't want another person to join us. We are enough."

"We are too much," I said, sighing. "I'll get rid of Tony, I promise. It's only for a few days; he's going on to Turin on the twenty-seventh. Now we'd better get back in there before he starts wondering what we're doing."

"You go," said Schmidt. "I wish to confer with Sir John."

"Sir John" had filled the glasses; leaning against the counter, arms folded and a supercilious smile on his face, he said nothing. I picked up the tray.

Tony had the Munich directory open on his lap and the telephone in his hand. I was sorry to see that he had already reached the stage of plaintive pleading. "Nothing? Not even a single, small...yes, I see. I'll try there."

He took the glass I offered him, glared at me, and dialed again.

Half of my mind was fighting off the nasty hints John had reawakened. Coincidences do happen. Tony wouldn't...The other half was wondering what wild yarn John was telling Schmidt.

A furious cacophony of barks and whines burst out, mingled with Schmidt's shrill expletives. John had let the dog in. Caesar didn't linger; in search of me, his best beloved, he came barreling through the swinging door. The back swing ended with a thud and a curse from Schmidt; I deduced it had hit him in the stomach, which is the part of him that sticks out the farthest.

Tony had not had the pleasure of meeting Caesar. He dropped the telephone and went over the couch in a vault that would have done credit to an Olympic athlete. Of course that attracted Caesar's attention — he loves people to play with him — and a chaotic interval ensued, until I could pry the dog from Tony.

When the dust settled, Tony and Schmidt

were sitting on the floor with Caesar between them, and Schmidt was explaining that Caesar was just a big lovable pussycat who happened to be in the body of a Doberman. Caesar was slobbering on both of them, alternately and impartially. I saw no reason to join in, so I sat down and drank my beer.

John had taken advantage of the brouhaha to escape, but not, as I hoped (or feared) out of the house. Before long, he came tripping down the stairs, fully attired. He was wearing the same thing he had worn the night before; I deduced as much, since he had not been carrying a suitcase, but I must admit it was the first time I had actually seen the ensemble. Black, all of it, from his track shoes to the cap he was carrying in his hand. I had expected he would bid us a fond farewell, since he was clearly dressed for the street; instead, he parked himself in the most comfortable chair and proceeded to be charming.

I sat there morosely drinking beer and wondering what the hell John was up to. Oh, I knew part of the performance was designed to calm Tony and persuade him to do what John wanted him to do, i.e., spend the night at the house. He succeeded in the former aim; I saw Tony's frown smooth out, to be replaced by a pseudo-tolerant smile as he studied John's graceful gestures and winning smiles and deceptively slender build. I thought John was overdoing it a bit when he started calling Tony "duckie" and patting him on the arm — John's great weakness is a tendency to get carried away by a role — but Tony has the usual prejudices against well-groomed men who bat their eyelashes at him.

That wasn't John's only reason for hanging around. He was waiting for something, I could tell. When the telephone rang, he stiffened perceptibly. At least it was perceptible to me; I don't think the others noticed.

She apologized rather perfunctorily for disturbing me, and then, as was her habit, got straight to the point. "I heard of your accident. I am so distressed it should happen. I telephoned you this morning but you did not answer—"

"I was here all morning," I began — then I saw the corner of John's mouth twitch, and I shut up. The telephone had rung; one of us — I think it was John — had reached out and taken it off the hook. Apparently he had put it back after I left.

"I am calling to ask for your help," Friedl went on. "I know my husband meant to do so. But I did not realize before that the matter was so serious. Now you are in danger too. It is a matter of life and death."

"Oh, really?" I couldn't think what else to say, not only because of the listening ears, but because she gave the impression of someone reciting memorized lines, not quite in order.

"You take it lightly," Friedl said, sounding more like her sullen self. "I tell you, they want to kill you!"

"Who?"

She went back to the prepared script. "I cannot say more over the telephone. I too am in danger. You must come – here – to the hotel. Bring a friend if you like, someone who can help us. Will you come? Tomorrow?"

"Well...all right."

In a sudden switch from the melodramatic to the brisk, she thanked me and hung up. I turned to find three pairs of eyes focused on me.

"Who was it?" Schmidt asked.

"None of your business, Schmidt. How about another beer?"

He was agreeable. I picked up the tray and went to the kitchen. John was right on my heels.

"How did you know?" I demanded.

"Was that her?"

"She. How did—"

"Pedant," John said. "Well, I expected something of the sort; didn't you?"

"No," I admitted. "She's invited me to be her guest at the hotel — dire hints of disasters past and present. Apparently she's decided to come clean; she admitted her husband had intended to write to me. Maybe I was wrong about her. She had no reason to trust me, walking in off the street the way I did."

"If you believe that, you are as innocent as a new-laid egg."

"You think it's a trap?"

"Could be." John did not appear particularly perturbed by the idea. "However, in my considered opinion, it seems more likely that they have decided to pick your brains instead of your bones."

"You have such a poetic way of putting things."

"In words of one syllable, then — *they don't know where it is.* Or, 'is at,' as you Americans say. Having searched in vain, they have concluded — somewhat tardily, I agree — that you may succeed where they have failed."

"I still don't see—"

"You've had a great deal on your mind lately," John said kindly. "Think. Why would Friedl go to such lengths to lure you to Bad Steinbach when she can murder you just as easily and far more safely, in Munich?"

"Cheerful thought. If they want to pick my

brains, why did they try to kill me yesterday?"

"Because they're a bunch of bloody amateurs," said John, with professional disdain. "They had been half-expecting, half-dreading your arrival; when you turned up out of the blue, they didn't know what to do. Someone – probably Freddy the Mindless and Muscle-Bound – acted on impulse. He's the sort of chap whose natural impulses would be lethal. Later on Friedl got in touch with the Mastermind, who pointed out a more responsible course of action. I trust you realize what that implies? It takes her some time to reach the man in charge. He isn't on the spot."

"If you mean Tony...I don't believe it."

John's demonic eyebrow soared skyward. "Of course you know him so much better than I, don't you?"

My nice neat living room looked like the scene of an all-night binge. It stank of beer – Caesar had knocked a glass over – and the place was littered with empty bottles and glasses, the ashes of Schmidt's horrible cigars, and the scraps of a bowl of pretzels. Schmidt had turned sentimental, as he usually does after three or four beers, and was looking at my photograph albums. He and Tony had their heads together over the Rothenburg mementos and were giggling as they recalled their encounters with the ghost of the *Schloss*.

"Yes, she married," Schmidt said with a sigh; he was talking about Ilse, Countess Drachenstein, who had figured prominently in the case. "A fine young fellow — he was a chemist in Rothenburg. I attended the wedding. I wore my white linen suit I bought in Rome —"

"Chemist?" Tony echoed. "Not the same guy we rousted out of bed in the small hours?"

"The same," I said.

John listened with bright-eyed interest. "Speaking of chemists," he began, and went on to tell an outrageous story about an art forgery that had made headlines a few years earlier. The part of the story he told had not been in the newspapers. "And," he ended, "it turned out he had latent diabetes; it was the sugar that did that trick."

Schmidt laughed so hard he turned purple. Tony laughed too, but he was still suspicious. "You seem to know quite a lot about detecting forgeries, Sir John."

John lowered his eyes modestly. "I'm just a dilettante, Professor. Jack-of-all-trades, master of none, as they say. As a matter of fact, I became interested because we had a slight problem with one of the family portraits — a Romney.... But that's another story. It's getting late. Shall we go, Herr Director?"

"Yes, yes." Schmidt chug-a-lugged his beer and bounced to his feet. "Where is my coat? Did I have a briefcase?"

Caesar went to help him look for them, and I followed John into the hall. "What are you up to now?"

"You wanted Schmidt out of the way, didn't you? Leave him to me."

"Oh, God," I said hopelessly, and said no more, because Schmidt appeared, trying to get into his coat, which was complicated by the fact that Caesar had hold of one sleeve.

We got Schmidt into his coat and convinced him he had not had a briefcase, and then they left, arguing about who was going to drive. Eventually Schmidt got in the passenger side and they drove off.

I returned to the living room. "Alone at last," I said.

Tony was looking at photographs. "I'd never seen these," he said, pleased. "We had a good time, didn't we? Why don't we spend a few days at that hotel in Bad Steinbach?"

It was all John's doing, of course. When he had found time to corrupt Tony, I did not know; but he had left the snapshots in plain sight, and that had finished the job.

Why did I give in? Not because I thought

there was the slightest possibility that John's vile hints had a basis in fact. I knew Tony. He was so damned honest it hurt. Even during the Rothenburg incident, he hadn't wanted the treasure for himself; he just wanted the fun and the prestige of finding it.

"And suppose," said a small evil voice inside my head, "that is what he wants now?"

The voice had a pronounced English accent. I countered, "So badly that he would shoot out the tires of Schmidt's car and endanger me?"

"I thought we agreed that was an impetuous, unpremeditated gesture. There are obviously several malefactors."

"Not Tony."

"What's his annual salary? The amount of money involved might weaken anyone's moral fibers. Even if he's too good for that sort of thing, consider the temptation of being hailed as the discoverer of the Trojan gold. Headlines, television interviews, a book, a film based on the book – and, under certain circumstances, a strong claim to the treasure for his museum."

I gave up the argument, not because I was convinced but because I seemed to be losing.

Short of picking a fight with Tony in the hope that he would storm out of the house and bid me farewell forever, there was no way of getting rid of him. Anyhow, he was just as

likely to go on to Bad Steinbach by himself. I
didn't want to postpone my own trip. For one
thing, I was worried about Herr Müller. I
should have taken steps to warn him earlier,
but with a wounded, starving Schmidt on my
hands early in the evening, and John later...
Nothing had happened to him as yet, but then
nothing had happened to me, either, until
after I had paid him a visit. I'd be a lot easier
in my mind if I could persuade him to get out
of town for a few days.

Besides, Friedl might be on the level. I might
indeed be as innocent (translation: stupid) as a
new-laid egg, but John had a cocksure, arrogant
way of stating theories as facts and of assuming
his interpretation was the only logical one. I
could think of others that made equal sense.
Friedl could be hopeless but harmless; Freddy
could be repulsive but right-minded. The villains could have been four other people.

So I said, fine, that sounds like a great idea,
and I called Carl the janitor, who became in-
coherent with pleasure at the idea of baby-
sitting Caesar for a few days. I said I'd bring
him over right away, since we wanted to get
an early start. This added concession almost
reduced Carl to tears. *De gustibus non est dis-
putandum.*

After we had dropped the dog off, we went

out to dinner at a little place the tourists haven't discovered, where the food is good and the prices are reasonable. Tony's capacity for food is almost as great as Schmidt's, though it doesn't show. As he stuffed himself with *Schweinebraten mit Knödel*, he kept mumbling about how good it was to be back in Germany, and recalling some of our past experiences. Usually I'm a sucker for sentiment and "remember when," but it irritated me that evening, and not only because Ann was hovering over the table like Banquo's ghost. It was almost as if Tony were deliberately avoiding certain subjects. Whenever I casually introduced the subject of crank mail and unusual letters, Tony went off onto another spate of nostalgia.

Much later, in what are termed the wee small hours of the night, I was awakened by soft sounds at my door — light scratching, the squeak of a turning doorknob. There was no further action because I had propped a chair under the knob. Sauce for the gander...

SIX

Saint Emmeram's beard was still ice-fringed; he had a long icicle on his nose as well. It had turned fiercely cold overnight; the world glittered with a cold, hard shine, like a diamond. Sunlight reflected from the snow-covered fields with a shimmer that stung the eyes. It was, as Tony said, a perfect day for skiing.

I had my skis strapped to the rack on top of the car, primarily as camouflage; I had a feeling I wasn't going to have much time for sport. Tony was planning to rent. Tony has this delusion that he is a great skier. I don't know what his problem is; it can't be his height because a good many fine skiers are tall. He kept talking about trying the Kandahar Trail, where the championship downhill races are held. I was tempted to tell him to go ahead and break his damned leg, so he'd be out of my hair, but then I decided that was not nice. Besides, a broken leg might keep him from traveling on to Turin, and who knows what I might find myself doing with a pathetic, bedridden, pain-wracked, engaged ex-boyfriend in desperate need of TLC?

He made no mention of his late-night visit, so naturally I did not refer to it. Ann's name was not prominent in our conversation, either.

Tony loved Emmeram's icy beard and the wreath of greenery draped around his stony shoulders. "I'm glad I thought of this," he said, as I pulled into the parking area reserved for hotel guests. "I always liked this place. Nice to see it hasn't changed."

"Herr Hoffman is dead," I said.

Tony turned a blank, innocent face toward me. "Who?"

"Hoffman. The host — the owner."

"Oh, the nice old guy who bought us a round the night before we left? Too bad. You know, this is a great place to spend Christmas. We can go to midnight mass at the church and . . . er . . ."

Freddy was not at the desk. There were a number of people waiting impatiently; the concierge, a stout middle-aged woman, kept poking nervously at the wisps of hair escaping from the bun at the back of her neck. When she got to me, she didn't wait for me to speak, but shook her head and said rapidly, *"Grüss Gott, I am sorry, but unless you have a reservation —"*

"I believe Frau Hoffman is expecting me. My name is Bliss."

"Ach, ja, die Dame aus München. Entschuldigen Sie, we are so busy—"

"Calm yourself, *gnädige Frau,*" Tony said soothingly. "We are in no hurry, and life is short."

Tony's German is schoolboy-simple, with a pronounced American accent that some Germans, especially middle-aged women, seem to find delicious. The concierge stopped poking at her hair and returned his smile. "You are very kind, *mein Herr.* You understand, this is a busy season for us and we are short-handed; I am the housekeeper, not a clerk, and what we are to do, with so many people..."

Tony listened sympathetically. Basking in his boyish smile and melting brown eyes, the woman would have gone on indefinitely if I hadn't cleared my throat and reminded her that customers were piling up again. She handed a registration form, not to me, but to Tony. It's a man's world, all right, especially in country villages. I took it away from him and filled it in. There was no bellboy; Tony allowed me to carry my own suitcase.

If Friedl *was* planning to murder me, she had taken pains to soften me up for the slaughter. The room was one of the best in the house —

a big corner room, with an alcove furnished with sofa and chairs, and a wooden balcony offering a breathtaking view of the mountains. I was distressed to observe that the balcony was decorated with plastic geraniums.

Tony didn't comment on the geraniums; he was more interested in the bed, a massive antique four-poster.

"Don't worry about getting another room," I said generously. "You can sleep on the couch in the alcove."

"It's only five feet long!"

"There's always the floor."

"Now, Vicky, this is ridiculous," Tony began.

"It certainly is. But I wasn't the one who established the rules. I suppose we could put a naked sword between us, the way the medieval ambassadors did when they bedded their royal masters' brides. Ann would probably love that one."

Tony picked up his suitcase and stalked out. When I went through the lobby, I saw him flirting with the concierge. He was so intent on the job he didn't see me, which suited me fine.

By the time I reached Müller's shop, I had worked myself into a state of idiotic apprehension; finding the place dark and the door locked, I banged and knocked for some time before I noticed the sign. It read, "Closed for the holidays."

I was about to turn away when there was a rattle of hardware inside. The door opened a crack; a narrowed blue eye and a tuft of bushy white eyebrow appeared.

"Ah, it is you," Müller exclaimed, and threw the door wide.

"I thought you'd gone."

"I am about to go — to my daughter's, for *Weihnachtszeit*. Come in, come in." He locked the door after me and then went on, "I had not intended to leave until tomorrow, but your friend persuaded me otherwise. He is waiting now to drive me to Füssen. A kindly gesture, though I cannot believe—"

"My friend," I repeated.

"Yes, he is here. Perhaps you wish to speak to him."

I indicated that I definitely did wish to speak to him.

The door to the shop was closed; Müller escorted me into a tiny hall that led to his living quarters.

Already the small parlor had the cold, waiting look of a place whose occupants have left it for a protracted period of time — dark, fireless, overly neat. Two comfortable chairs flanked the fireplace. In one — obviously her usual place — was the cat, bolt upright, tail curled neatly around her hindquarters, wide blue eyes fixed unblinkingly on the occupant of the other chair.

John was dressed with less than his habitual elegance; I deduced that the jeans and shabby boots and worn jacket had been selected in an effort to convince Herr Müller he was just one of the boys and hence trustworthy. He was staring back at the cat with a nervous intensity that reminded me of a character in one of the Oz books, who tries to cow the Hungry Tiger with the terrible power of the human eye. The cat appeared no more impressed than the Hungry Tiger had been.

Glancing in my direction, he said sternly, "You're late, Dr. Bliss. I expected you an hour ago."

"I had to...We stopped by...I'm sorry."

"If you're ready, Herr Müller." John got to his feet. The cat let out a raucous Siamese squawl. John flinched.

"Yes, I will get my suitcase. But I still cannot believe..."

"It's just a precaution," John said. "Our investigation is in the preliminary stages."

Shaking his head, the old man ambled out. "Who is 'our'?" I inquired. "Interpol, British

Intelligence, or some exotic organization invented by you?"

John whipped a leather folder from his pocket and presented it for my inspection. I must say when he did a job, he did it properly; the shield glittered busily in the light, and the ID card was frayed authentically around the edges. Even the picture was perfect — it had the ghastly, staring look typical of drivers' licenses, passport photos, and other official documents.

"International Bureau of Arts and Antiquities Frauds," I read.

"IBAAF," said John, returning the folder to his hip pocket. "It was your name that won the old boy's confidence, however. You're a district inspector."

"And you, of course, are my superior?"

"Regional inspector."

"That's modest of you. I had expected a title with the word 'Chief' in it."

"I have no time for idle persiflage," said John coldly. "You should have been here before this. Let me be brief—"

"That I want to see."

The cat yowled as if in agreement. John started nervously. "I'm staying here," he said rapidly. "At least for the time being. I want to have a look at the fragments of the *Schrank*.

It might be a good idea if we weren't seen together. Thus far, I am unknown to any of the gang—"

"The man who was shooting at us must have seen you."

"I was wearing one of those handy-dandy ski masks, remember? I might have been any casual traveler, rushing to the rescue. If you want to see me, come to the back door and give the signal—"

"What signal?"

"Anything you like," John said magnanimously. "Whistle 'Yankee Doodle,' rap three times—"

"Three, then a pause, then two."

"How unoriginal. I'll telephone or leave word at the desk should anything interesting arise." The sound of footsteps descending the stairs quickened his voice. "Watch for familiar faces. Be careful. Don't tell Tony I'm here. Let me know—"

"I'll report later this evening, sir," I said, as Herr Müller entered.

John tried to take the suitcase from him but was rebuffed. "I am not so old as that," the old man said huffily. "We can go now. I still cannot believe...Fräulein, do you know what it is, this mysterious missing painting?"

"No," I said, feeling it was safer not to elaborate. Lord knows what fantasy John had spun.

"My friend would not do anything wrong," the old man insisted.

"There is no question of that," John said smoothly. "I can't go into detail, Herr Müller, you understand, but we are certain that his involvement was accidental and, unhappily, fatal. He said nothing to you?"

"I have told you. I cannot believe..."

The cat jumped off the chair and walked stiff-legged around the suitcase, sniffing it and grumbling to herself.

"She knows I am going away," Müller said seriously. "She doesn't like changes. Remember, Herr Inspektor, she must have a square of raw liver each evening...."

A spasm of profound distaste rippled over John's face. "Er – Dr. Bliss, why don't you take the nice pussy cat to the hotel with you? She likes you."

Clara had given up her inspection of the suitcase and was rubbing around my ankles. I bent over to stroke her. "Don't you like cats, sir?"

"I am fond of all animals. That cat doesn't like me."

"Why, sir," I said. "You must be imagining things. Cats are splendid judges of character. I always say, never trust a person a cat dislikes,...sir."

The cat started toward John. The hoarse purr with which she had welcomed my touch changed tone. It was more like a growl. To be accurate, it *was* a growl.

"Perhaps she would prefer to go with you, Fräulein," said Müller. "It is her old home, after all."

"I imagine she'll go where she wants to go," I said. "Don't worry about her, Herr Müller. I'll help the inspector to watch over her."

"That would be most kind."

John had retreated into the hallway, and the cat had backed him into a corner. Crouched, her tail twitching, she appeared to be on the verge of leaping. Much as the sight entertained me, I was anxious to get Müller on his way. I scooped Clara up and put her in the parlor while John made his getaway.

The back door opened onto a walled garden deep in snow. Paths had been shoveled to the gate and to a chalet-style bird feeder, obviously Müller's own work, which hung from a pine tree. Its branches were strung with suet, bits of fruit and berries, and other scraps.

Müller hovered in the doorway, one foot in the house and one out. "I must make sure I turned off the fire under the glue pot."

"It's off," John said firmly. "I watched you do it."

"Fresh water for the cat—"

"I watched you do that, too."

The old man's eyes wandered over the dead garden. "I meant to take the *Weihnachtsblumen* to the grave today," he said slowly. "Now there will be no remembrance for my poor friend."

John was hopping from one foot to the other, whether from cold or the same formless sense of anxiety that nagged me, I did not know. "With all respect, Herr Müller—"

I slipped my arm through the old man's. "I'll take the flowers," I said. "I meant to do it anyway."

"You would be so good? For her as well — poor Amelie?"

"Of course."

"Not flowers, they would only freeze. Green boughs as for *Weihnachten* — berries and wreaths—"

"I know," I said gently. "They still do that in my home town in Minnesota. I'll take care of it, don't worry."

That promise got him out of the house. While he was locking the door, he told me how to find the cemetery. "The church is abandoned now, no one goes there except to tend the graves, and there are few left who care; Anton's grave will be the last, I think. For generations, the family of his wife was buried there, so he was

218

given permission to rest alongside her; but one day the mountain will crumble and cover church and graves alike. The fools have cut away the trees for their sports, tampering with God's work — they don't know or care...."

Between us, we urged him down the path to the gate and through it, into a roofless corridor of an alleyway lined for its entire length with high fences. These people liked their privacy. I could see that John approved of it, too. He wrestled the suitcase from Müller and put it in the back of his car.

Impulsively I threw my arm around the old man and gave him a hearty smack on the cheek. "Happy Christmas, Herr Müller."

"The blessings of the good God to you, Fräulein."

I didn't kiss John. District inspectors don't get fresh with their superiors.

That was one load off my mind. Grudgingly I gave John credit, not only for seeing the obvious without explanation, but for caring enough about the old boy to get him to a safe place. I'd have given him even more credit if I had not known he had an ulterior motive. Why he thought he could find a clue the searchers had overlooked, I could not imagine; but if anyone could, it was John. His natural bent toward chicanery had been developed by years of experience.

The lower end of the alley debouched into the Marktplatz. When I reached the hotel, I found Tony lying in wait. "Where the hell did you go?" he demanded.

"Out," I said shortly. "What's the matter, couldn't you get a room?"

"I got a room all right." He took my arm and pulled me aside. People passed us, going in and out and giving us curious looks as we stood nose to nose glaring at each other. "Why didn't you tell me?" Tony snapped.

"Tell you what?"

"Anything. Something. That Friedl was the new owner—"

"You know Friedl?"

"Well, sure. We all..." He grinned self-consciously. "Not me, of course."

"Of course. I'm sure she would have worked all of you in if she had had time."

Once again I had been caught with my pants down, figuratively speaking. (Obviously the metaphor applied more accurately to some of my former colleagues.) I had only been gone for half an hour; it was symptomatic of the luck I was having that Tony should have latched onto Friedl during that brief interval. Hoping against hope she hadn't spilled her guts, I murmured, "I didn't think you'd be interested, Tony."

"Not interested in somebody trying to kill you?"

"Oh, *Scheisse,*" I said. "What did she tell you?"

A Bavarian teenager trying to stash his skis in the rack beside the door narrowly missed decapitating Tony. Bawling the boy out relieved some of Tony's spleen; he turned back to me and said in a milder voice, "Suppose we have a beer and a little heart-to-heart talk. Friedl is anxious to see you, but not as anxious as I am."

The bar was crowded; we wedged ourselves into a quiet corner, mugs in hand. Sunset reddened the slopes of the Zugspitze and draped the sky wth gaudy cloths of scarlet and purple, but Tony wasn't moved by the beauty of the scenery. I let him talk. I wanted to find out how much he knew before I contributed to his store of information. That was fine with Tony, who seldom got a chance to conduct a monologue when he was with me. As I recall, the lecture went something like this:

"I don't mind participating in these mad extravaganzas of yours. Not at all. I'm always happy to give a friend the benefit of my superior expertise. A lesser man might resent being shoved into a mess like the one you've obviously got yourself into without some warning; I mean, the words 'sitting duck' come to mind. Or possibly 'decoy.' What I really resent is the insult to my intelligence. I knew something was going on. You and Schmidt and that — that effeminate character, with your heads together...who is that guy? Never mind, don't tell me, I'm not finished. You might at least warn a person that he's putting his head in a noose instead of pretending this was just a social visit—"

"Now wait a minute," I said, indignantly. "I didn't invite you to come. It was your idea."

"You could have warned me off."

"I could have," I admitted. "At the time I didn't know—"

"Is that the truth?" Tony scowled at me over his mug. "Nobody tried to mug you, murder you, or burglarize you until the day before yesterday?"

I was glad he had phrased the question that way, because I could look him straight in the eye and say firmly, "No. Nobody." Not that I wouldn't have looked him straight in the eye and denied anything he accused me of.

"Oh. All the same, you might have mentioned it."

"It could have been an accident. Some drunken hunter."

"Yeah. But Friedl seems to think not. Are

222

you sure you never got a letter or a package or anything from her husband?"

I looked him straight in the eye and said firmly, "No. I mean, yes. How about you?"

"Me? Why would I..." Tony considered the question. "No reason why it shouldn't have been me, come to think about it. According to Friedl, the object in question is a work of art — she didn't seem to know more than that. I met Hoffman last year, chatted with him...Hey. What about the rest of them — Dieter, Elise, Rosa..."

"I'm sure he liked you best," I said.

"I might not have taken notice of a letter," Tony muttered. "We get a lot of crank mail."

"I know."

"Just the week before I left, there were half a dozen or so. People seem to get weirder during the holiday seasons....An appeal for funds from that Psychic Archaeology crowd in Virginia, a curriculum vitae from some loony who thinks he should be appointed to the staff because he's the reincarnation of Herodotus, a copy of that photo of Sophia Schliemann — Hey, watch out!"

I had spilled my beer. "Sorry. Did you say Sophia Schliemann?"

Tony grabbed a handful of napkins off a nearby table and swabbed at his sweater.

"Damn it, Ann made this for me. . . . Yeah, you know, the one where she's wearing the jewelry from Troy. I don't know what the hell that was all about; there wasn't even a letter with it."

That answered one question, unless Tony was a lot sneakier than I had ever known him to be. "What else did Friedl tell you?"

"She didn't make a lot of sense," Tony admitted. "What did she tell *you?*"

"She hasn't told me anything yet," I said, with perfect truth.

"Well, let's go see her. Maybe the two of us can extract some information. So far it's a damned fishy story."

I was about to endorse this assessment when Tony's mouth took on the wistful curve that made strong women want to mother him. "It would be too good to be true," he said longingly.

Friedl did not rise to greet us. She gave Tony her hand at an angle that made it impossible for him to do anything with it except kiss it.

Usually I can tell when people are lying. Friedl defeated me; she was so accustomed to putting on an act that everything she said sounded phony. The gist of her long and rambling narrative was that (a) her husband had some hidden treasure, (b) she didn't know what it was, and (c) she didn't know where it was.

Though visibly moved by her quivering lips and pathetic story, Tony was not moved to the point of excessive gullibility. Tactfully he pointed out that old men sometimes suffer from delusions.

"He was not old," Friedl protested.

"Seventy-five?" I suggested.

"Not in his heart — in his love..." Friedl covered her face with her hands.

Tony patted her clumsily on the shoulder and gave me a reproachful look. Like all men, he is quite willing to believe that a young and beautiful girl will adore him when he's eighty.

Friedl restrained her grief, which had left not a smudge on her make-up, and proceeded with her story. She had not learned of the treasure until the past spring. It was something her husband had rescued at the end of the war and had kept safely hidden for forty years. Recently, however, he had begun to fear that his enemies had finally tracked him down.

"Enemies?" Tony said. "What enemies?"

Friedl opened her eyes so wide her mascara flaked. "The Russians. The Communists."

"Oh," said Tony.

I said, "Bless their red hearts, they make such handy villains."

The comment passed over, or through,

Friedl's head. She went on. Her husband would tell her nothing more for fear of endangering her, and when she suggested that he turn the treasure over to the authorities — she didn't specify which authorities and neither of us pressed her — he had angrily refused. The treasure was his. It had passed through many hands, the original ownership had always been in dispute, and now it was his by right of possession. He had as much right to it as anyone. He had saved it.

This part of the story had the ring of truth.

Then, late in the fall, Hoffman had changed his mind. His enemies were closing in. He feared for his life — and hers. He had spoken of getting in touch with me — was I sure, absolutely certain, he had not told me...

"I have no idea where it might be," I said. "That's the truth, Frau Hoffman. Are *you* sure *you*—"

"No. I mean — yes. Would I have called on you for help if I knew?"

The answer to that was so obvious no one felt the need of voicing it. Tony cleared his throat. "Forgive me, Friedl — Frau Hoffman—"

She interrupted him, looking up at him from under her lashes and reaching for his hand. "Please, you must not be so formal. We are old friends."

226

"Thank you." Blushing, Tony did not emulate her use of the informal *du*. "I was about to say — I don't see how we can help you. I must be honest; I am still not convinced your husband was — er — in his right mind. All this business about Communists—"

"Then who was it who shot at Fräulein Bliss?"

"Hmmm," said Tony.

"And," Friedl continued, "not long after my adored Anton's death, someone broke into his room and searched it. Several pieces of furniture were smashed to pieces. I thought at the time it was an ordinary thief — but after the terrible incident of the shooting...Please, you will not abandon me? You will help me to find it?"

"We'll try," Tony said dubiously. "Though, with so little to go on...Have the police no idea who could have fired those shots?"

Friedl shrugged. Watching her, I said, "Freddy isn't on duty today. Has he left town?"

She wasn't as dim as she appeared — or else she had had reason to anticipate the implied accusation. "Are you suggesting it was Freddy? Impossible. My own cousin—"

"I'd like to talk to him," I said mildly.

Her eyes fell. "I — you cannot. He has gone. There was — he has — someone offered him a better position. He was only helping me temporarily."

"Where has he gone?"

"Zürich." The answer came so pat that a new-laid egg might have believed it.

"Who is Freddy?" Tony inquired.

"I'll fill you in later," I promised.

"Freddy had nothing to do with it," Friedl insisted. "It was the Communists."

Every time she mentioned Communists, Tony's skepticism level shot up. "We'll try," he repeated. "If you think of anything else, anything at all—"

After a further exchange of insincere promises and protestations, we took our leave. I told Tony about Freddy, which seemed to cheer him a little. "Guy sounds like a thug," he said hopefully. "And his sudden departure is suspicious. Friedl is so trusting, anyone could take advantage of her."

"Uh-huh," I said.

It was possible — not that Friedl was a trusting innocent, but that someone could have tricked her. Her explanation of the destruction of the *Schrank* was feasible, too. I didn't believe it, but it was feasible. I saw no reason to disillusion Tony. He would only have accused me of being catty, jealous, and a few other things.

Freddy's departure was suspicious. He might

have taken fright after the failure of his attack and fled from a possible police investigation. Or, if John's theory was correct, he might have fled from someone else.

Once out of Friedl's cloying presence, Tony's spirits rose. "Communists aside," he remarked, "her story isn't as unlikely as it sounds. The Nazis were the biggest looters of art objects the world has ever seen. Hitler was collecting for his Sonderauftrag Linz, Göring was collecting for Göring, and everybody else was picking up the leftovers. A lot of the loot ended up in Bavaria; even Göring shipped his treasures to Berchtesgaden when the Russians began to close in on Berlin. Remember the salt mines at Alt Aussee? Over ten thousand paintings, dozens of sculptures – including Michelangelo's *Madonna and Child* – and thousands of minor works. According to one estimate, there were at least two hundred *official* caches of art treasures in southern Germany, and God knows how many unofficial ones. Some have never been found. This prize of Hoffman's needn't be a whole mineful; maybe it's a single piece, something that had special importance to him."

He was getting uncomfortably close to the truth. I hoped he wouldn't think of looking up Hoffman's name in the professional literature; that would turn his attention away from the paintings-in-the-salt-mine theory, which was where I wanted him to stay. The trouble with my friends, and enemies, is that they are too intelligent.

"It's a hopeless cause, Tony," I said. "These mountains are like Swiss cheese, full of holes, caves, and abandoned mines. It could be anywhere — if it exists."

Tony refused to be discouraged. The prospect of another treasure hunt, and of playing detective, was too exciting. "Don't be such a pessimist. Hoffman must have left some clue. He was an old man; he wouldn't take the chance of its being lost forever."

We had reached my room. I unlocked the door.

"I wonder how big it is," Tony mused.

"Bigger than a breadbox," I offered. "Are you coming in?"

"I have my own room, thank you. Friedl was more than happy to accommodate me."

He was infuriatingly calm about being exiled from my tempting proximity. In fact, there was a swagger in his step and a certain swing to his shoulders as he walked away....

"Tony," I said gently.

"What?"

"I have a feeling Ann would rate Friedl as a succubus, too."

230

Tony's smile was the sublime quintessence of smugness. "Why don't I ask her? I told her I'd call today. So if you'll excuse me for, say, half an hour – maybe an hour..." He disappeared into his room, leaving me to contemplate his closed door and the shame of my evil imagination.

We decided to drive to Garmisch for dinner. Actually it was I who decided; Tony was in favor of sticking around the hotel, in hopes of God knows what – another attempt on my life, perhaps. I wanted to get away. The town was preying on my nerves – not that it wasn't a nice town, but it was so small. Too small for the three of us – especially when John was one of the three.

Since it was still early, we poked around the shops for a while, and Tony, who was still smarting from what he considered my treacherous behavior, got his revenge by carrying out an act of atrocity from which I had dissuaded him on several previous occasions. He bought a pair of lederhosen.

Lederhosen are those short leather pants. Let me repeat the word "short." They do not come to the knee, or just above the knee, or to mid-thigh; they are, not to belabor the point, *short*. On Tony they were a cross between a visual obscenity and a bad joke; he had to buy the largest pair in the shop in order to cover the essentials, and they were so big around the waist there was room inside for two of him. He said it didn't matter, the suspenders would hold them up.

The suspenders, brightly embroidered with objects such as edelweiss, were part of the costume, which also included knee socks and one of those silly little hats with a feather or an ostrich plume or a *Gamsbart* (chamois beard) tucked into the band. Tony's had a white ostrich feather. When attired in the complete ensemble, he looked exactly like Peter, Peter, Pumpkin-Eater in a German edition of *Mother Goose* I had bought for one of my nieces.

He wanted me to try on dirndls — so we'd match, I suppose. I actually love those cute little outfits; the astute reader has probably realized that my nasty remarks about the waitresses were prompted by pure jealousy. A dirndl looks as absurd on me as the lederhosen looked on Tony, if not as indecent. I tried on a few, to shut him up; when I saw him in a whispered conference with the shopkeeper, I realized he was planning to buy me one for a Christmas present. I also realized I didn't have anything for him, so we cruised a few more stores and I took mental notes on the items Tony admired.

We stowed his parcel in the car. By that time it was dark, and the town was aglitter with thousands of Christmas bulbs strung from storefronts and lampposts. Snow crunched underfoot, the air was redolent with the smell of pine branches and wood fires; the colorful ski jackets and caps glowed like neon — raspberry, turquoise, hot pink — and the sound of carols poured from every door. It was very pretty and festive, and all I could think of was John's advice: Look out for familiar faces. Between the ski masks and the scarves and the caps pulled low over ears and foreheads, it would have been difficult to recognize my own mother. The season and the setting could not have been more convenient for someone who preferred to pass unrecognized.

We hadn't gone a block from the car before I saw a familiar face. He was as swathed in scarves as all the others; I recognized him by the globular red nose that flashed on and off.

He saw me at the same time. Dropping the arm of the woman who was with him, he came pelting toward me, arms extended, nose glowing. "Vicky! Adored and most elongated of womanly pulchritude" — he made it all one word, which you can do in German, if you aren't particular about syntax. "You changed your mind! You came!"

He flung his arms around me and burrowed his face into my chest.

It was merely a token gesture, since I was wearing three layers of clothing and my parka had a zipper that closed it tighter than a chastity girdle, but Tony decided to take offense. Twisting a hand in the back of Dieter's collar, he removed him.

"She came, and I came with her," he said, biting off the words so that his breath made irritated white puffs in the cold air, like a dragon hiccuping. "Cut it out, Dieter."

"I saw you," Dieter admitted. "I hoped you were only a figment of my imagination and that if I ignored you, you would dissolve into air. Where is my nose?"

He fumbled at his face. "Here," I said, handing it back to him. "Must you, Dieter?"

"Yes. Yes, yes, I must, or go mad with longing. . . ." He began pounding on his chest.

I indicated the woman who stood some distance away, her arms folded and her foot tapping. "Isn't that Elise?"

"It was Elise," Dieter admitted. "No doubt it still is Elise. You see, when you turned me down, Vicky, I had to find another companion. Don't tell Elise I asked you first. She would not like to be second choice."

Elise did not come rushing to greet us. "Look who I have found," Dieter cried, presenting us like trophies.

"Yes," said Elise. "Quite a coincidence that we should all be here again."

"It certainly is," said Tony.

"Why do you stand looking hard at one another like two strange dogs?" Dieter asked curiously. "That is no way for old friends to behave. Let us all kiss one another."

Whereupon he flung his arms around Tony and stood on tiptoe, his lips pursed. Torn between amusement and disgust, Tony finally succumbed to laughter; he pushed Dieter away and reached for Elise. "Good idea, old buddy."

He had to lift Elise clean off her feet to kiss her; when he put her down she was looking a lot more amiable. Giggling, she linked arms with Tony and leaned against him. "We were about to have dinner. You will join us, won't you?"

There was no way of getting out of it without rudeness, even if we had wanted to, which neither of us did. The coincidences were falling as thick as the leaves in Vallombrosa.

But as the meal progressed and everyone mellowed with wine and food, I began to wonder whether this particular coincidence might not be legitimate. Dieter was a keen skier, and

Garmisch was one of the most popular winter-sports areas in Germany. Elise's presence surprised me a little, but there again, Dieter's explanation made sense. They had certainly been friendly the year before; now that her marriage was kaput, she would be looking for entertainment.

I wondered whether Schmidt would approve of her new hairstyle. It was jet-black instead of pink, and arranged in the wispy, wind-blown style fashionable that year. She had lost weight, which in her case was not becoming. The hollows under her cheekbones were as deep as scars, and her wrists looked brittle as dry twigs. She laughed a lot.

Tony wasn't buying the coincidence, but he didn't make much progress in his subtle attempt to elicit information. One of his problems was that he had no idea what we were supposed to be looking for; it could have been a painting or a piece of sculpture, a rare coin or an entire frescoed ceiling. He twitched at the mention of Tintoretto and started at Saint Stephen's Crown. It was the most entertaining aspect of the evening, a lot funnier than Dieter's dreadful jokes.

During the course of the usual shoptalk and professional gossip, I had a chance to inquire after Rosa and Jan. Elise's comments about

Rosa were surprisingly catty, even for her; from what she said, I got the impression that a professional feud was brewing, probably over some earth-shaking issue such as whether a painting was by Rembrandt or by one of his students. Dieter professed to know nothing about her; since their fields of expertise were so different, they would not ordinarily meet professionally, and – as Dieter candidly and crudely remarked – Rosa had nothing else to attract a man of his tastes.

He had more to say about Jan Perlmutter. They lived in the same city, though divided from one another by a wall that was more than material, and communication between the museums of the two Berlins was not infrequent. According to Dieter, Jan had recently been passed over for promotion because of some petty political issue, and was very bitter about it.

The only other subject of interest arose when Elise asked where we were staying.

"Ah, the Hexenhut," Dieter said reminiscently. "Yes, it was a pleasant little place – especially that waitress – you know who I mean, Tony...."

He rolled his eyes and smacked his lips in a display that made it difficult for Tony to admit a like knowledge. I said, "You're revolting, Dieter. I suppose you mean Friedl."

"Yes, that was her name. Dear little Friedl. How is she, Tony?"

I took it upon myself to reply. The news of Friedl's marriage and bereavement didn't arouse much interest; Elise looked bored, Dieter giggled and made a ribald comment.

After dinner, we made the rounds of a few bars, and then Tony and I excused ourselves. We left Dieter doing the *Schuhplattler* with a group of costumed entertainers while Elise looked on with a sour smile.

As we began to drive back to Bad Steinbach, Tony said thoughtfully, "It can't be Dieter."

"What can't? Who can't?"

"You know what I mean."

"I'm not sure I do."

"Friedl said her husband planned to communicate with someone about the treasure. She thought it was you, but she may have been mistaken. Elise and Dieter were both at the hotel last year, and both are museum officials. What I'm saying is, it can't be Dieter."

"Why not?" We left the lights of the town behind and headed up into the hills; the stars spilled out across the sky like a handful of flung jewels.

"He's such a jackass," Tony said, in tones of deep disgust.

"He is that."

"Hoffman wouldn't confide in an idiot like Dieter."

"You think Elise is more likely?"

"No, not really. Now if Perlmutter were to turn up in Bad Steinbach . . ."

"Come, now," I said, sneering. "Don't tell me you've fallen for the dirty-Communist routine."

"Eastern-bloc scholars have pressures on them we don't have," Tony argued. "Suppose the item in question came originally from behind the Iron Curtain. Recovering it would give Perlmutter a lot of prestige, maybe a step up the party ladder."

Again he was getting too close to the truth. I changed the subject.

As soon as I got Tony tucked away for the night, I planned to pay John a visit. He was entitled to know what I had discovered. The presence of two more of the gang of six would get his mind off Tony as suspect number one. (At least that provided a reasonable motive for calling on John; if there were others, I preferred not to admit them.)

But it was to be an evening of renewing old acquaintances. When we walked into the lobby, the first thing I saw was an all-too-familiar face and form. Red as a rose and round as a berry — Schmidt and no other.

239

John had promised to take care of Schmidt. I hadn't inquired how he meant to handle the matter. Now I wished I had. Obviously the scheme had backfired.

Schmidt was so happy to see us. He waved frantically. "Here," he cried. "Here I am."

We joined him. "What are you doing here?" I asked.

"I came to help you, of course," said Schmidt.

"But I thought—"

"What is *he* doing here?" Schmidt glowered at Tony.

"Well," I began.

"You have told him!"

"No. No, Schmidt — now look, Schmidt—"

"It was our private affair. You and I and—"

"Never mind!"

"You told this fat old idiot about the deal and you didn't tell me?" Tony demanded.

"Fat and old? Who is fat and old?" Schmidt struggled to get out of his chair, but it fit his ample posterior so snugly he could only rock back and forth. His voice rose. "Fat and old, is it? I will show you. You will receive a strip of paper measuring the length of my sword. Choose your seconds!"

That was when I knew Schmidt was drunk — really bombed out, stinking drunk, not just mildly inebriated. He never challenges people to duels when he's just mildly inebriated. At my urging, Tony apologized; we sat down; Schmidt stopped rocking and relaxed. A look of mild perplexity replaced his indignant frown, and he muttered, "Now what was it I had to tell you? So much has happened, but Sir John must know—"

"How long have you been waiting?" I asked, trying to get his mind off the engrossing subject of Sir John.

"Hours," Schmidt grumbled. "Hours and hours and...No one knew where you had gone. Since I did not know where you had gone, I could not follow."

"True, O Schmidt," I said.

"I had a little to drink and to eat," Schmidt said, like a suspect under police interrogation trying to remember the activities of a long-past day. "I talked to the pleasant lady at the desk — she is the housekeeper, you know....But she intends to resign as soon as Frau Hoffman can find a replacement. I fear the poor young lady is not popular with the employees. It was expected that the hotel would be taken over by the nephew of the first Frau Hoffman, since it has belonged to her family for two hundred years. There is much resentment, I believe, since the second Frau Hoffman—"

"Schmidt," I said. "What are you talking about?"

Schmidt blinked. "About the nephew — or perhaps it is the grandnephew—"

"*Why* are you talking about him?"

"Now that," said Schmidt, "is a pertinent question. Why am I talking about him? I do not know. I should not be talking about him. There is a matter of greater importance — of consuming importance — of an importance demanding immediate action....*Ach, ja,* now I remember! Come, come quickly, I will show you. He is there — I saw him go in. He has not come out. I staked myself here to watch."

He surged to his feet, accompanied by the chair. Tony plucked it off his posterior and put it down. Schmidt ignored this with the lofty unconcern of a man who has more important matters on his mind. "There," he hissed. "He is there. I saw him go in. He has not come out."

He pointed toward the door of the bar. "But, Schmidt," I began. "There's another door—"

"Who?" Tony asked blankly.

"I will show you." Schmidt beamed. His face looked like the harvest moon hanging low over the hills of Minnesota. A pang of homesickness swept over me. Oh, to be in Minnesota now — away from intoxicated German professors and slippery English crooks and miscellaneous people trying to kill me....

We followed Schmidt to the bar. I fully expected that his suspect — some innocent householder who had beady eyes or a nose like Peter Lorre's — had had his beer and gone home via the street door. I was wrong. "There," said Schmidt, in the hissing shriek that is his idea of a whisper. "See — he is there!"

He was there, all right. There was no doubt as to whom Schmidt meant; his quivering forefinger and his intent stare pilloried a man sitting alone at a corner table.

He was worth looking at — tall and broad-shouldered, with a profile like that of a brooding eagle. A Wyatt Earp-type mustache framed a pensive, thoughtful mouth; brown hair curled over his ears and his high, intellectual brow.

"I've never seen him in my life," Tony said blankly.

I said nothing.

"Ho," shrieked Schmidt. "I told you I never forget a face. Only once have I met him. Only once, but I remember, and you, who have known him better, do not recall him. It is lucky for you I came here, *nicht?*"

"If you don't get to the point, I am going to kill you, Schmidt," I said.

"It is Perlmutter," Schmidt said triumphantly. "The assistant curator from East Berlin."

"You're crazy," Tony stuttered. "Perlmutter

is a blond, this guy is brunet. Perlmutter doesn't have a mustache, this guy—"

It was Perlmutter. The outlines of that splendid profile were burned into my brain.

They say that if you stare at someone long enough, invisible waves of something or other will stretch out and attract his attention. There must be something to it. Perlmutter looked up and met my eyes. The instant recognition that transformed his face would have removed any lingering doubts I might have had, which I didn't.

Before I could react, he was on his feet and out the door to the street. By chance or by design, he had selected a table in a spot convenient for retreat.

I wasted a vital couple of seconds trying to decide which way to go — across the crowded room toward the door he had used, or back through the lobby. Tony wasted a vital couple of seconds bouncing off Schmidt, who had started in one direction while Tony tried to go the other way. Schmidt then compounded the problem by keeling over, his face set in an imbecilic grin of triumph.

Schmidt does that sometimes. It is the inevitable conclusion to his bouts of really serious drinking. They are rare events and occur only when something has happened to upset him. I wished I knew what had upset him this time, but questions would have to wait. He wouldn't be coherent for hours. I had seen it happen once before, when he learned of the death of a favorite nephew in a car crash.

Well, there he was, hanging limply between me and Tony. We had each grabbed an arm as his round red form sagged floorward. We looked helplessly at one another over Schmidt's bowed head.

"What do we do now?" Tony asked.

"It's too late to follow Perlmutter....Oh, hell. We'd better get him to bed."

"Whose bed?" Tony asked warily.

It was a reasonable question. As we soon discovered, Schmidt did not have a room reserved, and the hotel was full-up. He may have had a reservation in Garmisch, but that was irrelevant since Schmidt was incapable of answering questions — or hearing them. He revived sufficiently to be dragged instead of carried; with one plump arm over a shoulder of each, we propelled him up the stairs to the second floor. Tony wanted to put him on the couch in my room.

"You have twin beds, don't you?"

"Yes. But—"

"Then he's yours. All yours. Every...adorable...chubby...pound."

The minute Schmidt hit the mattress he was gone. I took his shoes off and covered him with the blanket. Smiling beatifically, Schmidt heaved a deep sigh and began to snore.

An expression of profound melancholy transformed Tony's face.

"Does he do that all night?"

Tony had unpacked, in his characteristically haphazard fashion; from among the litter on the dresser top, framed in silver, the lovely heart-shaped face of Ann Belfort smiled winsomely at me.

I smiled winsomely back. "Snore, you mean? Only when he's drunk. Nighty-night, Annie — I mean, Tony."

Friedl had preserved one of the Hexenhut's pleasant old-fashioned customs; the chambermaid had turned down my bed and spread my nightgown gracefully across it. For the chambermaid's sake, I was glad I had brought my fancy new nightie instead of my old flannel pajamas. For my own sake, I was sorry I hadn't brought the jammies. The stove had been banked for the night, and as I knew from past experience, the room would be as cold as a frozen side of beef by morning, though it warmed quickly after someone revived the fire. I had usually managed to con Tony into proving his manhood while I remained snuggled under the downy warmth of the *Daunendecke*. Tomorrow I'd have to do it myself or wait for the chambermaid. Such are the disadvantages of celibacy.

I needed to see John. In this case, celibacy had nothing to do with it. Things were getting out of hand — suspects emerging from the woodwork, Tony narrowing in on the gold and on John (his accusations had been unnervingly accurate); and Schmidt...The old dear's rambling conversation had raised a host of new and ominous possibilities. One in particular, resulting from a casual comment I had been too preoccupied to notice at the time, came back to me now and made me all the more anxious to confront that sneaky, tricky, untrustworthy devil....I forced my clenched hands to relax. Maybe I was reading too much into a single statement. Maybe I had better not raise the point. He'd never admit anything anyway. There were other, equally urgent matters to discuss. What had happened to John's scheme for getting Schmidt out of our hair? Not that the little rascal hadn't been useful. I would never have spotted Perlmutter without Schmidt. That made five of the six.

I turned out the light and went to the window. Most of the town had gone to bed. The night was clear and cold. In the distance the snow-covered peaks of the Stuiben Mountains shone with a faint, eerie glow against the darkness. Far up on the dark heights of the Hexenhut, a single Christmas tree burned blue and scarlet and white, like a dollhouse miniature.

I realized that I had made a slight mistake in strategy — or is it tactics? I couldn't leave the hotel by the normal route without being seen and recognized. There isn't much to do in Bad Steinbach at midnight. Even a casual observer might wonder where I was going at that hour; and, as I had just learned, some of the observers might not be so casual. How was I going to get to Müller's shop unseen?

The answer was only too obvious. With a sigh and a shiver, I opened the window and went out onto the balcony. Investigation showed a nice convenient snowbank directly below. A single bulb beside a side entrance gave more light than I would have liked, but there didn't seem to be anyone around. That didn't mean there wasn't someone watching, but I had to take the chance.

I was about to lower myself off the balcony when it occurred to me that I might have a little problem returning by the same route. I went back inside, turned on the light, and investigated the backpack I carry on such excursions instead of a purse. There were a lot of peculiar items in the pack, but no rope. I hadn't really expected there would be. The only alternative seemed to be a towel or bed sheet. I balked at that idea; it was too much like the sort of thing Schmidt would think of, and a knotted sheet dangling from a hotel window was likely to attract attention. I would simply have to return through the front door and the lobby. It wouldn't matter so much if I was seen returning, so long as no one knew where I was returning from.

The snowbank was cold. I don't know why that should have surprised me.

Avoiding the lighted entrance of the hotel, I skirted the Marktplatz. A roofed arcade over some of the shop fronts cast a welcome shadow. There were a few other people abroad, but when I reached the mouth of the narrow, pitch-black alley, no one seemed to be interested in my activities, so I proceeded on my way. Only a faint glow from the snow underfoot marked the path. Despite my heavy gloves, my fingers were stiff with cold before I got the gate open and re-latched. Not a gleam of light showed from the house. I found the door, by touch, and knocked.

An icy breeze brushed my face and set the foliage sighing. Something hit the ground with a soft thud; I knew it must be snow falling from the laden branches of the trees, but my pulse skipped a beat or two. I was about to turn away when the door swung silently open into a space of absolute blackness.

The warm familiar smell of shavings and wood smoke wafting out of the house did not move me to enter. I stood squinting into the black silence until a hand wrapped around my arm and yanked me inside. My nerves were in such a state that I swung wildly at the dark. I missed him, of course; the door closed, two arms wrapped around me, pinning my arms to my sides, and two lips planted themselves firmly on mine. I had always suspected he could see in the dark.

"It is you," John said, after a prolonged interval.

"Who did you think it was?"

"One never knows." He continued to hold me immobile. I knew the futility of struggling against a man who knew more dirty, under-handed wrestling holds than Bruce Lee. Besides, I couldn't see a thing. Besides, I didn't especially want to struggle.

"No more hitting?" he inquired hopefully.

"Sorry about that. I find all this a trifle unnerving."

"You aren't the only one." He let me go. Then a light went on. It came from a door to the right — the door into the workshop, which

John had opened. He gestured. "In here."

He had made himself comfortable. The room now contained an overstuffed chair and a reading lamp, next to the workbench, where a tall slim bottle stood in incongruous juxtaposition to Müller's tools.

I was about to ask what had become of the cat when a muffled yowl and the sound of claws on wood gave me the answer. Clara was in the parlor, across the hall. Clara didn't want to be in the parlor, across the hall.

"A nice warm purring cat would add to the creature comforts," I suggested.

John pushed me into the shop and closed the door. I could still hear Clara. The complaints of a Siamese cat are hard on the ears – and, after a time, on the nerves. John said shortly, "That is not a nice warm purring cat."

"You can't keep her in there all the time."

John turned to face me, displaying a neat row of parallel scratches along one cheek. "Oh yes, I can," he said.

"But the poor thing..."

"Forget the damned cat," said John. "It won't be neglected; have you ever known me to be cruel to a living creature? Don't answer that...."

"A complete inventory would take too long," I agreed.

John's face darkened. His sense of humor was

decidedly under par that evening. "I haven't time to exchange feeble witticisms with you. Any news?"

"Quite a lot." I sat down in the chair and picked up the glass from which he had been drinking. "Delicate and fruity, with a fresh bouquet," I said appreciatively, after sampling the contents. "Piesporter Goldtröpfchen? Or do you call it hock?"

"I don't call it anything, I just drink it." He poured wine into another glass and hoisted one hip onto the table.

"Guess who I ran into this evening," I said coyly.

"I don't have to guess. I saw you being matey with your colleagues in Garmisch."

"Oh, those convenient ski masks," I murmured.

"As you say. One was the chap from Berlin — I recognized him from your snapshots. Who was the woman?"

"Elise. She's dyed her hair."

"Aha. That makes two of them. Three if we include your lengthy admirer."

"Four. Jan Perlmutter is in Bad Steinbach."

That didn't surprise him either. "I rather thought he might be."

"Did you rather think Schmidt might be here?" I inquired, hoping to puncture that

252

smug, know-it-all façade.

I succeeded. He stopped swinging his foot and slammed it to the floor. "Schmidt here? I told him to stay in Munich!"

"I know it must be a blow to your reputation as world's champion spinner of fantastic stories, but you obviously failed to convince Schmidt." I held out my empty glass and added generously, "He isn't easy to convince. Even a master liar like you—"

Frowning, John splashed wine into my glass. "I told him I wanted him to stand guard over your house — promised him armed desperadoes, attack, invasion, or some other form of entertainment. I fully expected the little elf would arm himself to the teeth and squat there indefinitely. You don't suppose..."

"Impossible. There wasn't a mark on him." I chewed on my lower lip; then I said reluctantly, "He was absolutely bombed by the time we found him. He doesn't do that without good and sufficient reason."

"What did he say?"

"He mentioned you. He didn't explain, though; he had just spotted Perlmutter and was all excited about him. Then he — well, he passed out."

"Wake him."

"No use. He's out for the next six hours, I've

seen it before. I'll talk to him in the morning."

"Bloody hell," John muttered. "I don't like this."

"I don't like any of it. How about you? Any luck?"

"Only in a negative sense. Look here." He put his glass down. The back of the shop was dark; when he pulled the chain of a hanging bulb, I saw that the pieces of the *Schrank* had been neatly arranged in something like the original order — the back against the wall, the two side pieces next to them, and, in between, a pile of rougher boards that were obviously the shelves. John picked up the topmost of these; it was a solid slab of hardwood three-quarters of an inch thick, unadorned and unfinished. He turned it to the light. The marks were clearly visible — slightly indented, faintly stained.

"Something stood on that shelf for years, probably decades," he said. "Something heavy and rectangular—"

"The treasure chest?" I said dubiously. "Boy, talk about jumping to conclusions—"

"I know it was a chest." John put the shelf down and indicated a smaller pile of scraps, off to one side. "Here are the pieces of it. The dimensions fit the marks on the shelf. Now observe — there is nothing up my sleeve...."

He carried the scraps to the workbench and laid them out. "Bottom, sides, top. It's oak, hardened with age. Even Freddy must have had a spot of bother chopping it up. Threads caught on splinters within indicate it was once lined with wool, possibly a piece of blanket." I opened my mouth to object; John raised a minatory finger. "Wait. The best is yet to come." From his breast pocket he took a small plasticized envelope, the kind jewelers use, and waved it. Sparks flared and danced. I snatched it from him.

"Gold!"

John resumed his pose on the edge of the bench, his foot swinging. "Gold. A grand total of five minuscule grains caught on splinters, or on the wool threads. No, don't open it, they're so light they'll simply float away. There's not enough to test, but from the color and the texture it appears to be virtually pure — twenty-four carat."

"No wonder they smashed the *Schrank*," I murmured. "It was there — my God, it was there all the time, while I sat listening to Brahms with Hoffman. Less than five feet away from me. . . ."

The small envelope swayed in my fingers; the gold twinkled like tiny stars. John took it from me and replaced it in his pocket.

"That would appear to be the case," he said coolly. "Friedl knew where it was kept; when she went looking for it, after Hoffman's – shall we stretch a point and say 'accident' – she found he had removed it. Hell hath no fury, et cetera; she may have been angry enough to kick the chest to bits with her own dainty foot."

"I can't believe he would be so casual about it! Right there in his living room—"

"Oh, that's comprehensible. He'd want it close at hand, where he could look at it and gloat over it."

"Well, that's very interesting, but I can't see that it gets us anywhere. Friedl may not know where he hid it—"

"Friedl does not know. Jest all you like, but my theory is the only one that fits the facts."

"We don't know where it is either."

"How about your elongated gentleman friend from Chicago?"

I tried to raise one eyebrow. Though I have practiced for hours in front of a mirror, the feat is still beyond me; both eyebrows slipped up. "If I didn't know better, I would suspect your harping on Tony's height betrays jealousy of a taller and better man. I'm convinced Tony is innocent, but he is no longer unwitting. Friedl got to him and spilled part of the beans. I'm going to tell him the rest."

256

Instead of objecting, John nodded. "You may as well. I do not share your blind faith in the lad, but if I'm right and you are wrong, he knows anyway. If you are right and I'm wrong, it's too late to remove him from the line of fire; the bad boys have seen him with you and they will assume he's a co-conspirator."

"I wish you wouldn't say things like that. I thought we had decided the attack on me and Schmidt was a single aberration."

John raised one eyebrow, without visible effort. "We hope that's what it was. If they are waiting for us to come up with a solution, we may all die of old age here in Bad Steinbach. I am completely without inspiration."

"Me too."

The glum silence that followed was broken by another outburst from the parlor. Even with two heavy doors in between, it sounded like a large child having a large temper tantrum. John flinched. "I can't stand much more of this."

"Maybe she wants out," I suggested.

"I know she wants out. As soon as I let her out, she wants in again. I have spent the afternoon letting her in and letting her out." John's voice cracked. "I can't let the creature sit outside the door howling, for fear the neighbors will hear and come to investigate."

"I never thought I'd see the day when the great John Smythe was cowed by a cat."

"It isn't the damned cat, it's general frustration. We aren't making any progress and I see no hope of our ever doing so. At what point do we call the whole thing off?"

"We?" I repeated. "You're a free agent, John. You can — and will — walk away whenever you choose. The only thing that puzzles me is why you signed on in the first place."

He turned slightly, to place his glass on the workbench. The fine hairs outlining his chin and jaw sparked like the shining scraps of Helen's gold. He started toward me. I waited till he was leaning forward before I slid ungracefully out of the chair and out of his reach. He lost his balance and sprawled awkwardly across the chair.

"Don't do that," I said.

"I didn't intend to." He sat up, but he didn't make the mistake of reaching for me a second time. "What's got into you?"

"Common sense, maybe," I suggested. "John, you make love very nicely. I don't know anyone who does it better—"

"And your experience, I presume, is extensive."

"Ooooh, how rude," I said. "That was unworthy of you, sir. As I was saying, I'm willing to play games of that sort with you whenever it suits me, but don't insult my intelligence by implying that our relationship means any more to you than — than that. If you did care about me, you wouldn't disappear into thin air the way you did and left me worrying — I mean—"

The hard, angry line of his lips relaxed, and I realized, too damned late as usual, that I had left myself wide open. That repulsive heroine of mine was affecting my speech patterns, if not my brain.

John stood up. "Darling!" he bleated. "I didn't know you cared."

I had one hand raised to smack his grinning face, before I realized that he had presented his cheek in gallant expectation of just that response. "Oops," he said in his normal voice. "Wait a sec — not that one." He turned the other cheek, the one that the cat had not scratched.

I let my hand fall. "Never mind," I said, with as much dignity as the situation allowed.

"Don't go," John pleaded, as I made a wide berth around him on my way to the door. "It's been a frightfully dull day, and these little exchanges are so enlivening. We could insult one another a bit longer and then retire—"

"I'll have to take a rain check. Schmidt will be at my door at around six A.M., and if I'm not there, he'll have the whole police force of Bad Steinbach out looking for me." Then I remembered my cooling stove, and added, "Unless you'd like to come back with me."

"Hmm," said John, scratching his chin and eyeing me doubtfully.

"Oh, well, forget it. You'd probably make me do it anyway."

"Do what?"

"Never mind." I opened the door to the parlor. Clara burst out and made a beeline for John. "Sic 'em, killer," I said.

SEVEN

Schmidt did wake me the following morning. It had taken me some time to fall asleep. The emphatic hammering on my door shattered a dream whose details I prefer not to recall and shot me out of bed before I realized what I was doing. Having gotten that far, I decided I might as well open the door.

"Ha, there you are," Schmidt said happily.

I stared blearily at him. He had changed into a bright orange ski suit, in which he looked like an animated pumpkin.

"We are having breakfast together in our room, Tony and I," Schmidt went on with ghastly cheerfulness. "Come. Come quickly, we have much to discuss."

I grabbed a robe as he towed me toward the door, and managed to get around me before he ushered me into his – their – room. Heavenly warmth wrapped around my shivering limbs. Some noble soul had fired up the stove.

Appropriately attired in lederhosen, suspenders, et al., Tony was seated at the table digging into a hearty Bavarian farmers' breakfast. It was no wonder he had been moved to start the stove; his bare thighs were still faintly blue with cold.

He was in a better mood than I had expected after a night listening to Schmidt snore. He greeted me with a wave of a fork on which a sausage was impaled. Such was my state of sleepy confusion that I was not at all surprised to see a Siamese cat sitting on the table next to the sausage.

"Sit down," said Schmidt. "We must discuss the case."

"I'm retiring from the case," I mumbled, sitting. Fortunately there was a chair under me.

"What? No! Give her coffee, Tony, she does not ever make sense until she has had coffee."

Tony obliged. Clara took advantage of his distraction to hook the sausage off his fork; she carried it across the room and sat down on the beruffled lace-trimmed hem of my robe to eat it. I was too far gone to protest. I said faintly, "I am retiring from the case."

"Have more coffee," said Schmidt.

"I will. But that will not affect my decision. I am retiring from the case because there is no case."

Tony and Schmidt said in unison, "You can't."

"Oh yes, I can."

"No, you can't," said Schmidt and Tony. Tony glared at Schmidt, who continued in solo, "The police are looking for you, Vicky, my dear. You must solve the case to free yourself from suspicion."

The cat rose fluidly from the floor to the table and clamped its teeth on the bacon Tony was holding. Tony tugged at it and swore. The cat growled but did not relinquish her hold. Schmidt giggled.

"A charming animal," he said approvingly. "Yours, Vicky? It was outside your door early this morning; I had hoped you would be awake, but you were not, and I thought I would let you sleep a little longer, so I brought it here with me—"

"Schmidt," I said softly. "Shut up. No. Don't shut up. Repeat what you just said."

"I thought I would let you sleep a little longer, so—"

"Before that. Something about the police."

"Yes, I expect they are looking for you."

"Why, Schmidt?"

"Because of the dead man in your garden, of course."

"The dead man in my garden," I repeated hollowly.

"Give her more coffee," said Schmidt.

Schmidt was full of admiration for the foresight of Sir John Smythe, who had warned him about the dead man.

"Well, not in so many words, of course," Schmidt admitted. "But he told me there would be a desperate attempt on your life, Vicky, and that I must come at once to tell you when it occurred."

"He told you I would be here?" I was still trying to get a grip on the situation.

"He did not have to tell me. I knew. He has a greater respect for my intelligence than some people."

"Wait," I pleaded. "Just stop talking for a minute, Schmidt, and let me think. Did you find...No, that's not the most important... How was he...What I want to know is, who was it?"

"You don't have to shout," Schmidt roared, clapping his hands over his ears.

"I'm sorry," I whimpered.

"Have some hay," Tony suggested. "It's very good when you're feeling faint."

Suddenly I felt better. It may have been the caffeine, but I think it was just Tony — the comradely grin, the familiar dimple, the tacit acknowledgment that the whole scenario had the lunatic logic of a Lewis Carroll plot. The cat jumped on my knee and began washing her whiskers.

"Let him tell it," Tony went on, indicating Schmidt. "He's been bending my ear with his tale since six A.M. He'd have rousted you out at that hour if I had let him, so you can thank me for your extra sleep."

"Thank you," I said meekly.

"*Bitte schön.* I might add," Tony added, "that if he had bothered to mention this little detail last night, instead of waiting until this morning—"

"There were more important things," Schmidt protested. "The spy from East Berlin—"

"Schmidt, you were so drunk you wouldn't have known a spy from a brontosaurus," I said wearily. "Never mind. Tell me now."

Schmidt made a long dramatic story of it, but there really wasn't much to tell. He had arrived at my house shortly after Tony and I had left. After Brotzeit, lunch, and a short nap, he had decided to take a little exercise. Jogging briskly and breathlessly around the block, he had attracted a pack of dogs. (Schmidt is irresistible to dogs; he is so round and so roly-poly, and he yelps so delightfully when they nip at his ankles.) Trailed by the fascinated pack, he had fled back to the house, but had been too distracted by the nips and barks and whines to unlock the door. In the hope that his admirers would lose interest and go away, he had slipped through the side gate into the back yard. One of the dogs had slipped through with him; from his vivid description, I recognized the animal as the beagle who lived three doors down. When the dog abandoned him and began digging furiously in a snowbank by the fence, Schmidt was curious enough to investigate.

I couldn't blame him for getting drunk. As soon as he realized what the snow concealed, he had bundled the dog out the gate, but its frantic howling provided a ghastly background accompaniment to his excavations. The stiff white flesh was the same shade and temperature as its icy shroud, but Schmidt had no difficulty recognizing the face of Freddy.

I patted Schmidt's hand sympathetically. He frowned at me and pulled it away. "It was a terrible sight. I am glad it was I and not you who found him, Vicky. His eyes were open and coated with a thin layer of ice...."

Shocked though he was, Schmidt had dug snow away until he found the dark-crusted stains on the breast of Freddy's fancy Hawaiian shirt. They came from multiple stab wounds, according to Schmidt — and I was willing to take his word for it. However, there was no blood on the snow. Freddy had been long dead and half frozen when someone tipped him over the fence into my back yard. It must have happened the night before, after I took Caesar to visit his friend Carl.

"So of course I left Munich at once," Schmidt finished. "To tell you what had happened. But I could not find you. You were not here. And by the time you came, I had seen Perlmutter—"

"Didn't you call the police?" I asked.

"No. Why should I do that? They would only detain me, asking questions. But I suppose they will find him before long," said Schmidt calmly. "And then they will want to talk with you. And when they find who he is, and that you were at the hotel—"

"Schmidt, don't be theatrical. I've got to go home right away. There is no sense in staying on here—"

"We can't leave yet," Tony protested. "Friedl — er — Frau Hoffman — has given me permission to look through her husband's papers. He must have left some sort of memo or note or map telling where he hid the gold."

"The gold," I said. "Right. I suppose Schmidt told you."

"Yes, he did. And I must say, Vicky, that your behavior has hurt and astonished me. I would like to believe that it was concern for my safety and respect for my altered status that prompted your reticence—"

"Believe it," I said, shrugging.

"I would like to believe it, but I don't. You've harbored a grudge ever since the Riemenschneider affair—"

"Grudge? Grudge, my eye! Why should I?"

"Because I proved my superiority," said Tony, with a smirk and a superb disregard for the truth. "Because we made a bet and I won."

"Like hell you won." The cat grumbled and dug her claws into my leg. I moderated my voice. "We collaborated on that affair. It was a joint success."

"That's what I mean. You can't stand sharing the credit."

"There is some truth in that," said Schmidt judiciously. "You do not share well with others, Vicky. You did not tell Papa Schmidt, or Sir John—"

"And that's another thing," shouted Tony. "Who is that character, anyway? What's he doing in this business? How did you meet him?"

"But I have told you," said Schmidt, winking furiously at me to indicate...something or other. Even when I'm at my best, I am sometimes uncertain as to the esoteric meaning of Schmidt's gestures. Enlightenment dawned as he continued, "Sir John is an under-the-blanket personage of an extremely secret organization—"

"So secret I've never heard of it?" Tony demanded. "He's lying to you, Schmidt. There is no such thing. He's probably some kind of crook; Vicky attracts them the way a dog collects fleas."

They went on exchanging insults and lies, which gave me a chance to consider this latest development. If anything, it only strengthened my determination to get myself, not to mention Tony and Schmidt, out of what was beginning to look like a nasty, dangerous, unproductive mess.

When they had wound down, I said, "If you two have quite finished, I'd like to make a statement. I said I was through, and I am. Through."

"But the murder of Freddy—" Schmidt began.

"Schmidt, there is no way anybody could suspect I killed Freddy."

"But the gold—" Tony exclaimed.

"What gold? We've built up a fabric of guesswork and surmise. We haven't the slightest clue, and there is nothing more we can do here."

"Not true," said Tony. Schmidt nodded vigorous agreement.

"What can we do?"

"Inspect Hoffman's papers."

"Lots of luck, buster. You can be sure Friedl had already been through them with a fine-tooth comb."

"I don't know why you are so prejudiced against the poor woman," Tony said. I rolled my eyes in speechless commentary. Tony reddened. "Even if she is – er – up to no good, which I consider unproven, I may find something she overlooked. I hope you won't accuse me of vanity if I suggest I am slightly more intelligent than she."

"No," I said. "I won't."

Tony wasn't quite sure how to take that, so he decided to let it pass. "We should also interrogate our colleagues."

"Now, Tony –"

"Look here, Vicky," Tony said in a kindly voice. "Let me spell it out for you, okay? You and I both got copies of that photograph of Frau Schliemann –"

"It wasn't Frau Schliemann."

"Well, Helene Barton of the Classics Department said it was."

"Helene Barton is a jerk. She doesn't know her –"

"Please, Vicky. The point is, if you and I got copies of the picture, maybe the others did, too – Dieter and Elise and Jan Perlmutter. My being here is a coincidence; I have to admit I didn't give that photo a second thought. Maybe Dieter just happened to fix on Garmisch for his holiday. But you can bet Perlmutter wouldn't be hanging around, and in disguise, at that, if he weren't up to something sneaky."

"Tony," I said desperately, "if your – my – our – theory is correct, one of them is a killer."

"Precisely. Therefore it behooves us to find out which one."

"It is Perlmutter who is the killer," said Schmidt. "He is in disguise. Or perhaps the one we have not seen – D'Addio. It is very suspicious that she has disguised herself so well we have not even seen her."

The brilliant illogic of this took my breath away for a moment. "There's another possibility, just as logical," I said. "Nobody we know is the killer. The photos were sent as a bizarre practical joke, or the delusion of a sick old man. Freddy's murder is unrelated to the hypothetical gold of Troy."

"Then why was his body left in your garden?" Schmidt asked.

"I don't know. Which is precisely why I intend to return to Munich this evening and make a full confession. I'll tell my friend Karl Feder the whole story and let him laugh himself sick at my girlish delusions of buried treasure, and then the police can get on with their investigation."

"She is speaking out of despair," Schmidt explained to Tony. "She is easily discouraged.

We will find a clue and then she will change her mind. Vicky, let us go to Garmisch and give Dieter the third degree."

"Sorry, I didn't bring my rubber hose. Besides, I have an errand to do this morning."

"Ah — to find Perlmutter. Perhaps that is better. I will come with you while Tony reads the old gentleman's mail."

"You can come if you like. I'm not going to look for Perlmutter."

"What, then?"

"I'm taking flowers to a dead man."

We were still arguing in a desultory, unproductive sort of way, and finishing the food the cat hadn't eaten, when the phone rang. It was Friedl, summoning us to The Presence. I agreed to accompany the delegation, provided I was allowed to get dressed first.

"There, you see, Tony," Schmidt remarked. "She is recovering. She will not abandon the quest."

"I'm going along to make sure you two don't dig yourselves into a deeper hole," I snapped. "And to keep you from committing me to a project I've no intention of pursuing. Now listen, both of you. You may not agree with me about Friedl's character, or lack thereof, but for God's sake don't volunteer any information. What she doesn't know can't hurt her."

"But of course," said Schmidt. "That is a basic principle of criminal investigation."

Tony's only comment was, "Don't be insulting."

We called on Friedl in a body, so to speak. She looked a little startled when we marched in, and I couldn't blame her; there was a decided nursery-rhyme air about the group — Peter, Peter; Peter's wife; and the pumpkin. She didn't notice the cat until Clara reared up and began clawing at the sofa. She let out a shriek, which didn't bother the cat one whit; when she reached for a poker, I intervened.

"I hope you don't mind," I said untruthfully — actually, I hoped she did. "The cat seems to have attached herself to me. I'll try to keep her out of your way."

The cat bothered her, all right. Clara was a living reminder of the old man she had deceived and betrayed, perhaps to his death. The feeling was reciprocated. Though she permitted me to hold her, the animal didn't relax into a nice furry bundle; her claws were out, her fur bristled. That was exactly the way Friedl affected me.

"It keeps coming back," she muttered. "I

suspect the cook feeds it. I would fire her if I could...."

"But she is an excellent cook," said Schmidt interestedly. "The Bavarian burger especially, that is a stroke of genius."

"Schmidt, Schmidt," I said, more in sorrow than in anger.

"Yes, you are right, Vicky; I am distracting myself. I must allow Frau Hoffman to tell why she asked to see us."

"I wished to know whether you had learned anything new," Friedl said.

"No," I said.

"That's not quite accurate," Tony objected. "We have discovered what it was your husband was hiding—"

I dropped the cat onto Tony's lap. It was a vicious, cruel, spiteful gesture; the information Tony had been about to disclose was information Friedl already knew, and if my assessment was accurate, *she* knew that *we* knew. I was furious with Tony for shooting off his mouth and ignoring my sensible suggestions, but I suppose that's no excuse.

After a while I got up and opened the door to let the cat out. Friedl went on mopping blood off Tony — an unnecessarily prolonged operation, in my opinion. The scratches weren't all that deep.

274

"As Tony was about to remark, we have decided that he was right the first time," I said. "We have found no evidence that your husband possessed anything of value, and if he did, we have found nothing to indicate what he may have done with it."

"But," Friedl stuttered. "But – but you–"

"I'm afraid I can't spend any more time on this, Frau Hoffman. I have my own work to do."

"I don't," said Tony.

She turned eagerly to him. "Then you will stay? You will help me?"

Her fluttering hands and flapping eyelashes had their effect on Tony's gullible heart. Also, he was moved by the desire to get the better of me. "Sure," he said. "You said I could go through his papers. Maybe he left a memorandum of some sort."

She gushed her thanks, then eyed Schmidt. "And you, Herr Direktor?"

"I have certain inquiries of my own to pursue," Schmidt said, trying to look mysterious.

She thanked him, though not as effusively as she had Tony (he wasn't as young and cute as Tony) and then asked me when I was leaving. I said I'd give it another day. "I promised – promised myself – that I would visit your husband's grave, Frau Hoffman. I thought I'd take some flowers or greenery. It's a custom where I come from."

I needn't have bothered inventing excuses. She said indifferently, "It is also a custom here."

"Would you like to go with me?"

From her reaction, one might have supposed I had suggested a visit to a morgue. *"Lieber Gott, nein!* That is — it is too painful for me. So soon after..."

She offered Tony free run of her office, but he declined, with thanks, and asked if the papers in question could be brought to his room.

"Whatsa matter?" I hissed, in the accent of the underworld, after we had left Friedl to her own devices. "You don' wanna be friendly wit' de little lady?"

"That's disgusting," said Tony.

He was right, so I abandoned the accent. "She seems a trifle tense, don't you think?"

"After murdering her lover she should be relaxed?" Schmidt demanded at the top of his voice.

Tony and I fell on him and carried him away.

"That's a libelous statement," Tony muttered, as we propelled Schmidt up the stairs. "Two libelous statements, in fact."

"Just one," I said. "She and Freddy were

lovers, all right. But she didn't kill him. She may not even know he's dead."

"Shall we tell her?" Tony asked. We shoved Schmidt into the room and closed the door.

"The less anybody tells anybody, the better off we are," I said sweepingly.

"That is a premise that can be carried too far," Schmidt grumbled. "You carry it too far."

"You know everything I know," I assured him mendaciously. "But for the love of Mike, don't blab to Friedl. I'll be damned if I can figure her out. Does she want us to go or stay? She sure didn't try to change my mind."

"She doesn't know her own mind," Tony said. "She isn't the one who is making the decisions."

I smiled approvingly at him. "You aren't as naïve as you look."

"I never said Friedl wasn't a crook; I said we couldn't be certain."

"I'm certain. And," I continued, before Tony could object, "you're right about her taking orders from someone else. Too bad we can't listen in on her phone. I'll bet she is passing on the latest news right now."

"Ha," said Schmidt. "You are again interested. You will not abandon—"

"Dammit, there is nothing to abandon! Oh, the hell with it. I'm off to the cemetery."

A procession of hotel employees carrying

cartons of papers arrived, and Schmidt and I left Tony gloomily contemplating the collection. Schmidt went with me to my room while I got my jacket and backpack; then he followed me downstairs and out of the hotel.

"You are really going only to put flowers on the poor old gentleman's grave?" he inquired.

"I really am."

"Not that I can believe you. But if you don't care if I come, then it means you are not going to do anything I want to do. All the same, Vicky, I will come."

"You're a suspicious old goat. Come if you like."

"No, that is not why. You go alone to this place so far from the village. I will come to protect you."

The idea of danger hadn't occurred to me until he mentioned it. I didn't know whether to scold him for scaring me or kiss him for caring. I kissed him on his bald head and arranged his cap to cover his ears. "You're a sweetie, Schmidt."

"I thought I was a suspicious old goat. I would not mind the rest so much if you did not always say 'old.' "

" 'Old' doesn't mean 'old.' " It means — it's a term of affectionate...of friendly...oh, never mind, Schmidt. I won't say it again, I promise.

Don't worry about me, I'll be fine."

He remained dubious; I had to pretend to see Perlmutter skulking in the distance before he would leave. "I will pursue," he exclaimed. "In that shop, you say?"

"No, he went up the street — that one. Hurry, Schmidt, before he gets away."

Off Schmidt scuttled, approximately as inconspicuous as a carnival balloon.

The clear bright skies were being invaded by herds of elephant-sized clouds. Some squatted on the mountains, hiding the high peaks; others moved sluggishly westward, swelling and multiplying. I had not been looking forward to the expedition and the dismal skies didn't increase my enthusiasm; but I had promised, and there was no sense postponing the job.

However, the idea of a little company had its appeal. I strolled across the square and made my way to the back of the wood shop. Clara was already there, staring at the closed panel with that ineffable air of concentrated expectation at which cats excel, and which seems to say, louder than speech, "If I wait long enough and hope hard enough, the anticipated miracle will occur — the door will open, herring will rain from the heavens, and I will be welcomed with the enthusiastic noises that are only my due."

It's sad to see such religious devotion go for nought. I knocked on the door. The cat didn't look at me, she was concentrating on expectation. After a while I remarked, "He's not there."

Clara didn't believe it. A piercing Siamese wail berated the cruelty of heaven.

Her howls produced no more result than my knocking. Either John was out or he didn't want to see either of us. The former conclusion seemed more likely, since, as he was well aware, prolonged complaint from the cat might arouse the curiosity of the neighbors.

So much for John. He was never around when you needed him.

The cat followed me down the garden path and along the alley. She stayed close at my heels while I canvassed the shops for wreaths. When I opened the car door, she flowed in and sat down in the passenger seat.

I have driven with cats before, or tried to; most of them like to get into cars, but they do not like to ride in cars. I reached across and rolled down the window on the passenger side, expecting Clara would hop out as soon as I started the engine. She didn't budge, even when I backed out of the parking space and turned into the street leading to the highway.

The clouds darkened and sagged lower. The cat started to purr.

Well, I had wanted company. Clara wasn't exactly what I had had in mind, but she was better than nothing. I hoped.

The main road into and out of Bad Steinbach wasn't a four-lane superhighway; but it looked like an autobahn compared to the narrow lane into which Müller's directions led me. It switched back and forth across the slopes of the Hexenhut, winding steadily upward between tall trees whose shadows turned the cloudy day to twilight dusk. I switched on my lights; the twisting of the road sent shadows darting, like sylvan monsters trying to elude the light. The cat kept purring. My skin started to crawl.

The old man had said, "You can't miss it," and he was right. Eventually I emerged from the trees onto a brief stretch of level ground — not the summit of the mountain, but a largish ledge, shaped like a half-moon and less than two acres in extent. The road skirted one side of it and then appeared to end, against the open sky. I cleverly deduced that there was a steep descent beyond.

I turned off the road and stopped the engine. In the silence the cat's hoarse purring seemed uncannily loud.

Straight ahead the mountainside rose, forming a natural wall around the scattered graves.

Tall trees marched up in stately parade; above and beyond, a wide swath of treeless white curved around the mountain's flank and then swung away, out of sight – the ski slope from the summit of the Hexenhut. I had not realized it came so close to the church. I had never skied that stretch, actually, and even if I had, I would have had no reason to observe the church.

It wasn't much. Perched uneasily on the edge of the drop, where the crumbled remains of a stone wall marked the far edge of the cemetery, it had neither age nor architectural distinction. Not even the usual onion dome, only a stubby broken tower. The windows were boarded up and snow had drifted against the walls.

I opened the car door. The silence was deafening. From where I was standing, I couldn't see the ski lift or the ski lodge atop the mountain. It seemed impossible that less than a mile away there were people laughing and talking and drinking beer.

The place was like a black-and-white photograph; there was no color anywhere, only shades of gray. Nothing moved except the scudding clouds and the tree branches swaying gently in the wind.

Then I saw that I was not the only one to remember the dead at the season of the Redeemer's birth. A few graves — a pitiful few — were blanketed and trimmed with boughs. The brave red bows and bright berries were like a snatch of song in a charnel house — or whistling in the dark?

I realized there were tears on my cheeks. Sheer terror, perhaps? I wiped them away with gloved hands, took a firmer grip on my wreaths, and set out across the snow.

The atmosphere was so thick I wouldn't have been surprised to see the cat unerringly select the grave of her master and fling herself down on the mounded earth like the dog in that morose old Scottish story. (Greyfriars Bobby was the name, I think.) Of course, she did nothing of the sort. While I searched for Hoffman's grave, she went wandering off in search of prey. But all the little mice and moles were tucked snug in their winter beds; when I finally reached my goal, Clara came to stand beside me.

It should not have taken me so long to find the right stone. It was the newest one in the graveyard, an austere dark granite slab with no epitaph, only the names and the dates. Hoffman must have had it prepared when his wife died. The carved lines giving the date of his death were raw and fresh compared to the other lettering.

The plot was enclosed by a low wrought-iron

railing, which I discovered by tripping over it; it was entirely concealed by fallen snow. The other stones in the enclosure belonged to members of the same family — Frau Hoffman's, according to Müller. The oldest visible date was that of a Georg Meindl, who had been born in 1867. There were probably older stones, now fallen and snow-shrouded.

After I had clumsily propped the wreaths against the tombstone I lingered, feeling as if there were something more I ought to do. I'm not much for praying, so I just stood shivering and wishing there were some truth in the wistful age-old desire for communication with the dead.

The Meindl plot was one of the ones farthest from the entrance to the cemetery. From where I was standing I could see clear out across the neighboring valley; a small settlement below looked like a toy village and, beyond it, another ridge of mountains raised dark, snow-streaked barriers. Apparently the road I had traveled descended from this point. A few of the lower loops were visible, but the section nearest me was hidden by the remains of the wall.

My wreath was the only memorial on the mounded earth above his grave. It looked cold and lonely; only the dainty footprints of the cat crisscrossed the white covering. The funeral flowers had been tidied away after they withered – probably by poor old Herr Müller. *She* wouldn't have bothered. Thank heaven for the kindliness of snow; it covered raw earth and weedy neglect with a benign white mantle.

Frau Hoffman's grave was equally stark at this season, but there were pathetic evidences of someone's tending. The stem of a small climbing rose twined around the dark granite. The rose was brown and leafless now, but during the past summer the green leaves and small fragrant blossoms would have softened the starkness of the stone. Dried brown flower heads protruded from the snow – not weeds, as I had thought, but chrysanthemums and asters – autumn flowers.

The cat ambled up to see what was taking me so long. A gust of icy wind rattled the dead stalks. She sat up on her haunches and swiped at a swaying flowerhead. I moved instinctively to stop her, but she scampered away from my hand, and I stood back, smiling wryly. Hoffman wouldn't mind. Life goes on. Better a warm living creature, rolling and playing, than silence and icy winds.

Clara had gone into a feline frenzy, rotating in a vain attempt to catch her tail, brushing the snow aside in a wide patch that bared the withered flowers and frozen earth. A white protrusion caught my eye and I bent to examine it.

It was a bulb — probably a daffodil, to judge from its size. Freezing, the ground had heaved and thrust the bulb out and upward. One less flower to brighten the springtime and testify to the hope of resurrection; it would never survive the winter's cold, exposed and vulnerable as it was. I knelt, thinking I would replant it, but the ground was frozen hard as stone.

Bad Steinbach looked like a teeming metropolis after the loneliness of the cemetery. I was glad to be back in civilization unscathed. My shoulders ached; I realized I had been driving with my head pulled in like a turtle's, in anticipation of attack. Thank you, Herr Professor Schmidt.

The town was livelier than usual, and as I watched people bustling around, setting up scaffolding and booths and arranging benches under the arcade, I remembered there was some sort of festival that night. *Weihnacht, fröhliche Weihnacht*...Mine wasn't looking very *fröhlich* at the moment, what with a frozen body in my garden at home and a number of live bodies harassing me in Bad Steinbach.

I opened the car door. The cat jumped out and went swaggering off, without so much as a thank-you for the ride or a backward glance. I wondered whether she would find John at home.

When I asked for my key, the clerk gave me a handful of messages. The first was from Tony. "Dieter and Elise came by, have gone skiing, we'll be at the Kreuzeck, why don't you join us?" I crumpled it and went to the next, which read, "Astonishing news! Have made great discovery! Come instantly to my room!"

The other slips of paper were telephone messages, all of them from Schmidt, all of them demanding I present myself instantly. "What the devil—" I said involuntarily.

"The *Herr* returned an hour ago and left the message," the clerk said wearily. "He has telephoned your room every ten minutes since. If you would be so kind, *gnädiges Fräulein—*"

I promised I would put a stop to Schmidt, and headed for the stairs. Schmidt and his astonishing discoveries; he had probably spotted all the members of the Politbüro lurking around Bad Steinbach.

Since he didn't have a room in the hotel, I assumed he meant Tony's, so I went there. A hearty *"Herein, bitte,"* answered my knock. I opened the door.

Schmidt was eating, of course. *Brotzeit.* The table was covered with beer bottles and plates, and across from Schmidt was Jan Perlmutter.

Schmidt greeted me with a shriek of pleasure. "It is you at last; I thought it was the room service. Look, Vicky — see — I have captured him!"

Jan rose to his feet and made me a stiff, formal little bow. *"Guten Tag, Fräulein Doktor.* I must protest the Herr Direktor's statement. It is not accurate. To say that he captured me is a falsification of the facts."

I studied him thoughtfully. "I liked you better as a blond, Jan."

"That is easily remedied," Jan said, straight-faced. "I am wearing a wig." He pulled it off.

"And a rotten wig it is. Is that the best a socialist Soviet republic can do?"

Jan looked blank. Dieter was right; the man had absolutely no sense of humor. But the tight golden curls clung damply to his beautiful skull and he looked good enough to eat. I smiled at him. "Sit down, Jan."

Jan sat. "He did not capture me. When I recognized the distinguished director of the National Museum..."

"I overpowered him," Schmidt explained, brandishing his beer stein. "With a chop to the throat and a partial nelson to the leg. I then applied a hammer-bolt and forced him to return here with me."

I said, "Shut up, Schmidt. All right, Jan, I

gather you were about to make a statement. Proceed."

"I will begin at the beginning," Jan said.

Well, he tried. The man had a logical mind; it wasn't his fault that Schmidt kept interrupting.

He began by taking a piece of cardboard from his breast pocket and handing it to me. "Yes," I said. "It's Frau Schliemann. . . . My God. It *is* Frau Schliemann!"

"Who?" Schmidt leaned forward and peered over my shoulder. *"Herr Gott!* This is not the same —"

"Schmidt, will you please refrain from unnecessary comments? Go on, Jan. Where did you get this?"

It had come to him in the mail. Unlike my photograph of the lady who was *not* Frau Schliemann, this offering had something written on the back. "What happened to the Trojan gold? Inquire of A. Hoffman, former assistant curator of the Staatliches Museum, Berlin 1939, now owner-manager of the Gasthaus Hexenhut, Bad Steinbach."

"Now you understand why I am here," said Jan solemnly.

"I'm damned if I do."

"But — did you not receive a similar communication?"

Schmidt's mouth opened. I put a doughnut in it. "Even if I had," I said truthfully, "I wouldn't have assumed it was an oracle from on high."

"You don't understand," said Jan.

"I told you I didn't."

What I failed to understand was that East German scholars, particularly those of the Berlin museums, had developed a mild neurosis about the Trojan gold. They knew the Russians didn't have it, which put them one up on the rest of us and also added to the mystery. Jan's boss, the director of the Bode Museum, was particularly sensitive about the subject; the very mention of Troy, Schliemann, or Helen initiated a fit of twitching and mumbling. So as soon as the photograph arrived, Jan carried it dutifully to his superior.

Schmidt couldn't let that pass. "Ha, I knew he would not have the initiative to come here on his own. They cannot go to the toilet without permission. However, Vicky, there is something admirable about the loyalty of a subordinate to—"

"Never mind, Schmidt," I said. "Are you telling me your boss fell for this yarn, Jan?"

Not only did he fall for it; the old boy practically had a stroke. He had been on the staff of the museum and had known Hoffman well.

After the war he hadn't bothered to look him up, since the relationship had been purely professional; if he thought about the matter at all, he assumed Hoffman had been killed. When Jan assured him that Hoffman had been rusticating in Bavaria for over forty years, he thought the circumstances curious enough to merit investigation. And, as Jan modestly remarked, who was better qualified than he to investigate? The letter had been addressed to him, he knew Hoffman personally — and he also knew the five other scholars who had stayed at the Gasthaus Hexenhut.

Not that Jan actually made that last statement. He didn't have to; I knew as well as if I had been sitting in on the discussion that this factor had been raised and debated. Jan was no dumbbell; he must have suspected he might not be the only one to receive a message.

He was rattling merrily along, his crisp curls coiling tighter as they dried, and he looked so beautiful I hated to scuttle his story. But I forced myself.

"Just an innocent little inquiry," I said. "All open and aboveboard."

"*Aber natürlich*. I have done nothing against the law—"

"Then why the wig? Why were you trailing me in Munich? Oh yes, you were, Jan; I saw you. What were you up to, that you didn't want to be recognized?"

I would like to say that Jan's reaction typified the police-state mentality, but I'm afraid it is typical of people in general: When somebody catches you pulling a dirty trick, blame them.

"You were conspiring against me," Jan said sulkily.

"Me and who else? Him?" I indicated Schmidt.

Jan shook his head. "No. Of course, your superior would be in your confidence. I did not blame you for that."

"Ha," said Schmidt, giving me a meaningful look.

"But when I saw Dieter enter the museum, and then Tony came, all the way from America, I knew all of you were together, against me. The Western capitalist oppressors—"

"That is a flat-out lie," I said indignantly.

"Yes? But they are here now, and also Elise and the Herr Direktor. For what have you come if it is not to steal the treasure from me?"

Schmidt emitted one of his fat, rich chuckles. "It has a suspicious look, Vicky. Admit it."

"Well...I suppose if someone has a strong streak of paranoia to begin with..."

Schmidt's open amusement went farther than my righteous indignation to convince Jan. He looked uncertainly from Schmidt to me.

"Are you telling me it is only a coincidence that you have met her? That you are not—"

"Conspiring? Hell, no, we aren't even co-operating! Nobody has the faintest idea of what anybody else is doing. I don't even know what *I'm* doing."

Jan studied me solemnly. Then his lips parted and stretched into one of his rare smiles. The effect was dazzling. "I am inclined to believe you."

"How very condescending."

"But, Vicky, you are the one I would have expected to be best informed. You knew the old man best; it was to you he talked, sent flowers—"

"You make it sound like some sort of November-June romance," I snapped. "We did talk. But he never mentioned the gold, Jan. Believe it or not."

"I do believe it. Because if he had told you then, you would not be here now." Jan leaned back in his chair and put his fingertips together pyramid-style, like Holmes getting ready to enlighten poor thick-headed Watson. His smile continued to dazzle, but his eyes were as hard and opaque as brown pebbles. "I will tell you what else I believe," he went on. "I believe you were all summoned here, as I was summoned. That Hoffman intended to divulge

293

to us the secret he had guarded for so many years. We are in a sense an international committee, representing some of the world's great museums, and he knew us personally. But Hoffman's death frustrated his intention. So now we are assembled, as he wished us to be, and the treasure is still missing. You don't know where it is either. I have observed you, all of you. Your actions have been as aimless and undirected as my own."

"Humph," Schmidt grunted. "He is no fool, this one."

I was forced to agree. Jan's theory was one that had not occurred to me — nor to the great John Smythe. It left a few minor odds and ends unaccounted for — like the frozen corpse in the back yard — but it had merit.

However, I was not moved to take Jan into my confidence and clasp him to my bosom (tempting as that idea might be). For once I didn't have to warn Schmidt to avoid the same error. His little blue eyes narrowed to slits, and he rumbled, "Yes, he is no fool. Watch out, Vicky. Next he will suggest we puddle our information—"

"Pool," I said. "Not puddle, Schmidt. Pool."

"But is not that the most logical thing to do?" Jan asked guilelessly. "Working together we may achieve what none of us can do alone. We are scholars, not criminals; our aim should be to restore a treasure that belongs, not to any individual, but to the world."

Schmidt's reaction to this beautiful sentiment was open-mouthed indignation. I looked around for something to put in his mouth before he could put his foot in it. However, he had eaten everything. So I kicked him in the ankle, and he began swearing in fluent *Mittelhochdeutsch*.

"I have no quarrel with your reasoning, Jan," I said. "But I'm afraid the cause is as hopeless as it is noble. As you have seen for yourself, I have no idea where to look. There are thousands of square miles of mountain scenery out there."

"So what do you suggest?" Jan asked.

"Me?" I opened my big blue eyes wide and looked innocent. "I'm baffled, Jan. So, as long as I'm here, I figure I might as well stay for a few days and enjoy some skiing and some Christmas cheer. The others will be going on to Turin on the twenty-seventh. I will return to my job — which I have rather neglected lately — and forget the whole thing."

"I see," Jan said slowly.

"You're welcome to join the crowd," I went on. "There's some sort of festival here this evening; I think Elise and Dieter are planning to have dinner with us and watch the show."

"Perhaps I will do that."

"Good. But – this is only a suggestion, of course – I don't think you ought to discuss this with the others. They are even more baffled than I am."

He agreed to meet us at the hotel at six. We parted with many expressions of good will.

After I had ushered him out, I turned to Schmidt, who was methodically finishing his catalogue of Middle-High-German obscenities. One advantage of an advanced education is that it provides you with such an extensive list of languages to swear in.

"Now what's the matter with you?" I demanded. "That little nudge didn't hurt."

"I am angry with you," Schmidt explained. "Vicky, you are a fool; don't you know that when a Communist invites you to share a meal with him, he is planning to eat your food and his own?"

"That evil suspicion did occur to me, Schmidt."

"He will give nothing away. He only wishes to pick your brain."

"There's nothing in my brain to pick."

"Humph," said Schmidt.

"It should be amusing," I said dreamily. "He'll be looking for hidden meanings in everything we say. Finding them, too, I expect."

"Your idea of amusement is very strange," Schmidt grumbled. "Why are you sitting here?

Why don't you follow him?"

"Why should I?"

"Because he...because you..." Schmidt bounced up. "If you don't, I will."

"Have fun."

"Humph," said Schmidt. Snatching his cap, he trotted to the door.

He opened it; then he stood back. Clara sauntered in, her tail swinging. *"Guten Tag,"* Schmidt said absently, and proceeded on his way.

"He wasn't home?" I asked.

The cat didn't reply. Jumping onto the bed, she clawed one of Tony's shirts into a nest, lay down on it, and went to sleep.

The beds had been made, but Schmidt and Tony had managed to create considerable havoc. Cast-off clothing littered the bed and the floor, the crumbs of Schmidt's snack were scattered far and wide, and poor Hoffman's private papers were all over the place. The majority of them had been returned to the cartons, not too neatly; I had the impression that they had been tossed there in frustrated disgust. Others littered the chairs and the beds.

I glanced through one of the untidy piles. It consisted of a dunning letter to a guest whose check had bounced, a receipt from an antique shop in Garmisch, and bills from several record shops. Poor Tony. No wonder he had given up in despair and gone skiing.

What to do, what to do? The long empty afternoon was mine to do with as I wished, but none of the options attracted me. Skiing with Tony and the others, in the gray, flat light that skiers particularly hate — with Elise glowering at me and Dieter arranging pratfalls for me and Tony sulking because he spent more time on his backside than on his skis...Pounding on the door of the house where John squatted like a toad in its hole? He probably wouldn't let me in, which would hurt my ego, or else he would let me in, and I would end up doing something I would regret.

To my disgust I realized that while my mind was wandering, my hands had been busy, tidying up the room. That's what early childhood conditioning does. I noticed with sour amusement that the sweater I had just rescued from the floor was the one Ann had made with her own fair hands. She'd have a fit if she saw how cavalierly Tony treated her love-offering; it smelled faintly of the beer I had spilled the previous day. I wondered if Ann sewed cute little tags onto her creations — a picture of crossed knitting needles and a motto, "From the needles of..."

There was a tag at the back of the neck, all

298

right. The sweater had been handmade. In Taiwan.

I stood quite still, clutching the sweater and trying to talk myself out of my evil-minded suspicions. There were a dozen different explanations for the discrepancy, the most obvious being that this was not the same sweater. My good angel, my better self, asked piously, "What difference does it make?" My other self — the one with the higher IQ — knew it did make a difference. And it knew how to ascertain the truth.

I dropped the sweater onto the floor and kicked it for good measure.

At first I thought it would be safer to make the call from a public phone, but after some reflection, I realized that it wouldn't matter if the conversation was overheard because it wouldn't mean anything to anyone except me — and Tony. So I went to my own room and put through a call to Munich. Some people might have taken advantage of the boss's absence to indulge in a long lunch hour, but not Gerda. She was there. However, she was not noble enough to refrain from pointing out at some length that while she was at her desk, working her little heart out, certain other people were gadding around enjoying themselves.

"Where?" she demanded. "Where are you? You left me no number, no forwarding address. What am I to do when people ask how to reach you?"

"Has anyone tried to reach me?" I asked, with a sudden uneasy recollection of the corpse in the garden.

"*Nein*. Not yet. But it is not professional, what you do—"

She went on scolding, and I went on thinking about Freddy. I am a great believer in not troubling trouble until it comes troubling you, and I certainly didn't owe Freddy anything — I had a strong suspicion he was the one who had tried to send me and Schmidt shuffling off this mortal coil — but I hated to think of him lying there cold and unwanted. It was the cold that had kept him from being discovered. If the temperature rose...

I didn't want to think about that. I said, "Gerda, will you look something up for me?"

Gerda loves being useful. She has her own little reference shelf, right beside her desk, and it only took a few minutes for her to find the information I needed, in the National Faculty Directory.

I thanked her and hung up before she could repeat her demand for an address and phone number.

So simple, and so damning. Professor James Belfort of the Mathematics Department at Granstock and his wife Louise had no children. Tony had lied to me from the beginning. Not only was Ann no knitter, she wasn't even a person.

EIGHT

I was on the bed, flat on my back with the cat on my stomach, when Tony walked in. The early winter dusk had descended, and I hadn't bothered to turn on a light. He fell over a chair, swore, fell over a table, swore, and finally found the light switch. I deduced that he had not expected to find me in residence, because he jumped nervously and let out a yelp when he saw me.

"What the hell...Are you all right? Is something the matter, Vicky? Are you sick?" He clumped to the bed leaving damp footprints across the floor, and put an icy hand on my forehead.

"I'm fine," I said. His fingers felt like those of a corpse. "Just thinking."

"You and Sherlock Holmes." Tony sat down on the edge of the bed. He was in a high good humor, so I deduced he had not sprained or broken anything that day. "I don't buy this sedentary ratiocination technique, Vicky; you'll never learn anything if you lie around here."

"You're leaking all over the bed," I said irritably. "Get up."

"It's just melted snow."

"I know it's melted snow, that's what I'm objecting to. Get up."

Tony rose to his full height.

"What time is it?" I asked, yawning.

"A little after five. Dieter and Elise are joining us as soon as they change. Listen, Vicky, I found out something—"

"I suggest you emulate them," I said, looking critically at the puddle forming around his feet.

"I will in a minute. I want to tell you what I found out—"

"Jan Perlmutter will be here at six."

"While you were lying here in slothful ease I found out...What? Perlmutter? Where? Here? How—"

"Schmidt captured him — or vice versa." Tony stood there melting and looking chagrined while I explained. I did not feel guilty for spoiling his big news. During my hours of cogitation, I had decided not to confront him with his low-down lies. There might be an innocent explanation, but I couldn't think of one, and I was very hurt by his behavior. If I couldn't trust Tony, whom could I trust?

Sir John Smythe? I had been a fool to suppose the leopard had changed its spots. Worse —

303

a besotted fool, so bemused by John Donne and his disciple that I hadn't noticed the fatal slip until long afterward. Perhaps John had been a little bemused too; it wasn't like him to be so careless. More likely he was just getting old. I would like to live to see the day when John alias Smythe let a woman cloud his crystal-clear selfishness.

I couldn't trust Schmidt either. He would double-cross me without a moment's hesitation if he could talk himself into believing he was doing it for my own good. Just as I would do it to him.

I couldn't trust anybody. And after all the efforts I had made to keep Tony safe and un-witting...

The narrative took the wind out of his sails in another way. Jan's theory anticipated the one Tony had cleverly formulated after talking with Dieter. "He and Elise both got copies of that photograph," Tony informed me.

"Oh, yeah?"

"I expected a little more enthusiasm. Even, perhaps, a touch of admiration. Something like 'Oh, Tony, how clever,' or 'Tony, you never cease to amaze me—'"

"You never do," I said grimly. "So you spilled your guts to Dieter and Elise?"

"Why not?"

"Why not?" I echoed. "Why not indeed? Why ever not?"

"You *are* sick," Tony said.

I pushed his hand away. "I'm not sick. Keep your clammy hands off me. So. Dieter and Elise are on the trail, too. Separately or in collusion?

Tony scratched his head. "They seem to be colluding now. It was Dieter's expedition to begin with. Elise paid no attention to the photograph — thought, as I did, that it was a typical crank communication."

"There was no message on hers?"

"I guess not. There certainly wasn't on mine. Dieter..." Tony pondered. "He didn't say exactly, but there must have been something. He called Elise and got her interested; talked her into joining him here."

"The sly little rascal," I said. "He certainly didn't invite me to collude with him."

"You don't collude well," Tony said with a grin. "Dieter likes to be Chief; Elise makes a better Indian than you." Then he added generously, "That's a good point; I should have asked Dieter how he knew it was Hoffman who sent the photograph."

"The same way Jan did, I expect."

"That's odd, though," Tony said. "Why would Hoffman give Perlmutter and Dieter leads he didn't give the rest of us?"

"I don't know."

I had another question, but I wasn't about to ask Tony – not since I had learned that Ann was a figment of his imagination. Perlmutter's photograph had been of Frau Schliemann, not Frau Hoffman. Maybe jerky Helene had been right about Tony's photo after all. What about Dieter and Elise – Frau Hoffman or Frau Schliemann? I would try to find out, though God knows why; I couldn't think what it might mean, if anything.

"A committee." Tony was communing with himself. "That makes sense, you know."

"Maybe it makes sense to you. Go drip on your own floor, Tony. I want to change."

"It is my floor," Tony said indignantly. With the air of a squatter establishing property rights, he dropped his soggy jacket onto said floor.

"Oh. So it is. I forgot I was in your room."

Tony unzipped his ski pants and tried to step out of them. Since he had neglected to remove his heavy, wet boots, the pants only wadded up around his calves. "You needn't be coy with me, Vicky," he said tenderly, struggling with the pants. "When I realized you were here waiting for me – Hey, don't go. I want–"

Though he was effectively pinned to the spot by the wet cloth around his feet, he has very long arms; one of them reached me as I was sidling toward the door and spun me neatly back into a fond embrace. It would have been as pretty as an old Astaire-and-Rogers routine had it not been for the fact I wasn't feeling as friendly as Ginger, and the additional fact that Tony's feet were immobilized. We toppled over onto the bed in a flurry of arms and bodies and breathless dialogue, profane on my part, conciliatory on Tony's, just as Schmidt walked in.

Instead of tactfully retiring, or bursting into laughter, either of which would have been appropriate, Schmidt rubbed his hands together and beamed from ear to ear. "Ah, it is nice to see you so friendly together. Don't mind Papa Schmidt, just go on with what you were doing."

This cooled Tony's ardor as effectively as the elbow I had placed under his chin. He stopped thrashing around and I assumed my feet.

"If we had been doing what you thought we were doing, which we weren't, we certainly wouldn't go on doing it with you refereeing from the sidelines."

"Then what were you doing?" Schmidt asked curiously.

Tony lay motionless, his arms over his face, like a dead knight on the battlefield. I'm not as hardhearted as I'd like to be. The total humiliation of the man moved me; I knelt at his feet and began working him out of his boots. It was a complicated procedure, since everything was soaking wet and his terpsichorean efforts had twisted his pants into overlapping coils.

"We were discussing the case," I said. "I told him about Perlmutter....Where did he go, Schmidt?"

"I lost him," Schmidt admitted. "I made a mistake, you see. I should have adopted a disguise. He had seen me in this suit—"

"Yes, that's all right," I said abstractedly.

Schmidt bent over Tony, lifted one arm, and peered down into his face. "Did you learn anything from Hoffman's papers, *mein Freund?*"

"No," Tony muttered. Schmidt let go of his arm, which dropped with force enough to make Tony grunt. "There's nothing there," I said.

Tony sat up. "So that's why you were here. Can't you trust me to do a job right?"

"No," I said coldly. "Damn it, there goes a fingernail. Take your own damned clothes off."

"Such language does not become a lady," Schmidt remarked.

"I don't give a—"

"Nothing?" Schmidt picked up a handful of papers and began looking through them. "Nothing at all? No maps, no keys for storage lockers, no code messages?" Neither Tony nor

I felt it necessary to dignify this question with a reply. Schmidt went on, "But what is this? *Ach, Gott,* it is a love letter! 'To my adored, my own Helen...' Ha, but that is significant! There is no Helen in the case. Had this dignified old gentleman a mistress, then? She may know—"

I took the paper from Schmidt's hand. "It's to his wife," I said. "There were only a few letters; I guess they weren't often parted. But she kept them, tied up with a blue ribbon."

"Oh." Schmidt's eyes filled. "How touching. Her name was Helen?"

"No, it was Amelie. Helen was his pet name for her. He quotes Goethe and Marlowe — 'Was this the face that launch'd a thousand ships...' Oh, stop blubbering, Schmidt, or you'll get me started. You're a sentimental old — a sentimental fool."

It wasn't Schmidt's easy tears that roughened my voice; it was the memory of the woman's face in the photograph. There had been beauty in that lined face once, at least to the eyes of the man who loved her.

I gathered up the rest of the letters. "I'm going to burn these," I said. "Friedl should have had the decency to do it, instead of handing them over to strangers."

Schmidt approved. Tony did not express any

opinion. He was still struggling with his boots when I left them.

I hadn't brought a dress, since I had not expected to attend any formal social functions. I rather wished I had when I saw Elise dolled up in mink and four-inch heels, but the weakness was fleeting; competition on that level is something I avoid, all the more readily because I don't own a mink coat. It did occur to me to wonder how Elise could afford one.

Dieter was sporting a Groucho Marx nose with attached mustache — a modest effort, for Dieter. When someone (me) objected, he said it was *Weihnacht,* and there would be other masked and costumed revelers in the crowd that evening. I doubted it; but Schmidt's face assumed a wistful expression. He asked Dieter where he had procured the nose, and they entered into an animated discussion of costume and magic shops that sold ghastly props for practical jokers.

Schmidt, who loves parties and is generous to a fault, had reserved a table and ordered champagne. Tony said very little. He was still annoyed with me, and he didn't care much for Elise. She appeared to be in a bad mood, too. Under her mink she was wearing a slinky black cocktail dress spattered with sequins — very inappropriate, in my opinion. Glancing at the unoccupied chair, she said disagreeably, "Is this for the skeleton at the feast?"

"No," I said. "We're expecting someone else. Jan Perlmutter."

That distracted Dieter from the subject of whoopee cushions. "Jan? He is here?" Unexpectedly, he began to laugh.

"What's so funny?" Tony asked sourly.

Dieter took off his nose and wiped his eyes. "You don't see how comical it is? All of us skulking about in disguise, keeping secrets from each other. It is most comical for Jan, he is naturally a spy at heart. How did you flush him out?"

Puffing himself up, Schmidt gave his version of the "capture." Dieter shouted with laughter. "Yes, it is very funny. Poor Jan, how his pride must be hurt. He hoped to find the prize and make off with it before we could stop him."

"Didn't we all?" I asked, glancing at Tony, who scowled back at me.

"Of course," Dieter said cheerfully. "Can you imagine the legal battles if it were found? Everyone has a claim – the Greeks, the Turks, the Germans – and the Metropolitan Museum or the Getty Museum would try to buy it; they have the most money to spend. But if one of us said, 'Ha, here it is, I have it, now what are you going to do?' it would not be easy to take it away. And if it were in East Berlin—"

"Sssh," I said. "Here he comes."

"Why should I ssssh?" Dieter demanded. "I don't say anything I wouldn't say to him. Ha, Jan, old comrade, how are things in the beautiful socialist society, eh? Have you won your dasha on the Black Sea yet?"

"No," Jan said. *"Guten Abend, Elise, Vicky, meine Herren."* Elise gave him a languid hand, and he bent over it, obviously relieved that someone was doing the proper thing.

"But how lovely to see you again, Jan," Elise murmured. "Vicky, why don't you move over, then Jan can sit between us? It is more suitable than having two ladies together."

In my opinion, it was questionable as to whether either of us qualified, but I did as she asked, and Jan sat down. They made a nice couple; unlike the other men, Jan was formally attired in a gray three-piece suit and a somber dark tie. He only needed a black armband to complete the picture, but even the rotten tailoring and dismal color couldn't mar Jan's absurd good looks. He'd look divine in the clothes like those of the King in the painting — rich brocades and glowing colors, and the chaperon headdress, with its graceful hanging drapery.

Tony on my other side gave me a sharp jab

in the ribs, and I realized that a silence had fallen over the table. Several people started talking at once; out of the corner of his mouth Tony muttered, "You look like a groupie staring at a rock star. Stop making a fool of yourself."

"I'll have plenty of help," I said.

Dieter banged on the table. "A toast," he exclaimed, raising his glass. "Let us drink to... to Heinrich Schliemann!"

Schmidt giggled and Tony's tight lips relaxed. Jan nodded gravely; but after Elise had drained her glass, she said pettishly, "I say to hell with Heinrich Schliemann. He started this—"

"Yes, but you can't blame him," said Dieter. He leaned over and planted a wet, smacking kiss on her cheek. "It is my fault you are here, *Herzgeliebte,* so you should say to hell with Dieter."

"To hell with Dieter," Elise said. I realized she was a little drunk. She must have downed a few before joining us.

Jan ignored the byplay. "I am glad you have decided to be candid," he said, addressing the table at large. "As I said to Vicky today, it is foolish we should not cooperate."

"To hell with cooperation," Elise muttered. "I think you are all crazy. This is a wild-goose chase; we are wasting our time."

"Oh, you hurt me," Dieter exclaimed, clutching his heart. "I have not wasted my time, *Schatzie*. What is the harm in this, if it gives us a pleasant holiday? Here — have more champagne."

"I believe I will," Elise said.

"You claim this is for you only a pleasant holiday?" Jan demanded, frowning. "You refuse to—"

"Oh, don't be such a suspicious old Marxist," Dieter said. "No one is trying to put one over on you, Jan. We came here for the same reason — we admit that — and now we know we have arrived at a dead end. Is that not so? Hoffman is dead, the treasure is hidden, if it was ever here to begin with, and that is all there is to it. Now I say forget it, enjoy yourself."

"But—" Jan began.

"But nothing. Have you an idea, a theory, you would like to propose? No? And you, Vicky — you, Tony?..." His bright, amused eyes moved around the table. "And you, Dieter? Dieter says no, he has no idea either. So let's forget it and have fun, eh?"

"Amen to that," Elise said loudly.

The arrival of the first course put an end to the discussion, if not to the disagreement. The band arrived, and began playing — a bizarre mixture of American soft rock and schmaltzy Bavarian waltzes. Filled with food and drink, especially the latter, Tony asked me to dance. I declined; Tony is even more of a menace on the dance floor than he is on skis. So he asked Elise, out of spite, and she was delighted to accept.

Dieter and Schmidt had gone back to discussing disguises, which left me tête-à-tête with Jan. He ate in silence for a while; then the band broke into a waltz — I think it was a waltz — and Jan said solemnly, "Will you honor me?"

"Why not?" I said.

The dance floor was so full we couldn't do much but stand in one spot and sway back and forth. Jan swayed rather nicely; I told him so, and he returned the compliment. He was holding me even closer than the crowded conditions demanded, and when his hand began making what my mother would have called "rude gestures," I said, amused, "I'm surprised at you, Jan."

"Surprised? That I am human, after all?" At close range the smile was drop-dead blinding. He went on, "Do you think I am some sort of machine? No, Vicky, I am a man; I feel as any man would feel in the company of a beautiful woman."

There was ample evidence of that. At that

interesting moment the music ended with a crash of cymbals, and Tony charged toward us, towing Elise, whom he thrust into Jan's arms. "Change partners?" he suggested.

Tony pressed me to his manly bosom and we went blundering around the floor to the strains of *"Du kannst nicht treu sein."* How appropriate, I thought sadly. How tragically, poignantly, painfully appropriate. Champagne always makes me sentimental.

Champagne makes Tony belligerent. "What were you doing with Jan?" he demanded. "You turn me down and then go groping around with that — that — You know what he's after, don't you?"

"The same thing I was after. We were both wasting our time, actually."

"Oh. You can't trust him, Vicky. He just wants—"

"Tony, will you try to get it into your head that this has turned into a farce? It's like one of those films about comic secret-service agents falling over each other's feet and out windows and into swimming pools."

We went back to the table. At least Schmidt was having a good time. Dieter appeared equally relaxed and happy, but Jan sat in frowning abstraction, replying to Elise's bright chatter with brusque monosyllables.

When we reached the coffee-and-dessert stage, I saw Friedl circulating among the guests like a good hostess. Hoffman had done the same thing, but with a grace and genuine good will his widow could only imitate, not emulate. Her smile was mechanical, her movements abrupt, and she kept glancing toward our table.

Jan had been watching her, too. "Is that Frau Hoffman?" he asked.

"She used to be a waitress. Don't you remember her?"

"No." Jan added, "One never looks at their faces, does one?"

"Especially not in Friedl's case."

"Bitte?" Jan said, looking puzzled.

"It was a joke, Jan. Not a very good one, though. Are you sure you don't remember her? She used to have brown hair — braids—"

"Oh, yes," Jan said indifferently. "She is the one who was Dieter's friend."

"Not yours?"

"I prefer tall blond ladies," said Jan, looking at me sentimentally.

I never know what to say to remarks like that; fortunately, they don't come my way very often. After a moment, Jan said in quite a different voice, "Surely he would confide in his wife."

Dieter caught the remark. "He would be a

fool if he confided in that one. She hasn't a brain in her head."

"Oh? And how do you know?" Jan demanded.

"Don't be such a self-righteous little puritan," Dieter said without rancor. "We all had a try for Friedl, including you; if you want to have another try, go ahead. But I can tell you, she would not be running this crummy little hotel in this dull little town if she knew where there was something of value to be sold. She would see her mother....Ah, Frau Hoffman! Please, won't you join us for a liquor? We are enjoying ourselves so much."

He liberated a chair from a nearby table and Friedl accepted the invitation with a gracious inclination of the head. Dieter, his round face now as lugubrious as an undertaker's, offered his condolences on her husband's death. A mildly embarrassed and wholly unconvincing murmur from the rest of us seconded the sentiment, which Friedl acknowledged with proper sobriety. Accepting a glass of brandy from Dieter, she said, "I remember all of you were here last year at this time. I hope you find everything satisfactory?"

We murmured at her again. "I am glad," she said. "It has been difficult for a woman alone. It is hard to get good help."

"But surely," Jan said, "many of the former

employees are still here. In such a small place, it is almost like a family, yes?"

I could see what he was thinking, the foxy devil. He was trying to find someone in whom Hoffman might have confided. It was the sort of thing a good thorough private investigator would do, but I had already considered the idea, and dismissed it. If Hoffman had not divulged the secret to his best friend, he was not likely to have confided in his cook or his driver.

Friedl answered him with a long string of complaints. Several of the older employees had left, the cook was threatening to quit, the younger ones preferred to work in Garmisch, where wages were higher and there was more excitement. Dieter patted her on the back in an avuncular fashion. "You are still young, Frau Hoffman. It is too soon to be thinking of such things, but believe me, time will heal your wounds. A woman of your attractions will not always be alone."

Friedl simpered. "You are very kind to say so, Herr Professor."

"But it is true. A little more brandy?"

He caught my disapproving eye and winked openly. His hand was still on Friedl's shoulder, squeezing and squirming in Dieteresque fashion. Friedl didn't object. She giggled and nodded.

"Humph!" said Schmidt, staring.

He wasn't the only one to find their behavior unbecoming. Elise said loudly, "We should leave if we want seats for the performance."

"There is plenty of time," Dieter said easily. "The seats are only for the town dignitaries; the rest of us commoners will mill around in a friendly confusion."

He handed Friedl her glass. Reaching for it, she was a little too eager — or perhaps her hand was a little too unsteady. Only a few drops of the liquid spilled, but one of Friedl's fake fingernails popped off and flew across the table, landing with a splash in Schmidt's coffee. His expression of disgust as he stared at his cup would have been funny if the whole performance had not been so repellent.

The incident put Schmidt off his food, and shortly thereafter, we left. Friedl tried to keep her hand out of sight, but I caught a glimpse of the denuded finger. The nail was bitten to the quick.

After the overheated, stale confines of the restaurant, the night air felt like wine. Clouds hid the winter stars, but the Marktplatz was as brilliant as a stage, and the dark slopes of the Hexenhut twinkled with lights like a giant Christmas tree. Even Elise forgot her ill humor.

"Oh, look," she cried, "what is it?"

"Torches," Tony said. "The young men carry them in procession through the forest and end up on top of the mountain where there is a huge bonfire."

"It is in essence a pagan festival," Jan explained. "The old pre-Christian commemoration of the winter solstice. On the longest night of the year, the fires were lit to welcome the returning Sun, who was the god of these heathens. The demons of darkness are most dangerous at this time, you understand, so the ignorant villagers make loud noises to frighten them away. No doubt there was once a pagan sanctuary on that very hill; the name Witches' Hat—"

"We've all studied folklore, Jan," I said.

"Yes, don't lecture to us," Dieter added. "This is supposed to be fun. Come, let us find a good place. Where does the parade go?"

"Down from the mountain, I think," Tony said. "It ends up at the church."

From pushcarts and stalls draped in greenery, people were buying trinkets and refreshments — mundane offerings like cotton candy and popcorn along with fragrant, freshly baked gingerbread and twisted canes of red-and-white sugar. Schmidt bought an enormous candy cane and a pocketful of gingerbread, which he munched as we made our way through the crowd. People filled the Marktplatz and the surrounding streets, whose steep slopes made an informal viewing stand. It was a cheerful, well-mannered crowd, but beer was flowing freely and I suspected there would be a few fights before the night was over. Ropes strung from wooden horses outlined a path through the Marktplatz and around the fountain; it ended, as Tony had said, at the church.

Christian theology had converted the spirits of forest and field into demons, to be expelled and exorcised. The hunters on the hillsides would drive them from their refuge and into the church, where the priest would cast them into outer darkness. Poor little harmless nymphs and satyrs, stumbling and squealing as they fled the hunters, cowering under the ceremonial lash of the priestly voice. Since the ceremony had to be repeated every year, one might reasonably assume that the demons weren't annihilated, only temporarily inconvenienced. I was glad of that.

I realized I had taken a little too much to drink. Contrary to popular belief, fresh air doesn't clear one's head; in fact, it concentrates the fumes. The others were feeling no pain, either; Jan's face was flushed and he had an arm around Elise, under her coat.

Alternately pushing and wheedling, Dieter forced a path through the milling bodies. His methods were deplorable — I heard him tell one large woman who was reluctant to give up her place that his poor old father was suffering from leprosy and wished to watch the festival once more before he died. He was referring to Schmidt, whose face did suggest some loathsome disease; the crumbs of the gingerbread had stuck to the patches of sugar from the candy cane and he looked absolutely disgusting. The woman backed away, whether from compassion or fear of catching the disease I would hesitate to say. Dieter's technique was effective; we ended up right against the ropes.

The twinkling torches twisted in snakelike symmetry, converging on the mountaintop. Then a great tongue of fire rose heavenward, and a roar of delight rose from the watchers. It was paganism, pure and simple, and it was very contagious; I realized I was yelling, too. As the voices died away, a spatter of firecrackers echoed across the valley. Like sparks from a spreading fire, or burning lava from the heart of a volcano, the torches reappeared and expanded out and down, faster now, as the runners took the downhill slope at perilous speed. The sounds of explosions accompanied them, growing louder as they approached the village – firecrackers, horns, and an occasional blast from one of the old-fashioned blunderbusses resurrected for the occasion. There were special organizations, called Christmas Shooters, in some Alpine villages; the members practiced all year with the old black-powder, ramrod weapons.

The crowd swayed back and forth, laughing and cheering. Children broke away from their parents and capered madly in the open space; they were promptly snatched away by an adult, but some of the younger men remained, daring the headlong rush that would soon be upon them. The priest came out onto the church steps, robed in scarlet and lace, holding the Book and surrounded by his entourage.

Then the head of the procession appeared. It wasn't a parade, it was a rout; they came at a dead run, their feet trampling the snow, their torches whirling, their faces flushed with exercise and excitement. The noise was deafening. Some of the youths waited till the last possible second to throw themselves aside, or to join the fringes of the rushing throng. Parents clutched their children tighter; girls squealed with half-real, half-pretended terror as the bright tails of the waving torches came dangerously close to them. As the procession thundered toward him, the priest stood his ground, smiling and raising the gilded crucifix; the runners came to a sudden stop, spreading out to fill the spaces reserved for them on either side of the church steps.

That should have marked the end of the performance, but instead of dispersing, the crowd pressed closer to the ropes, and nervous giggles replaced the shouting. The priest remained in his place, his crucifix raised. Then from the darkness beyond the Platz came a soft pattering of feet and an odd rustling.

They ran in silence, with a strange broken step, darting from side to side and then huddling together, but never slowing their frenzied speed. Wrapped in straw, like animated haystacks, with faces out of nightmares – long hairy muzzles, pointed fangs, horns crowning their brutish heads. They were armed, not with guns, but with chains, axes, hatchets, and long, sharp pikes.

One of them darted toward us, its hatchet raised. It had a stag's head, the great horns rampant, the glazed eyes fixed. The people around us gasped and swayed; I lost my footing and felt a moment of sharp, genuine terror as I feared I might fall under the close-packed bodies and booted feet. Then I was caught and held by someone's arms. The menacing figure spun back to join its fellows, and the bizarre procession passed on, to the open space in front of the church, where it was surrounded and menaced by the runners. The crowd cheered as the honor guard, the last of the forces of light, marched proudly past. They carried guns and wore a kind of uniform — apparently a select group from one of the Christmas shooting clubs.

That was the end of the parade, and people started moving away, toward the church. Jan continued to hold me close. His lips brushed against my ear. "Poor little Vicky, did the demons frighten you? Never fear, I will protect you from the darkness."

"I slipped," I said coldly. The truth is, I have always been terrified by witches and demons — or perhaps I should say by scary costumes. It stems from a Halloween outing when I was about eight and was cornered by a bunch of fierce twelve-year-olds dressed like skeletons.

Jan didn't believe me. "I have always desired you," he whispered hotly. "Later I will come to you. Tell me where your room—"

Even if I had been tempted by the offer, which I wasn't, being somewhat suspicious of Jan's motives, the sheer publicity would have put me off. Several of the group overheard — Tony, for one.

"Next time it gets to be too much for you,

just put a notice on the bulletin board," I said rudely and swung the heel of my boot against Jan's shin. He released me, a little more abruptly than I had anticipated; I staggered forward, bounced off the ropes, and found myself nose to nose with an individual wearing a ski mask patterned in shrieking colors of crimson and green. Two eyes blue as cornflowers gazed soulfully into mine; the mouth framed by the slit of the mask was twitching with some strong emotion. Probably suppressed laughter.

John melted into the crowd, as was his wont, and my dear old friends clustered around to confer about what we should do next. Dieter was all for hitting the night spots of Garmisch, and Elise, shivering and tottering on her ridiculous heels, seconded the idea of indoor entertainment. No one else was interested, so the two of them went off arm in arm. Jan had a hard time deciding which group to spy on; after wavering indecisively, he ran off after Dieter and Elise.

Their departure cleared the air considerably. I was still mad at Tony, but not as mad as I had been. Once I cooled off, a possible explanation for his inexcusable behavior had come to me — a relatively harmless and mildly flattering explanation. I decided to let bygones be bygones, at least for the rest of the evening.

Schmidt bought more of everything that was edible and pressed samples on us — gingerbread and candy canes and cookies and pretzels shaped like snowflakes and marzipan pigs wearing sugary wreaths around their sweet pink necks — and, of course, beer. The church was packed, not even standing room; but the doors stood open to the bright night, and we gathered with other spectators beside the steps and listened to the sweet high children's voices singing. *"Stille Nacht, Heilige Nacht," "O du fröhliche,"* and the lovely old cradle song — "Mary sits among the roses and rocks her Jesus-child. . ."

Schmidt was too choked by emotion to sing, which was fortunate, since he can't, but the others joined in; Tony hummed in a mellow baritone and I threw in a few wobbly notes of my own. When the mass ended, the congregation poured out, full of virtue and ready for fun; there was dancing in the plaza and an exhibition of marching by one of the shooting societies, and an incredible amount of eating and drinking. This was the last night of public revelry — Christmas Eve would be spent in family gatherings and quiet devotions — so people made the most of it. The merriment was still in full swing when I persuaded Schmidt we ought to pack it in. The children and older people and family groups had gone home and things were getting rather lively. A couple of fights had already broken out; I was afraid that, left to his own devices, Schmidt would start challenging people to duels and some other drunk would take him seriously.

A final nightcap in the bar consoled him, and we went upstairs arm in arm singing his favorite carol, a corny old pop song about the *Weihnachtsmann*. Tony didn't know the words, which did not prevent him from singing along. As Schmidt entered their room, bellowing the refrain — *"Didel-dadel-dum und didel-dadeldum—"* Tony caught my hand. "Can I...I mean, is it okay if I...I mean—"

"I know what you mean and no, you can't and no, it is not okay." I pulled my hand away and marched off. Honestly, I thought — it just shows what a mistake it is to be nice to some people. At the door of my room I turned. Tony was looking at me, his hands on his hips and a scowl on his face. If he had appeared apologetic, or pleading, or even disappointed, I might have weakened, but his pose of righteous indignation brought my anger to the boiling point.

"Shame on you," I said. "Faithless and forsworn already? How could you so easily forget dear little Ann, the knitter of sweaters?"

Out of consideration for sleeping guests, I did not slam my door. Dimly in the distance

I heard the reverberation as Tony slammed his.

The maid had left a single light burning; the room looked warm and cozy, but it was already cooling off. Tossing my jacket onto the bed, I quickly got into my nightgown and opened the window a crack. I was about to leap into bed when suddenly there came a tapping — as of someone gently rapping — at my chamber door.

"Go away, Tony," I called.

The tapping came again. It occurred to me that it might not be Tony. I unlocked the door and looked out.

Not Tony, not Jan, not John. Dieter.

I assumed he must be up to one of his unseemly jokes. He was dressed for it, in an overcoat that practically touched the floor and a fifties fedora pulled low over his eyebrows. The reek of beer was so strong I fell back a step. Dieter took this for an invitation; he slithered through the opening and closed the door. Then he turned the key.

"Oh no, you don't," I said, backing away from him. "Get the hell out of here, Dieter."

"I will take off my coat and stay awhile," said Dieter, with the profound air of a man quoting from the classics.

"I wish you wouldn't," I began.

He did anyway. My eyes popped. He was wearing the most hideous pajamas I have ever

330

seen — and I include Schmidt's, which range from the merely tasteless to the utterly unspeakable. Dieter's were lavender, printed with sketches of naked women and rude sayings in German, French, and English. I started to laugh. Dieter looked hurt. He put out one hand and pushed me, hard. I fell backward onto the bed; Dieter fell on top of me.

I was tired, and still bemused by the lavender pajamas; it took me a few seconds to react. When I did, I was surprised to find that my struggles to free myself were futile. He had both my arms pinned, and his mouth covered mine so that I couldn't express my exasperation. Exasperation was the word — not fear, nor even worry; he was stronger than I had realized, but I am not exactly a fragile little victim type. I decided to relax and bide my time. It wasn't until I heard the fabric of my nightgown give, with a nasty rending rip, that I got mad. That nightgown had cost me 380 marks.

Before I could slug him, Dieter suddenly soared up into the air. It was the most amazing thing I have ever seen. He seemed to hang there, arms and legs dangling, mouth horribly smeared with my lipstick, for the longest time. Then his feet dropped, his body swung sideways, and he toppled over backward.

I raised myself onto my elbows and stared at John. "Well! That was lovely. Rambo couldn't have done it better."

"Rambo would have blown him away." John frowned at his scraped knuckles and raised them tenderly to his mouth. "Which is what I should have done," he mumbled. "When will I learn to control these impetuous impulses? I suppose now you're going to tell me you didn't need rescuing."

"Well, no," I said apologetically. "Although it was a very nice gesture."

"Who is it?"

"It's only Dieter."

"Maybe you did need rescuing."

"Oh, it was just a silly joke. Look at those pajamas."

"They're a joke right enough. The absolute nadir of bad taste."

"Exactly. Dieter thinks I'm here with Tony. He probably set this up so that Tony would burst in on us and find us in a compromising position."

"Very funny," muttered John. "Far be it from me to criticize your personal habits, but the way these men keep popping in and out...Is Tony about to join us?"

"I shouldn't think so. But you'd better go. If Dieter wakes up and sees you—"

"He could hardly have missed me," John said caustically. "Had I but known you were entertaining, I'd have worn my mask."

"I think he's coming to," I said.

A mumble from poor Dieter confirmed the diagnosis. John glanced down at him. "No, he's not," he said.

"John, don't—" It was too late — not that he would have paid any attention anyway. The toe of his boot clipped Dieter's jaw in a carefully calculated, but very nasty-looking blow. Dieter subsided. I winced.

John sat down beside me on the bed. He started to speak, then frowned and fumbled under his thigh. "What the hell is this?"

I studied the object he was holding; things had been happening so fast, I had to think before I could identify it. "It's a bulb."

"I can see that," John said in exasperation. "Perhaps I should have been more explicit. Why are you hatching daffodils in your bed?"

"It must have fallen out of my pocket. How do you know it's a daffodil?"

"My dear old mum is a fanatical gardener. I've planted thousands of the damned things for her. There's no use carrying it around, Vicky, it's the wrong time of year."

"Well, I know that. I found it at the cemetery — on Mrs. Hoffman's grave. It looked so lonesome and cold—"

A moan from the recumbent form at our feet interrupted me. John said, "I should have kicked him harder."

"Don't you dare kick him again."

"I suppose I can't go on doing it indefinitely. He must have a jaw like Gibraltar. Honestly, Vicky, you can waste more time on trivial conversation than anyone I've ever met. Get rid of him. Like MacArthur, I will return."

"When?"

"As soon as you get rid of him." John rose to his feet, then looked searchingly at me. "Can you handle the fellow?"

"No problem. He's very drunk."

"Smells like a brewery," John agreed, wrinkling his nose fastidiously. "Very well, then — *à bientôt.*"

He faded into the night like a shadow, leaving a blast of cold air to remind me my torso was bared to the breezes. After examining the damage, I was tempted to kick Dieter myself. Annoyance made me less tolerant of his moans of pain and protestations of regret than I might otherwise have been; I bundled him ruthlessly out into the hall and watched with mean satisfaction as he set off on a slow retreat, ricocheting from wall to wall.

"You forgot these," I called, heaving his

coat and hat after him.

I suppose I needn't have spoken quite so loudly. As luck would have it, Schmidt chose that moment to open the door of his room. His exclamation of surprise and interest brought Tony to the door as well; the two of them stood there like Mutt and Jeff, staring from Dieter in his lavender pajamas to me, in what was left of my expensive nightgown.

I retreated and slammed the door. As I turned the key, icy air brushed my back and I whirled around, crossing my arms over my chest. "Close that window," I ordered.

He had already done so. "Cold?" he inquired. "Personally I find it a bit close in here." He peeled off his sweater and hung it neatly over a chair. "Stop right there," I said, as his fingers went to the buttons of his shirt. "This is going to be a business conference."

"You aren't dressed for it," said John.

"Where the hell is my robe?"

It was lying on the bed. I reached for it, and jumped spasmodically as a thunderous knock echoed at my door. "Vicky?" Tony bellowed.

"What do you want?"

"I want to come in."

"Well, you can't. Go away." I got one arm in a sleeve. It was the wrong sleeve. John, lips twitching, moved to help me — or so I thought;

335

instead of the robe, it was his arms that went around me. After an exploratory traverse, his lips settled into the hollow between my neck and shoulder.

"What happened?" Tony demanded loudly. "Are you all right? What did you do to him? What did he do to you?"

"Noth – ooop! – nothing." John was laughing soundlessly; the movements of his lips were horribly ticklish. "Stop that," I gurgled.

"What?" Tony shouted.

"Get lost, Tony. I mean it."

"That goes for you, too," I added, as the sound of heavy, offended footsteps thumped away.

John released me and sat down on the bed. "How do you do it?" he asked curiously. "Where do you find these farcical characters?"

"We are not amused," I said, finally managing to get both arms into the sleeves of the robe. "Do you suppose we can possibly have a sensible conversation now?"

"Yes, I suppose we'd better. There's no telling who will pop in next. Let's see – where were we? You were telling me about visiting Hoffman's grave."

"That's all there was to it. I visited the grave, I left my wreaths. That was a relatively peaceful interlude in a day otherwise full of surprises.

Don't you want to know why Schmidt got drunk last night?"

"Yes, I do, rather."

"He found a body in my back yard. A dead body."

"Anyone we know?"

"Do let's stop being so cool and sophisticated about all this," I grumbled, pacing the floor. "It was Freddy. According to Schmidt, he had been stabbed."

"I'm sorry, I can't work up much heated indignation about Freddy's demise," John said. "I saw he wasn't at his post today; I assumed he had fled or been sent away, but it doesn't surprise me to learn that someone found him an unnecessary encumbrance. Let's see....Schmidt found him yesterday. He must have been killed, and left on the premises, the night before. The murderer would hardly risk carrying out his activities in daylight; your neighborhood is too populous. So what was the noble dog doing night before last?"

"I had taken him to his sitter early in the evening. Which means," I added, before he could do so, "that the killer didn't know I have a dog; or he knew the dog was out of the way; or he didn't give a damn whether the body was discovered or not."

"That would seem to cover all the possibilities," John admitted. "Why don't you come over here and sit down? You're making me nervous."

"No, thank you. Let me get on with my report. If you'd stay at home where you're supposed to be, you'd have known all these interesting things earlier."

"Oh, were you looking for me?"

"Yes. So was Clara."

"I can't say I'm sorry to have missed Clara."

"She went with me to the cemetery."

"How jolly. I seem to detect a note of criticism, even of resentment, in your voice; is there something I'm missing?"

"Oh, no. Not at all. Let's see, what else is new? Oh, yes. Jan Perlmutter has come in out of the cold, or out of the closet, or whatever—"

"I know."

"How do you know?"

John threw up his arm as if to protect himself from a blow. "Your suspicion cuts me to the quick. I saw the gentleman with you this evening, and I recognized him from the snapshot you were good enough to share with me."

"Oh." I sat down on the bed. "So you admit you've been watching over me. Or is it following me?"

"A little of both." His hand moved across the small of my back.

"I said this is business—"

"A little of both," John repeated. "Yes, I saw Perlmutter. I found it amusing...." Somehow I found myself on my back with John leaning over me and the robe I had assumed with such difficulty half-off. He continued without missing a beat, "...seeing you all together, smiling at each other and lying..." He kissed me and went on smoothly, "...in your collective teeth with every word...."

I let out a screech. "Your hands are freezing."

"Oh, sorry. Let's try this."

The next sound I made wasn't a scream, but I supposed it might have been rather shrill. John's reply, if any, was lost in a thunderous crash. The door exploded inward and a large, round projectile hurtled through the opening. A large, round, orange projectile.

"You are safe, Vicky, I am here," Schmidt shouted. "There is nothing to fear!"

"Oh, Christ," John said. "Is that — does he have—"

He rolled off me and got very slowly and carefully to his feet.

"Put the gun down, Schmidt," I said apprehensively.

"Oh, it is Sir John," Schmidt exclaimed. "I am so glad to see you again, my friend."

John bared his teeth in a sickly smile. "I'm

delighted to see you, too, Herr Schmidt. Er — that's a very nice gun you have there. Colt forty-five, isn't it?"

Schmidt nodded, beaming. "Yes, it is a rare antique. Would you like to see it?" He offered it to John. I think he'd forgotten his finger was still on the trigger. The muzzle was pointing straight at John's nose.

"Lovely," John said in a strangled voice.

His hand moved in a blur of speed, sweeping the weapon neatly out of Schmidt's pudgy little paw. Then he turned pea-green and collapsed into the nearest chair.

"You don't have to be so rude," Schmidt said, hurt. "I would have given it to you."

"Where did you get it?" I demanded. Germany in its admirable wisdom has very tight gun-control laws.

Schmidt grinned and winked. "Ha ha, Vicky. I have my connections."

"It probably isn't even registered," I muttered. "Schmidt, what possessed you to come crashing in here?"

"You screamed," said Schmidt.

"I did not scream. I. . . .It was not a scream."

"Well, I see that now," said Schmidt. He gave me an admiring leer. "I forget that you have so many lovers. First Tony—"

John stopped mopping his brow and gave me

340

a thoughtful look, but said nothing. Schmidt went merrily on, "I knew it was not Tony, since he was with me. Dieter was very angry after you would not let him make love with you, he said many rude things which you did not hear because you had closed the door, but I was afraid he would come back and do what he said he would do to you, so I brought my gun, in case of trouble, and tiptoed here to listen at the door and make sure Dieter had not come back to assault you, and then when you cried out... Well, now you see how it was. Are you going to get up from the bed?"

"No," I said.

"Then I will sit here and we will have a conference," Schmidt announced.

"Schmidt," I said wearily, "the door is gaping open – I don't know how we are going to explain that – and I am somewhat inadequately clothed–"

"Yes, it is very nice," said Schmidt, eyeing me with candid approval.

"...and why Tony hasn't appeared I cannot imagine–"

"He won't come; he is sulking," Schmidt explained. "He said you were rude to him and so far as he is concerned the entire male population of Bad Steinbach can assault you. But he didn't mean it, Vicky."

"Go away, Schmidt," I said.

"I don't want to go away. I want to stay here and talk to Sir John."

"I'm afraid not this evening, Herr Schmidt." John had recovered himself; he rose with all his old grace, and had the effrontery to grin at me. "Shall we try my place next time?" he inquired politely. "This has been an evening I won't soon forget, but the novelty of it would pall with repetition."

"Go away, John," I said.

"Can I have my gun back?" Schmidt inquired meekly. John weighed it in his hand. I knew it was against his principles to carry a weapon — "the penalties are so much more severe" — but it was even more against his principles to give it back to Schmidt.

"I'll take it," I said, standing up with a martyred sigh. My nightgown promptly slid down to my hips, and Schmidt emitted a gentle moan of pleasure. I decided he had had enough excitement for one night, so I put on my robe and slipped the Colt into its pocket, over Schmidt's strenuous objections — to the robe and to the "sequestion of his piece," as he called it.

I got them both out, and shoved an armchair against the door to hold it in place. Schmidt had burst the tongue of the lock completely out of its socket. That was one thing he did well, falling heavily on things and breaking them. I went to bed. Nobody woke me. I didn't know whether I was glad or sorry about that.

NINE

I think I had a right to expect that after the carnival of comedy inflicted on me the night before, matters were going to calm down. Wrong; the second act of the farce began with the arrival of my breakfast. It surprised me a little, because I hadn't ordered breakfast.

I mumbled *"Herein,"* in response to the call, and then realized that she couldn't because the chair was blocking the door. So I got up and moved it.

The woman wasn't one of the waitresses — at least she wasn't one of the current waitresses. She did not respond to my sleepy *"Guten Morgen"*; carrying the tray with that never-to-be-forgotten skill, she pushed past me and slammed it down on a table.

"That's very nice of you," I began.

"Eat it and go," said Friedl. She folded her arms. "I need the room. It is reserved. You will please check out before *Mittag*."

There were two cups on the tray. I sat down

344

and poured coffee. "Are you joining me?" I asked.

"No."

"Then why...Oh, I get it. Not bad," I said judiciously. "As you can see, Frau Hoffman, I am alone. What's bugging you? Why aren't we friends anymore?"

"You can ask?" She flung out one arm in a dramatic gesture toward the door, sagging on its hinges. "I do not allow such things in my hotel."

"Oh, that was just Schmidt," I said. "He'll pay for it. He's got pots of money."

Now that the coffee had cleared my head, I could see her outrage was not assumed. Her chin was jerking spasmodically and her eyes were about to overflow.

"Something is wrong," I said. "Please, Frau Hoffman, won't you sit down and tell me about it?"

"But that is just it. You don't talk to me. I invite you here, I appeal to you for help and you betray me...."

Her voice broke into ugly, gulping sobs.

"You're right," I said quickly. "Absolutely right. I owe you an apology."

Her sobs subsided into snuffles. She looked suspiciously at me. "You apologize?"

"Yes. We've neglected you, I know that. But

believe me, Frau Hoffman, that's only because there is nothing to report. We've explored every lead we could think of and found nothing."

Tears had excavated deep tracks through her make-up. "That is what you say; but how do I know you aren't lying to me — keeping it for yourself?"

Friedl was herself again. I decided it was time to respond in kind instead of being so bloody polite. "You don't," I said. "Whereas I know you have consistently lied to me. I want to help you, but you must tell me everything you know."

"I have...." Her hand went to her mouth.

"I don't think so. What happened to Freddy? Why are you so frightened?"

"Freddy?" Her voice rose shrilly. "What does he have to do—"

My abused door swung open. "More screaming," said a familiar voice. "Again it is Schmidt to the rescue!"

It wasn't just Schmidt, it was an entire delegation — Tony, and behind him, looking uncharacteristically shy, Dieter.

"Nobody is screaming," I said irritably. "We were just talking. If you will all go away, perhaps I can resume what was beginning to look like a very interesting conversation. Girl talk. Do you know about girl talk, Schmidt? It's be-

346

tween girls — females. No men allowed."

Nobody took the hint. Dieter shoved Tony, who shoved Schmidt, and the trio came into the room.

"We will talk, too," said Schmidt. "We can put the cards on the table, since the spy is not here."

'He'll probably turn up any second," I said resignedly.

With the instincts of a homing pigeon, Schmidt zeroed in on the second cup and my hitherto untouched breakfast. He said indistinctly around a mouthful of pastry, "Let us have three more cups and perhaps an omelet, eh? Then we can sit back and have a pleasant—"

"Drop that telephone or I'll break your wrist," I said. "This is my room, dammit; I'm tired of people walking in and out as if—"

"I'm not leaving until everyone else leaves," Tony announced. He folded his arms magisterially.

"Why not talk now?" Dieter was frankly amused. He dropped into the armchair and smiled impartially at all of us. "Cards on the table, as the Herr Direktor has said. You were holding out on us, weren't you, Vicky? You are in confidence of this charming lady. Don't you think it is time you admitted the rest of us to her confidence?"

Friedl glanced at him askance. "I don't know anything," she muttered.

"That's true," I said. "Friedl — Frau Hoffman — asked me to come, and Schmidt and Tony were in on the deal, too. But she knows even less than we do. Only that her husband was mumbling about some long-lost treasure."

Dieter rolled his eyes and looked skeptical. "It sounds very peculiar to me."

"Your basic premise still holds," I pointed out. "If any of us knew where it is, we'd grab it and run."

Friedl's reddened, smeary eyes turned to me. "You would?"

"Now, don't give Frau Hoffman the wrong idea," Tony said. "We're not trying to pull a fast one. If we ran with it, we'd run straight to the proper authorities. Right, Vicky?"

"Oh, right. Sure." I added thoughtfully, "Whoever the proper authorities may be. . . ." I saw Friedl's head swivel toward me, her eyes narrowing. She might not be too bright, but she had a good ear for nuances — of a certain variety.

"We wish to help you, Frau Hoffman," Dieter said. "You know we are honorable people, with reputations to consider. Have faith in us."

"Well. . ."

"If you still want me to leave," I began.

"No. No, I didn't mean..." She glanced around the room and seemed to gain confidence from the silent approval and sympathy the men were beaming at her. "I would be pleased to have you stay on."

"For another day or two, then. Perhaps we can talk later — all right?"

I hoped she would take the hint, and her departure; the arrival of the committee had ended any hope of a confidential chat, but I had a feeling that Friedl and I might have things to say to one another under the right circumstances.

"Changed your mind, eh?" said Tony, after Friedl had left. "Now why—"

Schmidt had finished my food. "It is time for breakfast," he announced. "Let us adjourn the meeting to the restaurant and confer some more."

"Yes, why don't you?" I said. "I'll join you later."

Dieter was the last to leave. He looked doubtfully at the sagging door. "Did I do that?" he asked. He sounded as if he hoped he had.

"No. Don't you remember?"

His sudden rueful grin stretched the purpling bruise on his jaw. "I remember only that I made a fool of myself, as I always do with you. Did you have to hit me so hard?"

"I didn't..."

His eyes were wide and innocent. I amended my original statement; if he really didn't know there had been another person in my room, there was no need to tell him. "I have a few bruises of my own, buddy."

"Am I forgiven?"

"I think you came out worse than I did."

Dieter's hand went to his jaw. "Yes. I think so, too."

Glancing into the restaurant as I passed, I saw that Jan had joined the group. If I had entertained the slightest intentions of participating in that so-called conference, the sight of him would have squelched them.

Sullen gray clouds pressed down on Bad Steinbach. A scattering of snowflakes was blown into frenzied dances by the frigid wind. Gaiety prevailed, despite the cold; booths and stands still fringed the Marktplatz, dispensing food, drink, and variegated trinkets. It was Christmas Eve. The demons of darkness had been banished for a year, and tonight the birthday of the Child would be celebrated with midnight mass at the church and private family devotions.

There was no sign of life at Müller's shop — inside or outside. My signaled knock went unanswered. As I re-emerged into the Marktplatz,

I saw someone sauntering slowly across the open square. He walked toward one of the cafés and went in.

The small place was crowded, the few tables occupied. I joined the man who was standing at the counter — a man with a bushy gray mustache and heavy matching brows. His knit cap was pulled low over his ears. I ordered coffee and bread from the bustling waitress and waited until it had been delivered before I turned to him.

"Why aren't you answering your door?"

He had his back to the room, but his eyes remained fixed on the mirror behind the counter. There was a second door not far away; I knew if he saw anything that bothered him, he'd be out the door in a flash — leaving me with the check.

"I've moved," he said after a moment. "Too many people know where I live."

"What have you done with the cat?"

That inconsequential question drew a flash of blue eyes and a half-smile. "Locked her in the house with three days' supply of food and water. Müller will be back by then."

"Oh."

"What's wrong?"

"How can you tell?"

"I can tell."

"It's Friedl. She's wound so tight she's ready to explode. She burst into my room this morning in a fit of hysterics and ordered me to leave—"

"Well, what can you expect after that performance last night?" The gray mustache quivered.

"Oh, that was just an excuse. I tell you, she's terrified."

"Perhaps this is the time to apply pressure." There was no pity in his voice, only a cold ruthlessness. I knew he was right, but I hated him for being right — and I hated myself for agreeing.

"It's for her own good," I argued.

"Oh, quite. Poor little Friedl. . . . You won't gain any information about the whereabouts of Hoffman's treasure, but you might learn the identity of his murderer. If that detail concerns you . . ."

"It concerns me," I said curtly. "We could be wrong, you know. All the members of the group are behaving exactly as one might expect them to. How do we know there isn't an unknown third party involved?"

"Eighth or ninth party, rather. Whoever he is, he has murdered two people. Friedl may be next."

"That's what I'm afraid of. That's what has

352

me so..." The cup I was holding wobbled. John's hand closed over mine, steadying it.

"Then it behooves you to convince the lady — I use the term loosely — to spill her guts, before he can do it for her....Sorry. 'A man who could make so vile a pun would not scruple to pick a pocket.' "

"Amen. You're neglecting to watch the mirror."

"Oh, right." John released my hand and assumed his former position. After a moment he said, "I believe you are overly concerned about the danger to Friedl. Through her, he has access to the hotel and to Hoffman's papers and property. He'd be a fool to kill her so long as there is the slightest chance that she'll find something, or remember something, that might help him. But if he ever finds out where it is..."

"I hope you're right."

"I am always right," John said.

"You keep saying 'he.' You don't have any idea—"

"Not the slightest." His eyes remained fixed on the mirror. Mine remained fixed on him. He hunched his shoulders uncomfortably. "I use the masculine pronoun for the sake of convenience. By all the standards of detective fiction, the villain ought to be Elise. She's been less prominent in this affair than the others."

"The least likely suspect? No, that's Rosa D'Addio. She isn't even here."

The corner of John's mouth relaxed. "That sounds like Schmidt's logic. She probably ignored the photograph. Any sane scholar would."

"Exactly. Which brings us back to—"

"Your lot," said John. "Speaking of which, or whom—"

I glanced over my shoulder. When I looked back, he was gone.

I hadn't seen any familiar faces. I assumed John had pulled another of his little tricks to distract me so he could slither away.

When I got back to the hotel, I found that my buddies had finished breakfast and were staked out in the lobby waiting for me. I thought I caught a glimpse of Dieter's shrieking aquamarine jacket ducking back into the restaurant as I walked into the hotel; his wish to avoid me showed an unexpected sensitivity. Maybe Tony had read him a little lecture.

"Where is Jan?" I asked, sitting down on the couch next to Schmidt.

Schmidt chuckled. "In the kitchen. He is interrogating the cook, I think. A council of desperation! I have already questioned her, and the good woman knows nothing — except the recipe for the Bavarian burger, which she was kind enough to give—"

"Spare me," I said, wincing.

"That reminds me," said Schmidt. "I want my gun back."

I failed to see the connection, but I said firmly, "You can't have it."

"It is a valuable weapon, a museum piece. I want—"

"I'm not going to steal it, Schmidt. Just keep it until...until later. And *that* reminds *me*..." I scowled at Tony. "What possessed you to let Schmidt out of the room with that weapon last night? He could have killed somebody."

Tony had to raise his voice to be heard over Schmidt's sputtering protests. "I hoped he would."

"Thanks a lot."

"He wouldn't shoot you." Tony thought a minute. "Unless it was by accident. Vicky, I am not going to comment on your sexual activities—"

"You damn well better not."

"Because that is a private matter between you and your conscience. But I would like to know, if you will pardon my curiosity, what made you decide to stay on at Bad Steinbach."

"Yes, I would like to know that, too," said Schmidt. "You have found a clue? If you have, and you keep it to yourself, you can find yourself another position. I will set fire to you."

"Not 'set fire,'" I said automatically. "Oh, never mind. I don't have a clue, Schmidt. I will come clean with you, though. I think Friedl may be having second thoughts. She's wound tighter than one of Dieter's trick snakes. It's barely possible that, properly persuaded, she will break down and talk to me. Me," I added, clutching Schmidt's collar as he started to rise. "Confidences of that sort are best induced on a one-to-one basis."

"Why not me to her?" Schmidt asked hopefully.

"I think Tony to her would be more effective," I said. "But give me a crack at her first, okay?"

They agreed. Then Schmidt said, "Can I have my gun back?"

"No."

"Humph." He glanced at his watch. "Ha. It is time for *Mittagessen.*"

"Schmidt, you just ate a huge breakfast," Tony protested.

"But it is now almost *Mittag.* Come, I will take you both to lunch. Then . . . Then what shall we do?"

"You guys can do anything you like," I said agreeably. "I'm going to Garmisch. I have to do my Christmas shopping."

"Christmas shopping!" Tony was incredulous.

"This is Christmas Eve," I reminded him.

"Ha, yes," Schmidt said eagerly. "And to-night we have the roast goose and the presents and the Christmas tree. . . . I will find a tree, a little one, and we will put the ornaments on it—"

"I thought you were going to your sister's."

"I will call and tell her I am dying," said Schmidt. "I would rather be with you, Vicky."

"Me, too," Schmidt." I smiled at him. "And I'd rather be here than trying to explain to the Munich police why there's a dead man in my garden."

"So that is why you stay," said Schmidt.

"It's a good reason. What do you want for Christmas, Schmidt?"

I figured it was safe to leave Schmidt un-attended. After lunch he would have a nice long nap, and then his shopping would keep him busy for the rest of the afternoon. Tony asked to go with me, expecting, I'm sure, that I would fob him off with some excuse or other. He was disarmed, poor innocent, when I said it was fine with me. "But you'll have to go off on your own part of the time," I warned him. "I'm not going to buy you a present with you looking over my shoulder."

Tony smiled shyly.

As soon as I'd gotten rid of him, I went to the magic shop Dieter had mentioned. They had what I wanted; I also bought Schmidt a light-bulb nose like Dieter's and a few other props. After that, I let myself go; what the hell, it was Christmas Eve. When I got back to the car, loaded with parcels and wrapping paper, Tony was waiting for me.

"You really did go shopping," he said in surprise.

"You must stop doubting me, Tony. I told you I wanted to get something for you. Here it is....No, no fair peeking."

It was a sweater, made in Taiwan. I had the tag all made out: "From Ann, your imaginary fiancée in the Far East."

Tony had packages of his own; he showed me what he had bought for Schmidt while we drove back. It was getting dark. Clouds shrouded the sky and hung low over the mountains. The lights of Christmas trees and candles, placed in the windows of every house to honor the Child, defied storm and darkness. The radio was playing carols, and even the voice of the announcer predicting heavy snow in southern Germany didn't spoil my mood. Damn it, I thought, I'm going to have a happy Christmas Eve. I'll forget about poor frozen Freddy and all the rest of it for a few hours. Caesar would be having the time of his life with Carl, feasting on goose and pudding and anything else his canine heart desired. He would then be violently sick — on Carl's floor, not mine. And John would be — where? Probably freezing his butt in the snow while he spied on me or on someone equally harmless. Serve him right. That cynical creature was as far removed from the gentle kindliness of Christmas as the pagan deities the priest had exorcised.

For the first time that year, and under rather inauspicious circumstances, I found I had some genuine Christmas spirit. Tony and I parted at our respective doors after agreeing we would meet in an hour for the start of the festivities. He promised he'd keep Schmidt out of my way until I had finished wrapping my presents, and I promised I wouldn't peek through his keyhole or otherwise cheat until he called to tell me he and Schmidt were ready.

Humming unmelodiously but cheerfully, I spread my purchases out on the bed — including a box of chocolates, Vicky's present to Vicky. The bright wrappings and colored ribbons, an American contribution to old-fashioned German customs, looked pretty and festive. I had even remembered to buy a small pair of scissors and some tape.

Dusk deepened into darkness twinkling with lights. Far away in the distance, muted by the closed window, I could hear the sound of a radio or tape playing Christmas carols. I thought of poor Clara, locked in the dark house all alone. Perhaps I ought to get her and let her share the goose. One of the neighbors must have a key. And if I did happen to run into John... Nobody should be alone on Christmas Eve. I might even ask him to join us. Schmidt would be tickled pink to have him. Tony would be furious.... It would be an interesting combination − a real witches' brew of personalities. Not such a good idea, after all. Besides, it was unlikely I would see him.

I was busily wrapping packages when the telephone rang. Expecting Tony, I didn't recognize the voice at first, or understand what it was trying to say. Then the hoarse, rattling sounds shaped themselves into words. "Please − come − help me...."

"Friedl?" I exclaimed. "Is that you? What's wrong?"

"Yes...come, please...." There was a muffled thud, as if the telephone had dropped from her hand, and after that nothing but silence.

I dropped my own phone and bolted for the door. No time to tell Tony — no time to do anything except get to her, as fast as I could. God, she had sounded as if she were being strangled, even while she was trying to speak to me.

The lobby was full of holiday celebrants, gathered around the tree in the center. The bar had spilled out into the lobby, and people were raising glasses, singing, and laughing. By contrast the private corridor was ominously quiet. Not a soul was visible, not a whisper came from Friedl's apartment. The door to her sitting room was ajar. I eased it open.

Tony was bent over the couch — over something lying on the couch. Hearing me enter, he straightened and turned around. Great drops of perspiration beaded on his forehead, and his face was a horrible gray-green. But it wasn't as bad as the face of the woman on the couch. I recognized her by her frizzy blond hair and by her clothing.

"She's dead," Tony said.

I touched Friedl's wrist, searching for a pulse — futile gesture, but one I felt I had to make. "She's dead, all right. It must have happened within the past few minutes."

"I didn't do it," Tony said. "She was on the floor —"

"You picked her up? Oh, Tony!"

"I didn't think." Tony raised one hand to his forehead. "She called me — asked me to come down here on the double — sounded absolutely frantic, I hardly recognized her voice. You believe me, don't you?"

"I believe you." My response was automatic. As I stared down at the swollen cyanotic face, I was remembering what John had said earlier that day. "If he ever finds out where it is..."

It would seem that he had found out.

And so had I. I could only marvel that it had taken me so long.

TEN

A clicking sound, like castanets, made me start. It was Tony's teeth. Poor baby, he wasn't accustomed to death in such an unattractive form.

Well, neither was I. They say one's mind works with unnatural quickness in times of crisis. Mine doesn't always oblige in that way, but I knew we were in deep trouble. Not that there was any danger of Tony's being convicted for Friedl's murder; he hadn't done it and they couldn't prove he had. This was a delaying tactic, and it was more than likely...

"Get out of here," I ordered. "Quick, run."

I followed my own advice, but Tony just stood there, frozen with shock. Before I could return to him and remove him forcibly, there was a crash of crockery and ringing metal. Instinctively I ducked behind the open door. One of the waitresses stood in the doorway. She hadn't seen me; her bulging eyes were fixed on Friedl's hideous face. The tray had fallen from her hands.

The sight of her distress jolted Tony out of his. He took a step toward her. She screamed and fled. She went on screaming all the way down the hall.

"No, wait," I gabbled, grabbing Tony as he stumbled toward the door. "It's too late. This is what he wants...."

I could see the scheme in its entirety. I should have known the person who had set Tony up wouldn't neglect to provide a witness. Running away now would be the worst thing Tony could do. Not only would it be taken as an admission of guilt, but if he was a fugitive, pursued by the police, one well-placed shot would give the authorities their murderer — dead and unable to defend himself. The safest place for Tony now was the slammer.

There was no time to explain. Already I could hear running footsteps and cries of alarm. I held on to Tony. "Wait, no time," I insisted. "Wait."

He didn't struggle. All his natural, law-abiding instincts demanded that he stand like a man and face the music.

What I did was a dirty, low-down trick, but I had no choice. The crowd surged in — guests, waiters, busboys — all shouting in horror and distress — and surrounded Tony and the corpse. His poor white bewildered face was the last thing I saw as I slid quietly out the door.

I had to risk going to my room. I met no one on the stairs or in the hall, but when I opened the door, I saw Clara lying on my bed in a welter of tangled ribbon and shredded wrapping paper.

"Dammit," I exclaimed. "How did you get in here? You're not supposed to eat ribbons; they can block your intestines."

Clara raised her head. A curl of scarlet ribbon dangled from her mouth like an outré mustache, and it seemed to me that there was a distinctly critical look in her eyes.

"Right," I muttered. "Right. No time..." I snatched up my jacket and backpack and ran out.

How had she gotten into my room? The window was closed. John had locked her in the shop....

As I trotted through the lobby, I heard Schmidt's well-known voice in the distance. He'd keep an eye on Tony. I wished I could have him arrested, too. But the danger was not in the hotel, I was sure of that; it was heading up the mountain, to the same place I was going.

The twinkling Christmas lights and warmly lit windows of the houses I passed were poignant reminders of a misspent life. If I had settled down to domesticity, I'd be in just such a pleasant cottage, baking cookies and patting the dog and kissing the kiddies, instead of skidding along icy roads under a sky dark as death, on my way to a rendezvous with a murderer.

The traffic was surprisingly light. Not so surprising, actually; it was Christmas Eve, sensible people were safe at home. I swore — at myself — and swerved to avoid some idiot who was standing in the middle of the road waving his arms. As I turned sharply into the narrow track leading up the mountain, it occurred to me that the idiot had been wearing a uniform of some kind.

The wheels hit a stretch of ice and the car went into a skid. Despite the cold, I was sweating when I pulled out of it, and I forced myself to let up on the gas. There was no hurry. He couldn't be more than fifteen minutes ahead of me, half an hour at the most. And what he had to do would take a long time, even if he had thought to bring the proper equipment. Needless to say, I had not. It wasn't the gold I was after, it was the man. Not that I had the slightest idea of what I was going to do if I found him.

With a sharp stab of relief I remembered that Schmidt's gun was in my backpack. Good old Schmidt.

The road was bad. I had to concentrate on

keeping a steady pace, fast enough so the car wouldn't stall on the slope, slow enough so I could handle the frequent skids. Only my own headlights broke the darkness ahead of me. I must have gone half the distance before a flash of light in my rearview mirror betrayed the presence of a following vehicle.

Could I be ahead of him? Certainly I could. My foot had started for the brake; the car wove wildly when I returned it to the gas, a little too emphatically. It made no sense to stop; if I did, I'd never get started again, and there was no place to turn until I reached the cemetery. Perhaps it was the law behind me — the cop I had narrowly missed. Such dedication over a simple traffic violation? I sincerely hoped so, but I wasn't counting on it.

I had to keep both hands tight on the wheel, but how my fingers itched for that lovely gun. Time enough for that later, I told myself, and set my mind to considering alternative strategies. Or was it tactics? I can never remember which is which. Any attempt at innocent coincidence — "Fancy meeting you here" — was O-U-T, out. There was only one reason why anyone, including me, would visit the abandoned churchyard on such a night — and it wasn't the desire for a quiet spin in the country. No, it would be a direct, honest confrontation for once, no pretense, no kidding around. I would have to get him – or her – before whoever it was got me.

I think if I had known who it was, I wouldn't have been so nervous. Dieter or Jan or Elise? I wasn't afraid of any of them, or of any hypothetical third party. I was afraid of the unknown. And of the possibility that it might be someone I did know but had not wanted to suspect.

The following headlights behind me alternately shone out and vanished, as I swung around the tight upward curves. The car wasn't making any attempt to catch up; it stayed at the same discreet distance. So, I thought, not the police. No flashing lights, no siren.

Intent on the car behind me, I almost passed the cemetery. My turn was too sharp and too fast; the Audi slid sideways into a huge snowbank, and the engine died.

I had closed my eyes involuntarily. When I opened them, I saw nothing but snow. Mercifully, my door was still clear. I fought my way out, pausing only long enough to snatch my backpack and turn out the lights.

There was no moon to shine on the breast of the new-fallen snow, but the pale surface was lighter than the sky. The desolate church loomed like a crouching dinosaur, its tower the stiff, raised head. I floundered through the drifts, leaving a trail a blind man could follow. Maybe abandoning the car had not been such a great idea after all. But the prospect of being trapped inside, with the opposite door blocked, was even more unpleasant.

The night blossomed with light. I fell face down, burrowing into the snow.

After a while I realized the light was gone. The car had passed by. It hadn't turned into the churchyard; I would have heard the engine cut off.

I got slowly to my feet and brushed the snow from my face, and listened. The night was not silent. The wind blew shrill from the east, wailing under the eaves of the church and rattling the branches of the trees. It made a lonely howling in the night, like the poor demons of paganism, cast into outer darkness and bewailing their banishment from the throne of light.

As I stood there slowly congealing, I faced the unpleasant truth. I had panicked. I do that sometimes; what the hell, I'm not Superwoman. While I was thinking patronizingly about poor old Tony's inability to react quickly in a crisis, I was reacting too quickly, mounting my horse and riding off in all directions. I should have tried to find help. Though whether I would have succeeded, on Christmas Eve, with a new-laid murder preoccupying the small police force, was open to question.

Either I was all alone in the cemetery, or the other denizens of the region were singularly silent types. . . . Obviously nobody had arrived on the scene before me. There was no sign of activity near the lonely grave. It would require a blowtorch or a long-burning fire to soften the frozen earth before anyone could begin digging. The driver of the car that had been following me must have been an innocent local, homeward bound to his cottage on the other side of the mountain.

Obviously I couldn't spend the night squatting on Frau Hoffman's grave, waiting for the unknown to turn up. I could freeze to death before that happened, if it ever did. I decided I had better get back to the car. In the enthusiasm of new-car ownership I had stocked the trunk with a variety of suggested emergency equipment. Some of it might even be there. The blanket was kaput; I had used it to cover the seat one day when I took Caesar to the vet, and he had eaten most of it. But if memory served, I still had a small folding shovel and a few other odds and ends. If I couldn't dig the car out and get it back on the road, I might at least survive until morning.

It was at that point in my cool, deliberate reasoning that I heard something that was not the wind moaning in the branches. The wind wouldn't call my name.

The voice came from behind me – between me and the car. Did I panic? Of course I did. I started forward, my progress agonizingly slowed by the depth of the snow. Get behind something – that was my only thought. A snowbank, a wall – how about a tombstone? Plenty of them around.

"Vicky!" Unmistakably my name, though the wind snatched the syllables and played with them. High-pitched and distorted by emotion, it could have been the voice of a man or a woman.

I reached an area where the snow was slightly less deep – only about to my knees. The black square framed in whiteness was Hoffman's tombstone. The snow lay deep and untouched over the graves. One of my wreaths had toppled forward, only a black half-circle showed, partially veiled by the drifting snow.

I could hear him now, thrashing after me. I reached into my bag and found the gun. My hands were stiff with cold, despite my gloves. I realized I'd have to remove one of them to get my finger around the trigger.

"Vicky!" Then, at last, I knew the voice.

He was a dark featureless shadow against the paler blanket of snow, but I would have known that shape anywhere. His voice was rough and uneven, barely recognizable. "What the hell are you doing? It's thirty degrees below freezing; are you trying to turn yourself into an icecube?"

I said, "Friedl is dead. Murdered. Strangled."

"Ah." His breath formed a ghostly plume against the darkness. After a moment he said, "It's here. I should have known. The bulb."

"The wrong time of year, you said." My lips were numb with cold. "Bulbs are planted in the fall, before the ground freezes. I expect he put the chrysanthemums in at the same time. Even if anyone noticed, in this remote place, the signs of digging would be explained."

"And what more appropriate spot than the grave of his Helen," John murmured.

Had he read Hoffman's love letters? Not necessarily. His quick, intuitive mind was capable of appreciating the poetry of real life, even if he couldn't feel it himself.

When he spoke again his voice cracked with anger. "So you came rushing up here in the dead of night, with a blizzard forecast, to catch a killer. Are you out of your mind? Even if he knows—"

"She's safe until he finds out, you said."

"I said a lot of things. What am I, the voice

of God? He may have had other reasons for murdering her."

I said, "I have a gun."

"How nice." He had regained control of his breathing; his voice was almost back to normal, light and mocking. "I suppose you could use it to start a fire. But if I may venture to make a suggestion: A packet of matches would be more useful."

"I'm not so sure. What are you doing here?"

"I followed you, what do you think? You came haring out of the hotel as if your jeans were on fire and took off like a bat out of hell." The dim shadow shifted, and I said warningly, "Don't come any closer."

"For God's sake, Vicky! Do you want them to find us frozen in place, like Lot's wife and her brother? Let's go back to town and have a hot drink and a nice long—" His voice broke, in a long indrawn breath. Then he said quietly, almost reverently, "My God."

Even the great John Smythe couldn't have feigned that emotion. I glanced behind me.

It was almost upon us. I caught only one flashing glimpse before it engulfed me, but the sight burned an image onto my eyes.

Snow. A solid, opaque wall of whiteness, silent, deadly, moving down from the mountain heights.

Within three seconds it had filled my mouth and nostrils, weighted my lashes, hidden the world. I heard John call out, and tried to fight my way toward him, but the wind tore his voice to tatters and drove me to my knees. When I struggled up, I had lost all sense of direction. Groping blindly, I stumbled forward. My foot caught on a tombstone and I fell again. The faint far-off wail I heard might have been his voice, or the wind — or my own whimper of fear. I couldn't even see the ground, it was the same color as the air around me, but I felt it cold against my face as I slid forward. The blackness that filled my vision was a pleasant change after all that uniform white.

Warmth. Still dark, but warm and therefore wonderful. Surely there was a faint red glow, a specific source of heat not far away....I was afraid to open my eyes. Mother always warned me I'd go to the bad place if I didn't mend my sinful ways. Little did she know. After being frozen to death, hell seemed like...

"Heaven," I murmured blissfully.

"You aren't the first woman to tell me that," said John's voice.

I turned my head slightly and burrowed deeper into the lovely, prickly warmth of his sweater.

"How did you find me?" I asked drowsily.

"I believe the usual answer is, with great difficulty. To be quite honest, I fell over you. Lucky for you.... Lucky for both of us, in fact. It helped orient me; I was heading straight for the cliff."

"Where are we?"

"Why don't you open your eyes and find out?"

So I did.

The only light came from the flames of the fire by which I was lying. An empty, echoing darkness reached out beyond the light. At least it was enclosed; there was no wind and no snow, but it was warm only by comparison to the out-of-doors. Though the few details I could make out were indistinct, reasoning told me that there had only been one source of shelter near at hand.

"The church?"

"Mmm-hmmm."

"Where did you find the wood for the... Oh, John, you didn't!"

"I hadn't much choice. Luckily the pews were old wooden affairs. They burn very nicely."

"But you'll set the place on fire!"

"No fear. The baptismal font makes a handy little fireplace. Really," John went on in a meditative voice, "I had no idea how convenient an abandoned church can be. I must remember to look for one next time I'm benighted."

"Good God," I said helplessly.

"I couldn't agree more. If you are sufficiently recovered to tend the fire, I will go questing to see what other useful items I can find. I felt a fire was the most important thing. You were unpleasantly frigid to the touch when I towed you in."

I sat up. Once away from the warmth of his body, I realized the temperature of the air was well below freezing. I felt like a piece of bread in one of those old wire toasters, singed on one side and cold on the other.

He had removed my wet outer clothes and laid them on the floor near the fire. I heard him move away, cat-footed in the dust. He was whistling softly.

Well, I could think of worse people to be caught in a blizzard with. My lips twisted in a reluctant smile as I saw the crumpled papers next to the makeshift fireplace. They were pages from a hymnal.

I looked over my shoulder. The flame of his lighter gleamed like a star in the dimness, and I thanked God he had taken up smoking. "Haven't you got a flashlight?" I called, and then recoiled as the high ceiling threw the last syllables back at me like the voice of the Inhabitant himself.

"Yes. In the caaaar....Fascinating echo, isn't it? Yodayahlalala..."

He came back carrying an armful of wood, which he dumped onto the floor. "I wonder if I could invent a torch," he mused, squatting. "My lighter isn't going to hold out indefinitely. We ought to save it in case the fire needs to be restarted."

"What are you looking for?" I asked, as he straightened with a burning fragment in his hand.

"A bottle of sacramental wine would hit the spot."

"I doubt that a thrifty Bavarian would overlook anything like that. Besides, this isn't a Catholic church. Some offbeat local sect."

John came back to the fire to rekindle his makeshift torch. "Please," he said, in tones of the utmost sincerity, "Please don't start talking about the Old Religion. The ambiance is grisly enough without that."

"The Old...oh, you mean the witchcraft cult — the theory that it was a survival of pre-Christian religions. There are plenty of survivals around here."

His teeth gleamed uncannily with reflected firelight. "Yes, I saw you gibbering at the *Buttenmandeln*. Or was that just an excuse to fling yourself into Perlmutter's arms?"

He went off again before I could answer. I huddled closer to the fire.

The torch burned fitfully, now flaring up, now sinking to a sullen glow. Gliding through the darkness, it resembled a giant, diabolical firefly. A dry, inhuman squawl made me jump before I identified it as the sound of rusty hinges. The dancing light disappeared. An interminable time seemed to pass before it appeared again.

"Found the sacristy," John announced. "Or the off-beat local version of same. Not much there." He tossed a bundle onto the floor. Dust billowed up in an evil-smelling cloud.

"God," I said involuntarily. "It smells like a grave."

"Mold. Let's eschew suggestive similes, shall we, and say mold." John nudged the bundle with his foot. "Curtains. They're rotting and filthy – and moldy – but we're in no position to be fastidious. It's going to be a long, cold night."

"No wine?"

"No wine." He sat down next to me. I edged away.

"Now don't tell me you are going to come all over prim propriety," he jeered. "Bundling, I have been informed, is a thrifty old New England custom which ought equally to have applied in the frigid tundras of Minnesota."

"It's not unheard of," I admitted, moving into the circle of his arm. "I'll endeavor to overcome my qualms about doing it in a church. What's a commandment or two compared to death by freezing?"

"Fornication," said John precisely, "is not mentioned in the Ten Commandments."

"That's a relief."

"In fact," John went on, "if one analyzes the sexual regulations of the Old Testament, one finds that they are based on property rights rather than moral attitudes."

"Is that right?" I pressed closer against the warmth of his body.

"Adultery is prohibited because a man's wife belongs to him in the same sense as his horse and his ass and so on. The daughter belongs to the father, so sibling incest infringes on the old man's territory."

"But surely father-daughter relationships—"

"There's no prohibition against that." John added thoughtfully, "I checked."

I started to laugh. "This is an incredible conversation. Would you consider me vulgar if I asked why you investigated that particular issue?"

"That is not only vulgar, it is repellent," John said coldly. "Idle curiosity alone prompted

my investigation. It's my greatest weakness — but one never knows when a seemingly irrelevant bit of information may come in handy."

"I've noticed that."

He turned slightly and put his other arm around my shoulders, holding me close against him. His warm breath stirred my hair. After a moment he let out a long, tremulous sigh.

"God, I'm hungry," he said.

John claimed he had not eaten since breakfast because he had been too busy playing bodyguard for me. I took that with a grain of salt, but I was moved by his plight. I was hungry, too.

"I don't suppose you brought my backpack? Oh, you did — bless your heart."

"I had no choice. It was attached to you like a misplaced pregnancy." A tender and touching hope dawned on his face as he watched me rummage in the knapsack. "I could even eat that bulb."

"No, you couldn't. Daffodil bulbs are poisonous."

"So they are. I'd forgot. Another example of seemingly useless information proving relevant."

"Yes; one never knows when one might want to poison an acquaintance. Here."

John studied the object dubiously. "What is it?"

"Gingerbread. Schmidt kept forcing it on me last night."

"I loathe gingerbread. What's that white on it?"

"I guess some of the tissue I wrapped—"

"Hand it over."

I went on rummaging while he munched. His eyes widened as the pile of edibles mounted up. An apple, two-thirds of a fruit-and-nut chocolate bar (large size), more gingerbread, little packets of sugar (with pictures of Alpine scenes) and artificial sweetener, and two tea bags. I'm sure it was the tea that wrung an involuntary exclamation of admiration from John.

"O goddess! Lady of the Sycamores, Golden One, who gives food to the hungry and water to the thirsty—"

"It's nothing," I said modestly. "I thought I had...Oh, here it is. I'm afraid it's a little stale, and some of the jelly seems to have oozed out....If you can find a container, we might have a spot of tea."

John surged to his feet. "There are a few broken flower pots in the sacristy. And God knows there is plenty of snow."

I don't think he got all the encrusted dirt out of the pots, but as he said philosophically,

it gave a spurious look of strength to the tea. He was fascinated by my hoard.

"Are you clairvoyant, or do you always prepare for blizzards?"

"I always carry artificial sweetener. Not all restaurants have it."

"Then why the sugar?"

"I can't resist the pretty pictures on the packets. I'm making a collection."

John nodded gravely. "Of course. And the apple – the chocolate–?"

"Doesn't everybody carry things like that around?"

He dropped his head onto his raised knees, sputtering with helpless laughter.

"Have another piece of gingerbread," I said hospitably.

Life never ceases to amaze me. In my wildest dreams or nightmares, I had never expected to spend Christmas Eve in an abandoned church with an unreformed and unrepentant thief, dining on stale gingerbread and muddy tea. And I certainly would not have expected to enjoy it.

We talked for hours, huddled in front of the little fire, wrapped in cobwebby curtains and sipping tepid tea. He kissed the crumbs from my lips and held me close, for warmth, but we didn't dare lie down for fear we'd fall asleep and the fire would go out. It was as if two opposing armies had declared a temporary truce. He talked more easily than he had ever done, and I tried to avoid questions that would raise the barriers again. We talked about everything under the sun — even the weather.

"I've never seen anything like that moving wall of snow."

"And you are from the wintry wastes of Minnesota."

"Have you?"

"Once. That's why the sight of it petrified me. It was in the so-called mountains of western Virginia."

"What were you doing in Virginia?"

I slipped then, but instead of clamming up, he answered readily, "Visiting a friend. I do have a few, you know. I was only a few feet from the lodge — bringing in wood — when it hit, but for a few memorable moments I didn't think I was going to make it back."

And about abstruse academic subjects.

"Who is the Lady of the Sycamores?"

"Hathor, Egyptian goddess of love, beauty, and so on. I may have misquoted. My specialty is classics, not Egyptology."

"Greats," I said. "Isn't that what you call it? You went down with a first in Greats?"

"Well, not exactly," John said amused. "It

cannot be said that I went down from university, as the idiom has it; rather, I was pushed off the ladder of learning."

"Far be it from me to ask why."

"It wasn't extortion or fraud, if that's what you are implying. Just a little matter of a tutor arriving home before he was expected."

"I'm sure there is an Old Testament parallel."

"Oh, quite. Potiphar's wife. I was very young and naïve. I didn't take up a life of crime until after that," John went on cheerfully. "Someday I must tell you about my first scam. I don't believe I have ever equaled the sheer splendid lunacy of that concept. It didn't come off, unfortunately, but I'm still immensely proud of it."

And about his family.

"Is your mother's name really Guinevere?"

"It really is."

"I'd love to meet her."

"You wouldn't like her." After another of those meaningful pauses in which he excelled, he added, "She wouldn't like you either."

But not about the gold of Troy.

We recited poetry and sang, to keep awake. I taught John all the words to Schmidt's favorite Christmas carol, which he approved — "kitsch at its finest" — and he taught me the second part of the glorious duet in Bach's Cantata 140, where the soprano's *"mein Freund ist mein"* is echoed by the baritone's *"und ich bin dein."* My voice had suddenly descended from soprano to tenor during my last year in high school, so I took the baritone part and John sang soprano, both of us shifting octaves with reckless abandon. John was an excellent musician; I wondered whether he knew that my most secret, unfulfilled ambition was to be able to sing. He was kind enough to refrain from critical comment and I sang away with happy incompetence, no longer bothered by the ghostly responses from the rafters. "My friend is mine – and I am thine."

"Isn't that a little romantic for J. S. Bach?" I asked.

John was trying to play the oboe obbligato on a tissue-covered comb. He broke off long enough to remark, "Your theology is deficient, duckie. It's not a love song, it's all about the marriage of the faithful soul to Christ."

"It sounds like a love song."

"So it does," John said agreeably. He returned to the comb.

I fell asleep in the middle of a long lecture on horticulture – I remember he waxed eloquent on the subject of double digging, a technique on whose details I am hazy, but which, he said, his mother insisted upon – and did not waken until he moved to put more wood on the fire. I rubbed my eyes. "Sorry. I'm so tired...."

"You've had a busy day. Why don't you lie down?"

"The floor's too cold," I mumbled.

"Come here, then."

He was still holding me when I woke again to find that the darkness had been replaced by gray gloom. At first I thought the bright yellow streaks across the floor were paint.

"Sunlight," I muttered.

"It's morning," said John. " 'Arise, fair sun, and kill the envious moon.' Come on – be a big, brave girl – don't topple over–"

I was so stiff I could hardly move. Stiff, cold, hungry...I looked up at him from under my hair. He had risen to his feet and was methodically flexing his arms, grimacing as he moved them.

"Did you sleep?" I asked.

"How could I? 'My strength is as the strength of ten,' " John chanted, stamping his feet in cadence, " 'because my heart is pure.' "

The truce had lasted only one night, and the barriers were up again. I had expected it, but that didn't keep me from resenting it. Silently I extended my hand; briskly he pulled me to my feet, turned me around, and gave me a hearty slap on the backside.

"Dusty," he remarked. "Let's have a look outside. At this moment, I'd trade you and the gold for a hot breakfast."

I stood for a moment, stretching creaking muscles and looking around. The ruined building had been stripped of all portable objects, but even in its prime it had lacked the exuberant charm of the local Catholic churches. There was nothing to be seen except a bare floor littered with pieces of the fallen pews, bare stone walls, and boarded-up windows. Sunlight stretched long fingers through the cracks, and drifts of snow marked breaks in windows and roof. The fire had died to coals.

I pushed through the swinging doors and found myself in a narrow vestibule. The outer door was ajar, held open by a heap of drifted snow. John must have had to force it. No small feat, in that howling storm, with muscles already half frozen and my dead weight encumbering him. His footprints led up and over the drift. Shrugging into my jacket, I followed.

I had to shield my eyes with both hands. The world had changed overnight, into something so beautiful I forgot physical discomfort in sheer wonder. The sky overhead was a pure, cold blue, but behind the eastern mountains the bright shades of dawn framed the frosty peaks. The shadows on the white slopes were not gray but ravishing tints of pastel – pale rose, blue, lavender. The blanket of new snow dazzled like cold fire – swan-white, angel-white, glittering with billions of tiny sparkles.

My sunglasses were in the pocket of my jacket. After I put them on, I dared to open my eyes, and then I saw John. He was knee-deep in snow, even though he stood under the porch eaves where the snow was less deeply drifted. It undulated across the open court-yard in lovely dimpled dunes. My poor precious Audi was only an elephant-sized lump.

John stared dispiritedly at the scene, his hands shielding his eyes, and I decided this was not an appropriate moment to comment on the splendor of the view. "Where are your sunglasses?" I asked.

"In my car," John said, snapping the words off like icicles.

"And your car is..."

"Halfway down the slippery slope beyond, under a foot of snow," said John. "Were you aware that just over the hill the road drops straight down at a forty-five-degree angle?"

"Surely–" I began.

"I didn't see the church until I had passed it. I had no idea where you were going. I've never

driven this road before. I was going too fast —
as were you—"

From across the valley came a far-off, elfin
chiming of bells. " 'Oh sweet and far, from
cliff and scar,' " I quoted. "Merry Christmas,
John."

"So what shall we do?" I asked brightly. We
had gone back inside, and John was doggedly
feeding the fire, as if he meant to settle down
for a long stay. "You should put it out," I went
on. "We can't leave—"

"That is the situation in a nutshell," said
John. "We can't leave. Not unless you plan to
spend the rest of the winter in a snowdrift between here and Bad Steinbach."

"Oh, come on, don't be a sissy. It's a beautiful day and it can't be more than a couple of
miles—"

"Just a nice little downhill run on skis," said
John. "Unfortunately we don't have any."

"I do, actually. On top of the car. I never got
a chance to use them. Hell of a vacation."

His expression lightened briefly as he considered this new information, but it quickly
closed down again. "The plows and the Ski
Patrol will be out before long—"

"On Christmas Day?"

"Yes, I should think so. This is an emergency, and there are bound to be idiots like us who were caught in the storm."

"We can't just sit here and wait to be found."

"Oh, do use your head," John said crossly. "Even if we could dig one of the cars out, the road is impassable. I don't fancy a two-mile hike through drifts that are up to my neck, either."

"I could ski down and get help."

"It's too risky. If you got in trouble there'd be no one to bail you out. It doesn't take long to freeze to death when you're lying helpless with a broken leg."

"Are you always like this in the morning?" I demanded.

"No, it's just a performance I put on in order to discourage long-term relationships."

"I can't sit around here all day! I've got to get poor Tony out of the slammer—"

"Tony?"

"I walked out on him," I admitted guiltily. "The killer set him up — one of the maids found him standing over Friedl's freshly slaughtered body, and raised the alarm. He was surrounded by what looked like the beginning of a lynch mob when I left."

"Oh, I shouldn't think they'd lynch him," John said coolly. "They're very law-abiding in these parts, and Friedl didn't inspire that variety of devoted affection."

"Even so—"

"I'll tell you what we could do." John stroked his stubbly chin. "Start a fire outside — smoke signal."

"On Frau Hoffman's grave?" I asked.

He wasn't abashed. "Kill two birds with one stone, so to speak."

"Okay," I said.

"Just as well to have a look before you call the cops," John went on. "If you're wrong, you'll look a bloody fool — Did you say yes?"

"I said okay. Same thing."

We used scraps of the broken pews for shovels. The air was cold but utterly still; John had no trouble getting the fire started. It burned clear and bright until we piled pine boughs on it. As we worked, the chiming of distant Christmas bells made a macabre accompaniment. I hated what I was doing, even though I felt Hoffman wouldn't mind.

In between hauling wood from the church, I tackled my buried car. Clearing the ski rack wasn't difficult; there was only a foot of snow on top. On the lee side, away from the wind, a lonely fender protruded, and I was able to dig my way into the door. My emergency kit produced some dried fruit — "petrified" would be more accurate. I carried it to John, like a dog offering a bone, but this time he was not amused. Smeared with smuts from the fire, his eyes sunken and shadowed, he continued to tend the flames while he chewed.

I sat down on a snowbank a little distance away and watched. The moment I had resolutely refused to consider was approaching. It would take hours of slow heat to soften the ground. We would need shoves, trowels. And then...

Neither of us had discussed what we intended to do if we found the gold. There was no need. John knew what I would do.

I didn't know what he would do. The trouble with John – one of the troubles with John – was that he wasn't a cold-blooded villain. He wouldn't kill to gain his prize. At least he wouldn't kill me. I thought he was rather fond of me – as a person, I mean, not just as an enthusiastic lover. He might even have wavered, at odd moments, and toyed with the idea of letting me have the treasure. But I knew that when the time came, when the glittering thing was actually before him, there was a ninety-to-one chance that old habits would prevail over...call it friendship.

His lean cheeks were flushed with exercise and heat, but the underlying color was a pale gray. He was short on sleep and on food, burning calories like crazy — but it never occurred to me that I could defeat him in a hand-to-hand fight. Surreptitiously, my hand sneaked into my backpack. The gun was still there. Thank God I hadn't dropped it in the snow.

I don't know how long we were there. Sometimes John sat down by the fire to rest; sometimes I went inside to get more wood. The plume of smoke had been rising darkly for a long time before he came, schussing straight down the final slope between the trees and stopping in a spray of driven snow, skis almost touching in a perfect parallel. He wore ordinary ski clothing, but the face that looked out from under the hood of the parka was muzzled and fanged and dark with rank fur. In his right hand, instead of a pole, he carried one of the long pikes the *Buttenmandeln* had brandished.

I was bent over, adding wood to the fire when the apparition appeared, and it is a wonder I didn't fall face down into the flames. As the snarling muzzle turned toward me, I went reeling back. Even John the imperturbable was taken off guard. He had been perched impiously on the tombstone; struggling to rise, he slipped and sat down with a splash, his back against the granite. And there he stayed, because the point of the pike was planted in the center of his chest.

I got the gun out. Don't ask me how. I was pleased to see that my hands were dead steady as I sidled sideways, away from the smoke, to a spot from which I could get a clear sight.

My voice wasn't as steady as my hands. "Drop it," I squeaked. *"Hande hoch* — er—"

At first I was afraid I had made a slight tactical misjudgment; the graceful hooded figure started, and a dark circle spread out around the tip of the pike — accompanied, I must add, by a yelp from John. Then the shaggy muzzle turned toward me.

The vocabulary of violence is limited. I heard myself repeating the most ghastly clichés.

"I've got you covered," I pointed out. "You're dead meat, mister — uh — miss...uh....Go ahead, make my day."

John's eyes, the only part of him he dared move, rolled wildly in my direction. "For Christ's sake, Vicky!" I don't know whether he was objecting to the sentiment or to the hackneyed phrase in which I had expressed it.

The masked head tilted slightly, as if considering the options. A stand-off, I thought, still sticking to clichés. Now what do I do? I can't shoot....The top of the pike wasn't in very far, but one quick push would drive it home. The bloodstain continued to spread.

I don't suppose it took the other more than

a split second to come to a decision, but it seemed lots longer than that to me. He didn't release his hold on the pike. His left hand moved, pushing his hood back and pulling the mask from his face.

"You," I said.

The terrible thing was that he looked like the same good old comedian, rosy-cheeked, broadly grinning. "You didn't recognize me, did you?" he said. "These latex masks are wonderful. Keep the face warm, too."

"Please, Dieter. Put down the pike."

"But if I do, he may get away." Dieter's smile stiffened. "You know who he is, don't you?"

"I . . . yes, I know. How do you know?"

I fought to control my voice and my nerve, but it wasn't easy — there was something so grisly about Dieter's nonchalance, as he held John pinned against the tombstone, casual as a naturalist about to impale a beetle or a butterfly. He looked marvelous on skis, his usual clumsiness transformed.

"Why, I saw the rascal in court, when I testified against him in a case of fraud a few years ago," Dieter explained. "He had substituted a forgery for a valuable painting; the poor woman had kept it for years as insurance for her old age, and when she was forced to sell it, the truth came out. Such a filthy swindle. I could hardly believe my eyes when I saw him yesterday in Bad Steinbach. It is good you have the gun; keep him covered while I tie him up, and then we will go for the police."

The bloodstain was the size of a small saucer. John didn't say anything. He just looked at me.

Dieter's smile faded. He said awkwardly, "I am sorry, Vicky, if he was...If you were... It's the treasure he wants, you know. If he told you otherwise, he lied to you."

I said, "He's been lying all along."

"Vicky—" John began.

"You made a number of slips," I said. "That casual comment about how Hoffman turned up in Bavaria and married the innkeeper's daughter — how did you know it was his wife's father who owned the hotel? I didn't tell you. I didn't know myself, until later."

Dieter was smiling again. His fingers tightened on the handle of the pike; the bloodstain oozed outward, a scant millimeter at a time.

"There were other things," I said quickly. "You knew Tony's last name. You were too sure about too many things for which there was little or no evidence. You told me the matter wasn't worth pursuing, but you stuck close enough to me to be on hand when — when... Dieter, please — don't."

"Then give me the gun," Dieter said, grinning.

There was nothing else I could do. I said, "I'll trade you."

Dieter laughed aloud. "Try it, it's fun. There is satisfaction in inflicting pain on someone who has hurt you – your pride, your ego." With a brutal twist he wrenched the pike out of padding and flesh, and snatched the Colt from my hand.

I reached for the pike but it fell to the ground, brushing my outstretched fingertips. Dieter turned, took aim, and fired at point-blank range.

ELEVEN

I hadn't expected him to act so quickly. He had been having such a good time tormenting his victim, like a nasty little boy pulling wings off butterflies. The sound of the shot, less than three feet from my ears, threw me off balance; I went sprawling in the snow, groping for the handle of the pike. When I sat up, Dieter was pointing the gun at my stomach. John had fallen sideways, face down, across Hoffman's grave.

"Now you," Dieter said. "I would like very much to hold you in suspense awhile, as I did Albrecht—"

"Albrecht?"

"Perhaps you knew him by another name. He had many."

"Yes, I know."

I drew my feet up under me. My fingers closed around the butt of the pike. It left a delicate smear of blood on the snow as I pulled it toward me. Dieter pivoted, planting his pole, gliding out of range. "Amuse yourself," he said.

"I wish I had more time, but I must not linger — much as I am enjoying your desperate attempt to save yourself...."

"I hurt your stinking little ego rather badly, didn't I? I guess there's something to be said for feminine intuition; deep down inside, I knew you made me sick to my stomach."

His lips drew back over his teeth. Funny, I had never noticed how long and sharp they were. "If I am careful where I put the bullet, it will take you a long time to die," he mused. "Think of Dieter the joker, the butt of your laughter, as you lie bleeding in the snow by the corpse of your lover. Think of me enjoying the treasure you were good enough to find for me."

"No," I said. "I don't think so, Dieter."

The damned pike wasn't heavy, but it was long and hard to balance. I got to my feet and swung the thing into position. Dieter stepped back, grinning. For all my bravado, I was beginning to feel a wee bit uneasy. Could I have made some ghastly mistake? Surely not.... But John hadn't moved, not so much as a fingertip.

Dieter fired. I couldn't help cringing. It is unnerving to have a gun go off practically in your face, even though you know it is loaded with blanks.

I'd have done more than cringe — fainted, for

example — if I had realized that the harmless-sounding blank cartridges were capable of inflicting a considerable degree of damage when fired at close range. Luckily for me, Dieter aimed at my midsection, not at my face. The wadding bounced harmlessly off the thick layers of my padded jacket; sparks from burned powder set tiny spots of cloth smoldering.

The expression on Dieter's face when he saw me still upright and unharmed almost made up for the unpleasantness of the past few minutes, and for the ruin of my expensive ski jacket. I lunged at him, and missed by a mile. He was off-balance too; in a kind of frenzy, he emptied the magazine. The rolling echoes of the shots were followed by a deeper and more ominous rumble, high on the mountain. He'd start an avalanche if he wasn't careful. . . .

As I turned for a second try, Dieter threw the empty gun at me — a spiteful, childish gesture that gave me a certain amount of equally childish satisfaction. I ducked. Dieter planted his pole and skated away from me across the open ground. I started after him, but I knew it was hopeless. Once he reached the road, he had a straight downhill run — not the best of slopes, but well within the capability of a skier of his skill. Anybody who could have made it down the tree-encumbered hillside had to be first-rate. As John had said...

John.

He hadn't moved. A few of the blackened spots on his ski cap were still smoking, and the acrid stench of singed wool stung my nostrils as I tugged at him, trying to turn him over. He was a dead weight, heavy and unresponsive. Could I possibly have slipped up when I replaced the cartridges in the Colt — left one live one in the chamber? I knew — I knew! — I hadn't done so, but if he had taken the charge full in the face...Why hadn't the shopkeeper warned me that the blanks were so dangerous? I thought they just made a big bang. Of course, I had never expected anyone would fire the gun....

"Is he gone?" said a voice, quite literally from the grave.

Relief hit me so hard, every muscle went soggy. I collapsed onto the muddy ground beside him. "Yes, damn it. God damn you, John, what's the idea of scaring me like that?"

"Scaring you?" He rolled over. Knowing Dieter better than I did, he had flung himself aside in time to escape the worst of the powder burns, but the side of his face was speckled with angry-looking scorch marks. One had narrowly missed his eye. "Me?" he demanded, his voice rising. "Scaring *you?*"

"What was I supposed to do, tell you not to worry, the gun wasn't loaded? I thought Schmidt would try to steal it back, so I got some blanks from that magic shop in Garmisch and . . . I assumed you would assume . . . uh . . ."

John raised a tremulous hand to his brow. "My nerves will never be the same."

"I don't know what else I could have done," I argued. "I hoped I could bluff him, but I sure as hell couldn't shoot him, and he would have skewered you before I could get close enough to tackle him."

"I think you prolonged it on purpose," John said. His hand moved wincingly from his face to his chest. "Bloody hell. Once these down jackets are slashed, there's no way of repairing them."

I pushed his hand aside and began to unzip the jacket. "You did lie to me. You knew it was Dieter all along."

"I did lie to you, but I did not know it was Dieter all along. Ow — take it easy—"

"Crybaby." I unbuttoned his shirt and pushed the sodden cloth aside. "It's only a little hole."

"Another inch and it would have been a little hole in my lung. I don't know why I associate with you. Do you realize that I never have work-associated accidents unless you're around?"

"What, never?"

"Well...hardly ever. There is a nice clean white handkerchief in the inside pocket of my jacket."

"I might have known. The instinct of a gentleman cannot wholly be suppressed. Even with a liar—"

"It was for your own good. I tried to talk you out of it."

Without replying, I got up and went to the car for my first-aid kit.

"What next?" John inquired, still prone, as I buttoned him back into his clothes.

"I am going to take determined steps to leave this place within the next ten minutes," I said. "By one means or another. God knows what Dieter will try next. In case you wonder why I am not rushing hysterically for my skis, or making ineffectual efforts to dig my car out of that drift, it is because I am being very calm and weighing all possible alternatives before I fly into action in my inimitable way. And also because for once – just once – for the first time in our acquaintance – I want the simple, unvarnished truth. In this case, it is not merely curiosity that moves me to inquire. I have a distinct and genuine need to know all the facts."

"A persuasive argument," said John, nodding. His eyes rolled down toward the hand I had planted firmly on his chest. "That is also a persuasive argument. All right. The simple truth is that I heard rumors about the Trojan gold as long ago as August. In fact, I was approached by a former acquaintance, who claimed that he expected to gain possession of it shortly and asked if I would be willing to assist in — er — marketing it. I told him I had no time to waste on what-ifs, and to let me know when he actually had it in his hands.

"Now what you must understand, Vicky, is that the contact was made through certain channels that allow the communicants to remain anonymous. I never saw this individual, whom I knew only by a code name — Hagen. He had been involved with a little, er, business deal I invested in several years ago. I knew he was connected with a museum and I was fairly sure he was male — though even that information was carefully guarded. I never tried to find out more; that's part of the bizarre ethics of my profession, you know. One respects a colleague's anonymity.

"I dismissed the matter then; I had other things to think about. When you told me of your involvement, I realized, with considerable relief, that you really had nothing to go on. It wasn't until the end of the conversation that you casually mentioned your old academic acquaintances, several of whom had just happened to turn up, and an unpleasant suspicion entered my mind. If one of your friends was the individual I knew as Hagen, you could be in deep trouble. Ensuing development convinced me that my worst fears were justified. Hagen had failed to locate the treasure and was hoping you could do it for him. I decided to keep a brotherly eye on you—"

"And on the treasure."

John raised an eyebrow. "Your doubts cut me to the quick. The attack on you and Schmidt surprised me; it didn't fit my theory. Later investigation strongly suggested that a subordinate had gone off half-cocked and acted without authority. Freddy had already committed a major blunder by killing Hoffman before he could be persuaded to talk, and after he tried the same thing on you, Hagen realized Freddy's stupidity and arrogance could ruin everything. So out went Freddy. In the meantime...God, what's that noise? Avalanche?" He sat up with a start.

"Snowmobile, I think." I rose and shielded my eyes against the dazzle of the slopes. "We're about to be rescued."

"Vicky." His fingers, hard and urgent, closed around my wrist. "I withheld no relevant information. I wasn't trying—"

"Right." I freed my hand. "Sure."

The snowplows had been out. The main road was fairly clear and the Marktplatz was walled with ten-foot-high banks. People who live in areas of heavy snowfall don't let it upset their schedules; church was letting out when we arrived, and the *Platz* was filled with red-cheeked, cheerful people exchanging greetings and trying to keep the children from flinging themselves and their Christmas finery into the drifts. Sledges and sleighs mingled with cars in the parking area; the horses' collars were twined with greenery and bright red ribbon, and a team of magnificent white oxen attached to one painted sledge sported bells and bow-trimmed harness. The laughing voices, the snatches of carols, the bright sun and glittering snow made a perfect, picture-postcard Christmas morning.

We went straight to the police station.

At least the headquarters of the local constable was a quaint gabled house, not a grim barracks. There was a tiny Christmas tree on the sergeant's desk. He was the only one on duty; the remainder of the five-man force was at mass or out with the Ski Patrol searching for lost tourists. He took us for two of the latter and started lecturing us. The storm had been forecast, people had been warned to stay off the slopes; staring pointedly at my battered companion, he suggested I take him to the hospital in Garmisch.

John looked as if this struck him as a splendid idea, but when I launched into my story, he did all he could to back me up. It was some story. I had to do some impromptu editing to make it sound even halfway plausible. I didn't go into the business of the Trojan gold, figuring that would be too much for a bewildered local sergeant; time enough for complications when the *Landpolizei* were on the case. Instead, I concentrated on the mad-killer theme. The sergeant readily took to that idea; when he exclaimed, "Ah! A crime of passion!" I knew we had sold him. Everybody understands crimes of passion. Of course, John couldn't resist the chance to show off; baring his breast, he displayed his wound to the admiring gaze of the sergeant, who expressed himself as thoroughly convinced. We told him we would be at the hotel and left him in animated conversation with his superiors in Garmisch.

Tony was in Garmisch too. The sergeant said he had been taken there the day before, since the local lockup was already full of holiday revelers. I would have lingered to inquire about posting bail and such things, but John kept muttering insistently about food and drink, and I figured Tony could wait. I was sure we had not seen the last of Dieter. His tender little ego had taken another lump, and now he knew where the gold was hidden. I didn't know what he would do, but I knew he would try something. The police would be looking for him, but between the blizzard and the holiday, they would be shorthanded.

I was itching to get back to the cemetery with some tools — including a gun with actual bullets in it, in case Dieter had the same idea. However, as John kept reiterating, that matter could wait until we had figured out a method of transport and replenished our strength. I had to agree with him; I felt as though I would topple over if someone blew hard at me.

The clerk had a handful of messages for me. As I might have expected, all of them were from Schmidt.

"Where is Herr Schmidt?" I asked. "In the restaurant?"

The woman flung both hands shoulder-high in a dramatic shrug. "I saw him earlier, but... *Herr Gott, Fräulein,* it is a madhouse here. Frau Hoffman dead, and no one knowing what will happen next.... The police asked for you, too."

"That's all right, I've talked to them," I began.

John took me firmly by the arm. "If anyone else asks for the Fräulein Doktor, she will be in the restaurant."

Schmidt wasn't in the restaurant. The smell of coffee and fresh-baked rolls made me so weak in the knees, John had to lead me to a table. I tackled the food with a gusto worthy of Schmidt himself. As soon as I started to feel stronger, I started to worry again.

"What do you think he'll do?"

"God knows," John said placidly.

"What would you do?"

His eyes narrowed, acknowledging the covert insult, but he said only, "Go for the gold — to coin a phrase. It'll take him a while. There is no hurry."

"But you're not him."

"No, I'm not. I'm so flattered that you noticed the difference."

"We did a lot of the work for him, softening the ground," I mused. "Depends on how deeply it's buried. Transportation will be a problem. . . . How the devil did he get there this morning? It's all uphill from Bad Steinbach."

"And all downhill from the top of the Hexenhut. I expect he took the lift up, and then sashayed down to us. The smoke signal was a grave error on our part, but he must have had some idea beforehand."

"He overheard us talking about the daffodil bulb."

John's lips curled in an elegant sneer. He had visited the facilities, as my mother always calls them, and washed the soot and dried blood from his face; the sneer was one of his best.

"He wouldn't have wits enough to reason that one out. It's more likely that your initial visit to the cemetery aroused his suspicions; it wouldn't occur to him that your motives were as pure and charitable as they really were."

"Or he located someone who saw me leaving town last night. I almost ran over a policeman when I turned into the road leading to the cemetery; I'll bet that's the only place it leads to." I glanced toward the door. "Where do you suppose Schmidt is? It isn't like him to stay away from food for more than an hour at a stretch. Maybe he's taking a nap." I put my napkin on the table and stood up.

"It's the best possible place for him," John said, sipping coffee. "If I were you, I'd leave him there."

"No, I need him to help me convince the police to dig up that grave. He's got more clout than I have."

"Oh, very well." John reached in his pocket. "Er — I seem to have lost my wallet somewhere. . . ."

"Back to your old form," I said, scribbling my name and room number on the check.

I knocked on Schmidt's door. The mumbled grunt was the reply I had expected. The door wasn't locked, so I opened it and walked in.

Schmidt was napping, all right, hands folded on his stomach, mustache vibrating with the intensity of his snores. I didn't see Dieter until I was well inside the room. He had been behind the door.

John put his hands in his pockets and let his shoulders sag. "Stupid," he said critically. "I should have anticipated this."

"Neither of us is at our best this morning," I agreed. "I wonder where he got the gun?"

"It isn't his," John said. "Unless he was carrying it on him the whole time. I searched his luggage—"

The barrel of the gun slashed across the side of his face and sent him reeling back against the closed door.

"Lie down!" Dieter shouted, his face suffused. "On the floor, *schnell,* or I will knock you down."

John spread the fingers of the hand he had clapped to his face and peered at Dieter. "Don't you want to boast about your cleverness before you shoot me?" he asked in wavering but encouraging tones.

"You talk about me as if I were a child," Dieter cried. "You taunt me — you dare to make fun of me! I will kill you, I will kill all of you—"

"He might at that," I said, before John could come back with another of those cute, provocative, dangerous little quips. "Dieter, calm down. You've won. You are the winner, *número uno*, top dog, and top cheese of all time—"

"'...the bravest by far in the ranks of the Shah,'" murmured a faint voice from behind the bloody hand.

"It would serve you right if he did shoot you," I snarled. "Dieter, what have you done to Schmidt?"

Dieter relaxed visibly. "A few sleeping pills. It is easy to drug that fat gourmand; he will eat anything and he eats constantly." He added in self-congratulatory tones, "It is his gun. He took it from the drawer when he felt himself succumbing to the Valium, but he was so sleepy I think he would have shot himself in the stomach if I had not taken it from him."

I felt my throat closing up. Poor brave little Schmidt. Damn the courageous old galoot anyway. The fact that he hadn't tried to steal the Colt back should have warned me that he had another gun.

"I was going to take him as a hostage." Dieter gave Schmidt's rotund and recumbent form a resentful look. "But he is too heavy to carry.

So I decided to wait here for you. I knew you would come sooner or later."

"It's later," I said, as John continued to watch Dieter through his first and second finger. "We've already been to the police. They'll be looking for you."

"Not soon," Dieter said coolly. "It is *Weihnacht,* and the storm has made for some confusion. But you will come with me, Vicky, and then if anyone tries to interfere with me, I will kill you."

"Take him," I said, indicating John.

"Right," John said. "Take me...." And then the idiot spread both arms wide and sang, "Please do take me — I'm all yours if you—"

Dieter was too smart to risk it a second time. He had caught John off guard with the first blow, but he must have seen the flexed hands, poised and ready. He stepped back.

"Over by the bed. Lie down on the floor. Hands under you."

The barrel of the gun shifted toward me and John said, "Calm down, old chap. You don't want to shoot anyone."

"No, I don't. I would rather not attract attention. But if I am forced to shoot, it will be all of you. This gun is a very nice gun."

It was, too. Nothing but the best for Schmidt — an automatic pistol — a Beretta, as I later discovered — the kind that fires the whole clip so long as the finger remains on the trigger.

John obeyed. "Face down," Dieter ordered.

With an expressive look at me, John rolled over. He must have known what was coming. I didn't. I suppose I expected Dieter would bend over and bang him on the back of the head with the gun. Instead, Dieter swung his foot. He didn't hold back, as John had done with him; his toe connected with a sickening soggy crunch that spilled John over onto his back, his head and shoulders under the high antique bed. This time he wasn't faking. His twisted body and outflung hands were as limp as dead fish.

I rocked to a halt as Dieter wriggled the gun admonishingly. He glanced longingly at John's body, but decided not to risk another kick, much as he obviously wanted to. "Come," he said. "We will go now."

Lovingly entwined, we went down the stairs and through the lobby. Dieter's left arm was around my shoulders, his fingers caressing my throat, his thumb nudging the nerve ending behind the ear. His right hand was inside his jacket, Napoleon-style. I could feel the muzzle of the gun through both our jackets.

We had emerged from the hotel before I got my voice under control. "You'll never make it up there, Dieter. The road is too icy."

"I think of everything," Dieter said. His thumb jabbed deep, and pain lanced through my head. Reflexively my head turned, away from the pressure. He forced my face down toward his and kissed me on the mouth.

"You son of a bitch," I said, licking blood off my lower lip.

"But a romantic son of a bitch," said Dieter, grinning and nodding at an elderly couple who had paused to smile at the young lovers. He pushed me toward a sleigh strung with bells and bright ribbons. "See what I have hired to take my sweetheart for a drive. I think there will be time for more romance while we wait for the ground to soften. How would you like that, eh?" He went on to enumerate all the "romantic" things he was going to do to me. The lad had quite a vocabulary.

I gritted my teeth and yearned for the moment when he would help me into the sleigh. He'd have to take the gun out of my ribs for a second, and that was all I would need. Boots, fists, teeth...

I should have learned by then not to underestimate him. The moment my foot touched the high step, he gave me a shove that sent me sprawling forward across the seat, my breath stifled by a fuzzy fur wrap. With a hearty chuckle at my clumsiness, he hauled me upright, folded me in a fond embrace, and hit me on the chin.

I don't know what happened after that, but I'll bet we made a charming picture as we drove out of town — bells chiming, horses trotting, and me wrapped cozily in the fur rug with my head on Dieter's shoulder and his arm around me.

He must have hit me again or I wouldn't have stayed unconscious so long. I didn't wake up until we had reached our destination and Dieter had had his way with me. No, not that; but I found myself flat on my back with my wrists and ankles tied to stakes, all ready and waiting as soon as Dieter found time to attend to me. My jaw hurt and my back was so cold it felt as if it were stuck to the frozen ground, and the arch of bright blue sky, which was all I could see at first, made my eyes ache.

After a while it occurred to me that I could turn my head.

The fire had gone out. Dieter was at work, scraping off the top layer of softened dirt and ash. He had even brought tools, the clever boy. Not shovels and pickaxes; no archaeologist in his right senses would use anything so destructive, and this was an archaeological excavation of sorts. One careless thrust of a sharp instrument might penetrate the container and reduce the gold of Troy to a heap of golden scraps.

God bless Hoffman, he had buried it deep. The fire had softened only the top few inches of soil. Before long, Dieter had removed it, along with a handful of pitiful bare bulbs that would never be flowers. Reaching for an armful of kindling, he arranged it with a horrible travesty of Boy Scout tidiness and lit a match. When the wood had caught and was burning brightly, he rose to his feet and looked at me.

It would have made a great scene in my book — the heroine spread-eagled and helpless, awaiting a fate worse than death. (I was beginning to wonder how I could have found that phrase funny.) I was wearing more clothes than Rosanna would have worn, but I had a feeling Dieter would get around to that before much longer. There was only one positive aspect to the situation. He'd have done better to tie my wrists and ankles together. The stakes had not been driven deeply into the hard ground. I had already managed to start one wriggling.

"I need more wood," Dieter explained. "Can't use these wet branches; they make too much smoke. I'll be back in a minute."

John would have said, "Take your time," or "Don't hurry back," or something even wittier. I resisted the temptation. The workings of Dieter's mind were fascinating. He wasn't your usual mad murderer, no such thing. He was perfectly sane. The treasure was his main objective, and he really wasn't sadist enough to risk that or his precious skin for the fun of torturing me.

Cheerful thought. As soon as Dieter was out of my field of vision, I threw all my strength into the muscles of my right arm. The stake popped out with such unexpected ease my arm flew up into the air. I replaced it even more hastily than it had arisen and twisted it around so I could look over my shoulder. Smart of me. He was back sooner that I would have expected, his arms full of wood.

I got back into position, praying he wouldn't notice my arm was free. He went right on past; while he busied himself building up the fire and extending the scope of the fire, I continued working on the left-hand stake. It was exasperating, nerve-racking work, because I didn't want him to realize what I was doing.

All too soon, the methodical woodsman had things going to his satisfaction. I rolled my eyes and made faces as he approached, hoping to focus his attention on my distorted face instead of my right wrist. He knelt down with his back toward it, took hold of the zipper of my jacket and pulled it down.

Sometimes I really wonder if I am in my

right mind. I did not take the course of action I knew prudence and common sense demanded. I was only slightly less helpless with one hand free than with neither. I was wearing so many layers of clothing it would take Dieter quite some time to work his way down to the foundations; his preoccupation and my vigorous reactions would provide excellent cover for freeing my other limbs, or at least making a damn good try.

It was pure kneejerk reflex. The instant the zipper parted, my right arm flew up, without any conscious effort on my part. My fist hit him in the back of the neck. It wasn't a bad attempt, considering that my muscles were stiff with cold and restricted circulation, but of course it only stunned him for a moment. It also irritated him a lot. He jumped up, swearing, and then jumped back as I tried to grab his ankle. The damage was done, so there was no point in pretending to be submissive; I squirmed and struggled and yelled, and tried to get my right hand across to where the left was still pinned. While I was doing that, Dieter reached into his pocket and took out a knife. It was one of those Swiss Army things, with every attachment but a buttonhook.

The left-hand stake would not budge. It didn't take Dieter long to comprehend what I had known all along; he had just been startled for a minute. With a nasty grin he kicked my flailing hand aside and planted one foot on my stomach – not too hard, just hard enough to hold me down and make me wonder how many ribs were cracking – while he examined his knife. Trying to decide which of the little tools to use? Corkscrew, can opener...

I didn't really want to see which one he picked, but unholy curiosity kept my eyelids from closing. My right hand was out of commission; it was just one gigantic ache. I kept tugging at the stake holding the left one. Dieter unfolded one of the knife blades. That was a relief. I did hate the idea of the corkscrew.

Removing his foot from my diaphragm, Dieter circled to my right. Careful lad; he was going to take care of that limp, flopping right hand before he got down to business. If he hadn't moved, I would have missed it – the most spectacular entrance ever made by a hero rushing to the rescue.

I said spectacular, not impressive. John had to leave the slope, which curved westward above the cemetery, and follow the trail Dieter had taken earlier, through the trees. Only an Olympic-class skier could have done it, and only with the devil's own luck. John wasn't in Dieter's class, and for once his luck seemed to have run out. When I caught sight of him, he was in mid-air, skis crossed and arms flailing. He hit the ground with a thud that sent sympathetic twinges through my straining body. A huge cloud of snow billowed up to cast a merciful veil over the scene.

The sheer splendid ineptitude of the performance held Dieter frozen for a few moments. Not until the snow began to settle and a dim form appeared, groping but upright, did he remember he had a gun.

At least the fall had freed John's skis; the bindings are supposed to let go when that happens. He still had his poles. As he came wobbling toward us, blinking the snow from his eyes, Dieter's hand dipped into his pocket. I let out a screech of warning. Half blinded though he was, John reacted in time; one of his poles swung in a wide arc. The gun flew out of Dieter's hand and sank into the snow.

The side of John's face was not a pretty sight, but I knew he must have ducked in time to escape the full impact of Dieter's kick, or he wouldn't be where he was. He was not at his best, however. Dieter flew at him, knife, corkscrew, and all; he went over backward in another billow of snow. Dieter staggered back clutching the inside of his thigh. Slightly off target, that kick, but not bad under the circumstances. It gave John time to regain his feet.

They circled one another warily. Dieter held the knife low; knees flexed, left hand weaving, he looked very professional. John's movements lacked their usual spring; he was at a disadvantage in a one-to-one fight against an opponent who probably knew as many dirty tricks as he did and who was in much better physical condition. I wished that he had been able to overcome his prejudice against firearms. The ski poles kept Dieter from closing in, but they were not very effective attack weapons, the fiberglass shafts too light to strike a crippling blow, the tips more blunted than the older type that had caused so many accidents on the slopes.

The left-hand stake gave way. I sat up and stretched, trying to reach my feet. Muscles I had forgotten I owned screamed in protest. Oh, God, I thought, straining, Oh, God, help me, I swear — from now on, I'll do those exercises every morning.

One of the poles broke clear across as John brought it down in a vicious blow on Dieter's head. It staggered Dieter for a moment, but it staggered John more. Dieter knocked the jagged stub out of his hand and John fell back, avoiding Dieter's rush. Slowly but inexorably they were retreating toward the far edge of the plateau, where only the ragged remains of a stone wall stood between them and the drop to the road below. I redoubled my efforts, but twice zero is still zero, and all my muscles had gone limp and stringy like overcooked spaghetti. The fingers of my right hand were practically useless; I was sure a couple of them must be broken.

Dieter was facing away from me, John toward me. Seeing me struggling, he yelled, "Hurry up, can't you?"

I always knew that mouth of his would get us in trouble. Dieter risked a quick glance over his shoulder. Apparently he didn't like what he saw. His next move caught John off guard; he turned and pelted back toward me, leaving John beating the empty air with his remaining ski pole.

Dieter was after the gun. The snow was wet and heavy; the hole where it had sunk out of sight was as clearly visible to him as it was to me. I had marked the spot, since I meant to head straight for it as soon as I was free. Dieter got off one shot before John tackled him. He wasn't aiming at John; the bullet hit the ground less than a foot from my shoulder.

They went rolling and tumbling across the graveyard, Dieter trying to escape his opponent's grasp long enough to aim and fire, John trying to prevent just that. Dieter squeezed off a few more shots; I gathered that they missed, since John continued to press him back. The echoes rolled from hill to hill, and as they faded I heard another sound, the sound of distant thunder. That was strange, I thought. The skies were clear, there wasn't a cloud in sight. . . .

Looking up, I saw it begin — a small puff of white, so innocent and harmless, at the barren summit of the Witche's Hat. It wasn't a cloud. It was a mass of snow. By the time it reached the bottom of the slope, it would be studded with boulders like raisins in a pudding, with snapped-off branches and whole trees.

The cloud expanded. It was coming straight down the ski slope, the path of least resistance, but it would not follow the curve of the slope. By the time it reached that point, it would have gained enough momentum and mass to continue straight on down — into the cemetery. Perhaps the trees would stop it or minimize its impact; perhaps they wouldn't. All these years the surrounding forest had protected the church, but the ski run had changed that. Herr Müller had been so right — fools, tampering with God's work for their sport. . . .

One of the pegs came out, but I was still tethered, like a goat, by one foot. The two men were perilously close to the edge of the drop, on their feet, clinging like lovers. Dieter's raised rigid arm strained to free itself from John's desperate grip. I don't know whether Dieter was even aware of the dreadful thing roaring down toward him. John was; but he couldn't run for cover unless he let go of Dieter, whereupon Dieter would probably shoot him in the back, or else lie low until the avalanche had passed – and then shoot both of us.

It happened so fast. John's taut body gathered itself for a final effort. Dieter's feet went out from under him. The small of his back hit the top of the low wall, and for a split second he hung there. I heard him scream, even over the mounting roar from the slope; but it was a scream of rage, not terror, and he never let go his hold on John or on the gun, though if his hands had been free, he might have saved himself. They went over together.

I had about six seconds in which to decide what to do. That's longer than it sounds. It didn't take any time at all. I found myself on my feet and running like a madwoman, the broken stake flopping. On the top of the wall, I could see two pale patches that weren't snow. Slowly a head rose up between the grasping hands. I was close enough to see every detail; in fact, I felt as if I were looking through binoculars, everything was abnormally clear and sharp. His eyes opened so wide the pupils looked like cabochon sapphires set in milky mother-of-pearl, and his lips shaped words. I couldn't hear him but I knew what he was saying. Good advice, but I went on running, throwing myself flat when I reached the wall and reaching out with both hands. My fingers weren't broken, they worked just fine; all ten of them clamped around John's left wrist.

I didn't look over my shoulder. I figured the sight would just depress me. It sounded like an express train, rushing toward the heroine tied to the tracks; but there wouldn't be a hero galloping up on his great white horse this time. A couple of skull-sized rocks, the precursors of the main mass, bounced off the ground and flew over the edge. "Duck," I yelled. I knew he couldn't hear me, though our faces were only inches apart.

In the final seconds, the agonized lines of his face relaxed. His eyelids dropped, veiling his eyes, and he said something — not the expletives, orders, and insults he had been hurling at me — something quite different. It surprised me so that I almost let go of his wrist. "What?" I screamed. "What did you say?"

Then it was on us.

I pushed my face down into the snow.

The only good thing about it was that it didn't last long, though the howling assault seemed to go on forever. A couple of rocks bounced off my back, but I didn't feel them at the time because all the nerve endings in my body were focused on my hands and the cold, limp thing they held in a death grip. I was still holding it when the echoes faded into silence and I dared to raise my head.

The brunt of the avalanche had been broken by the trees above the cemetery. If the full force had struck, it would have swept both of us away with it. It was bad enough, however. I think the noise was the worst. My ears were ringing even after the thunder died, and I felt lightheaded and dizzy. My eyes wouldn't focus at first. Then I saw that most of the wall was gone. Only a few tumbled courses remained. There was no sign of John — no face, no white-knuckled hands.

He was still down there, though. I could feel his weight — his entire, dead weight, pulling at my arms. I must not have been thinking very clearly. Instead of calling his name, I croaked, "What was that you said?"

I do not know how the hell I ever got him back up. At first he was no help, he kept passing out. Finally, he got one toe into a crevice and I was able to grasp the back of his jacket. When at last he was sprawled on the ground at my feet, I looked over the edge.

Fifty feet below, the road was blocked by snow and fallen stone. Nobody would be coming that way for a while. The section of cliff above the road was almost perpendicular, a sheer drop of broken, jagged stone. A single blotch of color broke the gray-white monotony of the background – a patch of bright turquoise, unmoving and crumpled.

I bent over John and shook him. He groaned and tried to burrow deeper into the snow.

"Come on," I said briskly. "Let's hope the horses didn't bolt during all that pandemonium. You'll have to walk or crawl or something; I can't drag you, my arms feel as if they're about to fall out of the sockets."

When I returned to my room, he was still lying across the bed, booted feet dangling and dripping, stained jacket soaking the spread. I put the tray down on the table and bent over him. His lashes were stuck together in starry points. They lay quiet in the bruised and sunken sockets.

"John," I whispered.

There was no reply. I said, "Kitty, kitty. Here, nice kitty."

His eyes popped open. "If you let that damned cat –"

"She's not here. I just said that to tease you."

"Oh, God," said John. He closed his eyes again. "To think I once praised your sense of humor."

"Just rest easy."

"I intend to. I don't intend to move for at least three days. I may die here, quietly and peacefully –"

His voice faded.

"Hang in there," I said soothingly. "You can die later, after I'm through with you."

I had to cut the laces of his boots, they were so sodden and twisted. Midway through the ensuing process, he revived sufficiently to sit up so that I could ease his jacket off. Surveying my preparations, he remarked, "I do admire a well-organized person. But I don't see any thumbscrews or cat-o'-nine tails or –"

"I have everything I need. I wanted to make sure we weren't interrupted."

"I see," John said warily.

"You'll have to stand up for a minute. I want to change the bed."

He did so, without comment, clinging to the bedpost for support; I scooped the whole soggy mess of ribbons, papers, and wet spread into my arms and tossed it aside before replacing it with the blankets I had taken from Tony's bed. The sight of his bruised, lacerated body almost shattered my resolution, but I was determined he wasn't going to get away with it this time.

After I had tended the scars of battle, I propped him up with a couple of pillows. "Now," I said encouragingly. "The worst is yet to come. What about a glass of wine to stiffen your nerve? Come on, don't be so suspicious. I haven't added anything to it. You don't think I would poison you, do you?"

He wouldn't take the glass until I had drunk from it. "This has been very pleasant," he said politely. "But I wouldn't want to keep you from your other obligations. Shouldn't you—"

I smiled brightly at him. "You aren't keeping me from a thing. Tony is still in Garmisch, Schmidt is sound asleep – Clara is sleeping on his stomach – and everything else can wait."

"Vicky," John began nervously. "I honestly didn't intend—"

"Never mind that." I put my hands on his shoulders. "What was it you said, just before the avalanche hit? No, don't try to pretend you don't know what I'm talking about. You remember. Say it. Say it again, loud and clear."

John moistened his lips. "I . . ."

"That's a start. Come on, get it out."

"I don't . . ."

"Yes, you do."

"I . . . I need another glass of wine."

430

"No, you don't. You aren't going to get out of it by claiming you were drunk."

He closed his eyes. I put one finger on a lowered lid and pushed it up. There was no brilliance, no sapphirine glitter in the eye that glared back at me; it was opaque as lapis lazuli, resentful and bloodshot. Then a spark stirred deep in the azure depths; he pushed my hand away and imprisoned it in his.

"I love you," he said flatly. "I – love – you. Shall I elaborate? I have loved you. I do love you. I will love you. I didn't want to love you. I tried not to love you. I will undoubtedly regret loving you, but – God help me – I love you – so much –"

"That's what I thought you said," I murmured.

"So he has gone?" Schmidt demanded, pouting.

"He has gone. Back into the shadows whence he came – but ready, whenever the chance of profit beckons, to take up his role as Supercrook, robbing the rich to sell to the highest bidder –"

"You joke? You can joke, in the face of this disgrace, this – this fiasco?" Schmidt's pout turned to a scowl. It was hard to tell the difference, since both expressions involved lowering brows and an outthrust lower lip, but I was

431

only too familiar with my boss's countenance. He went on, his voice rising in pitch and in volume, "Never have I been so humiliated! I, the director of the National Museum! Gaping down into an empty hole, while vulgar policemen snickered behind their hands and went home to tell their wives about the crazy old man who thought there was a treasure buried in an innkeeper's grave....I believed you. That was my mistake. I should have known better. I should have known you would betray me...."

He went on in this vein for some time. I didn't interrupt, since in a way I felt I deserved a reprimand. It was Tony who came to my rescue. He had been released just in time to join the expedition to the cemetery, and I must give him credit; he hadn't so much as smiled when the grave turned out to be empty of anything except Frau Hoffman's coffin.

"Hold it, Schmidt," he said. "You can't blame this on Vicky. On the basis of the information we had, her deduction was eminently logical — and don't forget, we both went for it. So we were mistaken. The job had to be done."

Schmidt said, "Humph." I said, "Thanks, Tony," and I meant it; but his kindly, if somewhat patronizing, consideration for my feelings couldn't wipe out my own sense of chagrin. I would never forget the awful sinking sensation that seized me when I realized my brilliant if belated deductions had been flat-out wrong. The fact that everyone else, including John, had also been wrong, was small consolation. The policemen hadn't actually snickered, but there had been quite a few suppressed grins and meaningful glances.

Avoiding those glances, I had found myself scanning the hillside, half-expecting to see a lurking form or the gleam of sunlight on a head of fair hair. I had left John recumbent in bed, looking as frail and pathetic as only John could look, but I had not been under any delusion as to his intentions or his capabilities. Nor had I been at all surprised to find no trace of him when I returned to the hotel. The chambermaid had tidied the room and made the bed; there was not even a crumpled pillowcase to show he had ever been there.

"Well, then," said Schmidt briskly, "why are we wasting time talking? We must return to Munich at once — we must organize ourselves. The gold is out there somewhere; now that its presence has been made public, there is no hope of concealment, so we may as well invite cooperation, eh? Yes, yes; all the museums and universities will join in the search — fine-tooth combs — strong young graduate students...."

He rubbed his hands together, his good humor completely restored by the picture taking shape in his mind — hundreds of hapless underlings crawling over the mountains of Bavaria, under the direction of that brilliant mastermind, Anton Z. Schmidt.

Frankly, the prospect left me cold. If the gold was ever found, it would be as the result of ordinary, painstaking police-type techniques — investigation of Hoffman's activities over the months preceding his death, interrogation of everyone who had spoken with him, consultation with local guides and mountaineers who knew the terrain and could suggest likely hiding places. All very efficient and very boring.

"Hurry, Vicky," Schmidt ordered. "Why are you so slow? *Die Weiber, die Weiber,* always they delay—"

I put my mutilated nightgown into the suitcase and closed it. "I'm ready. Except for Clara. She was in your room, Schmidt; why don't you go and get her?"

"You are adopting her, then?" Schmidt asked.

"It was predestined," I said with a sigh. "I called Herr Müller this morning; he wants to stay with his daughter for a few weeks, and he doesn't trust the neighbors to look after Clara properly, and...To make a long story short, he talked me into it. He always wanted me to take her."

"That is good," Schmidt said seriously. "The poor Caesar, he will have someone to play with."

He went trotting out. Tony leaned back in his chair and ran his hand through the tumbled waves of his hair. "I still don't understand everything that happened," he grumbled. "I never suspected Dieter."

I hadn't either, but I didn't say so. I felt I had been humiliated quite enough already. "There are some things none of us will ever understand; the only people who knew the truth are dead. This isn't one of those neat storybook solutions, where the detective triumphantly ties up all the loose ends and exposes all the unknown motives. But the general outline is clear, isn't it? I was the only one to whom Hoffman sent a photograph of his wife. Either there was a return address on the envelope, or he intended to follow it up with a letter. I think — I'm almost sure — he was still hesitating. His initial infatuation with Friedl had cooled, he had realized she couldn't be trusted with his secret — but it never would have occurred to him that he might be in danger from her. He was anticipating only an inevitable, but hopefully not imminent, natural death, so he saw no need for haste."

"That seems reasonable," Tony admitted. "But you'll never prove it."

"I don't have to prove it. I said this wasn't a storybook ending.... In fact, I don't believe Friedl meant to kill Hoffman. She knew he was about to communicate with me, and she ordered Freddy to stop him. Freddy goofed — or perhaps he misinterpreted her orders. Neither of them was very bright. It was sheer bad luck for them that Müller found the envelope before one of them could retrieve it. When Dieter learned what had happened, he decided he had better come to Bad Steinbach and supervise matters in person. They weren't sure that I had received the photograph until I showed up, along with Schmidt; but Dieter had already taken the precaution of sending similar photos to all the others. He didn't have copies of the one of Frau Hoffman, so he had to settle for Frau Schliemann."

"Yes, I understand that," Tony admitted. "He wanted an excuse for being here, if one of us spotted him—"

"And it got Jan Perlmutter here as well. Jan was supposed to be the fall guy in case things went wrong. That's why he got a clue you and the others didn't get. Dieter never meant you to show up; and he only brought Elise along as camouflage."

"It's an awfully complicated, convoluted plot," Tony said.

"Dieter had a complicated, convoluted mind — as evidenced by some of his practical jokes. We'll never know for certain why he killed Freddy, but Freddy was a danger to him all along; he knew Dieter's identity and wasn't above a spot of blackmail. Tossing the body into my garden was just another little spot of confusion. Then Friedl started to crack. Her nice simple little plan of finding the loot and peddling it through Dieter had taken on alarming dimensions and the treasure was still missing. She was jealous of him — look at the way she flew off the handle after she found out he had come to my room — and more than a little afraid of him. She was ready to confess, I'm sure; he realized it too, and got rid of her; called both of us, imitating her voice, to set us up. The more suspects, the better."

"I guess that clears most of it up," Tony said.

"Not quite all." I folded my arms. "I didn't have a chance to give you my Christmas present, Tony, and now I can't find the card — Clara must have chewed it up. So I will eschew subtleties and say straight out, What the hell is the idea of lying to me about imaginary Annie?"

Tony blushed. "Oh," he muttered. "I was afraid you had figured that out."

"You were right. Well?"

Tony sprang from his chair and wrapped his arms around me. "You know why, Vicky. Damn it, you've been putting me off for years. I thought if you thought—"

"A little reverse psychology?"

"Right. Vicky, I'm crazy about you. You know that. I always will be. Won't you—"

"No. I'm sorry, Tony."

I didn't try to free myself. After a moment, his arms relaxed their hold. "It's him, isn't it?"

"He," I said, without thinking.

"Dammit, don't criticize my grammar when I'm baring my soul to you," Tony shouted. "And don't laugh at me!"

"I'm sorry. I'm not laughing at *you*, Tony."

"Are you in love with him?"

"Oh, sure. Not that that has anything to do with it."

Tony flapped his arms. "I don't get it."

"Don't try. It doesn't even make sense to me. Let's get going. We'll have a nice, friendly, belated Christmas Eve tonight, before you leave for Turin in the morning. I hope and trust that by this time the police have removed Freddy; his presence might cast a certain pall over the celebration. We'll stop by Carl's and pick up Caesar and introduce him to...What's taking Schmidt so long?"

438

" 'Peace! Break thee off,' " said Tony; " 'look, where it comes again!' "

He had recovered sufficiently to smile and to quote Shakespeare, so I decided my refusal hadn't broken his heart after all. "Angels and ministers of grace defend us!" I agreed. "What happened to you, Schmidt?"

As Schmidt pointed out, at some length, the answer was self-evident. He had Clara clamped under one arm, and his other hand held her jaws closed. Both hands were crisscrossed by bleeding scratches. Clara's blazing eyes and muffled growls indicated that though temporarily overpowered, she was not subdued. She didn't scratch me or Tony. She bit Tony, and she squirmed and howled when I tried to free her from the red ribbon tied around her neck. The bow was under her chin, and so lacerated I had to cut the ribbon off. It took all three of us to cram her in the carrier I had bought that morning.

"Cats hate bows," I explained to Schmidt, who was sucking his wounds. "It was a pretty thought, Schmidt, but—"

"Do you think I would be so stupid?" Schmidt demanded. "I did not put the ribbon on her. I thought you had. She was in the wardrobe; that is why it took me so long to find her, and when I did, she—"

"I see what she did." I turned the ribbon over in my hands. A small package had been tied firmly to the bow. Clara's teeth had penetrated, but not destroyed it. I ripped it open under the curious eyes of Tony and Schmidt.

Inside was a small golden rose, enameled in scarlet and crimson, with green leaves. An attached ring enabled it to be worn as a charm on a bracelet or as a pendant. It wasn't the sort of thing one could pick up at a local shop; the exquisite workmanship and soft colors showed the hand of a master goldsmith, probably a long-dead master, for it was old – Persian work, at a guess.

"How romantic," said Schmidt.

"Isn't it?" I agreed. Actually, I found the paper wrapped around the trinket even more romantic – it was a receipt from a famous antiquarian jeweler's in Manhattan, and it was marked "Paid." Nice to get a present I would not have to return to its rightful owner.... But I think the thing that touched me most was my hero's gallantry in taking on Clara singlehanded.

I tucked the packet into my pocket. "Let's go."

Schmidt seemed to feel that some further ceremony was called for. He couldn't decide in which direction to face, to address the absent and admired one; after spinning around a few times, he settled on the window. Raising one hand in solemn respect, he declaimed, *"Ave atque vale,* Sir John. The memory of your gallantry will live, green in our hearts—"

"You sound like a funeral sermon, Schmidt," I said.

Tony was still in a Shakespearean mood. "How about 'When shall we three meet again?'" he suggested sarcastically.

I don't think Schmidt recognized the source. "Yes, yes," he exclaimed. "Very appropriate. How does it go on?"

He and Tony went out together, Tony reciting "'In thunder, lightning, or in rain? When the hurlyburly's done, when the battle's lost and won...'"

They had left me to handle the carrier. I picked it up and followed them. The quotation was more appropriate than Schmidt or Tony knew. I had won this battle, and John had lost something more important to him than Trojan gold. Served him right....I wondered how the next round would turn out.